IN ANOTHER MAN'S SHOES

Andy Paulcroft

Copyright © 2023 Andy Paulcroft.

All rights reserved.

No part of this book may be reproduced, or stored in a retrieval system, or transmitted in any form or by any means, electronic, mechanical, photocopying, recording, or otherwise, without express written permission of the author.

All characters and events in this publication, other than those clearly in the public domain, are fictitious and any resemblance to any persons living or dead is coincidental
.

'...somewhere in this vast universe there's a duplicate of every one of you, in a world you've never even dreamed of...'
BEN SHAWCROSS

Contents

1 ~ The Story Begins	1
2 ~ The New Boy	8
3 ~ The Journey	12
4 ~ Confession	18
5 ~ Being Ben Shawcross	23
6 ~ Park Life	32
7 ~ Being Jonny Vincent	36
8 ~ Lonely	47
9 ~ The Perfect Murder	59
10 ~ My Wife Next Door	63
11 ~ Worrying	71
12 ~ Dinner With My 'Wife'	75
13 ~ Biology	89
14 ~ A Night Out With My 'Boyfriend'	93
15 ~ Insomnia	113
16 ~ We Need To Talk	119
17 ~ At The Water Tower	127
18 ~ Meeting Hadley Cooper-Wilson	137
19 ~ Newsflash	150
20 ~ Tuesday Night Dinner	156
21 ~ Marshmallow Cloud	172
22 ~ Repercussions	180
23 ~ Revenge	188
24 ~ Lunch With The Other Arnie	195
25 ~ Half Term	202

26 ~ Obsession	206
27 ~ Thursday Evening	208
28 ~ Beyond The Birthday Party	221
29 ~ The Broken Door	227
30 ~ The Other 'Me'	240
31 ~ Jonny	260
32 ~ Butterfies	266
33 ~ A Non-Leaving Leaving Do	273
34 ~ After The Midnight Dances	282
35 ~ Revelations	290
36 ~ A Talent For Nonsense	297
37 ~ The Sunday Visit	300
38 ~ Amy in Monochrome	307
39 ~ Guilt and Good Fortune	315
40 ~ An Ordinary Monday	325
41 ~ Daring To Blink	333
42 ~ Roadworks	334
43 ~ The Gateway	337
44 ~ The Station	343
45 ~ Five Months Later	347
46 ~ Six Months Later	351
47 ~ The Whole Truth	356
Acknowledgements	366

~ 1 ~
THE STORY BEGINS

Carmichaeltown: Jonny

As I left number 34 Chancelwood Road on that Monday morning, there was nothing to forewarn me of the madness I was heading towards.

The moon wasn't glowing with a magenta hue in the coal scuttle sky. The streetlights weren't flickering a Morse code caution. The neighbourhood strays weren't twerking against the bark of the cherry blossom trees that lined the street.

All was normal.

A light in my bedroom window suddenly illuminated the gloomy pathway. Arnie was awake. I briefly considered running back into the house to give him a huge early morning cuddle. If I had done so, the strange events of that day might never have happened.

I loved him so much.

I loved him, and I was losing him.

We'd had yet another argument the day before. Well, when I say we, it would be more accurate to say that *he* had another argument with *me* the day before. I didn't argue. I never argued. It was far too close to actually sticking up for myself for my liking. And it was that very characteristic that frustrated Arnie to a point where he nearly lost his calm Icelandic serenity.

It had started in the pub. We had gone for a couple of drinks before a five o'clock Sunday dinner. I was queuing patiently when a man barged his way towards the bar. I'd seen him in there before. He stank of an overload of testosterone and pungent aftershave. His banter floated far too close to cruelty, for my liking.

The bartender closed the till on the previous transaction and called out an automatic 'Who's next?' However, as he was staring straight at me, all I had to do was order my drinks.

'Six pints of lager, bud,' said testosterone man, 'and liven it up, we're dying of thirst back here!'

To give him his due the bartender gave me every opportunity to place my order. He even started to say 'I think this gent was first...' until I meekly shrugged to let him know that I didn't mind. He shrugged also and moved on to deal with an order that became even more protracted as rounds of shots were added to the list.

When I eventually took our long-awaited drinks over to Arnie, he was gently fuming.

'Why do you always do that?'

I shrugged again. It didn't help matters.

'Oh, for God's sake Jonny! Why do you let people walk all over you?'

'Does it matter?' I asked mildly, 'we've got our pints, haven't we?'

'It's not really about the drinks though, is it?' he said pointedly. 'It's about everything in your life. It's about being taken for a ... *fífl* ... all of the time.' Arnie sometimes reverted to Icelandic when he thought the English alternative wasn't expressive enough. 'It's about Gemma and Cameron and a whole load of other people who just take advantage of you.'

Gemma and Cameron were at the top of Arnie's disapproval rating at this moment in time. They had both borrowed sizeable amounts of money from me without, in Arnie's opinion, having any intention of paying it back. I, of course, had done nothing about chasing them for it.

As he always did, he let it go quickly after he had made his point, which meant we finished our drinks, the meal that followed, and the weekend, amicably enough.

It didn't stop me worrying, though.

In my heart of hearts, I knew that eventually he would get tired of waiting for me to grow a pair and disappear into the arms of someone whose bollocks were already fully formed. I just didn't know how to grow a pair.

I glanced up at the house next door. Amy and Elliot were our best friends. I had known Amy since our mothers had bought matching Paddington Bear romper suits, and Elliot since we shared a sandpit at primary school. I think my timid nature even irritated them from time to time; they were just too nice to tell me.

I pressed the button on my car key and opened the door. Arnie always joked that my car looked like I had taken it on a test drive and simply forgotten to return it. His, on the other hand, looked like a tsunami had hit the interior. It was totally at odds with his organised Nordic background.

We differed on our views about driving as well. I loved it, Arnie didn't. On Mondays and Fridays, he had managed to wangle an office day, so he was able to take the train. The other three days he visited clients, so the car was more necessary. The firm I worked for was one of those clients. It was helping him to overcome the idiosyncrasies of our coffee machine that had been responsible for the start of our affair, four years ago.

I turned the key and the car burst into life. One of the national radio stations blasted out from the speakers. Most of the music they played was from a time before I was born, but it had the bonus of broadcasting no adverts. Besides, the last epithet I would have chosen for myself was cool. Cheesy pop suited me quite nicely.

At the bottom of our road, I turned right and headed out of town. The argument with Arnie was still on my mind as I passed the sign that told me I was leaving Carmichaeltown. Next to it was a statue of local hero, Alec Carmichael. He was a five times Olympic champion, and was, I thought, the perfect example of why it wasn't always a good idea to stick up for yourself, your family or random strangers.

The ten mile stretch of road that lay in front of me was my favourite part of the drive. It was wide and straight and, in the dull light of the pre-dawn, mercifully quiet. It was during that part of the journey that I fully relaxed and turned a metaphorical switch, so that my thoughts moved from problems at home to the challenges at work. Sometimes I got so lost in my reflections that had anyone asked me, I wouldn't have had a clue where I was. I was aware of the road ahead and any dangers that might be lurking there; I just wasn't quite sure of where on the road I was geographically.

However, when I turned off the main road to use the shortcut through the village of Sandelwood, which cut a good ten minutes from the journey, I readjusted my concentration levels. The road was narrower and meandered in and out of sharp bends, which was why most people stuck to the main roads. The chances of striking a wild deer, especially at dawn or dusk, was highly likely.

I know I was concentrating that morning. I know I was on a rare bit of straight road that cut the village of Sandelwood in two. I know that the car I hit came out of nowhere

There was a sudden blinding flash of headlights that made me blink in horror. I've heard the phrase *my heart was in my mouth*. Well, mine was poking between my incisors. I can't remember trying to find the brake pedal. I just prayed. I think I might have closed my eyes when I realised that a crash was inevitable.

There was no crash.

There was no hideous scraping of metal against metal, no impact that would force my head against the steering wheel or dashboard. No agonising pain when the bonnet of the car concertinaed in on itself, crushing my body and making an escape unlikely.

There was nothing.

The darkness following the sudden and intense light, seemed so complete that it gave lie to the fact that the day was moving quickly towards the dawn. Instinctively, I looked in the rear-view mirror but there were no taillights disappearing into the distance. It was completely dark except for the edges of daylight that were beginning to appear in the sky.

Whatever I'd hit had managed to stop my car, despite the lack of braking from yours truly. I turned off the engine to limit the chances of blowing myself up, although I couldn't hear petrol trickling onto the stony road. I could hear nothing apart from the sounds of a gentle breeze buffeting the car.

I sat there motionless for a few seconds, breathing deeply to quieten the tremors in my arms and legs. I then located the handle on the door and opened it. The sharp January air made me shiver involuntarily which did nothing to settle my shaking hands.

I got out of the car and looked around me. If the other car had swerved to avoid me, there was no way it could have missed an elm tree on one side of the road or a telephone box library on the other. And yet, there was no sign of any carnage. No sign of anything at all.

I thought about reporting the incident but decided that I couldn't cope with the conversation.

'Is anyone injured?'

'No.'

'How badly are the cars damaged?'

'They're not damaged at all ... and ... oh ... one of the cars has completely disappeared.'

I got back into my car and had a vague impression that something was wrong. I tried once again to compose myself. I'd been very lucky, I had just been involved in a head-on collision and walked away from it without a scratch, either on myself or the car. After a few more minutes of deep breathing, I decided I was calm enough to continue my journey. I rarely took a day off work, and I certainly couldn't justify taking a sick day for a car crash that had never happened.

It was then that I realised what was wrong.

The car was facing in the opposite direction. I'd been heading towards work. Now I was facing towards home. I didn't realise that the car had spun around, but it must have done. But that wasn't the only strange thing.

The inside of the car was a mess. Not the wastepaper basket on wheels that passed for my boyfriend's car, but it certainly didn't possess the saleroom sheen that my own car normally did.

Old parking tickets were strewn across the dashboard and a stray piece of paper had appeared in the foot well on the passenger's side.

Weird.

Satisfied at least that the car wasn't leaking petrol, I turned the engine back on and the sound of a cartoon choir singing a happy song about the wonders of a stairlift filled the car.

Even weirder.

Everything else about the car was the same. It was the same make and model, the same furnishings, all the switches were in the same place on the dashboard. When I turned the windscreen wipers on to clear the early morning mizzle, the wipers sprang into action. I didn't start indicating to turn left. The radio station might have been on the wrong channel, but everything else about it was the same as it had been earlier.

Except, I was sure the clock had said 7:15 just before the crash. I liked to keep it about ten minutes fast because I thought it prevented me from being late for appointments. Even though I'd spent a few minutes wandering around Sandelwood, the clock still only said 7:10.

I shrugged, put the car in gear, then manoeuvred it towards the correct direction and moved away from the non-accident. As I drove, I managed to convince myself that I had felt the car spin around and that I'd been wrong about the time. I also managed to tell myself that I must have left a few parking tickets on the dashboard recently. I must have failed to clear them up immediately as I always used to do. Perhaps the stray piece of paper had blown into the car when I was looking around for other, non-existent cars in Sandelwood.

It was only after I'd parked the car in the office car park and walked around to the revolving doors, which fronted the building, that the slightly strange morning mutated into full-blown madness.

I went to push on the door, when I was first struck by the fact that my suit was a slightly different shade to the one I had put on that morning. The shirt was wrong as well. I was sure I'd put on a white shirt. I had certainly ironed a white shirt, the night before, while I was trying to convince myself that Arnie wasn't still irritated with me. I wasn't sure if I possessed a yellow shirt – or the tie I was wearing.

But it wasn't sartorial matters that bothered me most. It was the fact that the face staring at me from the full-length piece of glass that sat in the revolving door wasn't mine.

It was the grown-up face of a boy I hadn't seen for nearly fifteen years.

IN ANOTHER MAN'S SHOES

It was the grown-up face of one of the boys who used to bully me at school.

~ 2 ~
THE NEW BOY

Westcastle: Fifteen Years Earlier

Jonny knew he had made a mistake the moment he saw the red trainers turn the corner at the back of the kitchens.

You weren't allowed to take that route as a shortcut.

You weren't allowed to wear red trainers into school – but that didn't stop the boy who was wearing them.

Nothing stopped him from doing exactly as he wanted, certainly not the teachers.

Jonny had been chatting to Amy about a new boy who had joined their year group that morning. It was unusual to change schools in the middle of May and they had been inventing increasingly ridiculous scenarios to come to a satisfactory conclusion. They had started with the speculation that he'd recently been orphaned in a tragic road accident and ended with the theory that the boy's parents were professional assassins, who'd decided that having a teenager tagging along on their missions was bad for business.

When the final bell rang, Jonny and Amy were still happily in a fantasy land on the other side of the school.

Amy had a free period. Jonny did not.

Amy could amble along to the library in her own time. Jonny didn't have the luxury of ambling; which was why he chose to make his mistake.

Ben was alongside the boy with the red trainers. He was generally with him. He was supposed to be Amy's boyfriend, and when he was with her, he didn't treat Jonny too badly.

When he was in the company of the boy with the red trainers, it was a different tale.

Jonny thought about a quick retreat, but he didn't really have a talent for speed, whereas the boys who were facing him did. He thought about running into the school kitchens. A detention was quite an appealing alternative.

They were on him before he'd had a chance to make his final decision.

'Rubber Jonny!' The boy with the red trainers had grabbed Jonny by the arm and turned him so that it was twisted around his back. He then pulled Jonny towards him and leant over his shoulder, so that spittle dropped onto Jonny's face as he spoke.

'Isn't he pathetic Ben?' he asked.

Please don't let me cry. Jonny sent up a silent prayer to anyone who might be listening. *Just don't let me cry.*

'Pa-thet-ic!' Ben stretched out his words, taunting him.

Please don't let me cry.

'What do you think Benjy?' The boy with the red trainers laughed unpleasantly. 'Bin him?'

'Bin him, Tan.' Ben agreed.

Suddenly, Jonny's arm was released, but only so his tormentor could get better purchase on the whole of his upper body. Ben grabbed his legs, and he could feel himself being raised from the floor.

Tanner transferred the whole of Jonny's weight onto one of his arms so he could open the lid of the industrial sized bin with the other. He and Ben then manoeuvred Jonny so that his nose was alongside the ledge of the bin. May had been warm and the bins weren't due to be emptied until the next day. He could smell sulphur and sweet strawberries, rotten eggs, and human flatulence; musty earthy smells that crept into his mouth and threatened to make him vomit.

As if he was a bag of rubbish himself, they tipped him over the lip, and he landed on the pile of black bags. The pressure of his body weight caused a bag to split, and his nostrils were assaulted by an even more extreme stench. He felt the rotten food ooze around his neck, arms, and legs. He tasted bile in his mouth, and he heard Ben and Tanner whooping in delight as they ran away from the scene of the crime.

Jonny looked around at his stinking prison. As vile as it was, it was almost tempting to hide there, and not bother to find an escape. Almost. After all, escape would only lead to some other torture.

Reluctantly he pushed his hand down on one of the firmer bags and, using that as a crutch, forced himself to stand up. Getting his balance was difficult. His foot stepped on something offensive near the bottom of the bin and an oozing liquid trickled into his shoe. He pulled his foot out of the slime, but every bag he stood on seemed more slippery than chip oil spilt on a tiled floor. After skidding this way and that, he fell against the side of the bin.

He could almost feel the grease and mould soaking into his shirt. His face was a mere inch away from the grey, black, and white residue that studded the walls. He tried to ignore it because he discovered that wedging his body against the wall gave him support, and the best chance of finding an escape.

He stretched out with his arm and dragged the firm bag he had used as a crutch earlier towards him. Gingerly he stood on it, stretched a hand up and located the ledge. It was greasy to the touch. He tried to breathe in through his mouth and not his nose. Although he could still taste the foul stench on his tongue, it no longer threatened to overwhelm him. It was an improvement of sorts.

He pressed down on the ledge. His upper body strength was not good, and his hands were sliding like a pensioner on an icy pavement, so it was lucky that the distance he had to push himself was not too far. By the time he hauled his body over the ledge, he was so desperate to escape that he didn't sit on the side of the bin and lower himself gently towards safety. He carried on sliding forward and down on to the concrete below, adding cuts, scrapes, and bruises to his list of woes.

He pulled himself against the wall of the kitchens and sat there, wrapping his arms around his legs, and dropping his head into his lap.

It was at that moment he finally allowed himself to cry.

He cried for all the pain and humiliation he'd received at their hands over the last few years.

He cried for all the pain and humiliation he would continue to receive.

He cried because he couldn't see an end to it.

Suddenly he was aware of a body dropping down beside him.

Oh shit! They're back...

But the person who had sat down beside him, didn't hit him.

He didn't pull at his arm or deaden his leg.

He put his arm around him and gently eased Jonny's head so that it was resting on the boy's chest. If he was aware of the smell and the slime that Jonny was all too conscious of, he gave no sign.

He spoke softly and told Jonny that everything would be all right.

His name was Will. He was new to the school that morning.

He'd got a bit lost, he said.

~ 3 ~
THE JOURNEY

Westcastle: Ben

I shouted goodbye to my wife as I closed the door. I don't think I got a reply. *She isn't half becoming a mardy mare,* I thought, *she never seems to be happy.*

Tanner Hootley, my life-long best friend who lived next door at number thirty-two, thought that she needed to lighten up. I had to admit, he'd got a point.

Mind you, if Tan lightened up anymore, he would probably float off to Nova Scotia...

No strings, no ties, no nob head trying to tell you what to do. That was the mantra he lived by, and he was following his own advice that very morning. It was the reason his house was still in darkness. Three Sundays out of four he *dipped his wick in the flesh pots of the city*, as he liked to put it, and on those days he would stay over and meet me at work on the Monday. I wondered about the fourth Sunday, I had a feeling that the girl he met on those days, might be a more serious fling than all the others. He never talked about her, not even to me, and he usually told me everything.

In a way, I hoped he had met someone he would treat a little better than his normal *love 'em and leave 'em* style. He was now over thirty for Christ's sake. I didn't want him turning into one of those ageing Romeos who had to treat their long hair with a double dose of *Just for Men* every couple of days. I always thought they looked a little bit sad.

Also, if he did have more of a full-time lover, she might get on with my wife. Stop her sulking around the house all the time. She only went out socially when she met up with that soft git she worked with. Her life-long girlfriend, if you know what I mean. Maybe she would be happier married to him – after all – they worked together, played together, and gossiped on their phones about reality TV 'til it made me demented... But sadly, Amy didn't have a dick for him to play with.

I was being mean. I loved her. I truly did. But things were going pear-shaped, and I wasn't sure how to fix them.

I turned the key in the ignition and the sound of the local radio station filled the empty car. I turned it up a little louder. I didn't like driving alone. Normally, I would have Tan spouting a load of endless crap to jolly away the journeys to and from work. Although I never would have told him this, I liked it and missed it when he wasn't there. Instead, I had a faceless broadcaster spouting endless crap instead. On top of that there were the annoying adverts for female sanitary products, and interviews with brain-dead members of the public. There was a bloke telling everyone he'd spent his weekend re-organising his DVD collection into alphabetical order, and he assumed we gave a toss.

Oh yes, I missed Tanner's rubbish when he wasn't there.

I climbed the hill out of Westcastle and passed the town sign that told me I was leaving – just in case I couldn't have worked that one out on my own. As always, I glanced at the sculpture of Alec Carmichael and thought it a bit mean. The man had won five Olympic gold medals and got a cheaply made, dull grey statue. I wondered what he would have needed to do to get something a bit more special.

Once I'd left the town behind, it was the open road for ten miles, and it was at that time when I really noticed the lack of a travelling companion. On the radio, the latest contribution came from a woman who was bragging that she'd spent the weekend crocheting used carrier bags into school satchels for her grand kids. She was very pleased with herself – especially when the DJ praised her for saving money and the environment at the same time.

I thought she should have gone the whole hog and crocheted some signs saying *please bully me.* She was obviously determined to make their lives a misery – she might as well do the job properly.

I know that Tanner and I had been called bullies when we were at school. It wasn't something I was particularly proud of, and it was the side of Tan's character that bothered me most. I don't think he meant to be vicious – he was only having a bit of fun – and Lord knows we all need a bit of that. It was just, sometimes, he went too far.

I turned off the main road and slowed down as I headed towards Sandelwood. The village reminded me of one of the occasions when Tan had gone one step further than fair. I had nearly wiped out a woman having an early morning trot on her horse, last summer, and she'd given me a major bit of verbal. Tan gave it back, big time, but I must admit I did feel bad about it. I was in the wrong, and he'd made her feel like she was, not to mention the fact that it was only down to luck and good brakes that I hadn't murdered her horse. I drove slower through the village now, even when it was pitch black and we were unlikely to meet angry horse lady. Tan gave me stick for it of course. *'Hey Ben, we could do with a bit more horsepower! Careful, we don't want to end up in horsepital! You'd better not stirrup trouble again...'* OK, it probably wouldn't get him a spot at the London Palladium, but it made us laugh.

As I thought about the abuse he had given the horse-rider, I squirmed a little. I did worry that one day he would say the wrong thing, to the wrong person, at the wrong time. I also worried about some of the things he was doing at work. I liked a good wind-up, but I was basically an honest guy. Tan liked a good wind-up, and he had a few scams going on.

Some of them bordered on fraud.

I drove out of the village, and through a series of bends, that would eventually lead to the main road and the city. I paid a bit more attention to the radio when the sports report was broadcast. Tan and I went to a sports quiz in the local pub on a Monday night, and they often had questions relating to the weekend before. City had won well on Saturday, which reminded me that I must tell Tanner that I'd managed to get tickets for the fourth-round cup match via the internet last night.

It was at the end of that thought when I had a sudden empty feeling in the pit of my stomach. I realised I'd done something stupid. I'd left my wallet in the lounge last night after buying the tickets, and I hadn't picked it up this morning before I left the house.

Like a moron, I took one hand from the wheel and started patting my jacket pocket. It wasn't there. I knew it wasn't, but I patted it anyway. With the same lack of expectation, I patted my trousers. I think I might have noticed if it had been in one of my arse pockets, seeing as I would have been sitting on it for the last fifteen odd miles. Surprise, surprise, it wasn't there.

Of course, it wasn't there. It was at home, on the coffee table with the wonky leg.

I hated being without a wallet. It made me feel vulnerable. I knew I'd have to go home and get it, even if it made me late for work. I pulled into the next passing place and quickly texted Tanner, so he could cover for me until I got there, then turned the car around and headed back to Sandelwood.

I was probably going a little bit too fast. Angry horse lady would have said so. But I was on a straight bit of road through the village. I could see quite clearly. I remember my headlights flickering on the old disused phone box, so I know I was concentrating. I did glance at the clock on the dashboard, but that was only for a nano second.

Then, I hit a car.

I hit a car that came from nowhere. It wasn't there, and then it was.

I slammed my foot hard on the brake pedal, but the headlights of the other car were already close enough to blind me. I knew it was so close that braking wouldn't make any difference, but I tried, nonetheless.

I thought it was strange when I didn't feel the force of the head-on collision. I remember thinking that the reason I hadn't felt anything was because I was already dead.

As Tanner would have said. 'Nob head!'

It was at that moment I realised that my foot wasn't on the brake, and the car was still moving. That was strange thing number one. I clearly remembered braking and didn't remember taking my foot from the pedal. I pressed down on the brake to sort that out and the car stopped quickly, forcing my body towards the steering wheel.

Strange thing number two was that I could see the disused phone box in the driver's side wing mirror. I had driven past it, so it should have been on the other side of the car.

It was at that point that I realised I was facing towards work. That was all wrong. I was travelling towards home when I'd met the other car in the middle of the road.

Strange thing number three, or four, I must admit by now I was losing count … was the fact that the other car had disappeared. I got out of the car and walked back towards the phone box. Silly really, the car was hardly likely to be hiding behind a blade of grass by the roadside – but by now I think I'd lost the plot.

That feeling didn't improve when I noticed the phone box. It was full of second-hand books. When my head lights had lit upon it, only minutes before, it had been empty. I was sure it had been empty.

I decided I was not going to go to work in that state. I put my hand inside my jacket pocket to pull out my mobile phone, so I could ring Tan and get him to bail me out with one of his special excuses.

As my fingers wrapped around the phone, they touched something else that was also in my pocket.

A wallet.

I felt a little sick. That wallet was definitely not there when I'd patted my jacket earlier on.

When I pulled out my mobile phone, the first finger on my right hand slipped into an indentation on the back of it. My phone didn't have a fingerprint scanner, so I was surprised when the phone clicked into life. But that wasn't the thing that nearly made me barf into the bushes.

The phone's background picture was a photo of two men. The first, looked like one of the company's service providers. He tended to deal with Tanner, and I didn't know him that well.

I knew the other bloke in the cosy picture, although I tried to have as little to do with him as possible. He didn't like me because

Tan and I used to bully him at school. Mind you, that was nothing compared to what my father and Tanner did to him later.

He was my wife's best friend. Her girlfriend. The soft git.

I wasn't aware that he even knew the other bloke, let alone knowing him well enough to be snuggling up the way they were. But that wasn't the most pressing question I had on my lips at that moment in time.

That would have to have been: *what the hell was I doing with his phone?*

~ 4 ~
CONFESSION

Westcastle: Fifteen Years Earlier

Jonny couldn't breathe.

It wasn't a case of being breathless because of a futile chase up a steep hill, pursuing an already departed bus.

Jonny really couldn't breathe.

Tanner's hands were around his neck, lifting him off the floor. The pressure from thumb on skin made it feel as if his tormentor was boring a hole through to his jawbone.

His neck felt stretched, as if he were a fifteenth century martyr on a rack being tortured for his beliefs.

Jonny wasn't being tortured for his beliefs. Jonny was being tortured for simply existing.

The skin on his neck felt taut to the point of breaking apart – like an elastic band that had been forced around a beer keg.

He was sure he was about to pass out. The lack of air was making everything seem hazy and, when he managed to take short desperate breaths, he was aware of Tanner's face close his own. Too close. He smelt of teenage laziness and garlic powder from last night's pizza.

Jonny thought he was going to die.

Ben stood a little bit away from the scene. It was as if he was trying to remove himself from the situation. He was worried. He knew that Tanner was going too far, but he didn't know how to stop him.

He had always gone along with Tanner. In junior school they would tease their victims with words and funny taunts. Banter, his father had called it. 'Get in first my son,' he used to say.

Once they'd swapped short trousers for long, the taunts became physical. Nothing too vicious. A Chinese burn, a dead leg, a couple of moves that Tanner had picked up from watching pantomime wrestling on the telly.

And of course, there was the traditional head down the loo prank, or a trip into the bins. Harmless fun, his father had told the teacher when she had mentioned it at a parents' night.

But lately... It was ever since that new kid had joined the school. Will. There was something about him that unsettled Tanner. Something that made him feel he needed to exert his authority.

Will had befriended Jonny and Tanner didn't like it. He had waited until a rare occasion when Jonny and Will weren't together, and he made his favourite punchbag pay for finding a friend.

Ben understood that Jonny was an annoying little dweeb. If he hadn't been so pathetic, if he had shown a little bit of bottle, then maybe it wouldn't have come to this.

This, Ben thought, *was going too far.*

'Tan...! Tan...! Stop it! He's going to pass out in a minute.'

'Oh, for fuck's sake Benjy! Don't be such a pussy. Rubber's enjoying himself. Have a look, he's probably getting a boner being so close to a real man. Ain't that right Jonny?'

'I ... can't ... breathe.' It took all of Jonny's resolve to get those three words out. It made no impression on his attacker.

'Aah.' He said in false sympathy, stretching the word out. 'Can't you breathe Jonny boy? Shame!'

'Tan,' Ben said urgently. 'Stop it ... please!'

'You agreed that Rubber had been having it too easy lately.' Ben couldn't remember saying anything of the sort. It was more likely that he hadn't disagreed, and as always, his best mate had taken that as approval.

Tanner's voice then took on a sing-song childlike tone – mocking Jonny. 'Now that he's got himself a new fwiend.' He turned to Ben but kept his vice like grip on Jonny's neck. 'What does your girlfriend say, now that she has to share him?' He turned back to Jonny and continued talking. 'A little nerd like Jonny doesn't deserve to have two friends.'

'A vile shit like you doesn't deserve to have any friends at all.'

A new voice had entered the conversation. It was enough to make Tanner release the pressure on Jonny's neck. Tanner's hands might have still been around his throat, but at least Jonny's feet were back on the ground. Once again, he found that he was breathless. However, this time it wasn't because a pair of hands were trying to strangle him.

He felt it every time he saw Will. It was wonderful and yet it was awful. Jonny just wanted to be in Will's company, but whenever he was, he couldn't stop himself from prattling on like an old maid in a care home. It made him scared and yet it gave him hope for the future at the same time.

He was just afraid that the hope would end up killing him.

'I guess it makes you feel important,' Will continued. 'Making other people feel rotten. Psychiatrists would have a field day with you, Hoots, they really would.'

Will had discovered that Tanner hated being called by the corrupted version of his surname – so he used it any chance he got.

'Piss off arsehole.' Tanner released his grip on Jonny and turned to walk over towards the newcomer. Tanner was tall for his age. The tallest in the year and he was trying to use his height now to intimidate Will. 'You need to keep on the right side of me.'

Will ignored him. Far from being intimidated, he used Tanner's proximity to insult him.

He screwed up his nose and flapped a hand in front of his face. "Now, they could say that you strike out at people before they have the chance to ridicule you because you are conscious of your revolting halitosis.'

Ben watched the new boy in amazement. Nobody had ever talked to Tanner like that, and he had no idea how his friend would take it.

Will had no worries on that subject, he scratched his chin, pretending to think. 'Or it could be that you have a pencil thin dick and you're so embarrassed by it that you behave like a Neanderthal to cover up the fact.' He smiled pleasantly and moved towards Tanner, so their noses were practically touching. 'But I think that it's simply because you're a brainless arsehole.'

Tanner bragged that he had quick hands. He always joked with Ben that nobody knew when he was going to strike until they were holding an ice pack to their eye. He went to punch Will in a similar fashion, but the shorter boy merely used his hand to block the punch and Tanner's own momentum to twist the bully and send him sprawling onto the concrete.

'That's enough!' Ben ran over to Tanner as a gesture of support, but also to stop him retaliating. As big and strong as Tanner was, Ben sensed that Will had wit and guile on his side, and he didn't want to see his friend humiliated any further. 'Come on Tan, let's leave them to it...'

Tanner wanted to argue but realised that mere strength alone wasn't going to be enough on this occasion. He decided to bide his time. He needed to think of a way he could beat Will in the most public way possible. He reluctantly accepted Ben's hand to help him up. However, there was no way he was going to scurry off like a pathetic loser. Tanner pulled himself up to his full height and walked past Will, barging into his shoulder as he did so.

'Later, arsehole,' he said.

'Oh, I can't wait Hoots!' Will said, and then continued in a phony American drawl. 'Missing you already!'

'Thanks.' Jonny said quietly once he and Will were alone. 'That was brilliant. You were brilliant. I've never seen anyone treat him like that. It was awesome!'

Stop it! he thought.

He knew he was babbling once again but although it sounded stupid, even to his own ears, it was so much better than the alternative. Anything was better than saying the one thing he wanted to say. The one thing he knew it would be suicidal to say.

He said it.

'I really like you,' he blinked as if he couldn't believe he was being so reckless. 'I mean a bit more than like, really...'

He tailed off and tried not to look at Will's face. He didn't want to see the disgust in his eyes. He didn't want to see the disappointment etched on his features.

To avoid this, he closed his own eyes.

Will stepped forward a couple of paces and cupped his hands behind Jonny's neck. In some ways it was not dissimilar to how Tanner had held him just a few minutes before. In other ways it was as similar as an icepack and a bonfire.

Jonny held his breath. He was waiting for Will to call him a cruel name and laugh in his face.

Will didn't call him a cruel name, and he didn't laugh. He kissed him softly on the forehead, causing Jonny to open his eyes. With a small grin, Will moved his lips southward and kissed Jonny gently, yet passionately, on his lips.

'Good...' he said.

~ 5 ~
BEING BEN SHAWCROSS

Westcastle: Jonny

It was the fact that I recognised the chairs in the reception area that propelled me through the door when all I wanted to do was run away and hide. As soon as I entered the building I could see Gemma smiling her fake smile in the direction of a visiting CEO. He had suspiciously white teeth, a January tan, and enough personal assistants to have a one-sided game of ice hockey in the lunch hour.

Gemma had been one of the subjects of Arnie's Sunday afternoon rant. According to Arnie, there were two types of men in Gemma's opinion. There was the type of man she wanted to bed and the type of man who was there to be bled. I, obviously, fell into category two.

I didn't want her to see me so I sidled my way into the bay window, the other side of the revolving door, where I was hidden from her view. I sat down on one of the blue corporate sofas to compose myself and work out what on earth had happened. I looked around the large atrium complete with skylight and potted plants. It acted as the reception area of the company I worked for, as well as a few other businesses that shared the same building. Everything was the same as I remembered. It even had the picture that always made Arnie and me laugh. The picture was between the reception area and the lifts. It showed an imposing Manhattan skyscraper with the company logo in the top right-hand corner and the legend 'RD Eversen – The New York Office' in bold lettering along the bottom. It failed to mention that the great New York company offices only took up a small part of the building in the picture. It also failed to mention that they weren't shown in the picture at all. They were at the back of the building, overlooking the car parks and the trash cans.

I was thinking that the picture looked the same, the atrium looked the same. and that Gemma hadn't changed since I saw her on Friday, when a thought exploded into my head. *How on earth would Gemma, or anyone else for that matter, recognise me?* I had not seen Benjamin Shawcross since he went away, just under fifteen years ago. I didn't know where he was and cared even less. He certainly didn't work in this building.

Unless I had fallen into a demented parallel universe.

I had no interest in the type of science fiction conspiracy theories that could have come straight out of The X Files. They were fine as a piece of entertainment on a winter's evening but people who believed that Martians had shot JFK, or that corn circles were a mapping system for life forms from another planet, seemed to be a little bonkers as far as I was concerned.

All that being said – as I sat there in another man's body – I struggled to think of a rational explanation behind it.

I pinched my arm, and then pinched myself again. By the time I'd pinched myself for the fifth time, I could feel a red burning sensation in the soft flesh just above my wrist, but I still hadn't woken up.

I decided that I could safely say it wasn't a dream.

I thought I would try and ring Arnie. I needed his humorous common sense to lighten my mood and help me make sense of it all. However, when I tried to press the fingerprint scanner to make the phone burst into life, I discovered that it didn't have one. When I pressed the switch on the side of the phone to wake it up the old-fashioned way, I received another shock in a whole morning of them. The phone's background image was the badge of the local football team. Football and I weren't friends, too many hideous school memories accounted for that. But that was inconsequential. I should have been staring at the photo of Arnie and me, in Ibiza on our first holiday together. I wasn't. Although I knew that tapping out the code which unlocked my phone, when the scanner failed, would be futile. I tried it anyway. Unsurprisingly, it didn't work, and even if it had, I was sure that Arnie's mobile number would not be in the directory.

I sat there for a few seconds while I tried to digest this latest bombshell and assimilate exactly what I did know.

It was quicker to work out exactly what I didn't know. I didn't know where I, or Ben, or whoever I was, lived. I didn't know where he worked. Apart from an incredibly lucky guess, I had no way of getting any information from his phone. I felt in the jacket and trouser pockets, but he didn't seem to have a wallet. Great! I added a lack of money to my list of woes.

A wave of depression washed over me. How I wanted Arnie to be with me at that moment. If he'd been there, he would have treated the whole situation as a big adventure and I would have been swept along with his enthusiasm. However, he wasn't there and worse than that, I wasn't sure if I would ever see him again.

I metaphorically punched myself. I had a habit of becoming pathetic when things became difficult, relying on other people, rather than fighting it out for myself. And I knew that was something I couldn't do in this instance.

I grabbed hold of the bridge of my nose and pinched it, as if the action would force me to think. The only place where I might be able to get some answers, was the car. There might be something in the glove compartment with an address on it. Maybe, there was an envelope stuffed into one of the door storage areas or perhaps the sat nav system had been programmed with a 'take me home' setting.

Just as I was feeling a little bit better, knowing I had some sort of plan I could follow, my thoughts were interrupted by a very loud bang on the glass behind me. I had been so immersed in my musings that the sound came as something of a shock. I turned around to see what had caused it. I saw something, or more accurately someone, who made that shock seem as inconsequential as one more drop of rain after a torrential downpour.

Standing outside the glass, grinning, and making obscene gestures, was the grown-up version of a lad who had made my teenage years a nightmare.

Tanner Hootley. He had been Ben Shawcross's best friend.

What the hell was he doing here? How was it even possible?

I had no time to recover before he bowled his way through the revolving door, and punched me on the shoulder, a show of hearty good humour that should have been illegal on a Monday morning.

I remembered his punches. The ones I had received as a boy were not as friendly as the one he'd just given me, but I remembered them nonetheless. It made me feel sick.

'Benjy! What are you doing?'

I looked at him in bewilderment. The answer to that question was: *I have absolutely no idea.*

He looked at my puzzled expression and snorted. 'The text you sent. You'd left your wallet at home...' He stared at me meaningfully, but my inability to grasp the situation was beginning to frustrate him. 'You were going home to get it and wanted me to cover for you, remember?' The last word held the sarcastic tone that I remembered all too well. Luckily, he'd just given me a little bit of information I could work with.

It also helped me with two items on my never-ending list of queries. Ben obviously worked in this building, and it explained away the lack of a wallet.

I tried to remember the way Ben used to speak, the words he used to use, but concluded that after fifteen years, it was likely to have changed anyway. I decided to keep it as simple as possible.

'I had second thoughts, reckoned I could last the day without my wallet.'

Tanner whooped in sarcastic delight. 'Mr Ben Shawcross deciding to spend the whole day without being able to pat his security wallet – who'd have thought it?' His demeanour changed quickly, and he continued in a tone of fake disappointment. 'Such a shame, I had a brilliant bit of a Jackanory lined up as well.' I realised that there was no way I could stop him from telling me what his story would have been. In fact, stopping a herd of marauding buffalo would have been easier... 'I was going to say that things had got a bit spicy with your good lady this morning, she handcuffed you to the bed frame and then lost the key...!' He punched me on the arm again before continuing, although he was struggling to get the words out, he was laughing so much at his own comic genius '...you were waiting for the emergency services to rescue you!'

I was in hell. It was now official.

I managed a laugh that was as fake as a print of the Mona Lisa in a ten-euro gift shop. However, something else had occurred to Tanner, and thankfully he changed the direction of the conversation quickly.

'Anyway. What are you doing sitting down here, looking like a spare dick at a wedding?'

I hated to admit it, but it was a good question. 'Umm, well, I knew you'd have some brilliant excuse lined up, so I thought I'd head you off at the pass, before you got a chance to use it.' Under the circumstances, I was quite pleased with that one.

'Yeah, that's right, spoil all my fun, nob head.' Tanner laughed and started to move across the atrium. I wasn't sure what else to do, so I followed him and hoped I could pick up information as I went along. To be honest, I would have rather gargled with kerosene than spend an hour in his company, but my options were limited.

'Morning gorgeous!' Tanner called over to Gemma and we both received a smile that she'd only bestowed on me when I'd lent her a thousand pounds. Thinking again of Arnie's comment I decided that, in Gemma's eyes, Tanner and Ben were obviously bedding material – and I was not talking about a king-sized duvet from M & S.

I followed a step or two behind Tanner, so it didn't look too obvious that I didn't know where I was going. He strode towards the lift and, totally ignoring the people who were already waiting, barged into it. Tanner then stood by the control buttons in the doorway, so that everyone else had to manoeuvre their way around him.

I was a little more hesitant and only just managed to squeeze into the lift before the doors closed. However, I did manage to see that Tanner had stabbed at the button for the fifth floor.

It was the floor I normally worked on.

True to form, Tanner charged out of the lift without a thought for anyone else, so I was able to follow his lead while managing to look like I knew where I was going.

I realised that I would have a problem when I reached the office. I could hardly follow Tanner to his desk. But, I had no idea which of the numerous workstations that populated the crowded office Ben would work at. Tanner unintentionally gave me an idea when he crash landed his body onto the office chair at his station, while I hovered hesitantly in the doorway.

'Get me a coffee Benj!' It was obviously the normal procedure for the pair of them, but to buy myself some time, I risked changing their routine. My only other option was to ask him where my desk was. I decided it was especially important that I didn't raise any suspicions that something was different.

'Actually mate, I'm desperate for the loo,' I continued hovering and made my actions compliment the words. 'Would you do the honours today?'

The real me would never have said anything like that, and I realised by the look on Tanner's face that this was unusual in his world also. However, he accepted it well enough for me to risk a request that would give me the information I needed when I got back.

'Leave it on my desk, would you?'

I walked down the corridor to where the toilets had always been and was thankful to see that they were still in the same place. When I returned to the office, Tanner pointed at the coffee with a look of exaggerated subservience. 'There you are, oh lord and master,' he said in a tone that was totally at odds with his words.

I followed the direction of his finger and managed to hold back an exclamation of surprise.

I had sat at that desk on Friday. I had sat at that desk for the past five years.

I nodded my thanks and hurried gratefully towards the security of my own small space. I took a swig of the coffee and nearly spat it out again as it tasted unexpectedly sweet. Ben obviously liked about three sugars, whereas I preferred my drinks without any. *Still*, I thought ruefully, *at least sugar is meant to be good for shock.*

My next problem was sitting in front of me. All the work computers had two passwords, the company one and the personal one. I tried the company password and got straight in. When I was debating what to do next, I saw a few post-it notes stuck to the side of the monitor. Glad that Ben had disregarded all the memos about privacy and security that he would have received regularly, I logged in, and blinked.

The subjects of the emails were remarkably similar to the ones I had dealt with when I last looked at my computer. Reading some of the replies that Ben had sent, he hadn't dealt with them exactly as I would have done. But, it was close enough to make me think that I could get through a working day without anyone suspecting anything.

I pretended to study one of the messages that had come in over the weekend, but it was merely for the benefit of anyone who, for any reason, was watching me. I didn't take in a word. My mind was full of a thought I'd had when I was in the reception area earlier.

Unless I had fallen into some demented parallel universe.

It was the only thing that fitted. The head-on collision. The lack of another vehicle afterwards. The fact that my car was heading in the opposite direction and the appearance of random parking tickets and other bits of rubbish.

Somehow, I had fallen into a world that was so similar to the one I'd left behind, but also totally different. In this world, Ben Shawcross had stolen my life. In this world, my ex-arch enemy was once again his best friend.

But where was I in this world? I opened the *About the company* page on the RD Eversen website and looked for my name. There was no one called Jonny Vincent who worked for them. I also looked under Ben Shawcross, there was a mobile phone number listed, but nothing useful revealing where he might live.

I opened the draw to his desk and this time I struck gold. I found an envelope with the RD Eversen logo on it. It had been delivered through the internal mail system, but it did have Ben's home address written on the front of it.

34 Chancelwood Road.

He *had* stolen my life.

After the sweet coffee and the endless revelations, my throat felt dry, and I was feeling slightly nauseous. I wandered over to the water cooler, hoping that a glass of RD Eversen's finest H_2O would settle my stomach. I also hoped that it would transport me back to my own life in Carmichaeltown, but miracles were only going one way that morning.

I arrived there at the same time as Steve Coombes. He was a work colleague and friend in my other life. We had also gone to school together. Alongside Amy, he and Elliot had been the closest people I'd had to friends before Will, my first love, turned up. We were still close, and regularly did the grown-up dinner party thing. In fact, it had been Amy and Elliot's turn on Saturday night, although it seemed like a million years ago at that moment. He was quiet and gentle and, I thought, worth the risk.

I said hello and he nodded in return; it was only when I asked my next question that the conversation became a little strained.

'Have you heard from Jonny Vincent lately?'

I had never seen Steve lose his cool, and outwardly he was still calm, but there was a definite fire in his eyes and his tone was curt. 'Why on earth would you be the least bit bothered about Jonny after what you, your father, and Tanner did to him?'

I managed to mumble an inconsequential reply, but my head was reeling. Even though he hadn't raised his voice, it was obvious from his manner that he was seething inside on my behalf. I liked him for it, even if I didn't have a clue about the reasoning behind it. I didn't think he was referring to the childhood bullying. If so, why had Ben's father been mentioned?

'Anyway,' he said, dismissing me. 'Your wife would know. Don't you ever talk to her?'

His manner had unsettled me. I stumbled away from the water cooler; all thoughts of a refreshing drink forgotten. I walked back to my work station trying not to give the impression that I was drunk. I felt very wobbly, and it wasn't wholly successful. As I sat down, my shaking leg caught the desk. I was aware of a photograph falling over. It was hidden at the back, behind a City

FC pen holder. I stretched across to pick it up. As I did so, I looked at it properly.

If I was in some parallel universe, an idea my logical brain was struggling to come to terms with, then an awful lot of things were different in this version of the world. As well as the fact I no longer worked for RD Eversen – Elliot and Amy were no longer married.

They couldn't be. The picture was of Amy and Ben, together.

It was a wedding photograph.

~ 6 ~
PARK LIFE

Westcastle: Fifteen Years Earlier

'Ben's not mean when he's away from Tanner.'

Amy and Jonny were sitting by the tennis courts in the park. Wimbledon had just finished for the year, so all the would-be Federers and Sharapovas were still in the grip of tennis fever. It would take another couple of weeks before their enthusiasm would drain away, but now the courts were full.

School had finished for the day. Normally Jonny would have run away home. He was safer at home. Since Will had arrived, he felt safer everywhere.

Jonny chose not to answer Amy's comment. When you associated two people with causing you pain, it was difficult to differentiate between them. In a comedy double act, there might have been one who was funnier than the other, but everyone knew that he, or she, wasn't as funny on their own. Jonny reckoned the same could be said about bullies, but without the feel-good comedic factor.

Amy took Jonny's silence as disagreement. 'He's not,' she reiterated, but Jonny was unsure who she was trying to convince. 'When we're alone together he's lovely.'

Once again Jonny didn't answer her directly. He commented on the forehand cross court winner that a teenage Maria had drilled past a flailing parent. Amy got the message.

'You think I should go out with Elliot instead, don't you?'

Jonny shrugged. 'Elliot's nice. He's kind. His best friend is not a Neanderthal.'

'...and he does seem a bit lost since *his* best friend has started going out with Lottie...'

Jonny grinned. 'Ames, I don't think you should go out with Elliot just because Steve has got himself a girlfriend.'

Amy laughed. 'Of course not, you dingbat.' She paused before continuing. 'Elliot is lovely, like you said. He's kind, he's the type of boy that would do anything to make me feel special every day...' She paused again to choose her words. 'Ben can be like that as well you know, but he's also a bit edgy, a bit more exciting.' She looked at Jonny and could tell he was not impressed. She repeated her original question. 'You think I should go out with Elliot and not Ben?'

'Yes, I do, absolutely.'

Amy sighed and changed the subject. 'Anyway, enough about me. Spill the goss. Someone I know has looked a little bit loved up the past week or so!'

Jonny laughed, a little embarrassed, but then realised it was Amy he was talking to. He had admitted to Amy as a bullied twelve-year-old, with no self-esteem, that he thought he might be gay. He had told no one else. Ever since, he had hidden his gayness as if it were a terminal disease that he couldn't bear to speak about. Now, there were signs that he was finally happy to relax into his own body. He would never be overtly camp, that wasn't his nature, but the odd flamboyance had crept into his speech and the gestures that accompanied it. He wasn't trying to hide them anymore. He was beginning to like himself.

'Oh Ames, I am so loved up it's almost pathetic!' He gave a little laugh at his own expense. 'Will has changed my life. I've never met anybody like him.' His eyes sparkled with a love of life that Amy hadn't seen in him before. 'He just doesn't care about being gay. He is so: *if they don't like it, they're going to have to get over it!* I love that!'

'You are being careful Jonny, aren't you?' Amy was pleased for him, but she just wanted him to remember that she was his oldest friend, and therefore, had the right to mother him if she thought he needed it.

Jonny coloured immediately. 'Oh Ames, we haven't done *that* yet,' he paused, for a moment unsure of how much he should tell her, and then realised he could tell Amy anything. 'We've done a bit of mutual masty, and he gave me a blow job...' the last two words were mouthed more than spoken, '...but we haven't done the up yer bum bit yet...' Again, the embarrassing words were disguised as a muted nasal muttering, but Amy got the message.

'Well, when you do, make sure you wrap up...'

'Don't worry, Jonny will wear a rubber.' Jonny couldn't believe he was using a phrase that had been used to torment him, as a joke.

Amy laughed softly and squeezed Jonny a little tighter. Suddenly Jonny was aware of being pushed away from her as another body moved in between them.

'Move over Madonna!' Ben said loudly as he joined them. He then pushed Jonny towards the far end of the bench, just so there could be no mistaking his words. 'Let me show you how a proper hetero man cuddles his girlfriend.' There was no denying the degree of ownership surrounding the comment, but it was friendlier than normal. There was a lack of his natural aggression towards his girlfriend's best friend.

'I'm not your possession Ben,' Amy complained and then she nodded towards Jonny meaningfully. 'Can't you just be nice?'

Jonny had decided that three was a crowd and, looking at his watch, realised that judo club was nearly over. He thought he would head back to school and meet up with Will.

Just at that moment, the preadolescent Maria dumped an easy forehand into the net and embarked on a display of temper so loud, and vicious, that everyone in the area stopped to watch. The parent on the opposite side of the net was horrified and tried muttering conciliatory platitudes, but they had no affect at all on her stroppy offspring.

Jonny muttered 'Martina Nav*brat*alova' under his breath and was rewarded by seeing Ben laugh so naturally it was infectious.

Suddenly they were talking quite normally about Wimbledon, a TV show they discovered they both liked, and a movie they wanted to see. It might have been normal inconsequential stuff to anyone who was eavesdropping. But, as far as their relationship was concerned, it was nowhere near normal.

Jonny was beginning to relax in Ben's company for the first time. He saw, at last, what Amy had seen in him. He thought they could even become friends, in time.

Because he was enjoying himself, he missed the sound of footsteps warning of a new arrival. He noticed, but didn't realise, the significance of the sharp look that appeared on Ben's face. He missed the tell-tale stench of engine oil, and the scent of deodorant that had been hastily applied to hide it. Jonny had no idea that Tanner had joined them, until his lifelong tormentor treated him to a Chinese burn. After-school mechanics club had finished for the afternoon.

'Hiya Rubber! You all on your lonesome? Where's the Karate Kid today?' Tanner twisted his face into an unpleasant grin. 'Or should that be the Bukkake Kid?' He laughed heartily at his own joke.

Jonny risked a quick glance towards Ben. He didn't look overly happy to see his best friend and, for a mad moment, Jonny thought that Ben was going to say something to defend him.

The moment passed quickly, and Ben started to laugh.

~ 7 ~
BEING JONNY VINCENT

Carmichaeltown: Ben

The morning was becoming weirder than some of the trendy bollocks they showed on Sky Arts around chucking out time at the pubs.

As well as the reappearing wallet and the strange phone, I was sure the suit jacket wasn't mine. This led me to look at the cuffs on my shirt. The shirt was white. I would have bet my own liver that Amy had ironed my yellow shirt, the previous evening. Also, my wedding band was on my index finger. Had I put it there after my early morning shower? It looked slightly different as well, maybe it was the half-light ... but...

Weird shit, or what?

I ran back to the car. I'm not sure why. I only knew that I needed to get away from the village of the damned as soon as I could.

The village of the damned. Sandelwood. There was something niggling at me but, try as I might, I couldn't quite grab hold of it.

The car was clean. That was the next thing. I'm not a slob myself, but this car looked like it had been owned by Anita the neat freak. I slammed the door and started the car. As I glanced in the rear-view mirror, I felt sure there was something else. In the small piece of glass, I could see the road behind me, and my eyes. What was strange about that? I butted the thought away and got on with performing yet another manoeuvre in a morning that seemed to have been full of them.

Sorry angry horse lady, I thought, *I need to get away from here as quickly as possible.*

The sports news was on the car radio, which was a little weird. I'd been listening to the sports report just before the crash – it had been the reason I'd turned the car around after all. They normally only had one update per hour. Also, there was nothing about City's match. When they returned to the breakfast DJ, I realised that I was listening to a national radio station. The one that played stuff from the last century. The other strange thing was that the clock was fifteen minutes later than it had been, when I'd looked at it, just before the crash. I was sure I'd only been faffing around outside for about five minutes. Where had the other ten minutes gone?

For once, driving alone was exactly what I needed to do. I used the stretch of open road back to Westcastle to get my shit together. By the time I was nearing town, dawn had fully broken and I'd convinced myself that that I'd been hallucinating. My shirt cuffs even started to look yellow in the early morning light. I'd had a very heavy sesh on Saturday. Perhaps this was a sort of hangover. I was just suffering twenty-four hours later than I normally would have done. By the time I got home, everything would be back to normal.

I was beginning to relax and even grinned to myself about the stick I'd get from Tan when I told him about it. This disappeared completely when I got back to the outer reaches of the town and saw the sign.

'Welcome to Carmichaeltown.'

That sick feeling returned to my stomach. *What the hell was going on?* In the time it had taken me to drive to Sandelwood and back, some daft bastard had changed the name of the town.

I went a bit blank then. I drove down the road towards my house in a kind of trance.

I parked the car, locked the door, and headed towards the short garden path.

And stopped.

A man was closing the front door.

He was the man who had been wrapped around Jonny bloody Vincent in the photo on my phone.

He glanced up as he tossed the door keys into his coat pocket. A grin spread across his features, and he opened his arms in welcome.

'Well hello lover! I was hoping you might wake me up before you went, but never thought that you'd risk being late for work...'

His accent was Scandinavian, or somewhere up there. He was talking to me like we were in some sort of pervy relationship.

What was he doing leaving my house?

I didn't ask him that. I was too busy side-stepping his embrace. Instead, I told him the truth.

'I felt sick. I came home.'

The look he gave me was of disappointment mixed with sympathy. 'Oh, poor you...' He glanced at his watch. 'Sod it! I can re-arrange an appointment or two. I'll come back in with you and get you settled before I get the later train.'

No, you bloody well won't.

I don't know why I didn't mention my wife, or the fact that he was leaving a house he shouldn't have been anywhere near – but it was something to do with the white shirt, the tidy car, my ring being on the wrong finger, and the fact that the name of the whole town had changed.

One thing I was sure about. I needed to be alone.

'Go to work.' I said sharply and saw despondency, mingled with surprise, written all over his face.

Tough.

I fumbled in my pocket for the keys. They weren't mine, but at least the second key I tried, fitted the door.

I glanced back. The Scandinavian pervy guy looked as if he wanted to follow me into the house. I glared at him, and thankfully, he turned and walked down the short garden path.

I closed the door on him.

And fell against the wall in the hallway, as the horror hit me.

This was not the wall that I had left behind, only an hour before.

All the strength seemed to disappear from my legs, and I slid down the wall. I ended up on my arse, squatting on the floor.

All around me were pictures. They were on both sides of the hall, and they stretched up the staircase.

There were pictures of Jonny Vincent and Scandi boy: drinking in Ibiza, outside the Sydney Opera House, in a queue to get into the Sagrada Familia. Any holiday destination that had gay boy connotations – they'd been there. I knew these things. I'd watched BBC 4.

I couldn't cope with being near them – grinning and gurning. Looking so happy. Well at least Scandi boy wasn't so happy today – and as for Rubber Jonny...

I wandered into the lounge. There was no coffee table with a dodgy leg. There was no wallet on top of it. At least there were fewer pictures in there. But there was a large trendy mirror.

Reflected in it, I saw myself. Or rather, I saw Jonny Vincent. The strange thing was, by now, it wasn't a surprise.

I looked at him ... me ... closely. The neat mousey coloured hair, the green eyes that had confused me when I'd seen them in the rear-view mirror, and the small straight nose. Everything about him from the slim build and medium height, to the wing nut ears and passive pose, shouted that he was nice – if a bit wet.

Which was exactly what he was.

I didn't hate him, despite what people thought. I didn't even dislike him. There was a point in our lives when we could have become friends. We were way past that now.

I saw little of him. Occasionally I would see him in the distance, the odd time I picked Amy up from work, but their friendship was kept well away from my home. Amy said that it 'brought back too many memories for him' and then fixed me with her death stare.

I don't know why I always got the blame. It hadn't been my idea. I'd only found out about it when it was too late to do anything, but I still got the blame.

I had thought that Amy was going to leave me at the time. Sometimes I wonder if she ever wished that she had.

I was rambling ... to myself ... in my own house, which looked like it had been redecorated by the team from *Queer Eye for the Straight Guy* without my say so.

Far too much weird shit...

I've always liked science fiction: time travel, alternative worlds, portals, extra-terrestrials, and artificial intelligence. It fascinated me. I've always thought that there must be more to the world than everything we accept as normal. The universe is massive, and we are small micro dots in it. How can we say that this is all there is? I didn't tend to mention it much. I tried to talk to Tan about it once and he accused me of being sparked out on ketamine.

But as I stood there looking at myself, in the wrong body, I honestly believed it was the only explanation. I had crashed into another car. My car had disappeared, and I'd ended up sitting in a strange vehicle – like mine – but not mine.

I got that feeling again. The one I'd had in Sandelwood – the village of the damned. But it was no good. My brain was mush. I desperately needed help.

I had to find a computer. I went back into the hall and climbed the stairs. The pictures of sunny gay memories goaded me with every step. I was reminded of a nightmare scene from some skanky horror movie, where demons and mad clowns haunted the hero while discordant music became louder and louder. Whereas, I was being taunted by happy holiday snaps from Sitges.

The first room I entered, when I reached the landing, was as freakishly neat as Jonny Vincent's car and had an air of redundancy about it. There was a sofa bed opposite the window but it was set out as a sofa, rather than a bed. It was obviously only used for the occasional guest that Jonny might have to stay. The second room was the smallest room upstairs, bar the bathroom. They'd turned it into a study, like Amy and I had done. There was a computer that I was about to turn on when another thought hit me.

There was only one room left. Which would mean that Jonny and Scandi boy shared it. Why that should have come as a surprise I had no idea. I mean, Jonny was gay. From what I'd seen of Scandi boy, he was obviously more than a lodger, I just hadn't clocked that they would share a room.

Share a bed.

I knew I needed to crank up the computer quickly. Even before I started researching weird car swaps and alternative worlds, I needed to do something much more urgent.

I needed to book into a hotel.

I could not share a bed with a man. I mean, Tan and I had done it once, but we were pissed up on *Reverend Benbellow's Six Percenter* and had no knowledge about anything until the next morning. There was certainly nothing sexual about the whole episode.

I then thought to myself that it was typical. If I had to be involved in a weird body swap scenario, why couldn't I change places with a multimillionaire who had a yacht in the Mediterranean and women on tap? But no, I had to change places with a poofter, who lived in my own house and played hide the sausage with a Scandi Ice Queen.

I turned on the computer and hit my first problem. He used a password to get into his own computer! At home. Did he not trust his dear beloved or something?

I knew Jonny's date of birth, mainly because it was the same as my own. Tan used to tease me about it and call us twins. He didn't bother any more.

I tried every connotation of the date that I could think of without any luck. I sat back on Jonny's poncy designer office chair and concluded that the Jonny Vincent I remembered was the type of romantic klutz who would use his lover's details to protect his privacy – from the self-same lover.

I risked a trip into the *chambre de gay*. There were yet more pictures of the beautiful couple and their equally beautiful friends.

Including one of Amy and Elliot.

Elliot had been my chief love rival back in our school days. I'd won and he'd buggered off to Australia. *Long before this photo could have been taken.* As far as I knew, he had never returned, and yet the picture had been taken in Hazelmeare Park, on the other side of town.

Apart from the pictures, the room was normal. It wasn't the fantasy in pink that I had feared it might be. Mind you, the curtains matched the duvet cover, and the carpets and walls were in shades of blue that tied in with some of the colours in the design of the fabric.

There were pictures in matching silver frames on each of the bed side tables. I went to the one that held Jonny's photo, figuring it would be the side of the bed that Scandi boy slept.

I opened the top drawer and found his passport immediately. His name was Arnur Bjorn Pétursson, which I hoped I would never need to know, but filed it into my memory bank, just in case. He was two years older than me, and he was Icelandic. Oh well, close.

It took me a few tries, but once I had entered Arnur's initials and his full date of birth numerically, the barricades crumbled and I was let in. That was when I came across yet another brick wall. I tried all the room booking websites and they came back with the same response. 'No Vacancies.' I found some small B & Bs without websites and rang around, but I was given the same answer.

'Why is everyone full?' I asked the lady who owned the last B & B on the list, my final chance.

'Well, it's Alec Carmichael week, isn't it?' She said, sounding amazed that I didn't know.

Carmichaeltown.

I hadn't twigged, when I drove back into town, that it was now called by the name of the man with the dull grey statue. In my defence, there had been a few strange things occurring that morning. But now, sitting in Jonny Vincent's bedroom office, I was suddenly reminded of a thought I'd had on the way to work before *The Twilight Zone* had crept up on my world.

What would he have needed to do to get something better than a cheaply made, dull grey statue?

I was nowhere nearer the answer to that question and the attitude of the lady on the other end of the phone didn't encourage me to ask. But, to have a town re-named in your honour, and a whole week dedicated to you, made me think that it must have been something seismic.

My thoughts turned away from Alec Carmichael and back to the strange happenings in my own life. I tapped Sandelwood, alternative realities, and disappearing cars into the search engine. When the computer revealed its findings, I sat there with my mouth open; like a goldfish who was amazed by the plastic castle it had already passed fourteen times that morning.

It was then the haze cleared slightly and the memory I couldn't quite grab hold of in Sandelwood, became fully formed. I had seen half of a TV programme about the place when I'd got home from the pub one night, a few years ago. I was a bit beer-ed up at the time, so I couldn't remember many of the details. There was a lot of chat about it at the football club, mostly people taking the piss. It lasted about five minutes before the story disappeared into oblivion.

Mind you, there was nothing about a TV programme in the search results.

Just a link to an article from the local paper.

I followed the link. I got the impression that the story had been written by some cub reporter, out to make a name for himself. He was obviously hoping that, if it was outrageous enough, it might attract attention from the nationals.

Sandelwood Gateway – Fact, Fiction, or a Conspiracy Theory Gone Mad?

Conspiracy theories ... everybody loves them, but only a few people truly believe them. However, when they do, they can be completely convincing. Sit next to a believer at a friend's dinner party and by the end of the evening, with the help of a few glasses of Rioja, you are certain that the moon landings were filmed in a Hollywood car lot, Paul McCartney died in the mid-sixties and was replaced by a doppelganger or that Adolf Hitler survived the Second World War and lived out his days shepherding sheep on a small Hebridean island.

Lately a conspiracy theory with local connections has emerged. It centres around the village of Sandelwood, twenty-two miles south-west of Carmichaeltown. The starting point of the speculation is the disappearance of HMS Valorous, over fifteen years ago. The nuclear submarine disappeared in the Pacific Ocean, south of New Zealand, and no traces of it have ever been discovered. The theorists believe that HMS Valorous exploded, whilst underwater, and the shockwaves opened a gateway to an alternative reality. In fact, it opened two. One is believed to be situated at the site of the explosion, and the other, on the other side of the world. It is believed that Sandelwood is the direct antipode to the area of the Pacific where the Valorous disappeared.

'In the beginning, the alternative reality was a carbon copy of the world as we knew it. However, over the years subtle changes have taken place.' Hadley Cooper-Wilson, chairman of the Sandelwood Gateway Investigation Co-operative, believes this is due to people inadvertently changing realities with differing results. 'Sometimes the effect on the worlds can be minute, sometimes it can be massive.' Cooper-Wilson even believes that one of the most tragic events from recent history happened because of the gateway being opened. 'We believe the death of Alec Carmichael, was due to one such event and that all the small changes, combined with some of the more cataclysmic ones, are creating a slow burning butterfly effect between the two worlds.' Mr Cooper-Wilson says the Co-operative is studying data to establish a pattern from which they could determine when the gateway is most likely to open. 'I think we would discover a world that is both incredibly similar and totally different from our own...'

Many thoughts occurred to me as I read the report.

First: it was a 'thing'. I was in another world. I wasn't going bonkers.

Second: it sounded as if people were changing realities easier than you could fly to Benidorm for a lads' weekend in the sun, according to this Cooper-Wilson bloke. Sadly for me, nobody seemed to know how or why.

Third: Alec Carmichael. The Olympic hero who was capitalising on his fame back in Westcastle by baking cakes in a marquee or eating snakes in the jungle. In fact, he was on any celebrity show or quiz that his agent could get his pen out for. But here ... here he was dead.

I read further on down the article, but the Cooper-Wilson git seemed completely stuck up his own arsehole. There was one passage that caught my attention, although I almost missed it, as I'd been drowning in his self-important pseudo intellectual claptrap.

It was about how you should act if you became trapped in this alternative reality.

Unfortunately for Cooper-Wilson, it didn't impress the reporter as much as it impressed me. He even mentioned it in his summing up paragraph, by which time he wasn't even pretending to be nice. He was, out and out, taking the piss.

So, if you get stuck in this alternative reality, remember, try to fit in and act normally. If you try and change things, you might never get home. Mind you, if you're stuck in an alternative reality, how are you managing to read this?

I almost felt a little sorry for Cooper-Wilson.
After all, he was right.
I continued scrolling down the page. All the articles printed were variations on the first one. Other than that paragraph, there was nothing to tell me how I should act in this world. There were several mentions about the butterfly effect and how slight changes could end up making massive alterations. I didn't care what they said. There was nothing on God's little earth, or God's other little earth for that matter, that would make me sleep with a gay boy.

More importantly, there was nothing to tell me how I was going to get home.

I leant back in the office chair, placed my hands over my face and sighed. I suddenly felt completely alone, and very tired.

I must have dropped off. The next thing I remembered was hearing a car door slamming. I rubbed my eyes and looked out of the window – and the depression lifted.

Amy was walking up the road. I suddenly believed that it must have all been a crazy dream. I even laughed at myself: *Alternative world – nobhead.*

But Amy didn't come down the pathway that led to our home. She walked up the street a few yards further and went through the gateway of the house next door.

Why is she going in to see Tan? I thought, *she doesn't even like him.*

It was the blinds on the window that first made me realise that I hadn't been dreaming after all. Back in Westcastle, Amy and I had some second-hand curtains that my Mum had been throwing out.

I looked around the room. We didn't have *La Cage aux Folles* or *Beautiful Thing* on DVD either.

So, I thought. *If Jonny Vincent lives in this house with his Icelandic squeeze and Amy lives next door with Tan; then where did I live?*

What had happened to Ben Shawcross?

~ 8 ~
LONELY

Westcastle: Jonny

I have felt lonely before in my life. Many times. The first time was just after Steve came to my primary school. At first it was the three of us, Elliot, Steve, and me. But then, the two of them seemed to have a lot more in common, and three became a crowd. They weren't horrible about it, which is why we are still friendly, but for a while I felt abandoned. Then, I drifted more and more towards Amy leaving them to enjoy their shared hobbies without me.

When Amy got herself a boyfriend, I experienced loneliness for the second time. Especially as that boyfriend was Ben. However, Amy was better at compartmentalising than the lads had been, and she kept time for me, even when Ben and Tanner used to tease her about it.

I also felt loneliness quite keenly when my Mum and Dad emigrated to Spain. I was having a few problems at the time, including the fact that Amy had fallen out with me. Mum and Dad had always been slightly detached as parents and I'd often wondered why they'd bothered to have me in the first place. They didn't seem to need children to improve their lives, they only needed each other. However, I'd needed their support at that time, and they hadn't noticed. They'd been hell bent on a new life in Lloret de Mar and I was made to feel irrelevant. Our relationship has never fully recovered. Even now it is limited to a one-night stop over when Arnie and I return from Sitges, once a year.

The loneliness I felt that morning after I had fallen, completely unprepared, into another world was different. I hadn't just lost my part-time parents. I had lost my entire life.

I could feel the tell-tale burn of tears spreading from my sinuses, tightening across my forehead, and hovering on the edge of my eyelids, threatening to swamp me.

I sensed a hollow space in my belly, so tangible that I almost felt sick with it.

Along with all of that, there was an overwhelming perception of loss for the world I'd left behind. And for the friends who still existed in this strange new land, but with whom my relationship had changed completely. But my biggest sense of loss was for the friends who had disappeared.

For Arnie.

I got through the morning. I'm not sure how. I just kept my head down and tried not to get into conversations with anyone. This was easier said than done with Tanner. Any chance he got, he sidled up to my desk and used it like it was a waiting room at the city's Old Street station. He annexed half of it with his lanky frame and, over the course of a few hours, filled me in with all the gory details of the previous night.

He had picked up a lucky girl during a meat raffle, in some back street pub. The irony of this was not as lost on me as it seemed to be on Tanner. She had 'tits that were like two fried eggs on a Bactrian camel.' This, apparently, seemed to be a good thing.

He had treated the lucky lady to a quickie over some empty beer barrels, outside the back of the pub. He had then left her to rearrange herself, while he'd sprinted away to find his next conquest.

This one he found 'talking to a tourist' in a trendy pub with its own microbrewery. Not only did he ease the girl away from her would be boyfriend, but he also managed to liberate the wallet that was hanging out of the man's pocket.

'Nicked his wallet, nicked his girl...' Tanner said proudly.

Throughout the terminal tales of his night on the town, I wanted to scream: 'You made my childhood a living hell. If only you knew how many days I had wished you were dead...'

Trying to zone out from Tanner's bragging, I attempted to formulate a plan. This involved logging on to the internet and searching for any details about alternative realities in general, and anything to do with Sandelwood in particular.

The RD Eversen that I knew, were clear on the rules regarding staff using company computers to access the internet for personal use. It was on the instant dismissal side of not advisable.

On the plus side, I had found a six-figure code written on a post-it note and stuck to the side of Ben's computer. It was alongside his computer password, so I was hopeful that it might be the code that would enable me to unlock his phone. I needed to use the mobile data to get a few answers. My security conscious self was split between shuddering at his negligence, and being thankful for it.

All I needed now was a quiet moment when I could use it.

And that was my problem.

I couldn't risk accessing the internet through my phone while sitting at my desk because of the many Tanner style interruptions that I had suffered that morning. I knew that he would appear the moment I had typed the words 'alternative realities' into the search engine.

I even tried disappearing to the toilets in desperation. I had got as far as entering the code I'd scribbled onto a piece of paper, when there was a mighty bang on the door.

'Oi! Benjy! There's a green cloud crawling down the corridor. What the fuck did the wife feed you yesterday?'

During the morning, I had remembered what Ben had called Tanner back in the world of my youth. I also remembered bits of their banter that I had normally heard alongside the pain of a dead leg or pinched ear. From the way I had heard Tanner talk that morning, I guessed it had been the same in this world also.

'For Christ's sake Tan. Can't a man even have a shit in peace?'

I'd obviously got it close enough to avoid making him suspicious. Tanner might have laughed and taunted 'Loser!' in the direction of the closed door, but he accepted it. The two of them obviously still talked like that when they were together.

Sadly, it didn't make him go away.

He stood on the other side of the closed door, making derogatory noises about the supposed smells that were wafting from my general direction and comparing them to the stench generated by a man I'd never heard of. 'Do you remember Benj?

Tonker at your stag night? The twat thought he was such a big man, eating a chicken phall and washing it down with ten pints of Kingfisher. The smells that came out of him for the rest of the night were outrageous.' He then spluttered a nasty, contemptuous laugh. 'Do you remember? He got taken short on the way home and ended up dumping a load in the middle of the bowling green...' He was laughing as he was talking, so it was difficult making out a few of the words. But there was no mistaking the punchline of the story, even if it was slightly smothered by a climatic belch of laughter. '...just as the security lights came on!'

Told by someone else, in a different manner, it might have been a funny story. Told by Tanner with his obnoxious tone of arrogance and scorn – it was about as amusing as syphilis.

I managed a grunt of laughter, but it didn't matter, he'd already moved on to another hysterical tale involving 'our' other football club mates. I realised I would be getting no peace, so I gave up even trying. I left the cubicle, managed a jocular pat on his back before washing my hands and heading back to the office.

I had to get away from him. When he was called away to meet a computer support advisor in one of the private meeting rooms, just before lunch time, I thought I had my opportunity. Unfortunately, a colleague chose that moment to arrive for a discussion about targets and objectives, so I was thwarted once again. By the time she left it was lunch break, so I made my escape before Tanner returned. My plan was to find a quiet corner in the local park. I knew it would be practically empty on a dreary day in January, so thought the chances of me being disturbed would be thin.

I nearly made it. The lift doors were almost opened enough for me to slide inside; when I heard Tanner's distinctive bellow, which forced my head to turn in his direction.

'Hold up Benjy-boy. Where are we going to lunch today?'

I'd rather hoped that 'we' weren't going anywhere for lunch together. I even had an excuse ready on my lips for some such interruption.

'Oh Tan. I've no money, remember? I just thought I'd get a breath of fresh air. You get some lunch and I'll catch you later.'

However, I should have realised by now that losing Tanner was going to be about as easy for me, as losing a pile of metal filings is for a magnet.

'Don't be daft. I couldn't let my best mucker go hungry, could I?' His uncharacteristic show of generosity was sadly short-lived. 'I'll buy you lunch today – and then you can return the favour for the rest of the week.' He mistook the look on my face. He thought I was disputing the fact that I would be paying four times, while he would only be paying once. 'Interest Benjy. Interest.'

In truth, I was just horrified. He was displaying the tenacity of a small child on Christmas morning. I was already worried about the sleeping arrangements with Amy tonight. In a splutter of dark humour, I had visions of turning over in bed and finding that he had sneaked in between us and was waiting for his present.

I had no idea how I was going to rid myself of him.

The obvious answer would be to tell him where exactly he could go and what he could do when he got there. It was an attractive idea. But, apart from the fact that it wasn't quite my style, my overriding desire was to get home. Until I'd found a way to do this, I felt it was necessary not to attract unwanted attention.

Even if that meant I had to be friendly towards a moron.

It was an uncomfortable lunch hour. He led the way to a nearby pub and told me he was going to order two pints of real ale without asking me what I wanted. My mild objection, that I had to stay awake that afternoon and drive that evening, brought a look of sarcastic disdain. It made me worry that I'd fallen at the first hurdle in the style of a 500-1 outsider at Aintree.

'No need to ask you what you want to eat.' He mocked as he thrust back his chair with the backs of his legs and strode towards the bar.

'I guess not.' I muttered to his disappearing rear. In truth I was a bit relieved. I had no idea what Ben would have chosen to eat.

I wasn't quite so relieved when a huge plate of cod and chips appeared in front of me. I don't like fish. I never have. I don't like the smell or the texture and covering it with a greasy batter makes me feel like I want to gag.

In short 'the fisherman's super-sized catch of the day', would not have been my choice.

I stared at my dinner, wondering how on earth I was going to manage to get it down my throat without something embarrassing occurring. I was also thinking about the last time I had eaten fish in Tanner's presence. When the man himself spoke, he nearly made me choke before I had even lifted my fork.

'Hey Benjy! Do you remember that saddo, Jonny Vincent?' Thankfully, he was in full reminiscing mode and missed my look of horror. 'Do you remember when we forced him to eat a double portion of scampi?' He laughed with vicious glee and performed a grotesque mime of someone being ill. 'Pro – ject – ile!' He stretched the word out with unpleasant hilarity, causing a woman on the next table to scowl in distaste, while she took sparrow sized bites out of her chicken, mango, and endive salad.

I remembered it as if had happened that morning. I remembered bumping into the pair of them as they left the chippie, on the way home from school. I remembered Ben restraining me while Tanner ran back into the shop. He'd reappeared a couple of minutes later with a bag full of the breadcrumbed balls of sliminess.

But this had happened in my world. How did Tanner know about it?

As I was trying to assimilate this question, alongside the uncomfortable memory, I became aware that an awkward pause was threatening to become something more obvious. I asked the question that was at the forefront of my mind to break the silence.

'Do you ever think we were a little hard on him?'

Tanner scowled. The Tanner I remembered hated to be challenged. Fifteen years on, it seemed that nothing much had changed.

'What's up with you today nob head?' He leant over and nicked a chip from my plate. 'Get a grip.'

I tried to laugh and remembered a phrase he had used that morning. I hoped it would get me out of the hole I was digging for myself.

'Sorry Tan. You know what I'm like without my security wallet – I start saying stupid things.'

He grinned and nicked another chip. He had a plateful of his own to get through, but I knew that this was more about power than it was about hunger.

'Nob head.' He said again, but this time it was softer, with something approaching affection. I guessed I had got myself out of a tricky situation.

I also managed to get through the massive plate of dinner in front of me without throwing up. In fact, I quite enjoyed it. This and the fact I had managed the mug of sweet coffee earlier, made me ask myself another strange question. *Whose taste buds had I got, mine or Ben's?*

The afternoon followed the pattern that had been set during the morning. I would be about to abandon my work on behalf of RD Eversen, to have a sneaky peak at Ben's mobile phone, when hurricane Tanner would blow in and ruin any chance I had.

Eventually, clocking off time arrived, and I started to shut down my computer with a feeling of relief that I had managed to negotiate a difficult day.

Sadly, for me, the difficulties were not over.

Tanner appeared in his normal, subtle as a sledgehammer, style. My desk shuddered ominously as, once again, he lowered his frame onto it.

'Home James and don't spare Shergar!'

Luckily, I was putting a few papers in the desk drawer at the time, so once again he didn't see the look on my face. I took longer over the task than necessary, to give myself a chance to process this latest bombshell.

I assumed, from that statement, I was giving him a lift home.

Where on earth did he live and how the hell was I going to find out without asking him directly?

I managed a grunt and a grimace, but he was already heading towards the door. Once again, I followed behind him saying goodbye to my colleagues, more as a stalling technique than for any other reason. Tanner certainly hadn't bothered.

They don't like Ben and Tanner. It was a thought that had been hovering around my brain all day, but at that moment it exploded like a bomb of certainty. I hadn't had one conversation all day, apart from those with Tanner, where anyone had said any more than was necessary. Back home, people might have viewed me as a soft touch, but they laughed with me. They shared stories and jokes.

They looked me in the eye when they were talking to me.

Gemma was the one exception. By the time we reached the ground floor, she was on her way out of the building, but not before she gave us her best flirty smile along with a breathy 'Laters!'

Cut from the same cloth, Tanner and Gemma, I reckoned. I could imagine them being discovered in flagrante delicto, on top of the photocopier at some office Christmas bash or other.

And what about Ben? The look she gave him ... me ... certainly made me think it was possible.

I thanked God that I hadn't fallen into this world during the festive season and silently applauded the lack of parties in the dull post-Christmas period.

Tanner strode across the car park and went unerringly towards my car. I was given the parking space when I was given the job, so obviously they were interlinked in this world as well as mine. After all, Ben did have my job.

I realised that I was nearing the point when I could find out from Amy what had happened to Jonny ... to me.

I pressed my thumb onto the key and let Tanner in, jumping in the driver's side at the same time. From things Tanner had already said that day, I guessed that they lived near to each other, worryingly in each other's pockets to be precise, so heading back to town was a safe bet.

I started the car, headed out of the car park and then out of the city. Without thinking, my neat and ordered brain surveyed the vague messiness of the car interior.

'I must give this car a clean,' I said automatically.

Tanner looked around him in surprise. 'It's not that bad. Besides, you only had it done the weekend before last.' He paused and I sensed the unpleasant grin, more than saw it. 'Mind you, get the little lady to do it again. It's a very pleasant sight to see while I'm drinking my Sunday morning coffee, Amy leaning over to hoover out your car.'

Mixed emotions scrapped for supremacy. On one side, I hated the way he talked about Amy and the fact he thought that Ben would accept it. On the other hand, I'd discovered that he must live in Chancelwood Road, and probably in number 32, from what he was saying.

How had he and Ben got hold of both of my parents' houses?

My parents bought the house next door to my maternal grandmother when they married. When she died, she left her house to them, and they rented it out. When they moved to Spain, they rented me their house on the understanding that after twenty-five years, they would sign it over to me fully. When the tenants in number 32 moved out some years later, Elliot and Amy were looking for a place to live. My parents had always been fond of Amy, so they offered her a similar deal to the one they had offered me. Amy still feels guilty about it. She says that she worries she has stolen my inheritance. I laugh and tell her not to fret. 'It's a small price to pay to have good neighbours,' I had said. I meant it too. I've never been that bothered about being wealthy. I'm never going to have children. Arnie and I are comfortable. Elliot and Amy are the easiest people you could want to live next door. It worked.

But now I had Tanner living next door, which would be as far away from easy as you are ever likely to find. I listened to him rambling on about the week ahead, and my mood became bleaker by the minute.

That night we were going to a sports quiz together. 'Did you make sure you listened to all the football results at the weekend?' he asked. 'You know what that sneaky nob is like. They'll be something obscure from the National League North.'

The short answer was no. However, I just kept quiet and let the interminable ramblings rumble on.

Tuesday appeared to be the night that Tanner, along with Ben's Mum and Dad, came along for 'Tuesday Night Supper'. By all accounts it happened every week, and every week it occurred at our house with Amy catering for it.

It seemed a bit one-sided to me.

On Wednesday we worked on Tanner's Rallycross car. He had a race coming up in a fortnight and wanted it to be in 'wazzock wasting' condition in time for it. The Tanner I remembered from my youth was always tinkering with an engine, so that wasn't a surprise.

I would have to find an excuse for that one. I couldn't tinker – I barely knew the difference between the exhaust and the ignition.

I only knew how to tidy the interior.

Thursday was five-a-side football night. That was a sentence I'd never uttered or had uttered to me before. It sounded vile.

Friday was our 'boys' night out' at the pub and Saturday we went to see City, if they were playing at home. Sadly, this weekend was the international break, so no Premier League matches were being played.

I muttered that it was a shame and acted as if I had known that all along.

A question came unbidden to my brain. *Why were Ben and Amy married?* Ben spent most of his free time, along with all his working days, in Tanner's company. *They'd* have been better off married.

As we passed through Sandelwood, and the site of my non-existent accident, I thought about praying for another car to come out of nowhere to take me back home. There was one problem with that. Tanner would end up there as well. I wouldn't have wished that on anybody.

When the journey, which seemed double the distance that evening, finally neared its end, I was greeted with another surprise.

The town was called Westcastle once again. This was what it used to be called before it was renamed to honour Alec Carmichael. The name had been mentioned a couple of times during the day but to see it written in black and white, on a sign, made it seem absolute. Unchangeable.

When I parked outside my gate, Tanner leapt out and said: 'See you in a couple. You'll drive, won't you? Can't be arsed to walk.'

I know I was trying to keep it all as normal as possible, but I had to draw a line somewhere. I could not go to a sports quiz.

'Do you know what mate?' I said hesitantly. 'I won't tonight. I'm absolutely knackered. Day without my security wallet and all...' I trailed off with the already used joke that was sounding tired, even to my own ears. I thought I'd blown it. The look on his face was full of anger and suspicion.

'Tosser. Don't you dare let me down.'

'Yeah, I'm going to. I've barely looked at the sports reports this weekend. I'd be as much use as a fishnet condom.'

'Nob.' He was more disappointed than angry, and the suspicion had faded as well. I felt like I might have got away with it.

'See you tomorrow.' I said quickly and moved towards my gateway, before he could try and change my mind.

I heard a mumbled obscenity, but I was already unlocking my front door and ignored it.

I had expected the house to look different. I had known there wouldn't be any pictures of Arnie and me on the walls. I thought the bright colours might have disappeared as well. Even though all of that was true, I still felt like someone had punched me in the stomach when I opened the door and went into my home.

Not only had all the pictures gone, but there was little there to replace them. There was a couple of sad wedding photos and a picture of Ben's Mum and Dad at their twenty-fifth wedding anniversary party – but that was obviously a few years ago now. The hall looked dark and depressing, so I moved quickly into the lounge. That was no better. It needed a coat of paint for a start. There was a coffee table with a wonky leg, which looked sad and neglected but at least it had a wallet sitting on top of it. The room was dominated by a massive television that was so large it covered half the window. Even with full daylight and the curtains open, I'm not certain it would have let much light in.

But the biggest surprise of all, was the woman who came through from the kitchen diner to greet me. She looked older and her hair had lost its healthy sheen. However, it was more the pale and sallow skin that surprised me. She looked exhausted, like someone had squeezed all the joy out of her life and left her wrung out, like a window cleaner's cloth.

Where was the vibrant mother of three that lived next door to me in Carmichaeltown?

Where was my best friend?

~ 9 ~
THE PERFECT MURDER

Westcastle: Fifteen Years Earlier

'If you could get rid of a group of people totally, like Hitler tried to do, which group would you chose?' Tanner said this languorously, as if he was discussing favourite breeds of dog rather than possible victims of another holocaust.

'County supporters?' Ben laughed. To be honest he wasn't sure that he'd understood the question. It sounded too close to serious for his liking.

'No, you tool,' Tanner snorted rudely. 'I'm for real. Who would you get rid of without a second thought?'

'Oh, I don't know. Teachers?' Ben didn't mean it, but he knew that Tanner didn't have a good relationship with most of the staff, so he thought he would be on safe ground.

'It's homos for me.' Tanner said without blinking.

'Well, I never knew you were that way inclined Tan!' Ben guessed where this was going and he wanted to steer his friend away from it. He knew Tanner was still seething about his run-in with Will, and the fact he'd been beaten by another boy in a fight for the first time in his life.

Beaten by a boy who was an out and proud homosexual.

'Don't be an idiot, turd breath.' Tanner said irritably. 'I mean, I'd like to get rid of all the fairy faggot boys in the world.'

Ben glanced at him in concern. Tanner really meant it. He was getting angry just thinking about the subject. Things had settled down after the school year had ended. Jonny and Will had been inseparable over the summer and neither Tanner nor Ben had seen much of them. But school was back after the long break, their last year before A-levels. The hatred between Will and Tanner hadn't gone away, it had just lain dormant. Ben could see it written all over his friend's face. It was turning crimson, and he was breathing erratically. Ben knew he would have to change the subject and calm him down in case Will happened to hear him. If it ended up in another fight, Ben had a funny feeling that Tanner would fare equally badly during round two.

'What about the perfect murder?' Ben enquired. 'How would you commit the perfect murder?' Ben had chosen his change of subject carefully. He knew it would have to be something that Tanner was equally obsessed with. And this had been a recurring topic for the pair of them ever since they'd watched a TV documentary on unsolved crimes.

If Tanner realised his buttons were being pressed, then he was happy to let Ben press them. 'A poison that is completely undetectable and leaves no traces in the body afterwards,' he said with certainty.

'How many of them do you know?' Ben laughed, relieved that his ploy seemed to be working. 'I mean old man Hatcher hasn't got around to the lesson on undetectable poisons yet.'

'I have ze ways!' Tanner tapped his nose in the manner of a cartoon detective.

'Ground up glass.' Ben countered quickly, keen to keep the idea going. 'I read that over a course of time, ground glass will shred a person's gastrointestinal tract and cause internal bleeding. If you're patient enough, it will kill them. Leaves no trace either.'

Tanner snorted. 'Except for insides that have been ripped to shreds, you twat.' He paused for breath. 'I've heard that whole daffodil bulbs release poisons that are untraceable.'

'Don't you think someone would notice if their plant pot was empty and they had daffodil bulbs doing the front crawl in their Sunday gravy?' Ben laughed in friendly scorn.

Tanner ignored him and smirked unpleasantly. 'Maybe we could secretly invent a new gay plague.'

Ben sighed inwardly. The man was obsessed. He was just going to tell Tanner to leave it – the joke wasn't funny anymore – when another voice joined the conversation.

This time, Will *had* overheard them.

'Or...' he said in a calm and reasonable tone. Ben shuddered. He knew the tone was a warning that there was trouble brewing

'...you could force someone to eat a large amount of a food they hated – and watch as they choked on their own vomit.'

'He didn't choke.' Tanner argued, then laughed nastily. 'I thought he was going to though. It was hilarious.'

'Foul, spiteful, malicious,' Will said in a deliberately pompous tone. 'As well as being puerile and immature...'

'Aah, fuck off you arse.'

'My, my!' Will said with false admiration. 'Hoots, what a fabulous orator you are, you have such a lovely way with words. Inspirational!'

Tanner ignored the sarcasm and asked instead: 'What's it to you anyway? It's none of your business what we do to Rubber.'

'Oh, but you see, I've made it my business. Jonny is my boyfriend. Upset him and you upset me.'

Ben saw the look of distaste that crossed Tanner's face. Will saw it too. He knew he was winning, getting under the taller boy's skin, so he chose to ramp up the pressure.

'That's right Hoots. My boyfriend, the man whose cock I like to suck, whose testicles I like to massage with my mouth. The man whose perineum I...'

Tanner's every urge was to resort to his normal fall-back plan when he found he was losing an argument. And apart from anything else he just wanted to hit Will to make him stop talking. He raised a fist in preparation, but Will simply tutted gently.

'I wouldn't do that Hoots. We all know how that ended last time, don't we? Best not humiliate yourself again.'

'You were lucky last time. I wasn't ready.'

Even Ben could see how ridiculous that sounded given the circumstances of their last physical encounter.

Will chuckled and made good use of the gift Tanner had given him. 'Well, perhaps next time you should make sure you're ready – *before* you attack someone.' He then sobered. 'Give it up Hoots. If you just admit that you're an inferior species to us homosexuals you'd have a much happier life.'

Ben looked at his mate anxiously. He knew it would never happen. He knew that Tanner could never admit to being beaten.

'No friggin' chance. Name your challenge Gaylord.' He stared at Will and mimicked a hoodlum in a bad gangster movie. 'No one ever beats Tanner Hootley.'

A grin spread across Will's face. It was a grin that let Tanner know he had just given Will exactly what he wanted.

'OK. In that case. Let's say a week on Saturday, just to give you a chance to have a little practice.' The mocking tone was there to ensure that Tanner had no chance of refusing the challenge. 'The water tower in the woods. First one to the top is King of the Year. The loser has to admit his inadequacies in front of the whole of the Sixth Form.'

It was a simple bet, a stupid wager. Two lions brawling to win control of the pride.

It would change everything.

~ 10 ~
MY WIFE NEXT DOOR

Carmichaeltown: Ben

I dashed down the stairs, fumbled with the lock, and almost fell out of the door. I was desperate to know what had happened. Why was Amy living next door? Why was she living with Tanner?

It was only as I slammed the door shut that a completely unrelated thought hit me.

Why did I think that Tan was still living next door?

I mean, I – or Ben Shawcross – didn't live at number 34 anymore. Why should Tan still live at number 32? I thought back to the picture in Rubber Jonny's bedroom. Amy and Elliot at Hazelmeare Park. A horrible thought suddenly convinced me that Amy was probably living there with Elliot Harper, my love rival.

But. *I'd won and he'd buggered off to Australia.*

Because of this thought, it wasn't too much of a surprise when Amy opened the door, and I couldn't see the City banner which acted as the only decoration in the hallway of Tan's home. It wasn't a surprise that the first picture I saw was the skanky Hazelmeare Park photo. It wasn't even a surprise to see that the other pictures on the wall seemed to be of children. Three of them, as far as I could make out. Amy and I had never had children. When we got married, I thought we would have them. I wanted them. I still wanted them. I think Amy wanted them. It's just that it had never happened.

But Elliot, who must have been the man in this household, had managed it nicely. Three little Harper sproglets.

So, none of those things were a surprise. After the morning I'd had, I should really have been unshockable. But there was one thing that managed to leave me standing there, like a gormless contestant on a game show they should never have entered.

Amy herself.

She was beautiful.

Now, don't get me wrong. My wife is a very attractive woman. Tan is always going on about her wonderful arse – and he's right. But the version of Amy that stood in front of me was different. The only way I could describe it was that my Amy was in black and white, whereas this version was in full technicolour.

She smiled sympathetically when she saw who was standing on her doorstep.

'Oh Jonny, are you all right?' I gave a vague nod, but she was already moving on without me needing to answer her. 'I was just about to pop round. Arnie rang me and said you weren't very well.' She frowned, and this little bit of disapproval creased her stunning features. 'He said that you were a bit snappy with him. Not your normal self at all.'

So, I'd upset the Icelandic lover. Tough.

'Come on in,' she said. I continued to hover on the doorstep and she jumped to the wrong conclusion. 'Don't worry about me catching whatever you've got. The kids are like germ magnets. If it's around we've probably been exposed to it already. I seem to be pretty un-infectable – if that's even a word!' She nodded in the direction of the lounge. 'Go on through and I'll make you a lemon tea.'

Lemon tea. If anything was going to make me want to gag, lemon tea would do it. Even so, I didn't need too much persuasion. I was hoping that Amy could be the key to uncovering a little more about this new world.

But, apart from anything else, I wanted to spend some time with her. I'd only seen her for a minute, only heard her speak a couple of sentences. It didn't matter. I didn't need any more time than that to realise. She was the Amy I'd fallen in love with when we were still at school.

I sat on the sofa and looked around me. A classy gas fire dominated the main wall of the room. The coals were glowing, and the room was warm and inviting. Pictures of the children, and the whole family, were everywhere. It was as sweet and cute as a Labrador puppy covered in candy floss.

It made me feel a little bit sick.

There were so many questions I needed to ask, but I didn't think that asking them was a good idea. The main question I wanted to ask was whether I could sleep in Amy's house that night. Even on the sofa. Anything that saved me from sleeping nose to nose, not to mention cock to cock, with another man.

It was the Cooper-Wilson article that stopped me. *If you try and change things, you might never get home.* And I did want to get home. I suddenly realised, sitting in my wife's house, in another man's body – in another man's world – that I wanted my Amy back. Not the monochrome version I'd left in Westcastle that morning. I wanted the sassy, classy, fully-coloured vibrant woman she should have been. The woman she had turned into in Carmichaeltown.

Amy re-appeared with the lemon tea. It tasted all right. Surprising really, because normally I liked my drinks so thick with sugar that the remnants turned to concrete in the bottom of the cup. Whereas this was as sharp as an out of tune violin.

'So, what's up with you?' Amy prodded me in the chest. Her eyes blazed with a fury so fake that I could see the worry behind it.

'I feel crap.' I managed to mutter. *Would Jonny even say the word 'crap'?* I hadn't got a clue, but Amy was too caught up in her own thoughts to notice.

'I'm not talking about your illness, you daft bugger,' she said fondly. 'I'm talking about you and Arnie.'

Oh shit! Are you?

'He's worried you're going to leave him.'

Yes, I am. Hopefully.

'You know he loves you. He just hates the way people stomp all over you. And you just let them. That's why he goes on about things so much.'

Now that did seem to be like the pathetic, wimpy, Jonny Vincent that I remembered.

'Things?' It was all I could manage. I was hoping it might draw her out. Get her to tell me more information about 'my' life. Luckily, she didn't need much persuading.

'Gemma and Cameron borrowing that money. We all knew they had no intention of giving it back. The bloke in the pub yesterday, the twit in the 8 'til late last week. The nasty little yob and his mates that are always giving you verbal whenever you bump into them in town...' She stopped talking and fixed me with her gaze once again. It was making parts of my body react in a way that would give the game away. Gay men didn't normally get hard-ons from talking to beautiful women. She then took my hand, which didn't help matters. 'He loves you – you twit. I know you don't think you're worthy, but he really loves you.' She caressed my hand and whispered softly. 'Let him...'

I didn't know what to say. I guessed saying: 'But I don't love him' didn't fit in too well with the Cooper-Wilson model of how to get me home.

Amy took my silence as a sign that I didn't want to talk about it. She was right, but not about the reasoning behind it. She decided to change tack and started reminding me of all the wonderful things that Arnie and Jonny had done together over the four years they'd been together.

This was good, for a couple of reasons. She didn't seem to expect me to say much, so I could just lose myself in her voice, her eyes, and from time to time, her touch. It also gave me a brief history of the last four years in the life of Jonny Vincent. I thought that might come in useful, if I had to spend an evening with the icy arse bandit.

Eventually she came to a pause. She looked at me earnestly. I tried to think what Jonny might have said. He was such a wet lamebrain that I guessed he would have just agreed meekly.

'Yeah, you're right Ames.' I said.

I don't know what made me call her that. I've never called her that, but something in the back of my brain must have remembered that Jonny Vincent did, or used to, in the world that I had grown up in. He must have done so in this world as well because she smiled and snuggled up to give me an affectionate cuddle.

I hadn't bothered to change out of Jonny's suit, which probably didn't fit in with my 'sent home from work' ruse. It wasn't good for another reason either. The trousers were tight and didn't hide much; but other than that, I enjoyed it. Amy and I didn't cuddle very much these days. *Why on earth hadn't I cuddled her more while I'd had the chance?*

She shuffled around, so she could lean against my arm and place her head on my chest. In her mind it was totally asexual. She chatted about the weekend. Jonny and Arnie, along with Steve Coombes and his wife had come over for dinner on Saturday night. Steve and Elliot had been very good friends in my world as well, before Elliot went away, so it wasn't much of a surprise.

I managed to join in with a conversation about a dinner party I hadn't been to. I was very non-specific. 'That dessert was delicious, how did you make it?' Again, the sort of poncy thing that I thought Jonny might have said.

Amy then started to talk about her family. They had even called the oldest boy Jonny – poor bastard. After about ten minutes, I'd had enough talk about Elliot 'Mr Perfect' Harper and his boys. The question I'd first asked myself in Jonny's bedroom office, slipped out of my mouth before I'd decided whether it was wise or not.

'Do you know what happened to Ben Shawcross?'

Amy sat bolt upright, leaving behind a warm indentation on my chest.

'Bloody hell Jonny, whatever's made you think about him?'

'Oh, I don't know. I was thinking lately that he probably wasn't as bad as I remembered him, and I just wondered if you knew where he was.'

Amy's eyes screwed up in a quizzical manner, as if she couldn't quite believe what she was hearing.

'I was always telling you that, but you wouldn't have it. You said he and Tanner were as bad as each other. You said they were responsible for making your childhood a living hell.'

Hearing it said like that was brutal. It made me feel as guilty as sin.

Amy slumped back on the sofa. For the first time, since I'd been in the house, she wouldn't look at me.

'I felt you'd abandoned me you know, after it had happened.'
What the hell was 'it'?

'I guess, in a way, we were on different sides back then.' She suddenly turned her head and fixed me with the full force of her stare. Like a laser boring its way through bone and gristle to get inside my brain.

I just wished that I could get inside 'my' brain.

'You were obsessed with Will. And in my own way, I was obsessed by Ben. We weren't good friends to each other really.' She patted my hand briefly, and then wrapped her own hand around my fingers as if her life depended on it. 'I'm so glad we got over all of that in the end.' Amy smiled suddenly and said with gentle affection. 'I love you, you daft old queer!'

All the time I'd been in that house I had wanted her to say those words to me. It just would have been better without the 'daft old queer' bit being tagged on to the end.

'I love you too ... Ames.' I said.

No-brainer.

'Do you ever feel guilty about what we did to Ben later?' Her words stunned me so much that I nearly missed the rest of her sentence. '...I suppose that's unfair, it was all my decision, but you were very definite about your views on the subject.'

Unsurprisingly, I didn't know what to say. It was just as well that Amy was so caught up in her own world that she didn't notice the strange gurgling sounds that I was sure were coming from my throat.

'Don't get me wrong. I don't regret my marriage to Elliot. He is kind and wonderful and has made me happier than I ever thought I would be...'

Ok, enough of the gospel devoted to St Elliot – what exactly did you 'do' to Ben?

She gave the little cheeky laugh that I remembered. The little cheeky laugh that I hadn't heard for a long time.

'He can also be a bit wicked. To think I used to worry that life with Elliot might be a bit dull, not enough of the naughty boy about him. But he's everything I want and everything I need – and – he's given me three lovely sons.'

I wasn't sure I could bear hearing much more about Mr Perfect von Perfect.

I had just decided that I wasn't going to get an answer to my original question, so I was trying to think of a way to bring it up again, without making it seem too obvious. I was at the point when I'd drawn a blank and had decided to give up that Amy spoke once more.

'Ben's back in Carmichaeltown.'

I nodded and tried not to look too eager to hear any more details.

'It's funny you should mention him today,' Amy looked curious but not suspicious. 'I've been thinking about him quite a bit these last few weeks.' She sighed and twiddled her wedding ring around on her finger. It psyched me out a little bit. My Amy did that as well, normally when she was feeling worried, which seemed to have been quite often recently. 'I bumped into an old acquaintance of mine, who knew his Mum. She said that he'd come back to Carmichaeltown a couple of months ago. He'd managed to re-build his life and this was his final test. He wanted to see if he was strong enough to face everyone again.'

I looked at her face. For a moment, the full-blown technicolour had faded and when she continued the monologue, her voice barely had more power than a whisper.

'His Mum had said they were just so happy to have him home. It might have taken almost fifteen years since it happened, but she felt like she'd got her son back again.'

Amy still didn't tell me what 'it' was. But the last thing she said to me, before she trotted out to do the school and child-minder run, left me breathless with shock.

It was as if she was confessing something she'd thought about many times, but hadn't said out loud before.

'I just feel I cheated on him. I cheated on him and abandoned him, just when he needed me most.' As I was still lost for words, I thought that rubbing her hand sympathetically would save me from having to say anything. She looked up at me gratefully.

'Apparently, Ben's mum said they had him on suicide watch, eight years ago, when he first came out of jail.'

I said goodbye to her in a bit of a daze. I let myself back into Jonny's house and sat on the bottom step of the stairs. I took several deep breaths.

Andy Paulcroft

In Carmichaeltown, things were very different. They were certainly different for Ben Shawcross, my alter-ego.

What had he done? How the hell had he ended up in prison?

~ 11 ~
WORRYING

Westcastle: Fifteen Years Earlier

'Don't do it Will.' Jonny's words were soft and low and nearly disappeared into the collar of Will's school jacket. 'You don't have to prove anything.' He paused, then twisted his head upwards, so the last few words were clearer. 'Not to me, at any rate.'

It was morning break, the one time during the school day that Jonny kept exclusively for Will. He didn't want to disown Amy completely, so the other breaks he still spent with her, or he shared her with Will. She didn't see her own boyfriend much during the daytime. He was too busy running riot with Tanner, the King of the Arseholes.

The evenings were different. Ben seemed to remember he had a girlfriend as soon as the clock nudged five o'clock. Before Will had arrived, this was the time that Amy abandoned Jonny. There were half-hearted invitations, but Jonny knew that she didn't really want him to play gooseberry. Her boyfriend certainly didn't want it, and he had no desire to do so either.

Although Amy still deserted Jonny at five o'clock, it was no longer to an evening spent fretting. He no longer had to play a game of trying to guess tomorrow's torture.

Will would meet him every night after his martial art club of the day had finished for the evening. They would alternate between each other's bedrooms. They'd run up the respective staircase, armed with their school-book alibis. For the next two hours they would chat and laugh, tease and squabble, and kiss. Sometimes Will would release the homework from his bag and work on it while Jonny pretended to do the same. In truth, he didn't have the concentration required to work on Stalin's July days uprising, or the inclination to factorise $2x^2 +13r+15$.

His head was too full of other thoughts.

He would pretend to study his book but couldn't stop his eyes peering over the top of it to gaze at Will. His boyfriend had a habit of worrying the tip of his nose with his forefinger as he read, or biting the inside of his lips as he solved a problem. Jonny would lose himself looking at the smartly cut hair, onyx black, and as sturdy as porcupine quills. He would stare happily at the perfect skin unaffected by teenage blemishes. And then – there was the body…

Will's athletic frame stretched the hastily donned T Shirt and Jonny could see the outline of his nipples behind it, teasing the slighter boy with a subtle invitation. The soft dark hairs on his arms spoke of a manhood that was galloping, racehorse fast, towards him. As Will sat cross-legged on the bed, his jeans would ride up and expose a strip of his lower leg, also dusted with similar soft black hairs.

Will knew exactly what Jonny was doing, but he made him wait. Finally, Will stuffed his book back into his bag and interlaced his fingers around the back of his boyfriend's neck. Jonny felt the excitement of a small child who was seeing the gates to a fantasy theme park open for the morning. The merest touch of Will's fingers, as they stripped and explored every centimetre of Jonny's body, seemed to heighten everything around him. The scent from the atomiser, plugged into a spare electrical socket, mingled with the smell of a slow cooked beef bourguignon wafting from a neighbouring house. The soft rumbling of the washing machine downstairs accompanied the song on the radio being played by workers in the road. Then there was the taste of Will, the citric shower gel that mingled with the vague perception of lemonade on his lips.

And above all, there was the sense of danger. Every creak of the staircase warned of an impending invasion. Every footfall from anywhere in the house caused Jonny to believe that at any moment the door would crash open, and an irate parent would discover the two of them, their naked bodies exposing their homework dishonesty. However, it didn't ruin the moment, if anything, it made it even better.

There was that sense of danger at school as well. They had discovered an area at the back of the caretaker's shed where all the old furniture and chemicals were dumped prior to being taken away. It was strictly out of bounds. Even the smokers gave it a wide berth, after an unfortunate accident with paint thinners and a highly flammable padded bench seat. The only person likely to disturb them was the caretaker himself, and he liked to patrol the corridors during break time. He thought of himself as an extra teacher, but his unnecessarily acerbic manner had garnered him little respect, and the nickname of Genghis.

There was evidence that he had been busy over the last twenty-four hours. Will and Jonny were enjoying the unexpected comfort of a faded and coffee-stained settee that had been removed from the staffroom.

After his soft entreaty, Jonny pulled himself up onto his knees and placed his fingers around the back of his boyfriend's neck. He could feel the tickly bristles of a recent haircut underneath the palms of his hands and was aware of Will's soft breaths as they buffeted against his face.

Above everything else, Jonny was aware of the hypnotic power of Will's eyes. Almost as dark as the hairs on his head, they were serious and sympathetic. Yet, there was a hint of soft teasing that hovered somewhere underneath his lashes.

'I don't think I could bear it if something happened to you,' Jonny admitted. He no longer felt the need to edit his vocabulary before he spoke. Will never made him feel like he'd said something stupid.

As if to prove the point, any hint of soft teasing disappeared completely. Will replied in a voice full of understanding and empathy.

'Nothing is going to happen to me, do you understand? Nothing.'

'But you could slip and fall,' Jonny said earnestly. 'No one's done any maintenance on that wreck for years. The staircase could disintegrate as you're running up it.' He then changed tack and said in a voice full of a certainty brought on by years of abuse. 'Tanner will cheat.'

'He might want to,' Will nodded. 'But he wouldn't dare to do anything in front of everybody. I know that he will start fast, but he has no stamina. By the time we're halfway up that tower, he'll be staring at the soles of my trainers. He'll be choking on my dust and won't be able to do anything about it.'

'What about Ben?' Jonny wanted to be reassured but, ever since the challenge had been issued, his brain could only think of the ways in which his brief glimpse of a perfect life could be sabotaged.

Will nodded. 'Ben's faster. He would give me a good race. But...' he paused to let the words sink in. '...the challenge is between the moron and me, no one else.'

He removed Jonny's hands from around his neck and held them, massaging them gently, as if he could rub some comfort in as he did so. 'I want to make that bastard pay for what he's put you through. I want to make him lick your arse.'

Jonny grinned despite himself. 'I hope that's a metaphorical licking. I don't want his rabid tongue anywhere near my arsehole.'

Will smiled and said softly. 'That's exactly what I mean. You're kind and lovely but you've also got an acerbic way with words. You're funny. It's a crime that no one has ever seen that except Amy. They've made you hide your true self from the world; that's why I'm doing this. Because, when Tanner has admitted what a loser he is and apologised to you, I'm hoping it will give you the confidence to show the world the wonderful Jonny Vincent that I know...' Will bowed his head with uncharacteristic shyness '...and love.'

Jonny smiled nervously. He was still getting used to the feeling of being admired. Of being wanted. Will was barely eighteen, but he was more of a man than his own father had ever been. He had made him feel loved, and safe, for the first time in his life.

Jonny never wanted it to end.

~ 12 ~
DINNER WITH MY 'WIFE'

Westcastle: Jonny

'Your tea is on the table.' The tone of the voice matched the look on Amy's face. Empty and lifeless. I was reminded of my mobile phone when I had forgotten to re-charge it overnight. Drained.

Automatically, I moved towards her so we could exchange a 'Thank God I'm home' type of kiss. Even lately, when things in the garden hadn't been exactly cram packed with blossoms, Arnie and I still did that.

It was almost imperceptible but I was sure she moved her head when I approached her, and I ended up pecking the crevice where her two lips met. When I followed her into the kitchen diner, which was decorated in the same style of neglected retro as the rest of the downstairs, I was surprised to see that only one place had been laid on the table.

'Not eating?' I said neutrally.

'I'll eat later when you've gone to your quiz.' She then looked at me defiantly, as if I'd already started to argue with her. 'And yes, before you start taking the piss, I will have it on a tray, on my lap, while I watch the soaps. Just like a sad middle-aged housewife without a life.'

It was the suppressed rage that surprised me most. Apart from once or twice, around the time we fell out, I don't think I'd ever seen Amy angry. I'd certainly never seen the hard, brittle, undeniably sad woman who was standing in front of me. It broke my heart.

'I'm not going to go tonight,' I said, then relied on the excuse that Tanner had accepted easily enough, if somewhat grudgingly. 'I didn't bother to look at any of the sports results over the weekend, I'd be useless.'

Amy looked at me as if I'd told her that the Virgin Mary was my mother. 'Excuse me! Apart from playing football and getting pissed with your mates, you did nothing else all weekend.' She then muttered under her breath, although she didn't seem to care whether I heard or not, 'I do live here you know.'

I suddenly realised that conning Amy was going to be fraught with difficulties. Much more difficult than it had been with Tanner. The one good thing about Tanner was that he wasn't interested in anything anybody said that wasn't related to him. Conversely, Amy listened. And she and Ben had a whole history together that I knew nothing about.

I decided it was time to use the fall-back plan I'd thought up on the journey home, just for moments like this.

'Actually,' I said, 'I had a little bit of a car accident this morning...' The immediate look of sympathy on Amy's face was the first indication I'd had that their relationship wasn't totally doomed. Ben just had to start treating her better. Remembering that he had a wife might have been a start. 'Oh, nothing drastic, it's just shaken me up a little, that's all.'

'Is the car all right?' I immediately wondered whether I'd been wrong after all. Her husband had just told her that he'd had a car crash and her automatic reaction was to ask about the vehicle. Their relationship was fractured, there was no doubt about it. It certainly put my problems with Arnie into perspective. Compared to the Shawcrosses, our relationship was at the stage when Cinderella was easing her foot into a glass slipper.

'No, it's fine. I'm fine.' I assured her just in case she might actually have been worried. 'I ended up on a grass verge. I did bang my head on the steering wheel though and to be honest, I think it might have given me a bit of mild memory loss, there are some things I just don't remember.'

I thought I was being smart. I thought I could tie it all in with a question I was desperate to know the answer to. Sadly, I had forgotten what Steve Coombes had said, at the water fountain, when I'd asked him a similar question.

'Your wife would know. Don't you ever talk to her?'

I don't know why I was so keen to find out what had happened to my alter ego in this crazy mixed-up version of my own world. I should have been more interested in trying to work out how to get home. After all, I had been trying to buy myself time to log on to a computer all day. Now, at last, I had the chance to make up an excuse and disappear upstairs to investigate. I'd already got the impression that Amy would be quite happy to see the back of me.

But, instead of that, I tried to be too clever.

And walked straight into a mantrap of my own making.

'For instance,' I said, pleased with the smooth way I was manoeuvring the conversation. 'Tanner mentioned a lad we went to school with today – Jonny Vincent – and I don't remember him at all.'

The look on Amy's face was unreadable at first. It was only the slight straightening of her back, and the fact she was twisting her ring around on her finger, that gave me any clue to the stupid mistake I had just made.

'Oh, for God's sake,' she said, 'can't you just give it a rest?' But she wasn't really asking me the question. She was talking to herself, the walls, the table with the single place setting. Anybody or anything except the man she thought was her husband, standing in front of her.

'I'm sorry.' I said. It was a generic apology. I had no idea what I was apologising for. It simply seemed prudent to do so.

'He's the one friend I've got left, but you can't let a day go by without taking the piss over how much I see him.' She didn't seem to notice that I had spoken. It was only when she spoke again that she addressed her remarks to my face. 'Every day I have to put up with you calling him "the soft git," "Rubber Jonny" or that charming nickname that came straight from the mouth of Tanner Hootley: "my husband without the shagging rights".'

Finally, she was beginning to get visibly angry, but it wasn't on her own behalf. It was on behalf of her friend, Jonny Vincent. I felt so thankful to her for it, but knew I had to be careful. After hearing that hateful soubriquet, all I wanted to do was join in and have a bitch fest against Tanner. However, I wasn't 'Rubber Jonny'. I was Amy's husband. I was Tanner's friend.

'OK, you don't like him. Neither you nor Tanner can cope with the fact that Jonny is gay, even now. Well, as I've been telling you for years, he is. He's not going to change anytime soon and he's always going to be my friend. So, you'd better get used to it.' I was thankful for her rant. It meant that she wasn't expecting me to say anything, and she hadn't finished. 'So, whose hilarious idea was today's gem? No, don't tell me. This has Tanner written all over it. "Let the mardy mare think that you've had a car crash and lost your memory. Then, when you've sucked her in, pretend that you can't remember who her 'girlfriend' is." Hilarious.'

Having spent a day in his company, I thought Amy's impression of Tanner was close to perfect. It might have been a couple of octaves higher than his actual sarcastic drawl, but she had got the intonation and phrasing spot on.

She turned her head away and addressed the next remark to the cooker. 'Well, I hope you have a bloody good laugh at my expense while you're at your sports quiz tonight.'

I had to calm her down. I got the impression she'd been building up to this for a long time, not just days, but weeks, months, even years. If I didn't subdue her this conversation would end abruptly, with a slammed door and silence for the rest of the night.

And I needed, and wanted, to talk to her.

'Hey, hey.' I reached out and put my hands on her shoulders. She didn't pull away which was a start. She didn't nestle her head into my chest either. But she didn't pull away.

'I know that I've not been the best husband lately,' I started to say, keeping my tone as soothing as possible. It was a guess, of course, but from what I'd heard and seen over the course of the day, it seemed likely to be true. Whether Ben would have admitted it like that, was another matter. I thought it was a good idea to enforce the bang on the head story, to cover that point.

'I did have a car crash this morning,' I continued. 'And I have forgotten a few random things.' I plucked at a few half-truths and tried to make them fit my tale. 'For instance, I couldn't remember my personal password to log into the computer at work. Luckily, I did remember that I had written it on a post-it note and stuck it to the side of the computer.'

Amy risked a half-smile. 'You do that at work as well?' she questioned, but she did seem to be calmer.

I nodded. 'And Tanner did mention Jonny Vincent earlier.' I was lurching towards the tricky bit. 'Of course, I remember Jonny. I just didn't associate that name with your best friend.' My excuse was as thin as rice paper, but maybe there was something in the tone of my voice that sounded genuine. When I risked a glance at Amy, her suspicion seemed to be fading slightly. It wasn't disappearing completely, but it was certainly fading. 'And you're right, of course, I watched all the sports results over the weekend...' I attempted a lop-sided smile '...I just can't remember any of them.' And then to explain my original faux-pas, I added, 'I was a bit embarrassed about the crash and the memory loss. I was hoping not to have to tell you about it, if I'm honest.'

Amy pulled away from me gently and went to flick the switch down on the kettle, as if she needed something else to do to avoid saying anything.

'What I really want to do tonight is to lay that table for two people,' I nodded at the lonely place setting, before continuing. 'I then want to open a bottle of wine and have a drink before dinner, followed by a quiet evening with my wife.' It felt funny to use that word, but I was beginning to feel more comfortable with my alter-ego. So much so that I hazarded another guess, although again, I didn't think it was a complete shot in the dark. 'We haven't been talking enough lately.'

It did the trick. Amy stopped looking at the kettle, which was rumbling gently towards a climax, and briefly patted my shoulder. It was the most intimate gesture she had given me since I'd walked into the house. Without a word, she opened the cutlery drawer and took out another knife and fork. She flicked the switch on the kettle back to the 'off' position and put the unused mugs back on the mug tree.

My immediate reaction was to help her by getting the glasses and the wine, which was when I realised my next problem.

Where, on earth, did they keep the glasses?

I wasn't sure I could stretch the story of memory loss to cover the fact that I didn't know where anything was in my own house, so I hovered uncertainly. Luckily, my inactivity didn't seem to be at all unusual to my wife. She sashayed her way around my prone body with a ballerina's grace and seemed completely oblivious to the obstacle I was creating. Within seconds, the glasses had been taken from the cupboard above the sink and placed on the table along with another set of cutlery. Then, after a quick trip to the fridge, a bottle of Sauvignon Blanc was waggled in front of my eyes.

'You definitely want wine, not beer?' Amy queried with uncertainty.

Ben really needs to sort himself out, I thought. *Not only does he have a wonderful wife who he ignores, but he also has an idiot of a friend who he treats with a god-like reverence. On top of all of that, he doesn't seem to drink wine.*

I nodded. Amy turned the control on the oven down to its lowest setting, swept the glasses away from the table with her free hand, and led the way back into the lounge.

'So,' she said once we were settled, and our glasses had been filled. 'You had a minor car crash, where there was no damage to the car, but you banged your head on the steering wheel and now you can't remember odd things?'

I nodded again. I was hoping to move swiftly on. If pressed, it would have become clear that my story had more holes in it than the Titanic after its brush with an iceberg.

'I thought we could start with our childhood,' I risked saying. 'See how much I can remember, and how much I've forgotten. 'I then gave myself a metaphorical safety net. 'Especially the things you're sure I should know.'

I was now, at last, becoming accustomed to shocks after a day full of them. Tanner's knowledge of my teenage brush with death by scampi should have prepared me for what was to come next. Even so, sitting in Ben and Amy's lounge, listening to tales from a childhood that were so like the ones stored in my own memory bank – managed to surprise me once again. I had no difficulty in adding bits and pieces to the conversation, I merely had to be careful that the snippets I added were from Ben's point of view, and not my own.

Once we had both finished our first glass of wine, we moved back into the kitchen and Amy served the chicken casserole. She started talking about the period around the time of our A-levels and when we were leaving school. It was then that the similarities between the two worlds became fewer and further between.

Eventually, she moved quite naturally onto a subject that had been teasing my brain since Steve had mentioned it at the water cooler that morning. What had Ben, Ben's father, and Tanner 'done' to Jonny around that time?

'I probably shouldn't ask this, but, how much did you know?' I got the impression that Amy hadn't challenged her husband on this topic for many years. She glanced at me carefully, as if she was expecting a show of anger or contempt. 'I know you swore to me that you had no idea what your father and Tanner were plotting, and I believed you at the time.' She gave a little snort of self-derision at what she perceived to be her own gullibility. 'Mainly, because I desperately wanted it to be true.' She fixed me with a stare that threatened to overwhelm me with its intensity.

'I don't know.' I'd never uttered anything more truthful. 'I can't remember anything about it.'

Amy pushed her empty plate away from her. The tension that had gradually evaporated during our conversation had returned and her body language was defensive. When she spoke again, the anger and suspicion were there once more.

'You can't remember anything about it?' She mimicked my words scornfully. 'You can remember the seat in the park by the tennis courts where we used to take the mick out of the younger kids playing tennis, but you don't remember destroying my best friend's life?' I was close to losing her. I racked my brain to try and think of a way to bring her back, and nearly missed the fact that she had started talking again. 'You see, I don't know about this story about a so-called accident. I still can't help thinking that I'm being sucked in to one of your "jokes". I'm half expecting Ant and Dec to appear from one of the cupboards to reveal where all the cameras are hidden.' The volume of her voice dropped sharply, but her next words were crystal clear. 'You don't forget something like that.'

'Tell me, please.' I was praying that the sincerity in my voice would be enough to placate her.

She sighed, then seemed to decide to take my plea seriously. 'Jonny was going through hell at the time...' Amy paused. I was just about to ask her to elucidate, but the question got caught in my throat as she continued '...when his parents were killed while they were on a boating holiday.'

Although my relationship with Mum and Dad could never have been compared to the Brady Bunch, I wouldn't have wished them ill. To have them suddenly pronounced dead was a strange experience. Even if they were a different version of the parents I'd known, and tolerated, for the whole of my life.

Luckily, Amy mistook the strange look on my face as confusion. I felt she was starting to believe my amnesia story once again. I reined in the shock and tried to look suitably vague.

'I must admit I thought they were being a little self-centred at the time.' Amy continued. 'Jonny wasn't coping. He was on the verge of a breakdown. On top of which he was just starting his A-level year. But, rather than be there to support him, they decided to take their bloody boat for an autumn trip on the River Hazel.'

'What happened?' I asked.

'The boat blew up,' Amy said. 'There was some gossip that they were in dispute with the bloke who did the maintenance for them, and he'd turned nasty, but nothing was ever proven.' She paused, picked up our empty plates and stacked them in the dishwasher. When she returned to the table, she fixed me with the force ten stare once again. 'Are you sure you don't remember any of this?'

That was an easy one. My parents were in all probability irritating the hell out of their fellow Brits in the Años Dorados retirement complex in Lloret de Mar. They had not been pronounced dead while partaking in an ill-conceived boating trip on the local waterways.

I shook my head. 'Not at all.'

She shrugged but seemed willing to continue giving me the benefit of the doubt. 'So, there was Jonny, left to deal with everything on his own. His uncle was the proverbial chocolate teapot. Completely useless. Jonny did get some counselling through school, but...' she shrugged again '...it didn't really help him.' She tried to jog my memory once again. 'Do you remember your eighteenth birthday?' I did, but obviously not the right one. 'I was torn at the time. I wanted to be with you, but it was Jonny's birthday too, and he hadn't wanted to go to your party.'

She stopped talking and, for a horrible moment, I thought she was going to burst into tears. 'It was only afterwards that I found out the truth. He had spent his eighteenth birthday, alone in his room, with a bottle of vodka and some razor blades.' She blinked the threatened tears away. 'Do you remember what he said to me the next day when he showed me the small nicks on his wrist?'

It was rhetorical, but I shook my head in any case.

'Why couldn't I have been brave enough?'

I had to swallow away the threat of a few tears myself. It was weird. It was as if I had discovered a long-lost twin brother. A twin who had a history completely diverse to my own. Black to my white. I felt strongly connected to him in the strangest way and, because of the alien body I was inhabiting, I also felt responsible for a lot of what had happened to him.

'Jonny went through hell at the time. And I found out later that I knew less than half the story. Jonny didn't tell me everything until a few years ago.' Her wedding ring received another twist. 'I know we've decided to agree to disagree on the subject of your best friend, but...' she stared at me meaningfully. 'What Tanner did to him; it was evil.'

I got the impression that Amy had locked her views on the subject inside herself for a long time. She had grabbed this unexpected chance to air those feelings, like a control freak might latch on to a religious sect that was short of a leader.

I wanted to ask her for more details, but she had already moved the story on.

'Even though I didn't know the whole truth at the time, I was still worried about Jonny. I asked you if your father might get involved on his behalf. The words "absentee parents" had been invented for Tanner's own mother and father, and your dad was the closest thing he had to parental guidance. I thought it might help.' She slowly shook her head at her own stupidity.

'The next thing I knew, your dad had found Jonny a solicitor and very quickly the deed was done. Your dad had "acquired" two houses, to add to his portfolio, and Jonny had a two bedroomed flat in the centre of town." Her next words echoed my own thoughts. 'Not exactly what you'd call a fair swap.'

I was silent. Sometimes silence is useful to encourage people to continue to talk and sometimes silence can be used as a criticism. On this occasion, I used the silence because I simply had nothing to say.

'Like I said, you swore you knew nothing about it. You said that Tanner and your father hadn't let you into their scam. Over the years I have become less and less sure that I believed you.' Her eyes found mine deliberately, challenging me to tell her the truth at last. I swerved facts that I was completely ignorant of, and tried to use my fictional amnesia to my advantage.

'Perhaps that's why I can't remember anything about this,' I said hopefully.

'What, because you feel guilty about it?'

'Or...' for some inexplicable reason I wanted to leave Ben a marriage to come back to, if we managed to get that far '...perhaps, I felt guilty because I thought I should have known what they were up to.'

Amy didn't comment on that gem but continued her story instead. 'When we realised what was going on, I tried to get my parents involved, but you know what they were like...' The Mr and Mrs Crawford that I remembered were lovely, gentle people who had died too soon. It seemed that none of that had changed in this world '...they were no match for Jack Shawcross, the greatest know-it-all of our time...' I got the impression that she was playing with me, seeing how much I would let her get away with. When she spoke again, she admitted as much.

'Sorry, he's your dad, that was below the belt. It's just...'

'What?'

'You seem different, softer, more approachable – I've said a few things tonight that would have normally ended up in a full-blown row, which is why I've stopped bothering to say anything, but tonight...' She left the thought hanging in mid-air as another one hit her. '...you're talking differently as well. You're not phrasing things in your normal way, and your views haven't been copied from the gospel according to St Tanner.' She laughed gently, 'I like it.' Her face was almost becoming youthful before my eyes. The careworn grey-looking woman of earlier had disappeared. The Amy I remembered was re-appearing; vibrant, happy, and cheeky. 'I might batter you over the head again, if it brings out this side of you.'

I feigned a look of horror. 'Call the police immediately!' I cried. We were entering territory so close to our normal bantering relationship, that for a moment, I forgot who I was supposed to be. 'Ga ... husband bashing going on in here!' Luckily, she had other thoughts on her mind and didn't notice my near miss. She laughed at the exchange but sobered immediately.

'Your dad...' She started tentatively but, after an encouraging nod from me, she said exactly what she wanted to say. What she had wanted to say for a long time. 'Oh Ben, it's the fucking Tuesday night supper tomorrow.' The Amy I knew didn't swear much and because of that, when she did, it was even more powerful. I rubbed her hand supportively and she continued.

'Could you just back me up a little?' She was almost pleading. 'Every week I cook for, serve, and wash-up after Jack Shawcross and Tanner, his surrogate son. I have to listen to their misogynistic clap trap. The only other female in the room is your mum, and the poor thing is still so in awe of your wonderful father that she's no help at all.' She paused and looked at me pointedly. 'I know you don't exactly join in with the things they're saying, but you laugh with them.' She nodded to herself before repeating. 'You laugh.'

'I could cancel it,' I said hopefully. I'd been dreading it since the moment Tanner had reeled off the weekly social timetable earlier, so this seemed too good an opportunity to miss. However, Amy screwed up her face in humorous horror.

'Crikey!' She said, 'and risk lightning striking the house and a plague of locusts invading the patio?' This time, it was Amy's turn to pat my hand as she shook her head. 'No, I don't want to get you disinherited, but it would be nice to feel that someone was actually on my side. And maybe suggest that next week, someone else could host it. I mean, once in about fifteen years, it's hardly unreasonable – is it?'

I'd won her over.

It's that easy Ben Shawcross, you idiot. She still loves you.

We moved back into the lounge and as the evening wore on, we got closer and closer on the sofa until we ended it in a companionable cuddle. She started talking about what had happened in the book shop in town where she worked. It was one of the rare duplications between our two worlds. Next-door neighbour Amy dished the dirt on the staff and customers all the time, as if they were characters in our own soap opera, so I was able to join in a little.

I had to be careful though, there were some notable changes. The most prevalent one was Jonny. The reason I hadn't been able to find him, on the RD Eversen website, was because he worked with Amy at the bookshop. He was still living in the two bedroomed flat that he'd moved into under those dubious circumstances. Amy thought he was happy, in an unfulfilled, wobbling through life, type of way. He was still waiting for 'the one'. He just hadn't found him yet. Once again, it made me think of Arnie, and how lucky I was.

'I've had such a lovely night,' Amy whispered in my ear as we straggled up the stairs. 'I feel like I've got my Ben back.'

There is only one way this night is going to end, I thought nervously. Cuddling Amy had been very natural to me, we had done it all our lives, and we still did. However, sex was something that, for obvious reasons, we had never done.

It didn't happen. When Amy was in the bathroom I tried to get myself aroused, by thinking about Arnie, so that I didn't ruin the evening with an unresponsive penis. Amy barely noticed, she crawled into bed, gave me a peck on the cheek, turned off the light, turned her back to me, and settled down for the night.

She's got out of the habit, I thought. *In fact, their whole marriage has become a habit that she can't be bothered to break.*

But what would happen next? If I managed to find a way to reverse the crazy happenings of the day, then I would return to

Arnie, and Ben would return to Amy. I would have built her hopes up, just for Ben to shatter them on his return.

And what about Arnie?

He was sharing our bed with a man who, from the evidence I'd seen that day, had progressed from an apprentice homophobic bully to the fully-fledged reality.

Arnie could be in danger. Sex had definitely not become a forgotten afterthought in our relationship, a bit routine, but not forgotten. What if Arnie initiated sex, like he innocently would?

I was scared for him.

I was scared how Ben would react to that.

Sleep would not come. I homed in on Amy's gentle breathing, the screeching of the cats in the street and the ticking of an alien alarm clock. But sleep would not come. I tried to send a telepathic warning, from one reality to the other, in the hope that it would reach the man I loved.

To stop myself thinking about Arnie and the danger he could be in. I thought over all I had learnt today; about this world I was inhabiting.

So much of what Amy had said resonated from my own adolescence.

When Amy had chided Ben about the bullying he and Tanner had inflicted on Jonny, I was once again that frightened child – scrabbling on plastic sacks – trying to climb out of the bins.

When she had talked about Will's arrival, I remembered how my world had flipped from Hades to Utopia in a heartbeat.

There was something else as well, a memory from the evening that was floating around in my brain, threatening to disappear completely. I caught hold of the tail of it and reeled it back in.

Amy had spoken of a conversation she'd had with Ben. She'd been trying to encourage him to dissuade Tanner from going through with the stupid challenge, the one that Will had tricked him into accepting.

I was suddenly back in Will's bedroom fifteen years earlier.

'Don't do it Will.'

I gasped in realisation and sat bolt upright, glancing quickly over to Amy, to check that I hadn't woken her.

Up to that point, the two worlds had been identical.
But everything seemed to change, after that day at the water tower.

~ 13 ~
BIOLOGY

Westcastle: Fifteen Years Earlier

'Jonny is so worried, Ben.' Amy was cuddling into her boyfriend on the seat by the tennis courts. The post Wimbledon surge of the Sharapovas had dwindled away, and a light covering of autumn leaves was making the surface slippery, which further discouraged the plimsolled invaders.

Ben grunted. He had hoped he could persuade Amy away from the exposed bench they had made their second home and move to the bench that was hidden in the trees, on the way to the pitch and putt course. He had a mock Biology A-level paper that was haunting him, even though it was out of sight in his school bag. He was hoping he could persuade Amy to join him for a little bit of practical biology before he was forced to return to the theory.

Her latest statement was a good a way of telling him that she wasn't in the mood.

'You know what he's like,' she continued. 'He could worry about a car crashing on an empty motorway. The thought of Will racing up a rickety old water tower, chasing Tanner, has practically got him thumbing through his phone searching for an undertaker.'

'Tan won't back down.' Ben shook his head in certainty. He heard Amy blow through her nose in irritation and quickly defended his friend. 'Don't blame it all on Tan. Will has been winding him up ever since he arrived at the school and made Rubber Jonny his pet project.'

'Don't call him that,' Amy said automatically. She had been saying the same thing ever since a pre-pubescent Tanner had discovered the term whilst rifling through his father's not-so-secret stash of pornography. It hadn't stopped them then, and it wasn't going to stop them now. Even Amy had given up believing that it would. Even so, she still thought she owed it to her best friend to keep on trying.

'Sorry.' Ben's apology was just as automatic and just as meaningless. 'But don't you think it's a bit weird? The two of them loved-up like they are. I mean Shakespeare didn't write Romeo and Romeo, did he?'

'Alexander the Great was bi-sexual.'

'Bullshit!'

'He was! A load of historians agree that his bodyguard was also his lover. Alexander went to bits after he died.'

Ben snorted. 'Well Jonny's not Alexander the Great. Imagine him marauding through Asia and Africa.' He stood up quickly and crudely imitated a mincing walk while play fighting with an imaginary sword. He felt one of Amy's trademark glares bore into his back, so he abandoned the mockery, sat back down, and returned to his original point. 'Honestly Amy, Will is a bit of a wanker, but he's quite normal. He does sport, knows about cars. I'm sure he's only with Rubber because he knows it winds Tan up.'

'So, he pretends to be gay simply to get under Tanner's skin?' Amy asked with a sneer. 'What is wrong with you? Why can't you just let Jonny be happy? Why can't you accept that some people are gay, and they deserve to be happy too? Tanner has made Jonny's life hell for practically all of it so far, and you haven't exactly helped.' She prodded his arm as a reprimand. 'Now, he has finally found someone who treats him well. Just let him have that, at least. Let him have Will. Talk to Tanner. Talk him out of that stupid challenge. Please.'

Ben smiled gently and grabbed hold of Amy's hands before she could move them out of the way. 'This is why I love you, Amy Crawford,' he said. 'You don't care that people don't like Jonny. You don't care that he's the butt of everyone's jokes. You don't care that it's not cool to be seen around him. He's your friend and that's all you care about.'

Ben held her. Told her loved her. Smiled at her and the warmth from his gentle, beautiful face enfolded her like a shawl. At times like this, Amy understood why she wanted to be with him forever.

She turned her face towards him and kissed him lightly on the lips. Suddenly it didn't matter that they could be seen by everyone in the park. Ben returned the kiss, with increased force, and yet it was still loving and gentle. Amy jarred her lips against his and eased her tongue between his teeth. She ripped his school shirt from its resting place between waistband and boxers and her hand found the gap between shirt and skin.

He gasped as the cool of her flesh tickled his stomach muscles and her hand negotiated a route up to his left nipple. To stop himself from ripping her clothes off in a frenzied act of passion, he concentrated on the neat precautionary signs, in green and white, that were dotted here and there: *Do Not Walk on the Flower Beds* and *These Tables are for Café Customers Only.* He added another sign of his own making: *No Shagging in Full View of the Tennis Courts.*

The part of their brains that were still trying to escape the clutches of childhood, prevented all-out revolution and calmed their frenetic grappling. Amy contented herself with gently stroking Ben's nipple, and Ben himself wallowed in the glorious pain of denying his erection any chance of relief. Instead, he concentrated on the kisses. Her soft lips against his own. the vague taste of mint imperials on her mouth. In the brief break between kisses, he would lay his face against hers. He could then smell the scent of summer flowers on her skin, courtesy of a birthday bottle of perfume.

After a while, the skin above her lips started stinging gently. It was a tell-tale sign that the razor on his birthday present list was not an optimist's folly. She reluctantly pulled her lips from his and nestled her head against his chest. It was then that Ben continued their conversation.

'How you feel about Jonny,' he was careful to use her name for him, 'it's how I feel about Tan.' He curled her hair with his finger. 'I know he's not liked. I know people only talk to him in the hope that he won't pick on them next. I know that people would laugh at him, the way they laugh at Jonny, if they were brave enough.' He moved his fingers from Amy's hair to her chin and tilted it upwards so she could see the honesty in his eyes. 'His has no one, not really. You could replace his parents with a cheque book, and he wouldn't know the difference. My father is more of a dad to him than they've ever been, but it's not the same. He's a bit of a saddo really. He's almost totally alone.'

The eyes didn't waver, although Ben's lips curled into a soft smile.

'But, he has me.'

Amy sighed. Resting against Ben's chest she believed she had never been happier. She knew that underneath the mask of boyhood bullying, beat a heart that was good and kind. She knew he would grow into a loving man.

And he would keep her safe.

Ben wished that he could enjoy this moment more. He was with the girl he loved, who loved him in return. He knew he was bright. He relished the exams rather than feared them. He knew his future was full of hope and full of promise. 'Enjoy these years,' his father laughed, 'it'll never get better than this.'

The one fly in the ointment was Tanner, his best friend. Ben would do as Amy asked, and talk to him, but he knew he had no chance of getting him to pull out of the challenge. No more than Jonny had any hope of convincing Will to do the same.

Will was strong, he was quick, and he was intelligent. *What if Will won?*

Ben had no idea what Tanner would do.

~ 14 ~
A NIGHT OUT WITH MY 'BOYFRIEND'

Carmichaeltown: Ben

'Hi Honey, I'm home!' The fake American accent sounded even weirder when it came via Iceland with a hint of Westcastle, or Carmichaeltown, thrown in.

The love of my life had returned.

After I'd hauled myself back up to the office, two hours before, my mind had been a bit of a mess. And it wasn't just Amy's revelation about the other Ben's time in jail that was responsible for that.

An hour spent staring at the jolly family snaps on the walls of my wife's house had psyched me out as well. If I'd been honest with myself, I would have admitted that I was jealous. Jealous of what Elliot had taken from me in this world and jealous that he seemed to be making a much better job of it, in Carmichaeltown, than I had in Westcastle. Unfortunately, being honest with myself was a bit of a work in progress. There was a thought bashing around my brain.

How could I free Amy from her life of perfection and reunite her with Ben?

The underlying feeling, behind that thought, was the irritating fact that Elliot had won. He hadn't lost and buggered off to Australia.

And to be honest, the thought of that was killing me.

Cooper-Wilson's warning was ringing in my ear. *If you try and change things, you might never get home.* But he sounded like a bit of a numpty. He might not even have been right. Even so, I swore I'd be careful not to change too much, but there were two things I was desperate to change. I was even willing to gamble my return ticket to ensure they did, and didn't, happen.

Getting Ben and Amy back together was, of course, one of them and you didn't need to be Clara the Clairvoyant to work out the second one.

I could not sleep in the same bed as a gay man. I had realised that if I wanted a place to stay during Carmichael week, then it would have to be under the same roof as Reykjavik Roger. But not in the same room and, certainly not, in the same king-sized double. With a speed brought on by panic, I came up with an obvious excuse. If I blagged it well enough, it might even buy me a couple of nights. I had come home from work ill, so ill I would be. As I was obviously a thoughtful chap, I would sleep in the spare room, so I didn't disturb him.

Feeling a little better knowing that I had a plan, I turned my attention to the other Ben Shawcross. Facing the computer, I tapped in the name of my father's company. It wasn't visible.

The only time in my life that I have gone against my father's wishes was when, after uni, I had refused to join the family firm. As a result of this he had amalgamated with another company and the two businesses, trading as one, had gone from strength to strength. It had been a much better move for him than being stuck with a trainee idiot who didn't want to be there. I never tired of telling him how right I'd been, but equally, he always leaves me thinking that it was his idea in the first place.

After scrolling through several pages, I discovered *JBE Shawcross*, a much smaller fish in a similar pond to my father's company. The picture of the managing director gave me the proof I needed. Obviously, having a jailbird for a son hadn't been brilliant for business.

I kept it as low key and unremarkable as possible.

Dear Mr Shawcross,

I have heard recently that Ben is back in town. I am sure you will remember that we weren't the best of friends. But I would like him to know that I bear him no ill will. I also heard that he is interested in testing the water as far as meeting up with old acquaintances is concerned. Could you please let him know that I would like to meet up with him? If you could forward this e-mail on, I would be grateful.

IN ANOTHER MAN'S SHOES

Yours sincerely
Jonny Vincent

It felt weird, typing that name as my own. I re-read the e-mail and felt pleased with myself. It was the wet sort of language I could imagine Rubber using. If Ben was, as Amy's friend of a friend believed, keen to meet a few people from his life before jail, then it wouldn't send him running for the hills.

Without giving myself a chance to think things through, I added a P.S.

I know Amy is keen to meet Ben as well.

I quickly pressed the 'send' button.

I then decided to do a little bit more research into alternative realities, and more accurately, how to get home once you'd managed to get yourself flung into the wrong one accidentally. I couldn't find anything, so I sent an e-mail to Cooper-Wilson. I gave him a bit of flannel about reading the article, being interested in the subject, and I asked him for a meeting.

And that was when the Scandi Ice Queen chose to arrive home.

Cursing silently, I shut down the computer and went to the top of the stairs. Standing just inside the hallway was a good-looking man. The one I'd had a go at when I'd bumped into him on the garden path earlier. He was holding a bunch of flowers that were not the supermarket deal of the day variety, I occasionally bought for Amy.

He had thick dark blonde hair that was swept up from a broad forehead but clippered neatly above the ears. His nose was wide, and full, and his jaw was strong. His eyes were the archetypical Nordic blue, and he had a smile that would send any self-respecting queen into a limp-wristed frenzy.

Obviously, I was not an expert in the subject, but I would have said that Jonny Vincent was punching well above his weight.

'Lover!' The single word managed to convey both sympathy and encouragement. 'Amy said that you were feeling a bit better.' *Oh my god!* I thought, *were they linked by some weird sort of audio umbilical cord?* Amy and the Ice God seemed to be continually on the phone to each other about Jonny Vincent. It took the power out of my impression of someone walking down the stairs while being close to death. And the next sentence made me re-think the whole illness strategy completely.

'Pity, I was rather looking forward to an evening of mopping your fevered brow and treating you to some of my grandmother's old Icelandic cures.' I had no idea what old Icelandic cures might entail, but I had a sudden awful vision of ice baths and Arnur running up and down my back in his bare feet. I decided to abandon the plan of taking to my bed through illness and go with the fact that I was well on the road to recovery instead. At the back end of that decision, I remembered that Amy had called him Arnie, so I thought that I'd better do the same.

I'd made it down the stairs at that point and he held out the flowers towards me. 'These are to say, "Get well soon" and "I'm sorry for yesterday".'

I guessed that he was apologising for the argument that Amy had mentioned earlier. I had no idea of the details, so I covered that fact by taking the flowers and muttering that I needed to put them into water. I don't think that anyone had ever bought me flowers before but, it was always the first thing that Amy did, on those rare occasions when I bought some for her. As I searched the kitchen for a vase, I could hear Arnie in the hallway, taking off his coat and shoes.

I was so involved with panicking about the evening ahead that I missed the sounds of Arnie coming up behind me. I was filling the vase at the sink when he wrapped his arms around my middle, trapping my arms to my sides, as he nuzzled his face into my neck.

'Careful!' I snapped slightly as the water overfilled the vase and dribbled down my fingers. I could feel him grinning behind me as he released the pressure on my body. He leaned over to turn the tap off, took the vase from my hands, and put it on the draining board.

He turned me around so that I was now facing him. His face was inches from mine, and he fixed me with the full force of his smile. I was panicking so madly that I did feel a little sick. As he moved in to give me a kiss, I neatly sidestepped his advances and gently eased myself away from his embrace.

'Sorry,' I apologised hurriedly. 'My breath must be minging, I haven't had a wash all day.'

I could not be stuck in the house with him all the evening. Even before we got to the question of sleeping arrangements, there would be the worry of him jumping my bones while we watched everything from *The One Show* to *Newsnight*.

'Why don't we go out tonight?' I suggested. I figured I would be safer if we were out in a crowd. Hopefully his Nordic liberalism would stop short of terrorising me with public displays of affection.

'What?' Arnie grinned. 'Jonny Vincent, I do believe you're beginning to rebel at last! Going out to play when you haven't been to school?' It was funny to hear such a British phrase being said with Arnie's gentle smorgasbord of accents. I guessed it was all part of his charm, if you were that way inclined. 'Give me half an hour to have a shower and I'll be right with you.' He raised his eyebrows and grinned in a suggestive way. 'You could join me if you wanted to.'

I had no words to describe my feelings about that particular gem, so I panicked once again and blurted out that I'd had a shower just before he got home.

He looked at me strangely, then put his hand on my forehead, checking for a temperature that could have been responsible for sending me schizo.

'I thought you hadn't washed all day?' he said.

* * *

'A quick one at the King John before we have dinner?' Arnie asked after locking the front door and walking quickly down the path to catch me up. I agreed straight away. First, I was desperate for a pint after the madness of the day, and second, I thought it was a good way to make the evening last as long as possible before we had to go back to the *Maison de Gay*.

At first, the people who were milling about were few and far between on a Monday evening at the arse end of the New Year celebrations. This changed as we neared the town centre and the trade created by Alec Carmichael week was obvious.

Mingling amongst them were a few local people that I recognised. *Do you know, I thought, somewhere in this vast universe there's a duplicate of every one of you, in a world you've never even dreamed of? It used to be an exact duplicate of the world we know. But a gateway was formed. People swapped worlds – swapped realities – and it changed things. I could be changing things now, even though I'm desperately trying not to...*

As we settled onto the stools surrounding one of the tables, near to the window, in the King John, I looked around the bar. It wasn't one of the normal ones that Tan and I went to. They didn't have a sixty-three-inch screen showing around the clock sport, like the Chancelwood Arms at the bottom of our road, so it wasn't on our list. There was only one discreet television, but it was close to us. On the screen, the league champions were warming up, ready for their latest match.

'I think they'll win the league again this year.' Arnie said enthusiastically, nodding towards the TV.

'I don't know, I think that City could give them a close run,' I argued automatically, without thinking.

Arnie laughed and held up a hand in apology. 'Sorry lovely boy! I should know by now that you and football don't mix.' I must have looked vague, but that was mostly because I was nowhere near to coping with a man calling me 'lovely boy'. Once I'd got over that, I realised I'd muddled up worlds again. Luckily, Jonny Vincent's lack of sporting knowledge came to my aid.

'City are having a terrible season,' Arnie said gently and smiled genuinely. 'But thanks for indulging me and trying to join in, even if your career as a sports reporter would be a short one.' He took a swig from his pint. 'Right, I promise no more football talk.'

I never thought I'd give up a chance to talk about football, but I thought that it was just as well. Over in Westcastle, City were having an incredibly good time of it. I vaguely wondered what had happened in this world to bugger it up for them.

I realised that Arnie had started to talk again, and I zoned back into what he was saying: '...I know, I'm the worst gay man in the world, football mad, untidy as hell and I don't really like Eurovision.' He grinned again. 'Mind you, I even got expelled from Iceland for that one...!'

His eye caught sight of a flyer for a Dusty Springfield tribute act, and he stabbed his finger towards it. 'On the other hand, I know exactly what you're going to say.' *Well, at least one of us does,* I thought. Luckily, Arnie continued, 'I get a shed load of gay points due to my love of Dusty.' He fixed me with a look that hovered uncomfortably between flirty and needy. 'We have got to see her. Ple-ease.'

I strained to see the date on the poster. It was the Saturday after next. I smiled, agreed, and hoped that Jonny would get the pleasure.

I was careful, after that, to think before I opened my gob – think, as I thought Jonny Vincent would think – and I managed to survive the night with only one other near miss. It was when we were discussing what to eat, once we'd been given menus in the Thai restaurant. The waiter had greeted us like old friends and pretended we had booked a table. This meant we could bypass several groups of Carmichael tourists who were waiting to be seated.

'I think I'm going to go for the fish curry,' I said. Tan would have had something sarky to say about that. I always had the fish curry. Arnie, on the other hand, looked at me as if I'd said I was dating the Princess of Wales.

'You're going to have the fish curry?' he repeated in amazement. It was then that I remembered something from my teenage years. Something about Jonny Vincent and fish.

'No, you deaf idiot,' I laughed, trying a quick recovery. 'I said chicken curry, the Thai green chicken curry.' I gave him my best look of incredulity. 'When have you ever known me to eat fish?'

After that second near miss, I let Arnie lead the conversation. When things looked similar to how they were at home I joined in. When they didn't, I kept shtum. Eventually the subject got around to work matters. It seemed that Jonny Vincent in this world did the same job that I did in Westcastle, which would be useful when it came to going back to work the next day. Arnie was still a service provider to RD Eversen, but the person he dealt with wasn't Tan.

I wondered what had happened to my best mate. I'd still heard no mention of his name.

Arnie was a good mimic; he was also funny and a bit rude. His impressions of the people I knew were spot on. But, unlike Tan, he wasn't cruel with it. And Arnie was quite happy to take the piss out of himself, something Tan would never do.

I liked him.

It was a bit of a surprise. I don't think I'd ever met a gay man that I'd liked before. I'd always felt a slight sense of superiority towards them and perhaps it showed. On the rare occasion that Amy and I got invited out to a dinner party, there always seemed to be a random gay couple there. It was as if the hosts needed to advertise their twenty-first century credentials. It was no longer girl, boy, girl, boy on the seating plan – it now seemed to be girl, girl or boy, boy, with a carefully accidental mix of races and a white straight couple to top it all off.

Halfway through our curries, Arnie returned to the subject of our disagreement from the day before.

'I'm sorry I give you a tough time,' he said. 'I know you're doing it because you want to help people. I just hate to see you taken in.' He paused as if he was working out how to say what he wanted to say, without re-starting the disagreement. 'I know you said that Cameron had got in over his head and he had learned his lesson...' He shrugged his shoulders and wobbled his head from side to side as if he was having a silent discussion on the subject amongst himself '...and I know that at the moment he does seem to be behaving himself, but...' he fixed me with his impressive blue eyes, deadly serious for the moment. He then said purposefully, but gently '...you still haven't got the money back, have you?'

I muttered something Jonny- like and inconsequential.

'And as for Gemma! That girl is just a prize *vændiskona.*'

I didn't know what the word meant, but I could have had a good guess, and I wasn't going to disagree with him. Gemma and Tan had spiced up the office Christmas party a few weeks ago with antics that made people avoid the chocolate fountain afterwards. She'd tried it on with me, and just lately I'd found myself tempted. If today's madness had taught me anything, it was how much I loved Amy. If I did manage to get home, I wouldn't even blink in Gemma's direction.

But Cameron? From what Arnie was saying, he sounded the same as the office trainee I knew back in Westcastle. Young, camp, and catty. Willing to push his luck as far as he could.

I thought it was Jonny who had got it right on that occasion. Our conversation had brought back memories of a Friday afternoon at the office over in my world. Cameron was in a right old state. He was telling everyone that he needed a thousand pounds that weekend, or his life was over. Tanner naturally took the piss but even the kinder members of staff thought that Cameron was being his normal hysterical self. No one was the least bit inclined to lend him the money. When he came in on the Monday morning everyone laughed about the fact that he had survived the weekend. But he was different. He didn't laugh and joke, or wind Tanner up by trying to flirt with him. Six months later we found out that he'd been fired, and the contents of his desk were unceremoniously dumped into a black sack. He'd got involved in selling drugs so that he could pay off his debts. He'd got in so deep that the weekend before, he'd been arrested. The last I'd heard; he was still inside.

Of course, I didn't say any of this to Arnie, but it did make me think. It made me realise how the butterfly effect worked. Somehow I had got Jonny's job and I hadn't lent Cameron the money, whereas Jonny *had*. In one world Cameron's life was in free-fall, in the other he was trying to rebuild it.

I was also beginning to realise how important it was to be careful not to change too many things. *Just re-unite Ben and Amy,* I promised myself again, *and find a way to go through the week without getting too cosy with Arnie.* The instant rapport between me and Arnie led me to add one rider to my thoughts of earlier: *but try not to wreck his and Jonny's relationship at the same time.*

Simple.

It was the 'not getting too cosy' idea that led me to suggesting liqueurs after dinner. I let Arnie choose and apparently Jonny was a Cointreau man. I wasn't, but then I wasn't a wine for dinner man either. I was a 'staying out long enough to make sure that Arnie was too knackered to want sex' man. Arnie just seemed surprised that I was drinking quite so heavily on a school night, especially when I was supposed to be recovering from the fictitious fever I'd had earlier.

Maybe it was the mix of unusual alcoholic beverages. Maybe I was slightly drunker than I thought. Maybe I was still thinking of a way I could change the configuration of the sofa bed, and sleep in it, without Arnie noticing.

Whatever it was, after we had left the restaurant and were walking along the streets towards home, Arnie caught me off guard and grabbed my hand. At first I was quite thankful for the three figures lurking by the bins outside the 8 Till Late. While we were still a fair distance away from them I was able to clear my throat, nod in their direction, and use their presence as an excuse to disentangle my hand from his. Even though the skin-on-skin contact had been no more intrusive than a brisk handshake, I was uncomfortable about it.

No sooner had I sorted out that problem, a far uglier one reared its head.

The three juvenile delinquents had noticed us.

I knew them. Chance Bagley and his besties. Strangely enough, they spent a lot of their time hanging around the 8 Till Late in Westcastle as well. They'd never given me any shit. I was normally with Tan, and he would have had their scrawny backsides for breakfast, and they knew it.

But tonight, I wasn't with Tan, and they had seen our moment of intimacy.

'Fucking hell! I'm gonna chunder, pass me a bucket...!'

One of his mates egged him on. 'What a pair of inverts! Shall we do 'em, Chance?'

Obviously not too much had changed for him between the two worlds. He was still hanging around outside the corner shop, still called Chance, still a bit of a twat.

I could see Arnie glance at me, and I could tell he wanted to say something. He seemed to be asking for my permission.

No need to ask, I thought. *Be my guest.*

'Shouldn't be allowed.' Chance chewed on some gum and smirked unpleasantly. 'Rubber Jonny is a fucking disgrace.'

Oh my God! I thought, *they still call him that.* I couldn't believe that he hadn't managed to dump that nickname at some point during the last fifteen years.

It was then that a nasty realisation hit me.

Tanner and me. We still called him that.

We had reached the point where we would be forced to cross the road to avoid them. I could hear people leaving nearby pubs and the rattle of metal shutters inside the 8 Till Late as the manager continued locking up for the night. In front of us the three of them were straggled across the pavement, completely blocking it. They all stood with their arms crossed in front of them. Arrogant. Sneering. So pleased with themselves. It was pathetic.

I wasn't quite sure how to react. The way I thought Jonny would react, or the way I wanted to react. Normally, in a situation like this, I would have just followed Tan and see what happened. Maybe Jonny and I weren't so different. Except, it looked like Jonny was the leader in this partnership. Or to be more accurate, Arnie didn't want to do anything that might upset him.

But, at that moment he'd taken as much crap as he intended to take. Or more accurately, he'd witnessed Jonny being taunted one time too many. He glanced towards me again, touched me briefly on the arm and said softly: 'Sorry Jonny, I've had enough of this shit.'

He walked up to Chance so that he was within head-butting distance. For a moment I thought Arnie was going to do it. He didn't. He was just letting the nineteen-year-old wanna-be hoodlum know, that he was about as threatening as a toddler on a tricycle.

'What is your problem *heimskingi?*'

Chance's Icelandic to English translation was about as good as mine. But, he latched onto the foreign word to prevent his mates from seeing that he was a little fazed by the fact that Arnie was standing up to him.

'Speak English,' he drew the words out as if speaking to an idiot. 'If you want to live in this country, learn the language.'

'Oh nice,' Arnie grinned deceptively. 'Homophobia and xenophobia, wrapped up in a horrible little package.' He leaned into the younger man, invading his space. 'Why don't you say something nasty about women? Add misogyny to the list and score a hat-trick of offensiveness.'

Chance was rattled, there was no doubt about it. He hadn't understood a few of those words, even if they had all been in English. He glanced around at his mates, unsure of how he could walk away without losing face completely.

'Fuck off.'

Arnie chuckled. 'Lovely,' he said, then wiped the grin from his face and went on the attack. 'You all have to do it don't you? Pick on Jonny because it's what everyone has done since he was young. Because he's gay, because he's gentle...' he glanced around at me '...because he's kinder and nicer than the rest of us.'

'He's a fucking perverted faggot.' Chance was standing his ground, searching desperately for the put-down that would win him the war of words. But, sadly for him, his brain wasn't up to the challenge. 'You both are.'

'OK, you think that was perverted?' Arnie asked. 'Jesus! We were holding hands in the street not barebacking by the ornamental fishpond in Hazelmeare Park.' Chance looked horrified, especially when Arnie stared at him. On one hand he didn't want to look away as it would be a sure sign that Arnie was getting to him. On the other, he didn't want to stare at a man who had just mentioned gay sex in the same way a football fan might mention a pint at half-time.

Arnie showed no intention of easing off on Chance's agony. 'Well, try this for size. I love that man. I haven't said it enough lately, but I do. I love his intelligence. I love his style. I love the fact that his wardrobe is laid out in colour order and all our mug handles must be pointing in the same direction. I love the fact that every time he smiles he makes me feel like I've discovered the cure for cancer.' Arnie took a quick breath but barely stopped talking as he did so. 'And if you think that's sick, and if it makes you want to chunder, then be my guest. Because that's your problem, not mine.'

Arnie smiled gently in my direction and nodded a couple of times to enforce everything he'd just said. I've never been a great fan of people telling the world how they feel about somebody. When someone on the radio says they want to tell their wife who's listening in the next room that they love her, it makes me want to shout: 'Just go into the next room and tell her...' But this? I had to admit, Arnie's speech had given me a warm and fuzzy feeling. It's something I'd never admit to Tan. He roasts me royally if I ever show my softer side.

Chance wasn't impressed either. 'We shouldn't have to look at that sort of thing,' he said stubbornly.

'And "we" shouldn't have to look at your ugly face, but hey, that's life.' Arnie glanced towards Chance's gang members who had gone a little quiet. 'What do the girls of Carmichaeltown call him lads? No Chance?'

Chance was already feeling under pressure. He knew he'd lost the war of words. Now, Arnie was laughing at him. And worse still.

He'd made Chance's friends laugh at him as well.

'Funny man.' He said, finally giving way to the fury that had been brewing inside him.

I'd sensed the frustration. I'd now seen a glimpse of anger. I never thought that he might be carrying a knife.

I saw his hand dive inside his pocket. I heard a faint click. I saw a flash of metal as it caught the streetlight.

The first thing Arnie would have known about it was when he felt the blade nestle on the skin below his Adam's apple. But he barely flinched.

'Not laughing now, eh, pervert?' Chance growled and nodded towards his friends who grabbed an arm each, then pulled Arnie's jacket down over his shoulders, further trapping him and exposing his open-necked shirt. Both were back in Chance's posse once again and were happy to help him. It was as if they were apologising for laughing at their mate.

Jonny didn't fight. That was my over-riding thought. All those times we'd tormented him, and he'd never once fought back. But, if Jonny had been in Carmichaeltown and not me, him and Arnie would have been tucked up safe and warm at home – not out on the mean streets – so the question of changing history did not arise. I had to help Jonny's boyfriend regardless of whatever Jonny might, or might not, have done.

Luckily, Arnie's attackers had forgotten that I even existed. The two bully boys laughed unpleasantly, goading their beloved leader into nicking the skin at the top of Arnie's chest. Chance dotted his knife from one place to another. It was as if he was producing a painting by numbers plan for a small child to draw around.

Arnie didn't even blink.

I could already see spots of blood on his skin.

'Apologise Kraut. Say "I'm a pathetic pervert, who deserves to be deported."' Chance was enjoying himself. He didn't care that it was three on one. Didn't care that he'd had to use a weapon to get one up on Arnie. Wouldn't have cared even if he had realised that he was about two thousand miles out with his insult. All he cared about was getting revenge, for being made to look like an idiot in front of his mates.

'I prefer "Peter Piper picked a peck of pickled pepper" if you're looking for a good tongue twister.' Arnie said, refusing to be cowed, even if he had a good reason to be panicking.

I was panicking, and the knife wasn't nestling against my skin.

'You think I won't use this, don't you?' Chance said, once again digging the blade in, a little more forcibly this time, so that a larger blob of blood joined the others.

I wasn't so sure. In my mind Arnie was being brave, but a bit of a nutter. If he kept on taunting Chance with his smart mouth, I thought it likely that the idiot wouldn't be able to control himself.

I remember someone saying once: 'I'd rather face a sensible man who was armed with a nuclear device, than a stupid man who was armed with a knife.'

I had managed to move slowly around to the back of Chance, under the cover of him and his mates being otherwise engaged. I was now standing within touching distance. I just had to find a way to get his attention, and disarm him, without getting Arnie stabbed in the process.

In the end, it all happened before I had quite worked that bit out.

The taller of Chance's two minders was directly in my eye line while he was restraining Arnie. I thought he was so wired up watching his friend mutilate their victim that he wouldn't notice me.

I was wrong.

'Oi Chance! Watch out!' He yelled out in warning.

Chance turned quickly and as he did so, Arnie fell backwards into his captors.

I had one fleeting thought. *It was as if he'd been stabbed.*

I could see that Chance still had the knife, but he had been disorientated by the interruption. I knew I had to pounce quickly.

I stepped forward, raising my arm as I did so, and brought it down heavily on Chance's shoulder. He shouted out in angry surprise and dropped the knife. All I wanted to do was get rid of it. I dragged it back with my foot and then side-footed it towards the gutter, where it clattered to a stop, a few centimetres from a drain. I had a sudden idea that, if I dropped the knife through the grating, Chance wouldn't be able to retrieve it and use it. I turned and stretched out my leg, found the knife with my foot, and heard the comforting sound of metal on stone as it made its way towards the sewer.

Unfortunately, I had underestimated just how pissed off with me Chance was. I guess that seeing his prize possession dropped down a hole, where only the rats could find it, was the final straw. He launched himself at me, as I turned from doing the deed, and his body hit me in the chest as if I was a scrum machine.

The impact caused me to fall over my own feet, or the gutter, and I felt myself tumbling back with Chance on top of me. My backside took the brunt of the fall, so I was now bruised on both sides of my body, but luckily I managed to stop my head from banging back against the tarmac.

I quickly reached up to grab hold of Chance's arms and restrain him, before he was able to do any damage with them. We then became embroiled in a bizarre type of arm wrestle, with him trying to break out of my grip, and me trying desperately to hold on.

The slightly crazed concentration I saw in Chance's eyes was a cause for worry, and the spit that dropped from his mouth didn't help matters either.

One of the things I was struggling to get used to was Jonny's slender frame. What with all the five-a-side football, and the gym sessions that Tan had forced me to take part in, I would have normally been more than a match for my teenage attacker. Being trapped in Jonny's body I felt like a rock star who was forced to perform at Wembley without his favourite guitar, but with a plastic ukulele instead.

Gradually, I got used to the ukulele and using a few moves that Tan had taught me, I managed to twist and turn, forcing Chance onto his side. Once I'd got him there, I kneed him in the privates and he slumped to the floor, whining in agony. I didn't waste a moment. I jumped on to his chest and trapped his hands above his head, squashing them down onto the cold pavement.

It must have looked to him as if I were going to kiss him as I moved my face down towards his. He looked scared shitless. Obviously, nothing could have been further from my mind – but he didn't know that. I bypassed his face and stopped moving my head when I was an inch or so above his earhole.

'I am going to get off you in a minute,' I whispered viciously. 'And you – you're going to run as fast as your sad behind can run. Do you understand?'

The whimpering noise coming from his voice box told me all I needed to know. Once I'd kept my side of the bargain, he kept his. He ran off in the direction of town without stopping to see what had happened to his friends.

As soon as I was satisfied that he wasn't going to come back, I took a deep breath and risked looking in the direction I had seen Arnie fall less than five minutes before.

Let him be OK. I was almost praying. Please, let him be OK.

If you had told me when I met him on his pathway with a less than friendly greeting, that later the same day, I would have been worried about Arnie's safety, I wouldn't have believed it. But then, there had been a lot of crazy stuff going on that day. What difference did one more bit of craziness make?

Arnie wasn't there. In fact, there was no one around. And no sound. It was as if everyone in the town had been sucked up into a spacecraft by some passing aliens.

I idiotically wandered over to the spot where I'd last seen him and looked around me. The only thing nearby was a litter bin, and he certainly wasn't hiding underneath that.

I saw a spot of blood and remembered the knife picking at Arnie's skin before I'd sent it for a swim in the sewers. Glancing to the right of me, I saw another blood spot. And then a collection of them.

I followed the trail which reminded me of a Quentin Tarantino remake of Hansel and Gretel. It led me down an alley by the side of the 8 Till Late.

The lane was dark and spooky. The only relief from a total blackout came from the odd blob of light, borrowed from the streetlights on the main road. I was getting a bit freaked out. A couple of times I could have sworn I saw a shape lying in the middle of the path, but it was only my imagination and the shadows playing silly beggars with my mind.

Then I heard the animalistic scream.

I jumped. And my heart lurched so violently that it was a miracle it remained attached to my body. Something flew past my ear and disappeared into the darkness. It took a few seconds to realise that it was either a fox, or a stray cat, escaping from an unknown predator.

My nerves were shot to bits, and I was dreading what I might find when the Tarantino trail ended. I had a feeling in my guts that it would end at a body. And this body wouldn't be explained away as a trick of the light.

I was sure the blobs of blood were getting bigger. Granted, it was difficult to make them out clearly. They might not have been blobs of blood at all. Just after the lane reached the end of the length of the shop, it turned sharply to the left, following the shape of the building around to the back of it.

I was just getting ready to turn, preparing myself for what I might find, when there was a sudden rush of noise. A shape appeared around the corner and this time it wasn't a mirage. A body rammed against mine with such force that I fell against the wall that the stray animal had been running along earlier.

Peeling myself off the wall, as quickly as I could, I raised my arm as a warning to my would-be attacker that I intended to use it. My would-be attacker did the same.

We must have looked like two people in a *Saturday Night Fever* dance off.

I was about to strike out to get past the intruder and find out what had happened to Arnie, when the man in the shadows started shouting at me.

Although I was not an expert, it sounded like a shedload of swear words, all strung together. All the swear words sounded suspiciously Icelandic.

'Jonny!' He finished his continuous stream of words with the realisation that I was friend, not foe. He then put his arms around me in a bear hug of relief.

Of course, I'd hugged men before. When any of the lads scored a goal during our football sessions, be it five-a-side or the real thing, we'd jump up and down hugging each other like we were a gang of teenage girls at a sleepover.

But, as much as I liked Arnie, he was a gay man. A gay man who thought I was his boyfriend.

I decided to take no chances and pulled away, holding him at an arm's length under the pretext of checking he was all right. Apart from blood spatters on his chest, which were already starting to dry, he looked remarkably unharmed.

'What happened?' I asked.

He grinned the grin that I was getting used to. The one that mixed charm and self-deprecation with a splodge of wickedness. 'I don't think my "No Chance" comment was a particularly good idea under the circumstances.'

I answered it with an ironic grin of my own. 'You think?' I said, flicking my eyes towards the heavens as if it was the most obvious thing he'd said all night. 'So, what have you done with your friends?'

'Aah,' he said, letting go of me and leading the way back around the corner. 'I'm afraid I'm probably guilty of a little bit of illegal incarceration.'

On the left-hand side of the lane, at the back of the 8 Till Late, there was a little storage area. It looked like it was used to break down large boxes, ready for recycling. It was closed off by two metal caged doors at the front. The doors had lost any padlock that might have been used to secure them so Arnie had used his belt instead, wrapping it around the two doors and tying it at the front.

'I wanted to check you were all right. My belt was the only thing I had handy. I thought it might slow them down at least,' he said. It explained both the sight in front of me, and the speed he was travelling when we had our mid-lane head-on crash.

The sight in front of me, lit only by a dim security light, was of two little scrotes. They were looking very sorry for themselves, trapped inside a cage full of cardboard.

'I suppose I should call the police,' Arnie said doubtfully, and if anything, his prisoners shrunk even more at the thought of a night being banged-up properly.

Obviously, I wasn't too keen on calling the police either.

'Shall we just let them go?' I suggested and Arnie grinned.

'I knew you'd say that!' He looked at the pathetic looking toerags and smirked. 'To be fair, they're not looking like they could knock the skin off a rice pudding now.' Again, the English expression seemed strange when delivered with his eclectic mix of accents. He untied his belt and opened the door. I resisted the temptation of giving them a sarcastic wave and stood in solidarity next to Arnie, encouraging them to favour flight rather than fight.

To be fair, they didn't need much encouragement.

We watched them disappear around the corner of the lane and Arnie turned back to me. 'When I had a go at you yesterday for not sticking up for yourself enough,' the grin was there, but this time it held a hint of seriousness around it. 'I wasn't expecting you to start with a knife wielding maniac.'

'I thought I'd got you killed.' With a jolt of surprise, I realised that I was talking for myself, and not for Jonny. 'When you fell backward, as Chase turned, I thought he had slit your throat.'

Arnie smiled sympathetically. 'No, I managed to avoid it.' The smile turned into the cheeky grin. 'Fell over my feet, didn't I? Fell straight against Dumb and Dumber.'

The smile disappeared and he became serious once again. 'Since I've known you, it's the first time I've seen you fight for anything.' His voice sounded strange, and I looked at him sharply. The dull security lighting couldn't hide the tear that had appeared in the corner of his eye, and there was definite emotion blurring his speech when he continued talking. 'And do you know what? It was for me. The first time you stick up for anything – or anybody – and it was to protect me. Do you know how wonderful that makes me feel?'

The power of his words, and the strength of his gaze, made me turn away slightly. *It was strange,* I thought. *All I'd been trying to do that night was not to wreck Jonny's relationship completely. In fact, I seemed to have strengthened Arnie's love for him.* I didn't have a clue what would happen to their affair when Jonny re-appeared as the same old useless sap he'd always been. But more of a worry for me, at that moment, was how this night might end.

I was so concerned about the fact that he might want to get intimate, when we got to the privacy of our own home, that I missed the fact we were totally alone at that moment as well. Hidden in a back alley, safe from prying eyes.

The first thing I noticed was a strange scent. It was a mixture of lemon grass, amoretto, and coffee. Without thinking I turned my head back towards Arnie.

And collided with his lips as he moved in to kiss me.

~ 15 ~
INSOMNIA

Westcastle: Jonny

The day at the water tower was the day that changed everything. That thought wouldn't go away. I didn't know why it was, or what had happened, to make it so. I only knew that the stories Amy had told me of life before that day could have been copied from my diary, whereas any story that occurred afterwards had been taken from an entirely different book.

I tried another round of focussing on Amy's breathing, the screeching strays, and the monotonous ticking of the alarm clock, in the vain hope that they would lull me off to sleep. Once again, it didn't work. I lay sleeplessly in bed with a familiar, yet unfamiliar, shape next to me. I drifted back just twenty-four hours to when I had lain in a similar bed, in a similar room, but with a different person beside me.

I had been sleepless and worried the previous night as well. Compared to the problems I was facing now; those worries seemed inconsequential. They were as crazy as a rich man quaking because the value of his vault full of gold, had fallen by a penny.

Arnie loved me. Thinking about it now, in another man's bed, in another man's body, it seemed obvious. Thoughts that had appeared muddled and muddied, now appeared to be simple and straightforward.

The friendly rivalry he had struck up with Amy over matters of my welfare. The way they would ring each other to discuss notes if I was slightly short of my shining best. The fact that he would never leave my office, after one of his meetings, without stopping for a quick chat. The 'thank God I'm home' kiss seemed less perfunctory and more heartfelt. The fact I knew without asking that he was always on my side. Even when he argued with things I'd done, like in the bar the previous Sunday, it came from a place of concern rather than control. I smiled sadly to myself. Even the fact that I couldn't go into the bathroom without tripping over his discarded underwear, seemed loveable rather than slovenly.

Lying in bed that night, I realised how lucky I'd been to find him. How lucky I'd been that he had fallen in love with me.

The clock said two o'clock. I hadn't slept a wink since I came to bed, and I knew that I was unlikely to do so. My thoughts about Arnie made my desire to see him again so absolute that I had no doubt about what I needed to do. I had been waiting for a chance all day to research my predicament. Why waste a golden opportunity with futile thoughts that would resolve nothing?

I slipped silently out of bed taking care not to wake Amy. Like Arnie and I, they used the third bedroom as an office. I opened the door to the bedroom and avoided the swinging shirt that was hanging on a wooden clothes hanger ready for the morning. I couldn't believe that Amy did all of Ben's ironing for him. If I'd asked Arnie for a similar service, I would have received a reply that was unprintable. Some English swear words, some Icelandic, and some that Arnie had just made up because he knew I wouldn't be able to tell the difference.

As I had discovered at work, Ben had post-it notes with passwords on them, stuck to his computer. This time there were too many of them for it to be obvious which code was for what. This was a slight worry, to start with, until I realised that none of them related to his home computer. His home computer didn't need a code. I tutted to myself at his complacency but then remembered all the ribbing I used to get for not by-passing the security options on my PC at home.

'Don't you trust me?' Arnie used to ask in a distressed tone, as fake as a store-greeter's hello. He then nodded cheekily. 'Fair enough. Don't blame you.'

Once the computer was ready, I entered 'Sandelwood' into the search engine. There was an awful lot of information about something known as the 'Sandelwood gateway'. A man called Hadley Cooper-Wilson headed the Sandelwood Gateway International Co-operative. There'd even been a TV programme and I managed to find a link to it.

So that was it then, pretty much confirmed. During the crash, I had somehow managed to swap places, swap realities, with Ben Shawcross. I was now living his life, which meant that he, as I had feared, was probably living mine.

Oh God Arnie, what have I done to you?

Cooper-Wilson loved the sound of his own voice. It only took me about five minutes of the hour-long programme before I realised that. I decided to scroll down and read a few of the many articles written about him. At the same time, I listened to his self-important drawl with half an ear, making sure that I didn't miss anything important. I had a long running friendly feud with Amy who insisted that no man could multi-task as well as a woman. I argued that I could equal her capabilities. Unfortunately for me, Arnie and Elliot let down the male race somewhat. Arnie was so chaotic that it amazed me he managed to do his job at all, let alone well enough to win 'Employee of the Year'. Elliot could barely hold a mobile phone and dial it at the same time. Although none of us could decide whether that was due to a lack of multi-tasking skills or down to the fact that, in the world of technophobes, Elliot was king.

I suddenly ached to see my friends. Amy had already told me, in an attempt to cure my temporary amnesia, that Elliot now lived in Australia. He had a wife and, strangely enough, three sons. Up to that point I had been harbouring ideas of seeking him out and re-uniting them. I thought it might ease my conscience to know that I wouldn't be leaving her with an idiot of a husband who seemed to care more about his best friend, than he did about her. However, the fact that Elliot was living in Australia with a family of his own, made that brilliant idea a non-starter.

What if that point was moot? What if I couldn't return home? In some ways, I could happily manage being married to Amy, but what about sex? From what I'd heard already, the sexual side of their relationship was dead in the water, so I'd be starting from ground zero, in more ways than one. I thought that even I might be able to manage that. But would I be able to manage without gay sex? It had taken me a long time to realise it, but I liked being a gay man, I didn't want to disappear back into the closet.

Undoubtedly the most depressing thought of all was: *How could I cope with Tanner as a best friend, Tuesday night dinners and wall to wall football?*

I turned my attention to the computer and decided to assimilate every minute detail that I possibly could.

The earliest piece of evidence I could find was a local newspaper report. The reporter was obviously a friendly type, or a true believer, because he gave the far-fetched theories that Cooper-Wilson spouted an almost reverential respect.

Except, I realised with a shudder, they weren't far-fetched at all. They had happened. To me.

Looking at the timeline of all the entries, it seemed that the television programme had come next. According to all the reviews I was reading from the national dailies, it was slated roundly in this country. That might have been the end of the road for Cooper-Wilson's five minutes of fame, but it had been taken up by several conspiracy theory groups across Europe and even one in America. 'I call them "Coop's Troop",' Cooper-Wilson announced in another article. 'That's why I've incorporated "international" into the title of the co-operative.' You could almost feel the smugness vibrating from the written words on the screen. If the number of "Science Fiction, Science Fact" conventions he had spoken at was anything to go by, they had bought into the lovably eccentric Brit routine. In comparison, his fellow countrymen and women seemed to find it all a bit embarrassing.

Over the course of the next couple of hours, I discovered many things I didn't need to know. Such as, how the gateway was formed and alleged stories that Cooper-Wilson had garnered from people who had travelled between the realities. Of course, none of the claims were substantiated and none of the people were named. 'I always keep my sources anonymous,' Cooper-Wilson said, a point which some people praised for being sympathetic and other people slated as being convenient. He also said with, more than a touch of the theatrical, 'I am aware that a famous Westcastle man is, in fact, dead in another reality.'

He obviously wouldn't name the man.

I could name him. The fact that the town was no longer called after Alec Carmichael and I had heard nothing about Carmichael week, which would just be starting back at home, gave me more than a clue.

For a moment I was impressed enough to think that it might have been worth sending an email off to Cooper-Wilson, to see if he would privately give me details of his source. After throwing the pros and cons around in my brain, I decided that a dead celebrity was an obvious claim to make, especially when no one could prove or disprove his story. The last thing I needed was Cooper-Wilson riding on my coat tails.

At the end of all this, he still hadn't answered a couple of questions that were foremost in my mind: *How much did I risk changing in this world, if the opportunity arose? Was it dangerous to try and meet the version of myself that lived here?*

He did, however, address the question that I most wanted answered. According to 'extensive research' including testaments from inter-reality travellers, Cooper-Wilson had eventually – and very long-windedly – reached a conclusion. Once the gateway had opened it would reopen at the same time, one week after the original incident. But only if exactly the same people were present.

Twenty-four hours ago, my comfortable, practical mind would have struggled with the improbability of it all. 'Implausible and ridiculous' I would have said. But now, something implausible and ridiculous was the only hope I had.

I crawled back into bed at around four o'clock on that Tuesday morning. I was so knackered I was sure I would be able sleep, despite all the thoughts that were flying around my head.

And, it was that one piece of information that trumped all the rest. I wasn't thinking about that long ago day at the water tower. I wasn't thinking about Amy, or any of the madness that had befallen me that day. I wasn't even thinking about Arnie. It was simply that one implausible, ridiculous, piece of information that I repeated silently.

...once the gateway had opened, it would reopen at the same time, one week after the original incident. But only if exactly the same people were present.

Eventually it managed to send me off into a fitful sleep. But not before one final thought replaced the mantra that was swimming around my head.

I simply needed that piece of information to be available for Ben to find in Carmichaeltown. And I needed him to find it.

~ 16 ~
WE NEED TO TALK

Carmichaeltown: Ben

His lips were soft. That was a shock. Not that I'd ever thought about kissing a man, but I would have expected the feeling to have been rough and leathery, like kissing Desert Orchid's saddle. It wasn't.

The only real difference between kissing Arnie and kissing Amy was the fact that she didn't have sixteen hours' worth of stubble just below her nose.

I jumped back quickly and tried to avoid looking at him. I failed. He had been standing there with his eyes closed as he kissed me, but when he realised that I had pulled away, he opened them. The look of sadness on his face was like the one he'd worn a few hours before when I'd snapped at him, the first time I'd met him. *Tough*, I'd thought at the time, but I didn't feel like that now. And it wasn't only because of Cooper-Wilson's warning. It was something to do with the fact that we'd battled, and beaten, the L-plated bully boys together. It was the fact he had recklessly stuck up for the person he loved without a thought for his own safety. And even before all of that, I'd felt that whatever the situation, we could have become friends. That had been rarer for me, in the past few years, than a nun with triplets. Yes, I had Tanner and my football mates. They were good for a laugh but I never felt they were totally on my side. If Arnie had been my friend, I was sure that he would have been.

I tried to find an excuse that would wipe the look of hurt from his face. 'I'm sorry,' I started, as gently as I could. 'It's not you...' *Whatever you do*, I told myself, *don't say "it's me"*, before adding '...it's me.'

Poor Arnie, he looked like the shabby excuse for an excuse was more insulting than the speed I had ripped my lips from his mouth.

'We need to talk,' he said and walked past me, heading back down the lane. The hand he gently lay on my shoulder was a little bit of an afterthought, as if he wanted to prove he wasn't in a strop. 'Let's go home, have a coffee, and decide where we go from here.'

Shit, Shit, Shit! I thought. The hand on the shoulder might have been a good sign but 'where we go from here' didn't sound too hopeful to me.

I had expected the walk back up the hill away from town to be stacked with meaningful silences, but to start with, it wasn't. He returned very quickly to the chatty banter and quips that had started the evening. At one point, it even looked as if he was reaching out to hold my hand again. Luckily, Arnie thought twice about that one before I had to say anything.

'Mm, probably not a very good idea,' he grinned and plunged his hand back in his jacket pocket as if to prove the point. 'I mean we don't want to upset anybody with our perverted behaviour.' He paused. 'Holding hands in the street. Where will it end?'

'Pornographic.' I agreed, straight-faced.

'Triple X. Git your DVDs here!' Arnie sang out with the worst impression of a cockney market trader I'd ever heard. It seemed his good humour could be knocked, but never trampled down for long.

It wasn't until we neared Chancelwood Road that the conversation become more stilted, and Arnie seemed to be lost in his own thoughts. In a way, this was good because I needed the time to work out what I was going to say to him.

After we arrived home, Arnie disappeared to make the coffee and I slung my still unfamiliarly slender frame onto the sofa. He brought in a cup of sugarless liquid, so I hesitantly asked for a spot of the sweet stuff. 'Good for shock?' I suggested hopefully.

Arnie gave a funny little look, shrugged his shoulders, and fetched the sugar.

'I meant it you know,' Arnie looked on with that same curious expression as I dumped three heaped spoons of sugar into my mug. 'What I said to Dumb, Dumber and Drullukunta...' The Icelandic cussing needed very little translation. '...although, I admit, I could have chosen a better time to say it.' A self-deprecating shrug and smile came and went quickly. 'Every word is true you know. Every word.' His eyes were almost impossible to ignore. 'I love you so much.'

Just because I liked him, didn't make it any less weird to hear a man say such things to my face. I found it impossible to return the compliment. Instead of answering him in the way he would have wanted, I cut straight to the excuses.

'It's just been a strange day.' I said. *And,* I thought to myself, *you don't know the half of it.* Unsurprisingly, I gave Arnie the censored version. 'Feeling poorly to start with...' I would have normally said, *like a crock of shit,* but my brain was getting better at remembering Jonny's turn of phrase and translating my words into his own less expressive language. '...and then having to cope with those idiots.'

Arnie looked like he desperately wanted to move across the sofa and give me an understanding cuddle, but once again, he seemed to be waiting for me to make the first move. *He's going to have a long wait,* I thought.

'Amy thinks your feelings of self-worth are so low you'd need to be a coal miner to find them, that you feel you don't deserve to be loved.' Again, the shared confidences between the two of them about Jonny Vincent surprised me. Why they bothered with him at all was another, he didn't seem to have changed from the rather pathetic whiner that I remembered. I would have thought that Arnie could have had a whole army of gay boys gagging to be his boyfriend. And Amy? She should have had people queuing around the block to spend time with her.

So, what about you? An unwanted thought stabbed at my brain. *What's your excuse?* But it was true. Lately, I seemed to have managed to find reasons to be anywhere else rather than at home with my wife. *If I get back to Westcastle,* I promised myself, *that'll change.*

Back in the here and now of the alternative reality, I nodded and shrugged in a non-committal fashion. I was watching his body language in case I had to fend off another attack. I was listening to strange words that no bloke had ever said to me before.

What I didn't expect to happen was to find me, Ben Shawcross, included in the conversation.

'I blame those bastards who bullied you at school.' It took a few seconds for me to realise he was talking about Tanner and I. The shock was like a low blow to my belly. 'Just thinking about them makes me want to go around punching walls.' He meant it as well. Sunny, mild-mannered Arnie was like an August storm eyeing a Caribbean Island. 'The way they mimicked your every word, every gesture, every action. Hitting you and hurting you. Treating you like trash, so in the end, you believed you were trash. Even after fifteen years, I can still see the terrified boy you must have been.' He shrugged and rubbed his left eye. 'It kills me.'

I couldn't speak. I felt as worthless as a turd that a skanky dog had left on the pavement. There was an ache in my stomach, as if Jonny's body was also reminding me of the crimes that I'd been guilty of.

I'd only ever seen those days from my own viewpoint. Amy had tried to tell me how cruel we were being. But because she'd been going on about it since the day I discovered my first zit, I'd stopped listening. Hearing Arnie's version of events was like hearing the story for the first time. It wasn't a pleasant tale.

Tanner and I had been relentless. Arnie had been spot-on. We'd hit Jonny, punched him, spat at him, twisted his arms, bruised his legs, taunted him, and then, taunted him some more. Once, Tanner had peed on him.

We'd thought it was funny.

Arnie didn't seem to expect me to speak, which was just as well, because there was only one sentence banging against my tongue.

If only you knew who I was.

But he didn't know.

'It never stopped, did it?' Arnie's voice was quieter now, soothing Jonny with his sympathy. Once again, I could see his hands twitching, desperate to reach out to me, but also mindful that he shouldn't force the issue. 'Even after you hauled yourself out of the bins, you had to spend the day in foul smelling clothes.' The hard edge and the anger were back in his voice again. 'Even after you pulled yourself from the mud pit, and wiped yourself down, you couldn't wipe the dirt off completely. You certainly couldn't wipe away the humiliation.'

For a strange, unexpected moment, I wished that Jonny had been there to listen to it. He should have been the one to hear such a passionate display of support and love – not me.

'And the bastards...' Arnie was almost spitting at the thought of them '...I bet they loved it. Taunting you and seeing all the sheep in the classroom taunt you too.' He shook his head, as if he was trying to shake Tanner and Ben from his brain. 'I know Elliot and Steve wish they'd done more to help you and, if I was honest, I probably think they should have.' He shrugged. 'But ... it's so easy to be wise afterwards.' He looked up at me. 'Even though she's never said it, I'm sure that Amy wishes she'd dumped the scumbag sooner...'

I was sure that Arnie must have heard the sharp breath I took. *The scumbag ... that was me.*

But Arnie didn't seem to notice, he just looked sad and reflective as he continued '...it might have saved a whole shitstorm of trouble if she had.'

He took a sip of coffee. He appeared worried that I hadn't given him the green light to show his sympathy in a more physical way.

'I'm sorry to bring this all up again,' he smiled sadly. 'I'm sure the last thing you want to do is go through the hell one more time.' He looked up and I could see that his eyes were red around the edges. 'I know how difficult it is for you. I just wanted to explain that, although it must seem like I'm always going on about standing up for yourself, I do understand what you went through.' He smiled genuinely, like a sudden flash of summer. 'It's why I was so proud of you tonight.'

I felt such a fraud.

'But' he continued carefully. 'I'm also aware that I'm being a bit arrogant, assuming that I'm the man of your dreams.' He looked down at his lap, as if he was dreading asking this question, but knew he had to know the answer. He sighed heavily and decided just to come right out with it. 'Sometimes you can be so distant, and I'm never sure if it's the baggage of all that ... *drasl* ...

or if it's simply that you want to break up with me, but don't know how to. If it is, please tell me. It might well break my heart...' he smiled at himself, and I saw a brief return of the Arnie from earlier. 'I know, no pressure.' He finished the long monologue simply. 'I'd just rather know.'

My first thought was: *Here it was, my golden ticket out of Arnie's bed.* All I had to do was break Arnie's heart and wreck Jonny's future. I was sure that Arnie would be reasonable and move out as soon as he could find a floor to crash on. Win win.

Twelve hours ago, it would have been that easy.

Except it was nowhere near as easy as that now. I knew without a doubt, from the things that Amy had said to me earlier, that Jonny loved the man. The fact that Arnie could doubt this himself, was all part of his unassuming charm.

I felt so guilty.

Arnie had just described, quite brutally, how I had helped to destroy Jonny's childhood. Could I really destroy the rest of his life as well?

I was panicking at that moment, no question. But I knew I needed to speak. Remaining silent was as good as slap in the face, thank-you, and goodnight. I opened my mouth to say something – anything – when out of nowhere, the words started tumbling out.

It felt like they were being scripted by Jonny himself.

'I don't want to break up with you. I love you.' I could barely believe what I was hearing, but suddenly the words didn't seem quite so strange or difficult to say. I grinned and tried a little humour of my own. 'I don't think I would have faced down psycho-teen tonight if I didn't.' I paused briefly, but the words kept coming. 'I know that I'm distant sometimes and you're right. I think a lot of it does come from my childhood. Like tonight, when I'm reminded once again that some people still think that picking on me is good sport. They still think they can call me "Rubber Jonny".' I frowned, 'I hate it. I mean, I'm over thirty and yet sometimes I feel I'm only an inch away from the school gates.' I risked a look in Arnie's direction. 'It makes it hard for me to believe that someone like you could bear to spend more than five minutes with me. It makes me want to be on my own.'

And suddenly it was there, the opening I'd been searching for all night, my chance to escape without doing any terminal damage to their relationship. 'I'm really not being funny, but would you understand if I wanted to sleep in the spare room tonight? All that stuff...' I waved vaguely in the direction of town. 'Tonight, is one of those nights. I just need a little space.'

'You're not sleeping in the spare room!' Arnie seemed to trounce on my brilliant plan straight away. I was so busy preparing another plea that I almost missed the fact that his tone softened suddenly, as he continued speaking. 'I do get it. Totally. The past doesn't disappear just like that.' He clicked his fingers. 'I can understand that you might need space sometimes.' He started to get up from the sofa and said firmly, ending the discussion: 'But, it's your house. I'll sleep in the spare room.'

I was so relieved I could have cried. I felt I had to give him something. Some encouragement for the future. I started to get up as well, and gently brushed my lips against his cheek before moving quickly to pick up the empty mugs from the coffee table.

'I tell you what though,' Arnie grinned. 'You can help me with that evil bed-settee. Bloody thing nips my finger every single time!' He seemed happy, and I realised that even someone as outwardly confident as Arnie had their demons and their doubts. *He and Jonny should have talked more*, I thought, before realising I was the last person in the world who should have been offering that advice.

We carried on chatting as I helped Arnie set up the bed. He moved a few things, and I managed a goodnight hug, before we both disappeared into our separate rooms.

After I'd gone to the loo and washed my hands, I looked at Jonny's toothbrush. I rinsed it through thoroughly. It wasn't the gay thing, I'd always had a thing about using other people's toothbrushes, even Amy's. I then laughed at myself. I had Jonny's mouth. I had Jonny's teeth. Why on earth was I being so precious about using his toothbrush? I shrugged, turned the light off in the en-suite and crawled into the mercifully empty bed in the room next to it. My head was buzzing from the evening, from the whole crazy day.

I thought about Arnie's belief that Amy wished she'd split up with Ben earlier.

It might have saved a whole shitstorm of trouble if she had.

What was the 'shitstorm of trouble'? And what did it have to do with the fact that Ben had ended up in jail?

At some point, the two worlds had split and ended up as the world I had known yesterday and the world I knew today. But what had happened to cause it?

Earlier that evening, I received a reply from Cooper-Wilson to the e-mail I'd sent him. He was very keen on meeting up during my lunch break the next day. If he wasn't a complete nutter, I'd find a bit more about the two similar but totally separate worlds.

Lying in the darkness, I could smell a vague scent on the pillow. The smell of Jonny. As I lay there in his bed, with all the bits and pieces of his life around me, I thought about what I'd said to Arnie. The speech that had appeared fully formed in my mouth. I then wondered about Jonny and the labels I had stuck on him for so long.

I thought about the times I'd picked on him. It would be very easy to blame it all on Tanner, but I was there, I could have stopped it. Without even thinking too hard, I could remember twenty times I'd taunted him. And there were many, many, more over the years. I hadn't really stopped now, which was the main reason that Amy made sure we never met. And what had he ever done to deserve it? We had decided that he was weak and spineless ... and different. He might have been different to us, but who were the weak and spineless ones: the person who had to put up with year-on-year of schoolboy torture, or the people who had dished it out?

As I finally drifted off into a dreamless sleep, I thought of a quote that I remembered vaguely from school. I probably hadn't got it quite right, but it seemed spot on, as I lay in the darkness of that very strange night.

Before you are too quick to judge, walk a mile in another man's shoes.

~ 17 ~
AT THE WATER TOWER

Westcastle: Fifteen Years Earlier

The autumnal trees were dripping leaves of red, gold, and amber onto the wide track that led up through the woods to the run-down, disused water tower. As Jonny walked up the hill with Will alongside him, he was aware of how many of his year group were making the same trip.

'Whip his arse Will!' A whey-faced youth offered encouragement as Will and Jonny passed them.

Will gave him a smile and a thumbs-up before whispering to Jonny, 'Just you wait. If, in the very unlikely event, the flabby arsed wanker beats me, that one...' he nodded in the general direction of the youth '...will say: "Knew you could do it, Tan".' The over-the-top sycophancy was delivered with such brutal humour that Jonny couldn't help but laugh.

'You won't lose though, will you Will?' Jonny said. A lifetime of expecting the worst caused him to abandon the humour.

Will cuddled into him, oblivious to the fact that they were in public view. In fact, the sight of the two of them embracing or holding hands, had become such a familiar sight over the summer that no one bothered to mention it anymore. Except Tanner.

'Not a chance, J...' Will had started to call Jonny by the smallest diminutive of his name that was possible. Jonny liked it. It made him feel strong and special. 'This is going to be the tortoise and the hare, super-hero version.'

The worries were still there, but Jonny didn't really believe that Will would fail. He had never seen Will fail at anything since he'd known him. He wasn't expecting him to start that day.

Even so.

This was the second time that Will and Jonny had travelled up this track in the last twelve hours. Jonny wished desperately that they could be recreating their previous trip, rather than partaking in some ridiculous willy-waving competition with the school Neanderthal.

Jonny's phone had rung three times the night before. It was the pre-arranged signal for him to climb out of his bedroom window, carefully drop onto the shed below, slither down to the ground, and run towards the corner of Chancelwood Road ... and Will.

This had become a common occurrence during the warm nights of the summer. The fact that the autumn had trimmed a few degrees from the temperature hadn't yet dissuaded either Jonny or Will from continuing. They knew it would have to end soon. All the forecasts warned of October gales and rainstorms arriving during the week. However, the doom and gloom of the weatherman's pessimism, hadn't prevented them from dancing their midnight dance one more time.

The water tower hadn't been the only venue during their ballroom summer. Sometimes they would ride their bikes down country tracks, as black as obsidian glass, towards the lakes five miles out of town. They would skinny-dip for kisses, then laze on the bank afterwards, drinking beer and eating pretzels. They would sit with Jonny's legs wrapped around Will's body and Will's Olympic sized towel wrapped around them both.

'It's times like this I feel closest to you,' Jonny had admitted to Will a few weeks ago. 'It's like we are part of the same body.' The thought was on the sentimental side of twee but Jonny had, over the course of the summer, censored those sort of thoughts less and less.

'I give you Jonwill, the lardy-arsed beast with two heads!' Will laughed but added a schmaltzy codicil to ensure that Jonny knew he was included in the joke, rather than being the target of it.

'And one heart.'

Other nights, they would ride their bikes over to Hazelmeare Park. Will would padlock his bike to the railings, stand on the saddle and leap over the spiked top, landing gracefully on the grass below. Jonny was much more tentative, anticipating the agony of one of the spikes ripping through his skin. He would wobble his body onto the saddle, as unsure as a toddler taking his first steps. Will would stretch up to provide support. He'd lift Jonny over the fence and down to the ground beside him. Then they would run to the seat by the tennis court, where they would make love in the middle of the deserted midnight park.

'If only Ben could see what we're doing on his seat!' Will laughed afterwards. Jonny grinned, but decided to tell no one, not even Amy.

Last night they had shared beers by the water tower but hadn't gone through the barbed wire fence surrounding it. 'I'll leave that delight 'til later,' Will had laughed, 'when I get to show Hoots how a proper athlete runs.'

He had then stared at his can and curled his mouth up in distaste. The beer was called 'Legends' and the brewery had paid large amounts of money to several sporting heroes who advertised their brand. Jonny was drinking a can of the beer with a picture of Alec Carmichael powering his way to the first of his gold medals. Will on the other hand was staring at a picture of a footballer who had blotted his copybook a few weeks before, when he'd insulted an openly gay chat show host with homophobic comments.

'Twat!' Will said viciously and drained the can before lifting it to his face, as if he was addressing the man directly. 'Only one thing to do with you.' He jumped up and walked twenty feet away before placing the can, carefully on the grass, and returning to Jonny. 'Right J! Every time you hit the smug bastard with a small stone, I will plant a kiss on the body part of your choosing. Every time I hit etc etc...'

It wasn't much of a contest. Jonny would have struggled to hit a mansion with a mallet, whereas Will had a steady arm and was sure of his shot. By the time Will had hit the can for the fifth time, Jonny was still waiting for Will to give him his first kiss. With a dirty grin, Will lowered his eyes and pointed to the area he had chosen for attention.

If ever losing felt like winning... Jonny thought.

Jonny blinked himself back into the here and now. They had arrived at the opening in the woods, not far from where they had been just a few hours before. He could see Amy in the distance, standing with 'Team Tanner' at that moment. They waved at each other, and Tanner said something to her, before dragging Ben away for a private team talk. Jonny could see her shoulders stiffen as she stared after him. She turned towards Jonny and made a descriptive gesture, but the look on her face made it clear she was insulting her boyfriend's best friend, rather than Jonny himself.

The sixth form had turned out in force. Jonny knew that Will had been right. They all secretly wanted the new boy to win, but most of them would hedge their bets shamelessly if Will should happen to lose.

Nobody fitted that description better than Kyle Hammond. Throughout the whole of his school career so far, he'd managed to sit on the fence. 'It must be hellish uncomfortable sitting down,' Will had laughed, 'with all those splinters studding his bum.' He then added conspiratorially, 'if he doesn't end up in the Houses of Parliament, then stick me in a tutu and make me dance *The Nutcracker*.'

Kyle had taken on the role of MC for the proceedings, and he signalled that Will and Tanner should join him. Will gave Jonny a quick kiss on the lips before ambling over and holding his hand out to his rival. Tanner wasn't in the mood for niceties and ignored it.

'OK!' Kyle roared and everybody quietened immediately in preparation. The only sound was music from a radio that someone had brought along. After Kyle had directed a swift glare in the general direction of the noise, the radio was turned down, and the MC continued. 'We are here today because Will Flanagan has challenged Tanner Hootley to a race up the water tower. They will start on my first command.' He held up the referee's whistle he had requisitioned from the leisure centre storeroom, the night before, and waved it to the crowd. 'The gap in the fence that Will is aiming for is on the left and Tanner's is on the right.' He held up his arm and then answered a question that was volleyed in his direction. 'The distances have been verified; they are the same for both contestants.' The inquisitors fell silent, and Kyle continued. 'When the runners reach the top, they will cross the metal walkway to the other side of the tower and descend. The first person who arrives back to shake my hand, is the winner.'

He paused, then took two envelopes from his jacket pocket. 'I have two statements here that have been written by the participants. The loser will have to read the winner's statement, whilst kneeling on the grass, in front of you all. Is everything understood?'

There was a massive cheer and as Kyle raised the whistle to his mouth, the crowd chanted: 'Three – two – one...'

Jonny experienced a weird feeling in his belly as the whistle blew. It felt like a sudden, violent hunger, but the last thing he wanted to do was to eat anything.

He had no idea why he had suddenly felt so nervous. True, the staircase was ricketier than he'd remembered, and there were some sections where the protective railings had disappeared altogether, but Jonny didn't really fear that Will would fall. He had far too much trust in his boyfriend's sure-footedness for that. If Will lost, Jonny knew that he'd be able to read Tanner's humiliating diatribe in such a way that he would be able to use it for comedic effect. And if he won? When he won. Jonny knew that when that happened, all the sheep would flock towards Will, and Tanner's power to hurt Jonny would be over.

And yet Jonny felt nervous.

As Will had predicted, Tanner roared into the lead and Will himself, seemed quite happy to let him go. By the time Tanner reached his allotted entry point, the conversation had returned to normal and the boy with the radio had turned it back on again, full volume.

Jonny could hear the news headlines. On the hour, every hour. The newsreader was talking about Alec Carmichael. That was no surprise. There had been something about him on the news nearly every day since he'd won five gold medals in the summer Olympics.

Apparently, he had arrived back in Westcastle the day before after an extensive victory tour around the country. According to the bulletin, he had celebrated with his family at a restaurant in the centre of the town. All very nice, Jonny thought, but hardly newsworthy.

He flicked his attention back to the race. Tanner was already starting to climb the rickety metal staircase. Will was only just pulling himself to his feet after crawling through the broken barbed wire fencing. By the time Will arrived at the steps, Tanner had already reached the first landing where the staircase doglegged back on itself.

Jonny urged Will onward, but his boyfriend seemed intent on taking his time. *Too much time,* Jonny thought as he saw Tanner stretch his lead. All his shouts of encouragement were lost in the general cacophony that was echoing around the clearing. Jonny resorted to silent telepathy, to warn his boyfriend that he might be giving himself too much to do.

However, by the time they reached the next dog leg, Tanner had increased his lead by a couple of steps.

It changed so suddenly that Jonny could almost believe that his powers of thought transference were worthy of a storyline in *Star Trek*.

Jonny would have loved to believe that it was his urgency that caused Will to turn on the turbo, but he realised that Will was following a well thought out plan. He seemed to glide through the gears effortlessly and gracefully. Tanner, on the other hand, was showing signs that he was suffering from the fast start and the fact that he had climbed the first two flights like a maniac. By the time Tanner had reached the third landing, Will had cut his lead and was already on the second step of the staircase below.

He continued to close the gap inexorably, painlessly. His body fluid and rhythmic, in stark contrast to Tanner's lumbering bullishness. It seemed like the bull was in dire need of a lie down and a drink from a water trough. By the next turn, Will was only two steps behind him.

With a wonderful sense of joy, excitement and pride, Jonny could start to believe in the *lardy-arsed beast with two heads and one heart*. He felt like he was running the race inside Will's body. He could feel the power, he could sense that the distance between him and his rival was diminishing. He felt invincible.

Will had nearly caught up with Tanner, just as they reached the fifth landing. Jonny almost sensed the despair on Tanner's face when he realised that he would be beaten and beaten easily. It had never been Jonny's nature to crow, everybody had always made it clear that he had very little to crow about, until now.

He knew it was only adopted success and he was riding on his lover's coat tails. However, he had a sudden, incredible, desire to shout: 'In your face, you bastard!'

Will pressed forward as he started the sixth and final flight before the top of the staircase and the metal walkway that led to the other side. He pulled alongside Tanner. He seemed determined to win the race to the top, which would turn the race back down again into a formality.

The final flight had no handrail, but that seemed to hold no demons for Will. He stretched forward and eased himself ahead of his rival. All the time he had one thought in his brain playing repeatedly. *I'm doing this for Jonny.*

Jonny stretched himself to get a clearer view. An overhanging branch of a tree, between spectators and spectacle, was blocking his field of vision. It didn't matter. Tanner was beaten. Even without seeing it, Jonny could sense that his lover was increasing his lead away from the school bully. The King is dead! Long live the King!

And then...

The sense of panic didn't hit Jonny straight away. His initial thought was *No! Will! You're going to win anyway. You might get down even quicker like this; but Tanner will only accuse you of cheating.*

You don't have to jump from the tower.

The body appeared to be flying at first, before it dropped like a stone.

After the terrifying thud, there was a second of almost complete silence that was only broken by the thrum of the radio. Then, the screaming started.

Suddenly terrified, Jonny knew that he had to get to the site of the thud. As he started to move forward others appeared, as if from nowhere, blocking him in. He could no longer see the place in the distance where he'd seen the body, Will's body, fall. Jonny even started doubting himself. *Had it really been Will? Might it have been Tanner?* Jonny didn't feel guilty over the fact that he wished he had made a mistake. He hoped against hope that the body would turn out to be Tanner.

Still the hoards came. They moved like shambolic armies with no idea whether they were invading or retreating. Jonny stretched his head this way and that, trying to find a gap to prove to himself that it was Tanner's red tracksuit top that was sprawled on the ground, not Will's green sweatshirt. Every time he found a chink of light, another body closed in. They were like clouds that had skidded across the sky, to cover the promised patch of blue, just as the sun had threatened to escape towards it.

He moved his head towards another gap. The drawstring and toggles from a hoody whipped him across the face. The gap disappeared. His nerves and the smell of a pungent acne cream made him feel nauseous. He was stumbling over his own feet. They seemed to belong to an unapologetic alcoholic, and they made him bump into the backs of his nearest neighbours.

When the disorganised gaggle came to an abrupt full-stop, Jonny face-palmed the back of the girl in front of him. All he could see was fabric, but he knew that somewhere on the other side of the wall of bodies was Will – or Tanner. Mumbling an apology, he pushed his way past her. He then passed the next person, and the next, until he eased his head and shoulders out into the open and stopped abruptly.

Everything was ordinary. The trees were in the middle of a costume change ready for the winter. The sky was a watery shade of pale blue and the wind held enough of a chill inside it to rubber-stamp the fact that summer was on the way out.

Everything was ordinary.

Except for the body that lay on the grass.

The top half of it was covered by a green sweatshirt.

Will was lying close to the piece of ground where he had lain the night before. Jonny could almost believe he hadn't moved since their last kiss. Except, last night, Will had been lying in casual comfort. He'd had one leg over the other, and an arm around Jonny, protecting him from the damp autumn grass.

Today he was splayed as if he was an insect pinned to a piece of cardboard.

'No!' The word came out as a half shout, half scream. It brought the crowd to silence, and Jonny could hear the word return to him, as it bounced off the trees.

He half-ran, half-stumbled, towards the body before he fell to the ground beside it. As he pulled his head back up to look at Will's face, he thought for a wonderful moment that his desperate prayer had been answered.

Will was looking at him, trying to smile at him. Trying to let him know he had something important to say.

'Whoops.'

The fact that Will was still trying to play the scene for comedy, although he had just fallen six stories from a disused tower, made Jonny smile. But the smile was ripped from his face as the effort of speaking made Will start to cough and choke. It was a horrible sound. It was like the sound of a dropped flask being shaken. It proved that although it might look outwardly fine, everything was shattered inside.

Suddenly all was silent again. Will's body lay motionless. His eyes still stared but Jonny realised that they couldn't see him anymore. He knew, suddenly, violently – those eyes would never see him again.

He opened his mouth to scream. To yell against the dark. To swear at a god who he was certain was laughing at him. A god who had shown him what love was like, after nearly eighteen years of neglect, and then taken back his gift. It seemed to be cruel to the point of sadism.

No sound came out. He yelled and yelled but there was nothing.

He felt an arm around his shoulder, a weight pushed his face into the laundry-fresh scent of a cable knit sweater. A volley of platitudes hit him: 'Don't look any more. The paramedics are on their way. It will be alright.'

How can it be all right? Jonny thought and then he recognised the voice.

Ben.

He didn't want Ben to be nice to him. Especially as sympathy would remove the last brick from the dam. The brick that was preventing the wall from collapsing and the water from flowing out. Now, more than ever before, Jonny didn't want to cry in front of a man who had bullied him before, knowing that when the shock of the sudden death had diminished – he would bully him again.

He pushed him away, firmly, but not roughly. He stood back and felt his foot step on something metallic. When he looked down, he saw a beer can.

It had the picture of a homophobic footballer on the label.

The face of the footballer was crushed and crumpled into the grass.

~ 18 ~
MEETING HADLEY COOPER-WILSON

Carmichaeltown: Ben

I knew who Cooper-Wilson was the moment I stepped inside the coffee shop. He had a handlebar moustache that'd been dyed a shade of shocking pink, an orange cravat, and a stomach that spoke of a life spent crouched over a computer with a box of cookies beside him.

He had taken a seat in the centre of the café, desperate to be noticed. Gagging for people to realise how mind-numbingly intellectual, and freakishly eccentric, he was.

I took a deep breath and wandered towards him.

The day, up to that point, had been surprisingly OK considering the whole heap of trouble I had found myself in. Arnie had been up when I'd woken that morning. By all accounts, such a happening was as unlikely as seeing a nightingale during an Icelandic winter. Luckily, he pointed that out before I had a chance to say anything.

It seemed that nothing much kept the man down for long. He had been attacked at knifepoint, rebuffed when he'd swooped in for an after-crisis kiss, and then been kicked out of the marital bed. And yet, he seemed as buoyant as a teenager on a promise. I threw a cup of coffee and a piece of toast down my throat before I left, which made him raise an eyebrow. I got the impression that Jonny was a 'sit at the table with a bowl of muesli' type of guy.

He had followed me out and once again managed to plonk a smacker right on my lips before I was able to turn my head. I realised, with surprise, that it was becoming less weird and less unpleasant every time he did it. This was followed by the realisation that I had always assumed gay men were incapable of a gentle show of affection, without it turning into something more. A swift peck on the lips didn't always, it seemed, lead to an impromptu humping over the breakfast bar.

Once again, the journey into work seemed strange without Tanner, but twenty-four hours in another man's shoes had changed my feelings about my best friend as well. When viewed through someone else's eyes I realised that the reason he was seen as an unpleasant little shit, by so many people, was probably because he was an unpleasant little shit. Just because he wasn't like that to me, and I'd invented excuses for him since we were toddlers, didn't mean that everyone else was wrong.

Once I had swung through the revolving doors and reached the RD Eversen reception area, I treated Gemma to my best 'good morning' along with Ben Shawcross's trademark flirty grin. Maybe it looked a little strange on Jonny Vincent's face. I got nothing back.

Apart from her, everyone else had been friendly, much more friendly than I was used to. Steve Coombes had caught up with me as I left the lift and checked that I was alright after my absence of the day before. He talked about the Saturday night dinner party. I had picked up enough snippets from Amy to be able to have a normal enough conversation about the evening, as we wandered along the corridor and into the office together.

From scraps that Arnie had told me the night before, I had worked out that Jonny's desk was in the same place as mine was in Westcastle, and I headed towards it confidently enough. As soon as I saw the framed photo of Arnie, I knew I was on the money. I also knew that Tanner's replacement was called Kerie, as Arnie was due to meet with her that morning. She obviously liked Jonny, as well, because she seemed genuinely concerned about my health. Steve drifted off and I started a conversation with her. It probably went on longer than any conversation I'd ever had at work with anyone other than Tanner.

I had to be a bit careful. Not only was she fun and feisty but she was also a very beautiful woman. I didn't want to sit there looking like I was just about to drool all over her keyboard. It didn't sound very much like something that Jonny Vincent would do.

I pulled myself away from Kerie and tried to log into my computer. The problem came when I entered Arnie's initials and date of birth. His computer at home might have liked that one as a password, but the computer at work didn't. *Stick a ferret up my trouser leg,* I thought, *that man is obsessed with security.* I really didn't fancy calling computer support to tell them I'd forgotten my password, so I tried a few variations on the theme. I was at the point when I felt that one more wrong attempt would lock me out forever, when Arnie's full name and date of birth did the trick. I breathed a sigh of relief and looked around to check that no one had noticed. No one had. I glanced at a few sent e-mails and got an idea of how Jonny dealt with things. Talk about long winded. Why use three words when thirty would do, seemed to be the mantra he lived by. I spent the morning catching up, after Jonny's unexpected three-day weekend, and only had one more tricky moment.

It came towards the end of the morning. Arnie had arrived an hour before and given me a little wave. I'd managed to wave back – probably the gayest thing I'd ever done. He'd then disappeared into the meeting room with Kerie. By the time they'd reappeared it was practically lunch time. He perched on my desk until I finished the piece of work I was Jonnyfying.

'Right then,' he smiled, 'where am I taking you to lunch today?'

Shit, shit, shit.

'Oh, sorry Arnie, I should have mentioned. I'm working through lunch. I've got this meeting thingy...' I left it purposefully vague and hoped that Arnie wouldn't ask me to fill in the blanks. It was only half a lie, I did have a meeting thingy, it was just nothing to do with work. I'd never had a working lunch in my life, Tanner would have kicked off big time if I'd abandoned him to do unpaid work for RD Eversen. I hoped that Jonny was more of a workaholic than I was.

It seemed that he was. 'Never mind!' Arnie said brightly. 'It'll be a saddo sandwich in the park for one in that case...'

Before he left, I managed another lip-on-lip kiss and felt, once again, that I'd got away with it. No damage done. I waited for five minutes before I left the building, keeping half an eye out for a sarnie-hunting Arnie, as I headed towards the coffee bar.

Cooper-Wilson was as full of himself as I'd expected him to be. I could see how he'd managed to irritate the hell out of that reporter. Once we were settled and pleasantries had been done and dusted, I trotted out a trite tale of hearing about his society from a friend. 'I've always thought that there must be more to life than we think we know,' I said.

He launched into a re-hash of the article I'd read, and I could feel myself zoning out. He had one of those voices.

'...it's lucky for you that we've met up today because there's been an exciting development!' His change of tone brought me back into the world of Cooper-Wilson once again. Unfortunately, I'd zoned back in while he was taking a slurp from his bowl of carrot and coriander soup. Some of the soup had stuck to his moustache. Patches of orange gunge fought the pink dye for supremacy.

'Oh yes?' I faked interest and hoped it would be something worth hearing.

'Yes!' Another slurp and yet more gunge landed on his facial hair. It was putting me off my cheese and ham panini. 'One of my fellow believers has a "contact".' He said the last word as if the man was a member of MI5. 'This "contact", who must remain anonymous for obvious reasons, has "travelled".'

'Could I meet him, the traveller?' Maybe I didn't give the man the reverence that Cooper-Wilson thought he deserved, or maybe he was making it all up as he went along and there was no traveller. I got well and truly shot down.

'Out of the question, I'm afraid. Only I, and a few trusted contacts, are allowed to meet the "travellers".' I was getting a little sick and tired of all the pretentious emphasis he was giving to certain words. I was also getting fed up with his habit of elongating his vowels. It meant he took a hell of a long time to get through a sentence.

I only had an hour for my lunch break.

'So, what did your traveller friend have to say?' I asked casually.

'Well!' Cooper-Wilson leant forward, giving me an even better view of the soup globules. 'We have always thought that when the "genesis of the gateways" happened...'

'The nuclear explosion?' I queried. I was pretty sure of the answer but didn't think it would hurt my cause, if he was aware that I'd done a little bit of research.

'Exactly!' He did seem pleased. I got the impression that his believers were probably few and far between. People who took the piss were probably a lot more common. 'We always thought that two worlds existed alongside, but completely independent of, each other.' He paused for a slurp. 'Most of the anomalies between these worlds happened because of people "travelling", and the butterfly effects they created caused both worlds to differ from each other.'

Well, I knew that that was true, but I certainly wasn't going to tell my new friend about it.

'We thought that if someone died in a car crash in one reality, then it didn't necessarily mean they would die in the other reality...'

'OK,' I said neutrally.

'However!' He ripped off a piece of bread from his mini baton and waved it in my direction. 'This week we have discovered that this isn't always the case.' He stared at me, willing me to be as fascinated by all of this as he was. To an extent, I was. 'My "contact" has reported that his "traveller" has unequivocal proof that there are certain events that are "pre-requisites".'

I smirked inwardly as I added another of his phrases to the game of bullshit bingo I was silently playing as he spoke.

He leant across the table, invading my space and this time treating me to a close-up of his teeth and the small pieces of bread wedged between the gaps and the gums. 'This means that if someone should die in a car crash in one reality, they must die in a car crash in the other one. It might happen ten, twenty or even thirty years later, but it must happen. We think that only a very small percentage of people are "pre-requisitors",' he said and then added pompously, 'but my "contact" managed to convince me of the truth of it.'

Everything in my logical mind wanted to laugh it off as total rubbish. How did he, his contact, or his traveller know what was going to happen in thirty years' time for example? Had they added time travel to inter-reality tourism? But, as much as I might have mocked, I was here. I was not back in Westcastle where I should have been.

'You said, in the article, that the death of Alec Carmichael was the direct result of someone "travelling".' I laughed at myself. *Oh Lordy*, I thought, *he's got me exaggerating the freakin' word now*. 'Are you able to tell me about that?'

Cooper-Wilson sat back and beamed at me, this time without his normal air of superiority. He looked delighted that someone seemed to believe him. It was such a look of natural joy that I forgave him for being a bit of a pompous prat.

'Of course.' He leaned forward even further this time. I felt in grave danger of being sprayed with carrot and coriander soup. I edged back in my chair as Cooper-Wilson said, with a knowing smirk, 'it's about the words he used.'

'Who?' I said stupidly.

Cooper-Wilson sat back abruptly in his seat, which I was quite pleased about. I wasn't quite so pleased about the look on his face. It led me to believe that I was the most stupid person he had ever met.

'Marty Wilding.'

'Who?' I said again. First, I didn't have a clue what he was going on about and second, I experienced the surprise of hearing a familiar name when I wasn't expecting it. Marty Wilding was the name of my mum's cousin. Dad and I thought he was a bit of a family joke. Cooper-Wilson didn't know any of that, and he looked at me as if I'd asked him what my own name was.

'Marty Wilding,' he repeated, then added in a tone of delighted disbelief. 'The man who killed Alec Carmichael.'

'Mm oh yes, sorry.' I stuttered slowly, to hide the surprise of hearing cousin Marty's name being linked to the murder of an Olympic swimmer. 'Yes of course,' I managed to say. 'After fifteen years it's all a little bit hazy.'

'Hazy?' He questioned condescendingly. I supposed it was a big deal. A man who had won five gold medals, died in circumstances which had caused the local bigwigs to re-name the town in his honour. It was unlikely there were many people in the area that weren't aware of the story surrounding it, or the name of the man responsible. Luckily, Cooper-Wilson's love of being able to pontificate won out and he gave me the benefit of being as thick as shit.

'Alec Carmichael had arrived back in Westcastle the day before, after an extensive victory tour around the country. He was celebrating with his family in the La Casita restaurant in the centre of Westcastle.' He seemed to be giving me the version he normally reserved for the local toddlers' group – which was fine by me. 'According to the witnesses, a few minutes after Vince Garrity and his wife...' He paused, looked at me, and the baffled look he saw on my face encouraged him to spell out what he meant. He didn't even seem surprised by my stupidity anymore. 'Vince Garrity, Wilding's other victim, and Garrity's wife, Marie.'

I nodded, pretending I knew who they were, and he continued.

'A few minutes after they'd been shown to their table, Marty Wilding arrived at the restaurant. He seemed angry to see Vince and Marie. He pushed a waiter out of the way, charged over to them, and started shouting. A huge row developed. After a few minutes, Wilding stormed out and everyone breathed a sigh of relief.' Cooper-Wilson broke off and took a deep breath. 'However, five minutes later Wilding returned.' This time, the pause Cooper-Wilson took was purely theatrical. 'And this time he was armed with a gun. He screamed at Garrity, shot him, then aimed the gun at Marie.' Cooper-Wilson looked at me again, checking that I was beginning to get the picture. I was. 'At this point Alec Carmichael, heroically but fatally, intervened. He rushed at Wilding to disarm him. As Wilding turned to see what was happening, his gun went off, and Alec Carmichael was mortally wounded.'

In my mind, the pleasure Cooper-Wilson was getting from the tale was almost indecent. Two people had been murdered, and he was using it as a piece of entertainment on a Tuesday lunchtime. I'd returned to disliking him.

'From everything everyone has told me, shooting Alec Carmichael so shocked Wilding that instead of shooting Marie...' Cooper-Wilson leaned back on his chair again, pushing his empty soup bowl with his stomach as he did so. '...he turned the gun on himself and pulled the trigger.'

I think I was meant to applaud.

'That's so sad.' I couldn't resist giving him a small telling off for enjoying himself too much. 'But what makes you think that it's anything to do with the Sandelwood gateway?'

'As I said before,' my lunch companion continued patiently, 'it's about the words he used. According to witnesses, when Marty Wilding first started shouting at Marie, he was accusing her of having affair.' Cooper-Wilson looked at me pointedly. 'He said: "He even looks like me".'

The penny started to drop. 'And Garrity didn't look like Wilding at all.' I said.

I got a triumphant smile from Cooper-Wilson. 'Exactly!' He said. 'Once you discover their back stories, it all starts to fit. Garrity was known for being highly-strung. He was heading to Westcastle, from a plumbing job in the city, to meet his wife at La Casita. It was meant to be an apology for accusing her of having an affair. Wilding on the other hand, was known for being calm and gentle. None of his friends or relations could believe what he had done. Plus...' Cooper-Wilson waggled a finger underneath my eyes '...no one has ever found evidence that he knew the Garritys, so why did he shoot them? He was visiting a friend on the outskirts of Westcastle. Why did he even go into the town? It was in the wrong direction. He was expected at the family farm, which was in a village...' he paused meaningfully '...on the city side of Sandelwood.'

Marty, my mum's cousin, lived in a village on the city side of Sandelwood. I pushed that fact out of my mind for the moment. I was beginning to realise where all this was heading.

'Garrity and Wilding could have been in Sandelwood at the same time, earlier that evening,' I said.

'They must have been!' Cooper-Wilson beamed with excitement at the thought of adding another convert to the cause. 'They must have met at the gateway – and – swapped over realities.'

'So now,' I said. 'Garrity is in another reality – and – he looks like Marty Wilding.'

And in a similar way, Ben Shawcross is talking to you in a coffee shop, but he looks like Jonny Vincent. I thought.

'To quote Edward Norton Lorenz: "When a butterfly flutters its wings in one part of the world, it can eventually cause a hurricane in another."' Cooper-Wilson said, then explained himself. 'Vince Garrity could have driven to Westcastle and passed the gateway at a slightly different time to Wilding in the other reality. Nothing would have happened. But something infinitesimal occurs in either reality. That butterfly has fluttered its wings. Suddenly, they're both at either side of the gateway, at exactly the same time.'

And Ben Shawcross forgets his wallet and turns his car around, which means that he is on one side of the gateway, as Jonny Vincent is on the other.

'After the transition, Garrity, in Wilding's body, will be facing in the wrong direction. He might think it odd, but the mind is a strange thing. He probably convinces himself that there is a logical reason behind it, turns his truck around, and heads for the restaurant.'

I was with poor old Vince on that one. After all, I'd managed to convince myself that a phone box had moved to the other side of the road, the radio had changed channels and the car had tidied itself up automatically.

Cooper-Wilson interrupted my thoughts. 'When he gets to the restaurant, he sees a man sitting at a table with Marie. He thinks the man looks like him. He doesn't think logically. He doesn't think "Why did she arrange to meet us both at the same time?"'

'He loses the plot.' I add.

Cooper-Wilson nodded. 'Now, we must rely on a little conjecture at this point. Maybe it's the discovery that he had a double, or the fact that his wife didn't recognise him. Maybe he looked into a mirror and saw a stranger. We will never know. But...' Cooper-Wilson banged his hand down on the table again, worrying the waitress who had arrived to clear our plates, '...something happened outside the restaurant that made him finally lose control.' Cooper-Wilson was on a roll. 'Now, we know that both men owned pick-up trucks. The only difference between the two vehicles,' he paused dramatically, 'was that Marty Wilding kept a gun in his.'

I felt so sorry for poor Vince. I had been lucky. The realisation had hit me gradually, and I'd had time to get used to it. For Vince, discovering a double, not being recognised by his wife – and maybe seeing a stranger's face in a mirror – had all happened at the same time. When he discovered the gun, it must have seemed like a sign. It must have seemed like he was meant to use it to murder his wife and her lover.

And to be fair, when option two is *Oh, I swapped realities in that car crash and I'm now looking at myself from another man's body* – I could see why he went for option one.

Cooper-Wilson breathed out after all the effort involved in the big reveal and sat back in his seat. His one-man show had given me the answers to quite a few queries. I used the silence to change the subject and move it on to the other main question I'd had on my brain for the last twenty-four hours.

How could I get home?

'Have any of your travellers ever mentioned if there are any times when it is more likely that the gateway would open?'

Asking for a friend, I thought, as I saw interest glimmer underneath his lashes.

Cooper-Wilson went into a long and laborious spiel, but at the end of it I did have a definite plan that might help me. It wasn't fool proof of course, ensuring that I would be in Sandelwood, at the same time next week, because I needed Jonny to have heard the same story and be in the same place at the same time. 'It has to be at the same time to the very second.' Cooper-Wilson had said. I swore he was getting a hard-on, simply by appreciating his own brilliance.

It might have been a load of bunkum. But, there were too many things that Cooper-Wilson had said which struck a chord with my own experience. It was worth a shot. Next Monday morning, I would make sure I was at the gateway.

'You should come to our meeting tonight,' Cooper-Wilson said as we got up to leave.

'Oh, I'm really sorry,' I said, 'but I need to get back to Westcastle tonight.'

He looked surprised, as if I was turning down the hottest ticket in town. The thought of spending a night with Cooper-Wilson and his cohorts did not fill me with any joy. After all, I could have given them the Wilding/Garrity story from the viewpoint of the other reality. I was just choosing not to. After today's meeting, I was even more convinced that admitting my predicament to Cooper-Wilson would have been like slathering myself with fish oil and waiting for the eagles.

On top of all of that, I realised with a shock that I was quite looking forward to spending another evening with Arnie.

Once I was free of Cooper-Wilson and hot footing it back to the office, I thought through everything he'd told me.

I now knew what had happened to cause the shift between the two realities.

I had just discovered there were two versions of that night. In one version two men had been shot dead, the man who'd murdered them had committed suicide, and the town had been renamed Carmichaeltown.

And the other version? The Westcastle version – if you like. Ever since Cooper-Wilson had mentioned Cousin Marty's name, there had been a memory bouncing around at the back of my brain. It was something Dad had said when Mum mentioned their plans for the weekend, at the Tuesday night supper last week, when everything was normal.

'Oh, sweet Jesus! We don't have to spend the weekend with The Twins do we?'

The Twins.

The story had become a family legend over the years.

Marty, lived on the family farm with his parents. Years ago, a stranger turned up at the farm, just after Marty had arrived home one evening. The stranger was in a lot of distress and claimed to be Marty, although he looked nothing like him. The family thought that he was barking, but decided to let him stay with them, rather than report him to the authorities. Over the next few months, the stranger proved himself around the farm. He seemed to know where everything was without having to ask, he picked up the way the family worked and seemed to know which suppliers the family liked to use. He struck up a special bond with Marty. He thought like him, they used the same words and phrases. And, of course, they shared the same name. Over the years they became inseparable. Hence my dad's nickname. 'The Twins.' He thought the family were soft in the head for being taken in by a tramp.

I knew exactly when the tramp had arrived.

It was the night before the race at the water tower.

I first heard the story about a week later. I hadn't taken much notice at the time because I was still reeling from the fact that Will had fallen and died. But, my subconscious always associates the twins, with the race at the water tower.

So, the butterfly flapping its wings had created two very different versions of that Friday night.

What had happened at the La Casita restaurant in the Westcastle version? Alec Carmichael and his family would have been enjoying a meal, celebrating his Olympic success. Their lives weren't about to be destroyed by a crazed gunman. They probably never even noticed the woman who was sitting at a table on her own. Waiting for a husband who didn't arrive, who she would never see again. She would always think that he had left her, that he didn't love her anymore. She would never know that he had committed suicide in a world she knew nothing about, disguised as a man she wouldn't have recognised.

All of this meant that there must have been two different versions of that day at the water tower as well. Two different outcomes of the race.

How did the shooting of Vince Garrity and Alec Carmichael, affect a group of teenagers involved in a stupid challenge, sixteen hours later and about a mile away?

And it had affected them. One version had led to the Westcastle I'd left behind on Monday morning. The other version led to the Carmichaeltown I was going back to that evening.

Strangely though, it hadn't affected all of them. Of the people I knew, Steve Coombes' life had barely changed. He was happily married to Lottie, his first love, in both worlds. Whereas his best mate Elliot was releasing his very fertile sperm in Chancelwood Road, rather than in Australia.

And everybody else? Jonny Vincent had found his happy ever after in Carmichaeltown as opposed to his happy never after in Westcastle.

Amy? I was starting to begrudgingly admit to myself that Amy was happy here. At home – my home – Amy was not happy.

And me? The Ben Shawcross version of me. A few days ago, I would have said I was happy with my lot in life. *I mean, nobody's got it nailed on perfectly*, I would have said. *At least I wasn't in jail...*

And then there were two.

I wondered what had happened to Will. I had seen him fall from the water tower. I had seen him die. Had he not died in the other version of that day? Had he not tripped when he reached the stretch of staircase with no railing? But if he hadn't died, what had happened to prevent it? And what had happened to tear him and Jonny apart? I would have said that if Will hadn't died, he and Jonny would have been together forever. Just like Steve and Lottie.

I had heard Will's name mentioned a few times, in a 'someone who used to be around but isn't around anymore' type of way. But I still hadn't heard Tanner being mentioned – even when Arnie had been mouthing off about him – he hadn't said his name.

It was the same with everyone else I'd met. I got a strong impression that it wasn't just that they didn't mention Tanner. It was more like they wouldn't.

It was almost as if they were trying to erase him from history.

~ 19 ~
NEWSFLASH

Carmichaeltown's Genesis: Fifteen Years Earlier

Amy looked around the clearing by the water tower. There was quite a crowd. Pretty much the whole of the sixth form had turned up to enjoy the entertainment. She was aware that most people wanted Will to win. Amy wanted Will to win. He was her best friend's boyfriend. He was her friend.

Even so, she was torn. Ben wanted Tanner to win. *No* Amy thought, *it was more than that.* Ben was terrified what would happen if Tanner lost.

The night before was their night. Ben and Amy's night. It was how she thought of Fridays. It was the night that her parents played badminton at the sports centre. The night that Ben was allowed to come into their house, unchaperoned, and watch TV with his girlfriend.

Normally, they didn't do that much TV watching.

Ben had tried. He had burrowed his hands underneath her polo necked sweater and unhooked her bra. He had developed the knack over the course of the summer. He could now do it every time without fumbling her breasts roughly, or nipping at her skin with the hook of the clasp. He had learned and remembered the acts that bought her the most pleasure, while ignoring the ones that had caused her to murmur with disapproval. He was a caring and attentive lover but could also be carefully aggressive. However, it was always on her terms. He was mindful to ensure that she always felt in control, even though he liked to make it look like he was.

Last night, however, she could tell that he wasn't feeling it. Once, back in May, he had tried to make love to her during the Champions League final. It hadn't been successful, and she had pushed him away mid-kiss when his eyes had drifted towards an on-screen penalty. Last night had seemed a little like that.

IN ANOTHER MAN'S SHOES

Amy understood Ben's concerns and had sympathy for him. She was beginning to sense than Ben believed his friend would lose and was still searching for the magic words. The words that would convince Tanner to pull out of the challenge. But Amy knew the same thing that Ben knew. Such words did not exist.

Ben had been distracted all evening. From the moment he arrived, and she'd opened the door to the sound of sirens screaming up from the main road below, she had known that he wouldn't be in the mood. The news flash, from the television, that there had been a fatal shooting in the town centre hadn't helped either. No other details had been released.

She hadn't really understood how, but it had intensified his already sombre mood.

It's very sad, she remembered thinking, *but it doesn't affect us.*

There was a murmur amongst the crowd who were already there, and Amy looked up to see that Jonny and Will had arrived in the clearing. Jonny waved at her, and she waved back.

'Benjy,' said Tanner, obviously annoyed. 'Tell your girlfriend not to fraternise with the faggot brothers.'

Ben glanced anxiously at Amy and steered Tanner away from her, under the pretext of a last-minute team talk. Tanner had practised many times since the bet had been wagered. Ben had been with him all the time. He had coached Tanner on the most effective technique for climbing the tower and on Tanner's request, had run the course himself a few times, so that his friend could see from ground level how to find the best racing line.

Amy looked over at Jonny and made a gesture with her hands, nodding in Tanner's direction. Jonny smiled back at her.

Kyle Hammond then took centre stage, calling the competitors over and explaining the rules in a tone that reminded Amy of a local councillor she had seen on TV. She zoned out from his voice and looked over towards Jonny again, wondering if she should go and stand with him. He looked a little vulnerable and lonely since Will had ambled across to join his competitor at the starting gate. But, just at that moment, Ben appeared at her shoulder and gave it a friendly squeeze. He was letting her know that he would never tell her what to do, or what to think, no matter what Tanner said.

She accepted his show of solidarity amicably, leant her head against his chest, and stayed where she was.

'Three – two – one!' The crowd cheered and Tanner roared into an early lead. Conversation which had been muted for Kyle's spiel, started up again. A radio that had been turned off, was turned back on. Full volume.

Amy watched as Will followed Tanner towards the barbed wire fence, hiding her true allegiance for Ben's sake. The radio had been turned up so loudly that it was audible above all the wagers and predictions that accounted for most of the chatter in the clearing.

The jingle which heralded the start of the hourly news bulletin was being played. It was followed by the theatrical tones of the news reader who, for once, had something notable to announce and was determined to wring every drop of drama out of it.

'One of the victims in the La Casita restaurant murders has been named as Alec Carmichael, who had just returned to Westcastle after winning five gold medals in the Summer Olympics...'

For a second, the silence was so complete that the sound of the wind could be heard as it rustled through the tall trees. Then, a wall of sound broke free. All the talk of the race and the wagers was forgotten. It had been replaced by the excitedly incredulous tones of people checking that they'd heard the news correctly. They were in the heightened state of being connected, yet unaffected by the story. Almost as if they knew that, for years, they would be able to dine off tales of 'what I was doing when I heard that Alec Carmichael had been shot'.

Tanner was just about to crawl through the broken barbed wire, pleased with his fast start, and more pleased with the slow progress of fairy boy.

He was aware that a radio was playing. But was so focussed on getting the job done, winning the race, that he'd been able to block everything out.

Until this latest piece of news.

He turned towards the noise, almost unable to believe what he had heard. The hero of his summer was dead.

Only Will paid it no attention. He was using concentration techniques he had learned through his martial arts training. His ears were closed to all other sound. His eyes were closed to everything except the next marker.

Tanner suddenly realised that Will had eased his way through the fencing and was building up a sizeable lead. He turned his attention to Kyle Hammond, still in situ, waiting for the winner to return and shake his hand.

'Oi Hammond!' he yelled. 'Stop the race, I was distracted.'

Still reeling from the newsflash himself, it took Kyle a couple of seconds to realise that Tanner was talking to him. It took him less time to deliberate on his decision. He wasn't a big fan of Tanner Hootley, although he had always been very diplomatic in the way he'd dealt with him in the past. This seemed the perfect way of dealing with the man, while seeming to keep his neutrality intact.

'Sorry Tanner. Same for both contestants. No can do.'

Tanner shouted a loud obscenity before deciding that Hammond was going to do him no favours. He scrambled through the fence and got himself to his feet. Then he set off as if it was a fifty-metre dash, not a difficult climb up and down a crumbling water tower.

Jonny watched on from the middle of the distracted crowd. He wasn't far from the spot where he'd lain with Will the night before. When they'd met at the corner of Chancelwood Road at midnight, Will had been intrigued by an unexplained shooting in town. Once they had reached the tower, any thoughts of the shooting had been quickly forgotten. They chatted about companionable nonsense, laughed, drank beer, and threw stones at a beer can for forfeits. The target they chose had a picture of a homophobic footballer on the front.

The forfeits led to other things. *Other wonderful things.* It made Jonny grin just to think of them.

He then returned his attention to the race in progress. He thought about what Will had said only a few minutes before, as they'd walked up the lane. 'This is going to be the tortoise and the hare, super-hero version.'

But now, thought Jonny, *the tortoise is in the lead.*

He closed his eyes and dared to dream.

Tanner felt the first stab of discomfort as he reached the turn at the top of the second flight of stairs. He managed to ignore it at first and powered his way painfully up the next two flights. By the turn of the fourth landing, he had almost caught up with Will.

And then, Will just seemed to disappear.

As if he'd been playing with Tanner, the way a kitten might worry a ball of wool before discarding it for something more interesting, Will was waiting for an outward sign that Tanner was beginning to struggle. This arrived when Tanner stepped onto the fifth flight and got a sharp reminder of the cramp that was refusing to go away. The small yelp that came from his mouth was the signal Will had been waiting for. Effortlessly, he glided away from Tanner and headed for the summit of the tower. By the time he reached the final set of stairs, which led to the walkway that topped it, there was a whole flight of steps between them. Will could take care on the tricky section, where the railing had disappeared, and a slip or trip could have led to disaster.

The race was as good as over.

When Will emerged from the barbed wire tunnel, a minute or so later, the whole of the sixth form crowd erupted into a frenzy of cheering. The tragedy on the other side of town had been momentarily forgotten.

Kyle stepped forward to shake Will's hand. He turned that into an embrace and whispered into Will's ear: 'Well done mate! I'm so glad you won!' He really wanted to make sure that Will was aware of the part he'd had to play in the victory, but didn't think it was politic to do so.

Ben watched on in despair. He could see his friend hobbling down the last few flights of the descent and his heart ached for him. He knew that Tanner wouldn't want his sympathy but he was suffering for him nonetheless. Amy was beside Ben, holding him tightly, as if she sensed his agony. He knew that inwardly she was delighted, but thanked her silently for her support.

When Tanner finally emerged into the clearing, the sound of catcalls and derisive whistles were his only welcome.

Hammond brusquely shook Tanner's hand and led him to the patch of mud, in front of his peers, that had been designated beforehand. Ben could feel his humiliation. His own cheeks and forehead blushed with it, as if he shared the shame.

But he couldn't share the moment after his friend had knelt in the puddle. When Kyle had opened one of the envelopes from his jacket pocket and handed the sheet of A4 paper inside of it to him, Tanner had to face the group alone.

'I am kneeling here in front of you all, a beaten man. I mostly want to apologise to one man for making his life a misery. I only did it because, deep in my heart I know I could never have half the strength, courage, and wisdom that Jonny Vincent possesses. I am not worthy...'

Tanner scanned the letter quickly and came to a decision. He couldn't continue. To pantomime jeers, he stood up and tore the piece of paper in two.

'I'm not saying any of that crap... A man who was everything that none of you lot will ever be, is lying dead and you're up here playing games like children.'

Even as he used a man's death as his excuse, Tanner knew that his attitude would have been different had he won. He strode towards the crowd aggressively and pushed the first few people out of the way, until the others parted like a religious miracle, and he was able to leave the clearing.

Ben watched him go and looked at Amy. She nodded gently, giving him permission to leave her. He ran after his best friend, catching him up as he reached the first of the trees that lined the track. Instinctively, he gave Tanner a sympathetic hug.

Tanner shoved him away.

Jonny watched them go and turned back to see Will heading towards him. They embraced to the sound of the cheering crowd. Before Will had arrived, Jonny would never have believed that his contemporaries would have accepted his sexuality, let alone congratulate him for it.

But Will, Will was special. And he'd changed everything.

'It's over,' Will whispered into his ear. 'Tanner's reign is over. You won't have to worry about him ever again.'

~ 20 ~
TUESDAY NIGHT DINNER

Westcastle: Jonny

By the time I turned into the road that led to Sandelwood on the second evening of my life as a married man, I was beginning to wish they'd fitted ejector seats on five-door family hatchbacks.

The commentary emanating from the passenger seat seemed to be interminable. Tanner certainly possessed a descriptive turn of phrase and if you weren't gay, religious, disabled, a woman or an ethnic minority, there was a chance that you might have found him hilarious.

Although, to be fair, it wasn't only the above groups that were a target for his caustic wit. Very few people were safe. If you weren't in the 0.1% of the population who Tanner found totally acceptable, the chances were good that you would find yourself on the receiving end of a cutting and generally inappropriate one-liner.

He described Steve Coombes as: 'Wet as a deep-sea diver's jock strap.' One particularly good-looking secretary was, in Tanner's opinion, 'As hot as a porno star in a sauna.' And a seventeen-year-old trainee, who didn't make the best of his brains, was branded: 'As thick and unappealing as concrete porridge.'

All in all, I decided that as a grown man, Tanner was just as vile as his teenage counterpart. I imagined that he would have had a lot of mates, but very few friends. At that moment in time, among all the other problems that were entailed with being an inter-reality traveller, I numbered the fact that Ben was at the top of that very short list as the most perturbing of all.

The day had been pretty much wall to wall Tanner. The journey to work, the frequent visits to my desk, the lunch that I owed him in the same pub we had visited the day before. His sparkling wit accompanied me at every turn. The one advantage of paying for lunch was the fact that I also did the ordering, so I could choose what I wanted to eat. Even though the fish from the day before hadn't induced the vomit that I'd feared, I decided to play it safe with a veggie burger. A fact that brought scornful laughter from my dining companion.

'Veggie burger? Damn it Benjy, don't go all Greenpeace on me. Next thing I know you'll be voting for the Green Party, taking it up the arse and rocking up to work in a kaftan.'

Little did he know. To paraphrase the words of the old song: Two out of three wasn't bad.

How I wished I was sharing my lunch break with Arnie as we so often did on a Tuesday. He generally made sure his meeting with Kerie was just before lunch time, so that we could meet up afterwards.

I had talked to him. I couldn't stop myself. When he'd left the meeting room after his tête a tête with Tanner, I contrived to bump into him at the water cooler. I gave him a bright 'Good morning' greeting and he managed to mumble a similar phrase in return.

I knew my boyfriend well enough to know that he was hiding the fact that he would have been less surprised had he received the greeting from the water cooler itself.

When I lurched into a rambling monologue about a fictional problem that I was hoping he could help me with, I could also tell that he was torn. The Britishness that he had learned since he'd been living here, required him to be polite. The honest, no-nonsense, Icelandic part of his brain was dying to blurt out that Ben Shawcross hadn't bothered to talk to him at any time during the last four years, why should Arnie bother to help him now?

Luckily for me, the British side won out and he agreed to meet me for lunch the next day.

His attention was suddenly distracted by the arrival of the particularly good-looking secretary. 'Sorry,' he said. 'My lunch date for today is here. I'll see you tomorrow. I'm at a seminar on the other side of town, so I'll meet you by the front entrance at 12:30.'

With that, his smile transformed from polite to delighted as he greeted his lunch companion. Swooping an arm around her shoulder, he moved away from me, towards the lift and their lunchtime gossip.

The feeling that I experienced in my stomach was extraordinary. It was a sense of longing so acute it announced itself in the form of a sharp and vicious pain.

The smile that the secretary had just been gifted, should have been mine. Was mine. It was the smile that I'd seen transforming Arnie's face for the last four years.

It even occurred to me during the journey home, four hours later, that they looked like a couple. Had Arnie turned mysteriously straight in this messed up version of my own world? I guessed I would find out at lunch the next day.

'Oi! Earth to Benjy. I hope you're paying more attention to the road, than you are to me...' I snapped back to the here and now with the realisation that I had zoned out rather too successfully from Tanner's never-ending monologue. So much so that I had missed the fact he had asked me a question.

'Sorry Tan.' I tried an apologetic grin that nearly killed me. 'It's been a long day.'

Tanner grunted. 'You've been a bit weird the last couple of days.' He shrugged, and let that one go. 'I asked you what sort of dirty dessert your wife has got planned for us tonight?'

Oh Christ! The Tuesday night supper. I'd been so wrapped up in thoughts of Arnie that I'd totally forgotten about the delights of a Tuesday night in Westcastle.

'You're one lucky bastard, Benjy Shawcross,' Tanner returned to his previous train of thought. 'A wife who's dirty in the kitchen and dirty in the bedroom.'

Despite my non-aggressive attitude to life – I wanted to punch him.

When I arrived home, I discovered that I wasn't the only one who was feeling violent. However, whereas my victim would have been my travelling companion; the force of my wife's wrath was being felt by a tray of choux buns that had decided not to rise.

The screamed obscenity hit my earlobes, along with the distinctive sound of a metal tray clattering against the kitchen wall, as soon as I opened the front door and stepped inside.

Among all the other things I was finding difficult to get used to, Amy's anger was the most upsetting. I moved quickly through the lounge and into the kitchen diner. The table had already been laid for five people in readiness for the delightful soiree the evening had in store for us.

By the time I had reached Amy, her immediate rage had subsided. She was squatting on the floor, hands over her face, with her fingers digging into her eye sockets. It was as if she was trying to physically stem the flood of tears that threatened to overwhelm her.

I called her name softly to let her know I was there, but she still jumped slightly as I tried to ease her to her feet.

'Hey,' I said carefully, 'it's only dinner for … my parents. Nothing to get stressed about.'

As she had done on a couple of occasions the night before, she looked at me with a curious expression. As if she didn't really know me.

'That recipe always works,' she ignored her thoughts on my unusual behaviour and nodded instead towards the sad, flat, discs that were now spread over the cooker, work surfaces, and floor. 'Two batches I've made today. Look at them. Bloody useless.'

I wasn't sure if she was describing herself, or the poor discarded dessert.

I retrieved one of the choux buns from the floor and tried my best goofy grin. 'On the other hand,' I said gently, 'stuck together, these would make a killer pair of flip flops for the summer.'

Amy looked up sharply, as if she expected to see mockery sneering from my face. When she didn't find it, she allowed herself a small grin and collapsed against my shoulder.

I gave her a sympathetic hug. 'Surely we've got something calorific, creamy and extremely bad for them, in the freezer,' I enquired as she pulled herself away. She stopped and gave me a horrified stare which wobbled uncertainly between play-acting and being deadly serious.

'Give Jack Shawcross a frozen dessert? Are you out of your mind?'

'Blame me,' I said easily, 'I'll tell him I was desperate for a Black Forest Gateau.'

She looked at me with the expression that I was getting used to. It was the one that told me she couldn't quite believe what she was hearing and was checking that she wasn't being set up to be used as the butt of a joke, later in the evening.

Satisfied that the 'new' version of her husband was still in evidence, she moved towards the fridge freezer and started rifling through the freezer compartments.

'Could you be desperate for a raspberry and white chocolate torte?' She asked, waving the life saver in my direction.

'I'm desperate for a raspberry and white chocolate torte actually.' I replied deadpan. In return I received a grin that was becoming more and more genuine every time she used it.

'Look,' I said, my success in calming Amy causing me to forget the role I was playing. I just wanted to help. 'Why don't you go and relax in the bath. Tell me what needs doing and I can take over from here.' Over in Carmichaeltown, Arnie and I had a deal. He would do the day-to-day dinners, if I took over on the nights we entertained.

I should have known that Ben and Amy would not have such a deal.

'Mm,' Amy said, 'I'm still trying to remove the results of your only attempt at catering from the side of the microwave. I think I'll pass, thanks.' She then grinned at me, taking any sting from the words. 'I mean, they might irritate the hell out of me, but I don't actually want to kill your parents...'

When the doorbell rang, an hour and a half later, Amy was as relaxed as I had seen her since I'd arrived in Westcastle. I, contrarily, was a bundle of dread and nerves. All I had to do that evening was convince a couple of people, I hadn't seen for nearly fifteen years, that I was their son.

I wasn't expecting it to go well.

The last time I'd seen Jack Shawcross had been on TV after the trial. His son had just been sent to jail and even I had managed to find a little sympathy for a man I'd never liked. He had the look of a dancer who was religiously following the choreography, even though the orchestra had gone on strike.

The Jack Shawcross who entered his son's home that evening had been restored to the arrogant, bullying force of nature that I remembered from my childhood. He strode into the house, leaving his wife hovering on the doorstep, as if she was unsure whether she had been invited as well. I remembered her as a gentle, nervous woman, who barely said a word. I was pretty sure her name was Joyce. Over the years, it seemed as if she had tried to transform her character through wearing vivid coloured clothing and extensive make-up. However, the lipstick was too bright, the eye shadow too thickly applied, and the tight perm was completely the wrong shape for her head. The final impression was of someone who had got ready for the evening, whilst riding on a roller coaster.

And, it still hadn't managed to change her character.

As she apologised her way into the house, it was clear that after thirty-odd years of marriage, she was still under the misapprehension that her husband was God.

'Hold up Driver! Room for a small one on top?' I had just been in the process of closing the door after her, when a bellow from the pathway let me know that we had another visitor. I was tempted to pretend I hadn't heard him and slam the door with all the might I could muster.

Fortunately, or unfortunately, I was too polite to do so.

'So, Benjy, what tasty treat has the little lady got in store for us tonight?' Tanner said, a variation on the question he had asked me in the car.

If there's any justice, a nasty case of Campylobacter, I thought viciously.

Tanner hadn't waited for an answer, which was probably just as well. Instead, he went straight into the lounge to greet Jack and ignore Joyce. I closed the door and followed him in. It seemed that Jack had the same question on his lips as his surrogate son. He was asking the 'little lady' herself for details of the menu, as I re-entered the room.

'Beef Stifado, Jack.' Amy's tone was polite enough, but I got the impression it was a little bit of a strain.

Jack burst into a loud guffaw of laughter. 'Beef Stiff – hard – oh!' he mocked rudely. 'Get that recipe off your gay boy best friend did you Amy?'

'Hey Jack,' said Tanner, joining in the fun, 'I better Rubber Jonny loves a bit of stiff – hard – oh!' They then indulged in a bout of fist pumping. Two members of an exclusive mutual admiration club, acclaiming their joint comic genius.

I noticed that Amy slipped away wordlessly in the middle of their merriment. I also noticed that Ben wasn't included in their joke. That would have made me feel better disposed towards him but for one thing.

Why did he let them get away with it?

I also let them get away with it, but I told myself that I was only doing what I thought Ben would do. It was nothing to do with the fact that I hated confrontation of any sort.

I muttered something about helping Amy and disappeared into the kitchen. My wife was straining the potatoes over the sink. She looked calm enough, but there was a tightness around the mouth and a jerkiness in her movements that led me to believe otherwise.

'Hey Amy!' Jack's bellow from the lounge could have been heard three doors down. I saw Amy flinch as she reached for the potato masher. She sighed, and called back with more friendliness than her body language suggested she was feeling.

'Yes Jack?'

'I hope you got that beef from Maxwells. No supermarket shit?'

The masher slammed down onto the potatoes to demonstrate the anger she was feeling. She then put that anger into words. Hissed, whispered words. I got the impression she wouldn't have cared if they were heard by the people in the next room. But for her husband's sake she was keeping it *sotto voce*, for the moment.

To her father-in-law she called out in an affable enough fashion: 'Yes, all fresh from Maxwells today, Jack.'

To me she hissed: 'Once. Five years ago. I served meat I'd bought from the supermarket.' She accompanied the next line with a bash of the masher drumming out each word. 'But every frigging week he mentions it.'

I decided to go for the quirky, humorous ploy again to try and defuse her temper. After all, it had worked earlier.

'Are you mashing those potatoes, or trying to extract a confession?'

She laughed. That wonderful natural peel of humour that I heard from Amy all the time at home. She then sobered up and looked at me.

'I don't quite understand it. If you'd said that to me last week, I would have snapped your head off. But there's something different about you, yesterday, and today.' She paused, and then seemed to realise what that 'something' was. 'I'm not getting the impression that you're laughing at me. I almost feel that you're on my side.'

I pulled her face towards me with my finger. I wanted her to see how genuine I was. How sincerely I meant every word.

'I am on your side. Always.'

She smiled, pulled her hand up and covered my own. Holding on to my gaze with her eyes, she lost the smile and whispered softly.

'Then – support me in front of them – even if it's only once during the whole, horrible evening.'

I agreed I would, and she nodded, before becoming sidetracked by Jack's latest diatribe as it floated in from the lounge.

'So Tan, I told you I was going to experience the joy of another weekend with The Twins, didn't I?'

Amy groaned. 'Here we go. From one of Jack's favourite rants to another. Poor Marty and Marty. Just because their family situation doesn't follow your dad's rules on "how you should live your life".'

As far as I could make out Jack was talking about Joyce's cousin Marty, and his extended family. The extended family included a man, who seemed to have turned up from nowhere. Jack didn't seem to be implying they were gay. He seemed to be mocking them for another reason entirely. Apparently they shared the same name and, according to Jack, Marty mark two thought he was Marty mark one.

This interested me for two reasons. Marty Wilding, a farmer, was the man who had killed Alec Carmichael and Vince Garrity back in Carmichaeltown. He had a hailed from a village near Sandelwood. The same village where, apparently, Joyce's cousin lived.

Just as I was getting excited, my sensible side warned me about asking too many questions. First, I could hardly ask about my own family. Second, it probably wouldn't end up helping me.

Marty, the version who might have arrived from another reality, had never made it back there.

And that was the only information I wanted from him.

When Amy had predicted that the evening would be 'horrible', she had been very accurate. The dinner party was tortuous. It was dominated by Jack, who had a view on everything, and everybody. Mostly, however, he had a view on the evening's menu – and how Amy had cooked it.

'Oh. You cooked the broccoli earlier and reheated it in the microwave.' He said disapprovingly, serving spoon hovering over the vegetable dish. His comment was not proof of his catering genius, it was merely proof that he had seen Amy take the vegetable out of the said appliance less than a minute before.

'Not Maxwells' best,' was his verdict on the beef. 'But maybe Amy, it's the way you cooked it.'

'Such a pity you didn't add a little double cream to the mashed potato, I always find that it perks it up a little.' He talked as if he spent most of his days rustling up gastronomic delights in the kitchen. However, as he had already described the kitchen as 'Joyce's domain', I doubted whether he'd be applying for his own personal Michelin star any time soon.

I should have stuck up for Amy. I'd promised her I would, and I spent the evening promising myself that I would protest the next time he said anything derogatory. I just couldn't seem to put the plan into action.

The evening was crawling past slower than a tortoise on a tightrope. Everyone had finished their main course and Amy jumped up to clear the table. Taking her lead, I stacked the vegetable dishes and followed her into the kitchen area.

'Son, Son,' Jack chided me. 'What have I told you about not encroaching on a woman's territory? They don't like it.'

It was Amy who answered him, when it should have been me. 'No Jack, it's fine. It's quite nice. After working all day, then cooking, I'm happy to accept any help that's going.'

'Working?' Jack queried, his tone just on the polite side of mockery. 'I'm not sure you can call selling a few books, while having a good old gossip with the girlies, working – eh Tanner?'

As much as my own silence had annoyed me throughout the interminable evening, Tanner's sycophancy had been almost unbearable. He thought of himself as Jack Shawcross in training, there was no doubt about it.

'Nothing like what you and I do, Jack,' he agreed.

Considering the fact that Tanner had spent most of his day leaning on my desk with his mouth in overdrive, I could barely believe what I was hearing. Except that it was Tanner who had said it. Tanner was a man whose uncompromising views on how other people should behave, didn't equate in the slightest to the way he lived his own life.

I returned to the table, to clear the rest of the dirty dishes, and had to endure more snide comments. Once again, I said nothing. In fact, it was Joyce who supported me, despite receiving a condescending look from her husband.

'I think it's nice Benny, don't listen to him.'

'Oh, for goodness' sake Joyce,' Jack made it clear that he didn't like to be contradicted by his wife. 'He's thirty-odd years old. Do you still have to call him Benny?'

Joyce stared down at her place setting; normal order restored. I took the stack of plates into the kitchen, put them on the kitchen counter, and received a look from Amy. Her meaning was very clear.

Support me.

I tried to ignore the truth-drug eyes and took the white chocolate torte she handed me. I'm not sure I had believed her warnings, about the way Jack might react, although his niggly comments regarding the rest of the meal should have given me a clue. I have never been a great fan of those cookery programmes where people sweated blood over a tasty treat, only for some so-called expert to find fault with it. If I ever went to someone's house for dinner, I was just grateful I hadn't had to cook it, or pay for it, myself.

Jack, it appeared, didn't think like that.

I had got no more than three paces towards the kitchen to pick up the bowls, and the cake slice, when I heard Jack call my wife's name.

'Amy,' his tone was somewhere between a whinge and full-on scorn. 'Was this pud – frozen?' He might as well have asked if she'd injected it with Novichok.

I ignored my growing irritation, both with Jack for continually criticising my wife and with myself for being unable to defend her. I trotted out the pre-prepared excuse and although it silenced Jack momentarily, it didn't stop him from behaving like a spoilt brat while the rest of us tucked into the dessert quite happily.

Joyce was trying to help by making suitably appreciative noises. However, as I smiled gratefully at her, Jack made his feelings known.

'Oh Amy...' petulance and reproof came together in the most irritating of ways. 'It's still frozen in the middle.' He then jabbed at the offensive dessert with his spoon. I had just been breathing a sigh of relief, believing that we had managed to defrost the dessert successfully in the limited time we had had available. Jack, however, was behaving as if he'd discovered an igloo hidden in the middle of his torte.

For the rest of the meal, I could see Jack out of the corner of my eye. He was pushing the offending offering from one side of his plate to the other, then mashing it with his spoon as if turning it in to soup would make it more palatable. Eventually, he put as much of the bashed about dessert in his mouth as he could. He then proceeded to make choking noises, to impress upon the rest of the dinner party that eating the pudding was practically killing him.

A sudden and completely alien sense of anger washed over me. It was almost a surprise when I heard a voice speaking. Not only because the voice was raging with fury, but also, because the voice was Ben's. Mine. As my mouth vomited the words, part of my brain vaguely realised that I had no control over what I was going to say. It was terrifying and liberating at one and the same time.

'That's it! I am sick to death of you criticising ... Amy ... my wife. Every bloody Tuesday you expect her to cook for you and clear up afterwards. And *nothing* is ever right. I mean, let's look at tonight. The beef wasn't tender enough for you, the mashed potato wasn't creamy enough – the friggin' broccoli was heated up in the microwave... I mean when exactly did you become Auguste Escoffier?

The voice – my voice – stopped suddenly. As the echo floated across the half-filled glasses before fading away, I tentatively looked around at the other faces, struck dumb by my outburst.

Joyce looked worried, Jack looked shocked and angry, while Tanner was mercifully speechless for the first time since yesterday morning. And Amy? Amy looked as if she was trying to mould her face into a look of surprise, while suppressing a massive grin that threatened to give the game away.

More in control now, I softened the tone of my voice, while ensuring that my next point was not up for discussion.

'I would like you to all to leave my house now.'

Jack recovered quickly. The spoilt child who had been playing with his pudding was replaced by the company boss who was dealing with an insubordinate employee. The bullying swagger had returned in full force.

'Your house?' The tone was nasty with a warning of worse to come. 'And tell me please, who ensured that you got it for a price you could afford? Who bought it for you and allowed you to pay him back on very easy terms? Who charged you an interest rate unheard of from any bank?'

The Jonny Vincent of the day before yesterday would have crumbled at this point, and it seemed that Ben Shawcross had been crumbling in the face of his father for the whole of his life. I didn't feel like crumbling. For the first time in my life, I felt like fighting.

'Oh, I'm very aware of who sorted it all out for me, Dad,' I looked at him pointedly. 'And how exactly did you do it? By conning a vulnerable young boy out of his inheritance. Does that make you feel proud...?' I paused to accentuate the bitterness I felt on behalf of my doppelgänger, '...because it makes me feel sick.'

Jack stared at me as if he couldn't believe the words that were coming out of my mouth. I couldn't believe the words that were coming out of my mouth, but I wouldn't have changed one of them.

When he realised that his son was not going to back down in his normal way, he slammed his serviette down onto the table and turned to his partner-in-crime.

'Come on Tan, my boy. I know when I'm not wanted.' He recovered his equilibrium quite quickly and gave Tanner a conspiratorial smirk. 'On the plus side, we can manage to fit an extra couple of pints in before closing time.' He then turned to me. 'You can get over yourself and join us when you've calmed down.'

I had discovered earlier on in the day that another Tuesday night ritual was that after the meal, the men relocated to the Chancelwood Arms, while Joyce and Amy did the clearing up.

I decided to stab tradition very firmly in the back.

'No thanks Dad,' I said testily. 'I'm going to help Amy clear up.' I then manufactured a sharp intake of breath as if I'd just had a brilliant idea. 'Tell you what though, why don't you take Mum with you? It'll make a nice change for her, rather than having to clear up after you, all the time.'

He either didn't notice the sarcasm or chose to ignore it. Jack had recovered quickly from my outburst, whereas I was still having to grip onto the back of one of the chairs to stop my hand from shaking.

'Don't be ridiculous Son,' he barked, normality restored. 'You don't want to get in the way of their girly chit-chat.' Again, he looked towards his surrogate son to back him up. 'Does he Tan?'

Tanner looked on the verge of agreeing with him when I received support from an unlikely direction.

'Do you know what, Jack?' Joyce said brightly, 'I would love a drink.' She smiled at me meaningfully. 'Give Ben and Amy a chance to have a proper chat.'

I suddenly realised that Joyce was probably more aware than anyone gave her credit for. She knew the precarious state of her son's marriage and wanted to help. I was warming to her by the minute.

In contrast, Jack remained in the icy part of the kitchen from where Amy had taken the ill-fated torte, as far as I was concerned.

He was not happy. I had no doubt that he'd been hoping that the rest of the evening would be full of beer swilling and banter. I thought it highly probable that Jack was one of those men who rued the day when women had been allowed into public houses.

Tough, I thought.

Between us, Joyce and I managed to usher Jack and Tanner out of the door.

'Don't think you can use your little strop tonight to get out of our trip to your grandmother on Sunday,' he said as he left the house. 'I will be expecting you to pick me up, twelve-forty-five as per norm. Don't let me down ... again.'

It was another of those pieces of information I had picked up, during the last thirty-six hours. The monthly trip to see Jack's mother in her nursing home. She was close to death's door, by all accounts. I wasn't looking forward to it, but I certainly wasn't going to deprive the old woman of one last visit from her grandson.

I nodded in his general direction and was about to close the door behind the three of them, when I realised that Joyce was lingering on the doorstep.

'You and Amy will come to ours next week,' she said. 'Won't they Jack?' She turned towards her husband, but he was halfway towards the Chancelwood Arms. Undeterred, she repeated the invitation and added meaningfully: 'I've been wanting to invite you for ages.'

I smiled and kissed her cheek. It seemed that I wasn't the only one who had discovered a backbone that night.

After I had locked the door, I walked back into the kitchen diner. It was like walking into the house next door, Amy's house, in the world next door.

The Amy that smiled at me was my Amy. My best friend.

'Thank you, Ben,' she said quietly. 'Thank you so much.'

She moved towards me and wrapped her arms around my neck. She kissed me lightly on the lips once, and then again, and then a third, fourth, and fifth time. Tiny butterfly kisses that tickled the creases on my skin. Suddenly, she moved her head away from my face, slightly to one side, as if she was assessing my reaction.

I didn't really think that she needed to study my face to gauge how I was feeling. There was another part of my body that was making it obvious to her how aroused I was.

This is crazy! I thought. *I am a gay man. Gay men don't normally react like this when being kissed by a woman.*

I'd had no chance to prepare myself. No chance to dream of Arnie. This was all about Amy, and how Amy was making me feel.

But Amy is my friend. I thought. *I love her, but not for one moment in my life have I ever wanted to make love to her.*

As Amy unzipped my jeans, I realised that if I stopped her, there would be no excuses that would be able to make it right. Nothing would take away the embarrassment and humiliation.

I also realised that stopping her, was the last thing I wanted to do.

* * *

As I lay in bed later, I was once again fretful and unable to sleep. But, whereas the night before had been due to worry, that night was due to guilt.

I felt like I had been unfaithful to Arnie. I wasn't sure what I could have done to prevent it, short of taking a massive step towards destroying Ben and Amy's already fragile marriage. However, I felt guilty non the less.

I felt guilty about Amy as well. Even though I had worried last night about building her hopes up in the knowledge that Ben would destroy them on his return, I had carried on building.

As she had lain against my chest after we had made love, Amy glanced up at me.

'We haven't done that for months,' she said.

'I know!' I grinned. 'Why on earth has it taken us so long?'

It was a bit of a fishing expedition if I'm honest. The Ben and Amy I remembered as teenagers couldn't keep their hands off each other. How had they turned into celibate thirty somethings?

'Well, I don't know about you,' Amy said, sitting up so that she could look at me properly. 'But I know why I haven't been interested in sex lately.'

I didn't have to say anything, I just nodded gently, and she continued.

'Oh Ben,' Amy sighed. 'I've felt like an outsider in my own marriage. You seem far more interested in spending time with Tanner and your football club mates. I don't seem to feature in your life anymore.'

She had paused. She seemed to be on the point of saying something else, opening up completely. But she didn't, she simply kissed me once more on the lips and disappeared into the bathroom to clean her teeth.

What was she going to say to me? I thought later as I lay there in the dark, in more ways than one.

It was my last waking thought of the evening.

It was a thought that would haunt me later in the week.

~ 21 ~
MARSHMALLOW CLOUD

Westcastle: Fifteen Years Earlier

After Will's funeral, everyone was invited back to the Flanagans' house for the wake. They had laid out a buffet of mixed sandwiches and assorted Danish pastries in the back room, directly under Will's bedroom. The French windows had been opened so that people, who weren't put off by the autumn mizzle, could spill out into the garden.

Jonny thought back to the last time he had been in this house. He'd been happy then. Yes, there had been that shred of a worry about the upcoming race. But he'd been happy. He was already beginning to forget what happiness felt like.

He looked across at the ransacked buffet table. It felt all wrong. It was almost as if people expected a reward for attending. And Will didn't deserve that. Will deserved to be honoured. He shouldn't have been used as an excuse for people to ram as many freebie triangles of bread and ham down their throats as they could manage.

Kyle Hammond was standing next to the table with his girlfriend, Dakota. She was a vacuous brunette whose one ambition in life was to appear in a reality TV programme. She was older than Kyle and had left the school the year before Will had arrived. The small fact that she had only met Will and Jonny once, when she and Kyle had bumped into them in Maudesley Street, didn't prevent her from ensuring that everyone knew how much she was suffering.

'I nearly went to the race,' she said breathlessly to the friends who had come to support her through the trauma. 'If it hadn't been for the fact that I had pre-booked a manicure, I would have actually seen it happen!'

She looked up and saw Jonny and mistook him for a waiter. She indicated to him with her eyes that she was in desperate need of a prawn vol-au-vent.

He wanted to scream at her: *I did see it happen, you stupid bitch. And I loved him. I didn't just meet him briefly outside Marks and Spencer. I wouldn't have needed to phone a friend to pick him out of a police line-up. I – loved – him.*

He passed her the plate.

Jonny hadn't wanted to come. He had steeled himself for the funeral. He knew he would have felt wretched later, had he failed to say his last goodbye. But the wake, he had only come along because his father was desperate to get some advice from Jack Shawcross. Mr Vincent was in the middle of a dispute with the mechanic who serviced his boat and he wanted to chew the bones of it with Ben's dad. 'An exchange of ideas from one businessman to another,' was what his father called it. Getting free advice from someone who thought they knew everything about everything – that was the way Jonny saw it.

Jonny knew there would have been an argument had he refused to join his parents – and he just couldn't be bothered to have it.

He glanced over and saw Amy watching him intently. Her face was moulded into the concerned expression she had been wearing for the last few weeks. Ben was by her side, as he had been for the last few weeks.

Jonny hadn't been aware of much since Will had died. Each voice he'd heard appeared to be muffled and distorted, and everybody he saw seemed vague and indistinguishable. It was as if he was viewing his life through a marshmallow cloud.

However, Ben was one of the things he had noticed. The hated bullying sidekick had become softer, friendlier, and more caring. Between them, Ben and Amy had got him through each day.

Jonny wasn't fooling himself. He knew that this change of heart was mainly to do with the fact that Tanner had kept a low profile during this time. When his long-time antagonist had climbed down from the water tower after the accident, he'd appeared to be shocked and genuinely upset.

'He misjudged the step and tripped over it. Before I knew what was happening, he was gone.' Tanner had said repeatedly, sitting on a tree stump in the clearing, rocking back and forth. Ben had gone over to Tanner and held him until the rocking had stopped, but they hadn't seen a lot of each other since that day.

But Jonny knew that Tanner's armistice was only temporary. When Amy and Ben had eased him back to school, at the beginning of the week, his nemesis had kept a sympathetic distance at first.

But yesterday, he'd noticed signs that normal service was about to be resumed. For once, Ben and Amy had not been at his side when he walked down the corridor, his world still vague and hazy. He had seen Tanner walking towards him, and the haze momentarily cleared, bringing acute memories of the days before Will. He found himself staring at Tanner and he could see that beneath the sympathetic mask, there was already a slight sneer playing on his lips.

Just wait, it said, *everyone will forget soon enough.*

And then I'll have you.

Jonny smiled a soft watery smile in Amy's direction and sent a silent message across the room. *If it hadn't been for you two*, the message said, *I don't know where I would have been.*

His parents had been useless. His father was obsessed by the fact that his boat mechanic had overcharged him by a few man hours on a 'simple job that could have only taken a few minutes.' His mother had been more worried by the fact that an expert on ceramics, who was due to talk at her women's craft club meeting, had cried off with a nasty case of shingles. Neither of them had enough time to be concerned about their son.

'It was a stupid thing to do,' was one of their opinions. 'And the water company should have done more to prevent it.' That was another. 'Leaving the barbed wire broken and the tower in ruins. Well, it was an accident waiting to happen.'

'But I loved Will.' Jonny tried to explain. He wondered if the hazy world he was living in was making it difficult for him to explain himself.

They laughed in a slightly condescending manner. 'I'm sure he was a very nice friend,' they said. 'But you'll have plenty more friends, just you wait and see.'

They talked to him as if he was five years old and his best friend had dumped him for a girl who had a paddling pool in the back of her parents' garden.

Jonny wasn't surprised. It wasn't that they had been outwardly homophobic since he'd emerged from the closet. It was more that they believed that a gay relationship wasn't as serious as a 'normal' relationship. In their eyes, it didn't really count.

'I think he's only doing it to be trendy,' he had heard his mother tell her friends in the early days of his relationship with Will. She might have been talking about a new hairstyle, or a pair of high waisted skinny jeans, rather than a sexual preference.

Jonny mouthed across to Amy that he was going up to the loo. He avoided the tail end of the locusts, who were determined to get the last cinnamon lattice without being too obvious about it, and made his way out into the hall.

As he climbed the stairs he had a sudden flash of memory, so clear it was hard for him to believe it wasn't happening.

Will and Jonny, running up the stairs. Spurred on by a daft challenge to be the first one to swallow dive onto Will's bed.

He could hear Will's voice and smell his antiperspirant. When he looked at the top of the stairs, he could see him.

Jonny closed his eyes. This was too much. He looked so real, so life-like.

When he re-opened his eyes Will was still there, standing at the top of the stairs with a strange look on his face.

'You're Jonny aren't you?' Will asked confusingly. *Surely Will would remember me.* Jonny thought.

He stared at Will. He wanted to reach out. He wanted to hold him in his arms and convince himself that it wasn't a cruel illusion.

He had almost plucked up the courage to do it, could almost feel Will's body against his own, when Will spoke again. The bitterness in the voice was like a slap in the face, and it ensured that Jonny kept his arms where they were.

He had never heard Will talk to him in such a way before.

'I don't know how you can dare to show your face. My brother was only doing that daft challenge to protect you.' The accusation was obvious. Suddenly, the identity of the man was obvious too.

It wasn't Will.

Will had four brothers and two sisters. 'My parents weren't ones for hobbies,' Will had laughed when he'd told Jonny. His six siblings were older and scattered around the country. Will was the only one who'd moved with his parents, when his father had a sudden promotion. He hadn't wanted to come. He hadn't wanted to leave all his friends in the middle of his 'A' levels.

'I'm glad I did now,' he'd admitted softly as he stroked Jonny's cheek during the technicolour summer when Jonny's life was full of hope for five, brief, wonderful months.

He mumbled an apology and Will's brother looked as if he wanted to say more but turned aside instead so that Jonny could pass.

Jonny stood on the landing watching as Will's brother reached the bottom of the stairs without a backward glance. Jonny was dazed. Was it because of the blame in the brother's eyes? Was it the shock of having Will returned to him, only to be snatched away again? Or was it the cumulative effect of both of those things on the top of a horrible day? Suddenly, Jonny didn't want to go to the toilet. Didn't want to do anything, except hide away from everyone and remember Will, in his own way, on his own.

He walked down the corridor towards the one room he knew that none of the mourners would dare go. It was also the place where he thought he could remember Will clearest of all.

However, he hadn't been prepared for the power that was present in the room.

The power of Will's presence.

The upturned paperback on the bedside table, opened at the last page Will had read, an unfinished story that mirrored his own. The half-drunk glass of water slightly clouded with the dust motes that had collected since that day at the water tower. The judogi that would never be worn again. The CD cases that were strewn around the room like musical confetti.

Jonny looked at the wicker laundry basket, in the corner of the room. The boxer shorts that Will had worn on the day before he died had got caught on a jagged piece of cane and they hung down like a quoit dangling from its peg. Jonny could suddenly visualise Will throwing them there, leaning back on his pillow and launching them in the general direction of the basket. He would have been thinking about Jonny and their midnight tryst at the water tower. He might have been thinking about the challenge he would face after sleeping. But, he would not have been worried about it. He would have been confident, excited, and determined to give Jonny his day in the sunshine – his revenge.

It would never have entered his head, for a minute, that the clock had already clicked off the first hours of the last day of his life.

Jonny picked up the underwear, caressed it between his thumb and forefinger and brought it up to his face. He inhaled deeply, and nearly collapsed with the intensity of the fragrance. It smelt of Will, of course, but more than that; it smelt of sex.

He staggered towards the bed and lay down, still holding the garment to his nose. He had the smell of Will. He could taste Will's kisses on his lips and the room itself was alive with ghosts of the noises that used to fill it. There was only one thing missing.

He lay there, immobile, and barely breathing. Not sad – not anything.

Eventually he must have fallen asleep because when he awoke it was dark outside. For a beautiful moment he thought he saw Will's head on the pillow next to his but soon realised that this time, it was just a cruel illusion. The pain of the discovery mingled with a pain from his stomach. It reminded him why he had climbed the stairs in the first place.

However, a wave of depression made it impossible for him to move. He knew he had a choice. He could either struggle his way to the toilet, or he would wet himself in Will's bed. He knew the option he needed to choose; he just didn't know where he would find the energy to complete the task.

Suddenly, unexpectedly, the door opened, and the gloom was lifted by a light that was shining in from the landing. Jonny could see a feminine silhouette blocking the soft glow. Although he was struggling to understand many things, some inbuilt detector warned him of the words of outrage that would soon be coming his way.

She didn't see him at first. She seemed to float into the room in a somnolent fashion, while Jonny held his breath, and waited.

She sat down on the bed and her back touched his legs as she did so. She jumped up then, and Jonny could hear the hiss of shock that emanated from her throat at the same time.

He was aware of her fumbling for the bed side lamp, and when it illuminated the room completely, he could see the anger and fear masking Mrs Flanagan's attractive face.

When she saw who it was – her expression changed completely.

'Oh sweetheart,' she breathed out softly. 'I've just come up to be near to Will. Is that why you're here?'

Jonny was amazed. Not only that she should be so understanding – but also because she understood.

She looked around the room, taking in all the minutiae of Will's short life. 'I suppose I should really clean this room, at least do his washing for the final time,' she looked at the pair of boxer shorts that had fallen onto the bed next to Jonny's body. 'I just can't bear to do it. I just can't bear the thought of tidying Will away.'

Jonny could see the sorrow and the despair, but he could also see the determination and the thoughtfulness overshadowing those two emotions. She was Will's mother.

'Your mum and dad went on, pet...' there was a slight air of unuttered criticism. 'I think they thought you'd already left.' Jonny didn't believe that for a moment, he just thought that Mrs Flanagan was too kind to say that they obviously didn't give a damn about him. 'That nice girl and her rather attractive boyfriend searched for you though,' she added. 'Now, they were really worried about you.'

Jonny was making a mental note to text Amy as soon as he could, when Will's mother changed the subject completely.

'Do you ever want to scream?' she asked.

Jonny thought back to that moment at the water tower when he opened his mouth to do just that, and no sound came out of it. He nodded.

Mrs Flanagan grabbed hold of his hand suddenly. 'Shall we scream together?' she asked. Without waiting for a reply, she sucked in her breath and held it for a few seconds before releasing a sound full of anger and anguish. But also, rather strangely, of joy.

He could feel her nails dig into his flesh. He was aware of an intense pain. But the pain wasn't another source of torment. It was liberating. It was wonderful.

He thought of Will rescuing him from the bins at the back of the kitchen. Cuddling up to Will on the sofa in the dumping ground. Watching Will as he did his homework, on the same bed that Jonny was lying on at that moment. Making love to Will at the water tower, and in the park at midnight.

All these thoughts, along with the woman who was holding his hand and exposing her vulnerability to him, encouraged him to do the same.

Slowly, he opened his mouth – and for the first time since Will had died – he managed to scream.

~ 22 ~
REPERCUSSIONS

Carmichaeltown: Ben

Arnie and I were just finishing our dinner when the doorbell started ringing and someone began pounding on the front door. In fact, pounding was an understatement. The person responsible was in a right old strop. They were banging like a heavy metal drummer who'd lost their kit and was using the first thing that came to hand. Which, it seemed, was Arnie and Jonny's front door.

I'd not suggested going out to dinner. I hadn't felt the need. During our quick, on the hoof breakfast that morning, Arnie had brought up the subject of our sleeping arrangements.

'I really do understand you know. For now, it's enough for me to know that you see your future with me.' He smiled, pure Icelandic warmth glowing from his eyes. 'I'm happy to stay in the spare room. You tell me when you're ready.'

I hoped that all being well, Jonny would be ready for a night of gay lovemaking, anytime from next Monday evening onwards.

So, I hadn't suggested going out to dinner. After last night's experience, I wasn't sure I could have coped with the excitement.

As it happened, we didn't have to go out to find that excitement. That excitement found us…

Arnie was the first to the door. He opened it while I hovered around the entrance to the lounge. There was a man standing on the step who looked like an advert for raw protein flapjack and body bulking whey powder.

His body was definitely bulked.

'Are you the Norwegian salami sucker?' the bulked man asked aggressively.

Again, Arnie gave me the same look as the night before. The one that said: 'Can I?'

IN ANOTHER MAN'S SHOES

Looking at the size of the Incredible Hulk in front of us, I didn't think it was such a good idea. But, from what Arnie said next, I could tell that my brain hadn't told my face that fact.

'I am Icelandic,' Arnie replied. 'I don't like salami,' he pulled himself up to his full height unapologetically. Even with the advantage of the step, he was still an inch short of his adversary, but it didn't stop him from baiting the Hulk. 'But I do like to suck cock.'

Arnie had told me the night before that he'd never been punched. The main thought in my mind, at that moment, was that the Icelandic people must have been a gentle breed. I was amazed that he hadn't been lamped, at least once in his life.

He was funny, unflappable, and a tiny bit suicidal.

I thought I'd better intervene in the style of Jonny Vincent, or the man himself could return to find a boyfriend with no teeth.

'I'm really sorry,' I said, shooting Arnie a look that said: 'Cool it'. 'What is this all about?'

The man stared at Arnie and then answered my question.

'This pervert, locked my son up last night.'

This time, Arnie didn't look towards me for permission. He'd had enough. And I couldn't say I blamed him. He had been attacked by three nasty little bastards and was now being made to feel like he was the guilty party. His body language was clear. *I'm taking no prisoners and to hell with the consequences.*

'Excuse me,' he said with a carefully reigned in sense of anger. 'Your son and his two mates insulted me and threatened me at knifepoint. My lover...' He rolled his tongue around the word, making it ooze with sex. '...came to my rescue but was attacked himself. When I had managed to get the better of the two idiots who were fighting me, I admit I did lock them up, but only so that I could check that Jonny was OK.' He glanced at me again and I could see the grin of a taunt playing on his features, as he turned back to the Hulk. 'Once I was sure that two pathetic gay boys had managed to get the better of three knife-wielding head cases – I let them go.'

The Hulk was going to punch Arnie, I could see it in his eyes. But just as I was anticipating a trip to A&E, the light was switched on in Amy's porch. Her door opened and the lady herself, with Elliot behind her, looked out.

'Is everything alright?' she asked, walking down the path a few steps, and speaking to Arnie across the thigh high wall.

'No, it's not all right.' Despite his words, the Hulk eased back on the aggro, sensing he could have an ally if he played his cards right. 'This homo...' he nodded towards Arnie '...locked my son and his mate in a cage last night. I was just having a few words with him about it.'

'Oh right,' Amy said calmly. 'You mean your lad was one of the horrible little halfwits who tried to attack my friends last night?'

I'd forgotten about the Amy/Arnie hotline. It had obviously been busy that day. If the Hulk had been expecting a homophobic alliance, he was about to be disappointed.

'You've only got your poofter friend's word that they were attacked. My lad tells a different story.'

'My friend's word is good enough for me,' Amy said staunchly.

She was momentarily distracted when a small child emerged from behind Elliot's legs and wandered down the path to join his mother, before his father could stop him.

'Oh no Jonny love, go back in the house, will you? Mummy's having a serious chat with this nice gentleman.' The description might have been pleasant, but the tone suggested that Amy would have chosen a slightly more colourful turn of phrase.

But, not in front of the children.

Elliot rescued the child and waited until he was safely behind frosted glass before he joined his wife on the pathway. He rested his hand on her shoulder in solidarity.

The Hulk nodded at the front door. 'You've got a young 'un. How would you like it if this nutter...' he jabbed a finger towards Arnie's face '...tried to lock him up?'

Amy appeared to give the question a decent amount of thought. 'Well, I'm sure that Arnie would come and see me, or Elliot, if he did have a problem with any of our kids.' She paused, still outwardly giving the problem serious consideration. 'But, if any of them were to go off the rails during that confusing teenage period and I ended up in your situation, then I hope I wouldn't blindly accept everything they told me. I hope that Elliot and I would realise that our kids are not automatically going to be perfect.' Amy pointed at Arnie's chest. 'I mean, look at the evidence in this case. Look at the knife marks underneath Arnie's Adam's apple. That supports his version, not your son's. Look at the company your son keeps. Listen to what the locals have to say about Chance Bagley.' Amy paused and said reasonably: 'I think you should possibly think about all these things. Then you can decide if he's as innocent as he swears he is. If you don't think he is, you should probably give him hell, and make sure he gave Arnie a full apology.'

She was magnificent.

It seemed that the Hulk didn't agree with me. He grunted and argued and refused to listen to anything Amy was saying.

'You're not listening, are you?' Amy had arrived at the same conclusion. 'You don't care whether your son is lying or not. You just want it to be true so you can try to intimidate two men whose lifestyle you don't approve of.' She blew through her nose in annoyance. 'It's no wonder you've raised a pathetic little bully-boy.'

The Hulk was used to people accepting what he said without question. He wasn't used to a gutsy woman who was having a go. He skipped the discussion stage and went straight to the insults.

'Oh, shut up you sad old fag hag.'

I saw Elliot tense up and Arnie moved a step closer to the man mountain on the other side of the wall. I wanted to brain him myself, so I moved forward to join Arnie. I could see the slight surprise on Jonny's lover's face. He still hadn't got used to Jonny being quite so reckless. This was all fine and dandy, except I wasn't sure that even the three of us working together would be able to deck the Hulk.

'Hi Amy, is everything all right?'

A man had appeared at the bottom of our foot path. I recognised him. He lived next door to Tanner, but we didn't talk. Tanner had upset him by chipping a golf ball straight into his greenhouse, just after the man had moved in. Tanner had then aggravated him even more by refusing to stump up for the repairs. Amy and I had also been ostracised, because of the company I kept.

In Carmichaeltown, without the threat of low-flying golf balls, everything in the garden seemed to be neighbourly between them.

'Oh, hi Greg,' Amy called out gratefully. I don't think she had given her husband and their two best friends much chance either. Greg wasn't in the Hulk's league, but he obviously shopped at the extra-large end of the clothes rack, and he was another body. 'This bloke reckons that Arnie is in the habit of randomly going around and incarcerating young men for no reason.'

Greg nodded. 'Oh yes, I was talking about that to Malc.' It seemed that Amy and Arnie weren't alone when it came to owning jungle drums that were in good working order. The whole neighbourhood seemed to be at it. 'We reckoned that if Arnie had done that, he would have had a very good reason.'

I looked at the man, known to me as 'Greenhouse Greg' and a thought hit me. I knew Malc as well. He lived just down the road. Tan had nicknamed him *Jabba the Hutt* and I was hard pressed to even raise a hand in recognition, when I passed him in the street. Yet here, there seemed to be a real community feel about the neighbourhood. The reason behind the difference was suddenly obvious. Tanner and I didn't live here – Elliot, Arnie and Jonny did.

Amy nodded gratefully towards Greg, while the Hulk looked around at everybody and realised he had nobody on his side. With bad grace, he turned and stormed back down the path.

When he reached the road, he turned towards Arnie and shouted: 'Don't worry gay boy. I'll wait until the PC brigade aren't around and I'll have you.'

For almost the first time, Elliot spoke. He spoke loudly enough for his voice to carry down the pathway, towards the Hulk. 'You won't though, will you?' he asked and then answered his own question. 'Because if anything happens to either of these two,' he indicated us with his hand, 'we'll go straight to the police. And if our testimonies aren't enough for them,' he tapped his mobile, 'I've got all your threats recorded on this little beauty.'

I was grudgingly impressed. The Hulk was grudgingly furious. Without another word he stormed down the street, almost knocking Greg into a stray wheelie bin that had been abandoned since recycling day. He then disappeared into the night.

When Greg had recovered from his near miss, he gave a little wave before heading up the street towards his home.

Arnie shouted his thanks and then turned to our neighbours.

'And thank you very much. I think I might have been cruising for a bruising the way I was going.' I was beginning to get used to the pick n mix phrases that frequently came from Arnie's mouth. He then turned to me. 'And thank-you too, sweetheart.'

He could have been taking the piss, I was so used to Tanner's banter that for a moment I thought he probably was.

I argued that I had done nothing, but he shook his head. 'You were here, right by my side. I would have expected you to be hiding in the lounge, hoping that I wouldn't get involved.'

Oh, for God's sake Jonny, I sent another message to my absent alter-ego. *Grow a pair.*

'You two fancy a drink?' Elliot asked. 'I could certainly use one just about now.'

To be honest, it was the last thing I fancied. To witness my wife in her perfect house with her perfect husband and perfect family. It would bring home to me once again, how much I had cocked things up.

But, turning down the invite would have seemed strange, and I could tell that Arnie was keen. I smiled, nodded, and said: 'Thanks, that'll be great.'

Arnie leapt over the wall, so I followed him. I got some strange looks from the other three. Obviously, Jonny would normally walk the long way around rather than risk chipping a fingernail on the thigh-high obstacle.

But even that wasn't as curious as the looks I got when I congratulated Elliot on having the nous to record the Hulk's threats on his phone.

'How long have you known him Jonny?' Amy laughed. 'Do you really think that Elliot Harper, technophobe extraordinaire, would be able to find the video button on his phone, let alone record it?'

Elliot grinned. 'My wife is very harsh, but sadly, very fair.' Jonny's apparent lack of knowledge of Elliot's technical abilities, considering they had been friends for nearly thirty years, was luckily being glossed over by the group. 'I was blagging it, of course, but thankfully the brick shithouse didn't realise that.'

Jonny Junior was building a rocket ship out of plastic cubes when we entered the lounge. His two brothers padded down from their bedroom when they realised that the shouting in the street had led to the arrival of unexpected visitors. This was seen as a good excuse to avoid sleeping for another half an hour, at least.

'Uncle Jonny!' Jonny Junior leapt up as soon as he saw me and barely gave me the chance to sit down before he had curled up in the crook of my arm, leaning his head against my chest, arm stretched out across my neck.

'Oh Christ JJ,' laughed Elliot, 'give the poor man a chance to get comfortable before you throw yourself on top of him – you're so like your mother.'

Amy laughed, poked her tongue out at her husband and checked if I was OK.

'I'm fine.' I grinned and suddenly realised, that I was fine.

Jonny Junior was babbling nonsense into my sweater. Arnie was delighting the younger boys with ridiculously bad magic tricks, while Elliot poured us drinks before cuddling up against his wife on the sofa.

It was so sweet; it should have given me a headache.

But it didn't.

I was enjoying being there. I suddenly realised I wasn't feeling jealous anymore. As the evening flew past, I worked out the simple things in life I'd been missing. The simple things that I'd always taken the mick out of in the past. Simple things like giving your godson a piggyback up to bed, once his mum and dad had decided that the children had stayed up long enough for a school night. Simple things like laughing the night away with some good mates, once the kids were asleep.

It was only when I made my own way up to bed in the house next door, a while later, that I had a horrible thought.

I had been so arrogant, so determined that Ben Shawcross should not be beaten by Elliot Harper when I'd sent that email the day before. The one where I'd asked to meet up with Ben and gave him the impression that Amy wanted to see him too.

Tonight, before we'd had dinner, I'd caught up with Jonny's personal emails. The other Ben had replied to the message I'd sent. He seemed really chuffed that Jonny had got in touch. Ben also mentioned Amy and that he would really like to see her sometime soon, but for now he seemed happy enough to meet up with Jonny on his own. He suggested Friday evening.

Had I opened a can of something horrible, and what effect would it have on the good people of Carmichaeltown – and me? Cooper-Wilson, in that newspaper article, had warned against changing things. But, of course, I had known better. I had totally ignored his advice.

I could see how good Elliot and Amy were together. When I'd written that PS, pretending that Amy wanted to meet up with Ben, it was all about what I – Ben Shawcross from Westcastle – wanted. It was nothing to do with making Amy happy. And it should have been. I should have wanted to make Amy as happy as she deserved to be. And, for Amy in Carmichaeltown, happiness was being married to Elliot Harper.

Had I reached the conclusion too late? Had I already set things into motion that could rip their family apart?

But, as I worried about that, I also knew that I needed to go through with this meeting. I needed to find out why Ben Shawcross had spent just over six years of his life, in prison.

~ 23 ~
REVENGE

Carmichaeltown: Fifteen Years Earlier

Tanner was alone in the classroom when Jonny arrived. A month ago, this fact would have sent him scurrying back into the corridor to wait for Will before making his entrance. However, that was before the wonderful day at the water tower. The day that had changed everything.

The school Neanderthal had been very subdued since. Jonny was shocked to realise that he no longer suffered from the debilitating fluttering in his stomach, or the sandpaper dry scratching in his throat, whenever he was near to his erstwhile nemesis.

That day he even risked a friendly 'Good Morning' before heading towards his desk. He was busy taking a few things from his rucksack, contemplating Will's arrival from early morning judo practice.

He failed to notice three things:

The first was the fact that his tie had got caught on the desk as he'd sat down.

The second was Tanner's reaction to his greeting. His recent restraint had nothing to do with being a reformed character. He simply hadn't managed to find Jonny on his own until that morning.

The third was that Tanner had left his seat and crept up behind Jonny, who was unaware that anything was amiss until he felt a waft of air ripple past his right ear. Jonny didn't have time to realise that the ripple was caused by Tanner's right arm plunging downwards, until a compass pinned his tie to the desk.

'Don't think anything has changed.' The voice in Jonny's ear told him. 'Your bum-boy lover can't be with you every hour of every day. Remember that.'

However, things had changed slightly. As Jonny was listening to the latest in a long list of threats that he'd received over the years, the door opened. Previously this would have meant nothing to Tanner, but since the day at the water tower, he knew he had to be more careful.

The lad who had entered the room was one of the sheep who had changed his allegiance more violently than most. Despite Tanner's best efforts, the lad had seen the compass being unpinned from the desk. When Will had reached the classroom a few minutes later, he was informed of the fact before he'd barely had a chance to make it through the door.

Will hadn't acted immediately. He had wandered over to the window and waited until the classroom had filled up. He then spoke, his clear and articulate voice cutting through the mumble of conversation.

'Ghengis is neglecting that patch of land below this window,' he said, waving a hand in the general direction he was referring to. 'There are weeds growing so high that there's a real danger we could lose one of smaller kids from year seven.' He then wandered towards the teacher's desk and leant on it, as if he was in complete control of the class.

'I've often wondered,' he continued casually, 'if you hung a six feet bag of shite out of the classroom, whether he could tickle the nettles with his nostrils.' He stared meaningfully at Tanner.

'Oh yeah?' Tanner stretched himself, completely unconcerned. 'You and whose army, Gaylord?'

'Oh, I don't know.' Will said it easily, as if he wasn't bothered either way. This would give him an easy get-out clause if nobody decided to follow his suggestion. 'Simply throwing an idea around just in case there was an army out there.'

Nobody moved for a second or two. Tanner returned Will's stare, a smug smile hovering around his face.

A solid lad with bad acne stood up first. He'd been christened Margarita by Tanner from the moment that puberty had played its first cruel trick. Gradually a few of his mates joined him and they all moved towards the desk in the corner of the room. As they surrounded Tanner, he felt the first flickering of unease. He looked at his tormentors defiantly, then realised with a sense of shock, that more of their classmates were joining them. Tanner wrapped his feet around the legs of the desk and gripped the tabletop as tightly as he could, determined that he would not be moved.

One by one Tanner felt his fingers being straightened and pulled away from the solid surface, while other members of the makeshift army set about untangling his legs. With an equal amount of pushing and pulling, they finally managed to separate Tanner from his chair.

Jonny looked on, amazed. This would never have happened before. None of them had even uttered a word in his defence until Will had seized control of the class. He loved it.

He had to admit, as he watched them struggling to control their writhing captive, that it didn't look much like an organised army of ants working together to transport their much larger prey. Their efforts had the finesse of a dodgem car, which had been stuck in a corner and was trying to bludgeon its way towards the centre of the rink.

Even so, he thought, *it's working.*

When Tanner realised that he was moving inexorably towards an even more humiliating fate, he decided his defensive methods would have to become a little more extreme. He started spitting.

In the manner of a teenager in need of an exorcism, he twisted his head left and right spraying his tormentors to convince them to leave him alone. Someone quickly found a handkerchief, which was unceremoniously stuffed into Tanner's mouth. He could feel it soaking up his saliva. He could feel it threatening to choke him. He knew that his last line of defence had gone.

He was then pushed, dragged, and shuffled towards the open window. By the time Tanner had managed to manoeuvre the gag to a part of his mouth where it was possible to spit it out, his head and shoulders had been forced across the ledge. He turned his head so he could rid his mouth of the obstruction. He could then see the patch of weeds and nettles below him. He watched as the handkerchief floated from his mouth and onto the wasteland.

'Tch Tch,' he heard Will say in mock concern. He was still leaning against the teacher's desk, controlling events without becoming physically involved. 'Those window restrictors are very poor. Someone should tell Ghengis.' He arched an eyebrow and grinned towards Jonny. 'I mean, anyone could accidentally dangle the most unpopular boy in the year out of a window.' He shrugged. 'Such a worry.'

Jonny hadn't believed that they would go through with it. He hadn't believed that Will would let it go that far. However, no one seemed to be stopping them, certainly not Will himself. And Jonny wasn't sure he wanted him to.

Tanner arched his back upwards, trying to postpone the moment when gravity would take over control. However, he realised he was completely helpless. He was aware of someone lifting his right foot, quickly followed by its mate. He could feel his lower back as it scraped over the windowsill. The sensation moved southwards over his buttocks and down to the tops of his thighs. Eventually he dropped his head and the wilderness in green appeared to reach up and swamp him.

He stopped struggling when the scraping feeling reached his ankles. He knew that the only thing preventing him from falling in an ungainly heap towards a prickly landing place, were the hands he could feel clamped around his legs. It wasn't a long distance to drop, but he would be travelling head first. Even if he didn't suffer a concussion, he knew he would spend a long afternoon searching for dock leaves.

To say nothing of his already fractured self-esteem.

As if to batter it even more, he could hear someone shouting through the open window.

'Hey Will! It looks like Hoots is flying!'

With that, he heard many of his classmates imitate an owl screeching. It was a sound he seemed to be hearing more and more.

Tanner believed he was in hell.

'What the f...?'

Tanner heard the muffled exclamation from the man he thought of as his only friend.

Ben had arrived in the classroom with Amy. They were running late due to the fact they had indulged rather too enthusiastically in some early morning smooching. Just behind them lurked Kyle Hammond. He was running late because he had been pinning a poster on the debating club notice board. One look at the scene in front of him, convinced Kyle that the poster would stand out a lot more if he moved it precisely one inch to the right.

He disappeared quickly, to do just that.

There were only two other people who seemed oblivious to the mayhem that was happening around them. Elliot and Steve were engrossed in a design that would make their microlight aircraft a little more aerodynamic. The fact that their classmates had turned feral, and a boy was hanging upside down from a window, didn't seem to interest them in the slightest.

On hearing Ben's censored expletive, one of the on-lookers turned to look at him. The boy had a strange complexion. When his summer tan faded, his skin always seemed to take on a jaundiced tinge. When Ben and Tanner first met him, a few years ago, they had christened him Bart.

'Oi Will, it's the other one.' Bart said. 'The Carmichael killer's cousin.'

Ben had discovered the identity of Alec Carmichael's murderer the day after the race at the water tower. His mum had been distraught, and all the extended family had been shocked. 'Mild-mannered Marty just wasn't like that,' they'd all said.

Hearing the type of comment that Bart had just made was a normal occurrence since the news had become public knowledge. Ben always dealt with it by shrugging, smiling, and saying nothing.

He shrugged, smiled, and said nothing.

Bart continued. He was regretting not getting fully involved in the fun earlier on and had spotted a chance to get himself into Will's good books. He nodded towards the window.

'Shall we give Hoots some company, d'you think?'

Three other unemployed on-lookers joined him before Will had had a chance to speak, and they all headed in Ben's direction.

Ben didn't make a fuss. He didn't shout and scream. He simply glanced at a worried looking Amy, spread his hands in an open gesture and smiled at his would-be attackers.

'Feel free if that's what you want to do lads. But be warned, I had a very explosive curry last night and it's getting a little bit lively in my underpants...' He paused, to ensure his point was made before continuing '...and it sure ain't sexual.'

Ben's would-be attackers stopped dead in their tracks, looked at each other and all decided the same thing, at the same time. Observing, rather than participating, seemed a much safer option.

'Will?' Ben turned to the figure leaning against the teacher's desk and nodded a silent question relating to the group at the window. Will sighed, nodded, and signalled that his lieutenants should haul their floundering prey back into the safety of the classroom.

Ben willed Tanner to laugh the incident off. He tried to ease himself through the crowd of spectators to keep his friend calm. However, before he managed to penetrate the outer ring of them, he heard a guttural roar and felt the crowd break apart. Tanner violently pushed his way towards the centre of the room. Ben tried to manoeuvre himself into Tanner's eyeline, but he could see that the red mist had swamped his best friend. His eyes were wild, his face was flushed, and every movement exuded violence.

Tanner pushed a girl out of his way. She had been at the back of the crowd and was the final obstacle between Tanner and freedom. He then picked up one of the tables from the front row of the classroom and launched it in Will's direction. His tormentor twisted his body away from danger, a smirk on his lips, and the table bounced off and across the desk before coming to rest adjacent to the white board.

The crowd loved it. They hooted and hollered as Tanner stormed from the room, cries of 'Hoots!' battering against his ears.

Amy stepped aside to avoid being treated in the same way as the girl near the window. She caught Jonny's eye as he glanced in her direction. His face was a mask of pure joy. She wanted to be happy for him. She knew how much he'd endured over the years. She didn't want to deny him his small piece of revenge, and besides, she had no affection for the youth who had thrashed his way out of the classroom.

But she couldn't help thinking. Pushing someone into an industrial bin for amusement or dangling them from a window.

What exactly was the difference?

~ 24 ~
LUNCH WITH THE OTHER ARNIE

Westcastle: Jonny

'So, have you got over your strop then?'

If I'd been hoping that Tanner had been so disgusted by my lack of hospitality, on the previous evening, that he'd refuse to travel to work with me – I would have been sadly mistaken. His unmistakeable bulk was visible in the streetlight as I left the house on Wednesday morning. I kissed Amy on the lips as she was preparing to leave at the same time. The book shop where she worked with my double, the other Jonny, opened its doors early so that office workers could enjoy a coffee and muffin in the tiny café area at the back of the shop. There, they could peruse a list of new releases and reviews before they had to leave their fantasy worlds and head for real life. Jonny and Amy had been rostered on for the early shift that morning.

I replied to Tanner's greeting with a non-committal grunt and got into the car. Tanner followed my lead. Pulling the seat belt across his stomach, he spoke in a tone I hadn't heard him use since I'd arrived in Westcastle. He almost sounded serious.

'He might not have shown it Benjy, but your dad was really upset by the way you talked to him last night.'

'Tough,' I said. 'He was vile to Amy. He deserved it.'

Was there something in the Westcastle water? I thought. There was an argumentative tone to my voice that I would never normally have used.

It certainly managed to clamp a muzzle to Tanner's mouth. The incessant commentary that I'd been subjected to during every journey so far, was mercifully lacking that morning. When we were about five miles from the Sandelwood turn-off, I thought I would use that to my advantage.

'I don't think I'm going to help you with the car tonight,' I said tentatively. 'I want to spend more time with Amy.' When he didn't immediately object, I thought I might as well as well lay all my sick notes on the table in one go and get it over and done with. 'In fact, count me out of the footie and the Friday night sesh with the lads as well.' Talking with Ben's voice was becoming easier the more I practised it. I took a deep breath and concluded my monologue of disappointment. 'In fact, count me out of everything for the next few days. I'm having a week off.'

'Nobhead.' However, it wasn't the playful cussing from earlier in the week. Tanner's catchphrase oozed resentment. He was not a happy bunny.

Mercifully for me, that resentment kept him quiet. It was only when we'd passed through Sandelwood, and joined the main road that would take us into the city, that he spoke again.

'Make sure you don't bail on your old man on Sunday.' He said pointedly. 'You take him to see your grandma, no matter what sad sort of second honeymoon you seem to think you're on.'

It was almost endearing. The way he was looking out for his friend, mentor, the man who had been his second father. Sadly, he managed to spoil it straight away, by opening his mouth one more time.

'Mind you,' he laughed nastily, the old Tanner making an unwelcome return. 'You'll probably be fed up with Wifezilla by then...'

That left just one more piece of bad news to give him. I waited until we were walking down the corridor towards the office, in the hope that I could dump it on him and then run off to the safety of my workday.

'I've got a meeting at twelve-thirty,' I said. 'So, I won't be joining you for lunch today.' I purposely misunderstood the look that told me he was ready for an argument about it. 'Don't worry,' I held up a placatory hand. 'I'll buy you that extra lunch I owe you next Monday.'

Please God, I prayed, *let me be safely back in Carmichaeltown by then and Ben can enjoy that delight.*

* * *

Tanner ignored me for most of the morning. I guessed that this was intended to upset me when, in fact, the opposite was true. Apart from one attempt to discover the identity of my lunch companion and a couple of snide comments about being the company's golden boy, my working morning was Tanner-free.

For once, fate was on my side. He'd been called away for a midday meeting and hadn't returned when the clock clicked over to twelve-thirty. I left my desk with the speed of a bionic cheetah and headed in the direction of the lift.

As I walked across the atrium on the ground floor, I could see Arnie waiting for me on the other side of the revolving doors. I was surprised by the intensity of the anticipation that caused a fluttering in my chest. I hadn't really had that sort of reaction since the early days of our affair. The chorus line from Joni Mitchell's *Big Yellow Taxi* stuck itself to my brain, as I bundled my way out to meet my boyfriend.

The boyfriend to whom I was a stranger.

I greeted him in the manner of a straight man who wanted a favour and offered to buy him lunch in return. I then hurried us away from the building before Attila the Tanner could arrive.

Avoiding Tanner was very much in my mind when I led the way to the small French café that Arnie and I favoured for our Tuesday lunches in Carmichaeltown. It was very unlikely that Tanner would choose to lunch there.

They didn't serve cheap beer.

When I was nearly at the door, I realised something was different. A stench of overly perfumed soaps was wafting from the building, rather than the smell of the house speciality bouillabaisse.

I manoeuvred a quick change of direction, both mentally and physically, and headed towards another independent café I knew further down the road. I was still finding it hard to get to grips with the idiosyncrasies of reality hopping. A picture framing shop and a small florist were still in their rightful places, as was thankfully, my second-choice cafe.

What infinitesimal difference had resulted in one business disappearing completely, whilst the others had thrived? Alec

Carmichael was alive in one reality and an idolised martyr in the other. Had the ripples created by this difference been responsible for all the changes I had seen? Or, like me, had several people swapped realities in the years since the submarine exploded? Had each swap changed the worlds – some to a lesser and some to a greater extent? What was I changing because of my holiday in Westcastle? What was Ben changing during his time in Carmichaeltown?

I purposely moved my thoughts away from that particular type of torture. But, I decided that I would try to be friendlier to Tanner, and Ben's dad, to minimise the ripples I would leave behind. If I managed to leave them behind.

'I must say, I was a little surprised when you asked for my help yesterday.' Arnie said with characteristic directness, once we had ordered our food and disposed of the small matter of business that had been my pretext for our lunch together. 'You've never done anything more than breathe in my direction in the four years that I've been visiting your office.' He grinned and released a small snort of amusement. 'Mind you that's better than your mate. He can't seem to decide whether full PPE will be enough protection during our meetings, or if he really needs to invest in a hazmat suit.'

I must have looked confused, but I was just losing myself in his incredible eyes. He leant forward, teasing the man he thought of as Ben, with a cheeky smile and a comedy whisper. 'He doesn't want to be contaminated with the G. A. Y. thing.'

Well, I thought, *that answers one of my questions from yesterday.*

I laughed uneasily, mindful of any ripples I might be creating, then replied with an opinion that belonged to my alter-ego and not myself.

'Oh, he's a good guy really. I'm sure he doesn't think that.'
Yeah, right.

'But...' I continued, giving Arnie some sort of explanation, '...I've been thinking for a while that we've become a bit insular at work. You're right in a way, and please don't repeat this, I think people see us as a double act. One can't exist without the other.' I shrugged. 'I'm beginning to think it's unhealthy.'

If someone told Arnie something in confidence, he wouldn't repeat it to anyone. It was one of the many good things about him. So, I knew that Arnie wouldn't be spouting this gossip into the ears of the beautiful secretary he'd lunched with the day before.

One of the many good things about him.

As lunchtime wound on, his many attributes revealed themselves, along with his appealing quirks. It was as if I was seeing them for the first time. The way he would brush his head with irritation, due to his one stray lock of hair. It always refused to join the others that were neatly swept away from his forehead. The crinkle in the corner of his lips that was a sure-fire warning of a wickedly cheeky comment coming your way. The Carmichaeltown/Westcastle burr that was noticeable when he said words like roar, or torn, and the hint of Iceland that was prevalent in any words with 'oi' sounds in them. His habit of playing table-top piano in anticipation of the plate of food that was being set down in front of him.

In the middle of the far wall of the café there was a timepiece in the style of a station platform clock. I glanced at it and realised that my lunchbreak was coming to an end, and I only had another fifteen minutes in his company. I silently swore at the clock for moving so quickly. With a sense of dread that I didn't fully understand, I started to ask Arnie whether he had a 'significant other'.

'No, I'm afraid not.' He shook his head. 'In the four and a half years since I've been over here, I've managed two major affairs. One who wanted to date me simply to shock his parents, and another one who was a Judy Garland impersonator. He was a lovely man, but he had a rather unsettling habit.' The corner of his lips started to crinkle. 'He named his penis Toto.'

We both laughed, but he sobered quickly as he continued. 'The reason I left Iceland is a pretty routine, pathetic story of heartbreak...' he smiled his self-deprecating smile '...you know, the one where your lover runs off with your life-long best friend. I stuck a pin into the jobs section of an international business magazine, which led me here. I got a flat in Westcastle because it was cheaper, and I'm not much of a city boy.'

I hoped that Arnie didn't hear me suck in my breath, and he wasn't able to tell that my heart was beating like an obsessive cleaner in front of a dirty carpet.

I knew that story. I'd heard it many times. First, when he had told it to me, and on numerous other occasions when he'd met new friends. The lover and his best friend, the pin in the paper, and the flat. He'd moved out of that flat, only a few weeks after we met.

And that was the only difference. He was still living in the flat – because we hadn't met.

Arnie grinned. 'I suppose it was too much to ask that I would find the love of my life, simply by moving to another country...'

I'm here you bloody idiot! I'm here.

As much as I wanted to say it, I managed to keep quiet, and he continued.

'...I'm afraid to admit it, but it hasn't happened.' He smiled sadly. 'I'm beginning to think it might be time to move back to Iceland.'

A strange thought suddenly occurred to me. Everything about Arnie, and his story, were the same as the man I had left on Monday morning. However, there was a definite distinction between the two Arnies. There was a certain sadness and regret hampering the man who was sitting in front of me. I had never seen that side of him. And, as far as Arnie was concerned, there was only one difference between the two worlds.

Me.

Even I, whose self-esteem was somewhere between the lower ground floor and the bottom of the lift shaft, could see the earth shattering, yet unmistakeable fact.

In Carmichaeltown, I had made him happy.

'Would you like to meet me at the King John in Westcastle on Saturday night?' I blurted out. I didn't want him to run back to Iceland. I didn't really know why, except a mad idea had suddenly exploded in my head.

'I'm not sure,' Arnie said carefully. He looked up and unerringly found my eyes. He fixed me with a shrewd expression, and I knew exactly what he was going to say before he said it. 'I tend to stay away from married men. I never seem to find that it ends well.'

I tried to laugh as innocently as possible. 'Oh, Christ no! I meant just as friends.' I tried a shrewd expression of my own. 'I got the impression you could do with a friend.'

'I have friends,' he said with fake indignity. 'I have my neighbour, Mrs Stephanos – and her parrot.'

'There's a Dusty Springfield tribute act playing,' I said quickly, playing my trump card before he could fit in a final refusal. I had no idea whether it was true or not. I only knew that I needed to see him again. Soon.

He looked at me with a curious expression that said: *How the hell did you know that I'm a life-long Dusty aficionado?* He grinned, conceding defeat. 'You've got me with Dusty.' The grin then morphed into a warm and friendly smile. 'I would like that very much. Thank you.'

I felt a bit of a fraud at that moment. Not only because he might turn up at the King John and have to endure a Dusty-less evening. But also, because despite what I'd said, the mad idea I'd come up with did involve him having an affair with a married man. More specifically, me, disguised as a married man.

It had seemed to solve so many problems when the idea came to me, just a few moments earlier. I was worried about Amy. I was worried about her husband returning and treating her just as he had before.

Could I protect her by staying in Westcastle?

Could I adapt Ben's friendship with Tanner so that it would be tolerable for the part of me that would always be Jonny Vincent?

Could I convince Arnie, against his better judgement, to have an affair with me?

I'd spent much of the week looking for a way to get home. Should I abandon the attempts to grab my own life back, and grab another man's life instead?

~ 25 ~
HALF TERM

Westcastle: Fifteen Years Earlier

'The Flanagans are moving,' Jonny said in the dull monotone that seemed to have become his favoured way of speaking since the accident. Any expression at all seemed to require more effort than Jonny was prepared to give it.

'Oh,' Amy said neutrally. In truth, she was certain it was a good thing. Since the day of the funeral, Jonny had spent practically every spare moment at the Flanagan house. He and Mrs Flanagan would sit on Will's bed. Together, but completely alone. They didn't speak, didn't really look at each other. Occasionally their fingers would meet, and they would wind them together in an almost subconscious need for sympathy. But even that action wasn't acknowledged. Both were lost in their own maze of memories.

Amy looked around Jonny's bedroom. Part of the reason she had arranged to come around that morning was to keep him away from the Flanagan house. She didn't think his obsession with visiting Will's room was good for Jonny's mental health, or Mrs Flanagan's, for that matter. It seemed that Will's family agreed with her. Mr Flanagan had applied for a transfer so they could be nearer two of their sons and one of their daughters. The company he worked for had moved with sympathetic haste, a position had been found, and the house was on the market.

Even Jonny could see the logic. He just couldn't shake the feeling that another person was abandoning him.

Amy subtly moved the subject away from the Flanagans and towards his own family. 'Have you heard from your Mum and Dad?' She asked. Their dispute with the mechanic was still on-going. The bill remained unpaid. But, the Vincents had decided to continue with their holiday plans on the River Hazel.

Jonny shook his head.

'I don't know why you didn't spend your half term with them on the boat,' Amy said. 'Anything to take your mind off Will.'

'I don't want to take my mind off Will,' Jonny said sharply. It was the first time his expression had changed since Amy had arrived. 'Besides,' he said, his voice returning to the safety of the monotone. 'They didn't ask me.'

Amy had her own views about the suitability of the Vincents for parenthood. They seemed to regard certain aspects of child rearing as optional extras. They would have ticked the boxes marked 'Child accepted for Cambridge', 'Child books place on Olympic team' and 'Child marries lovely girl and produces equally lovely grandchildren'. However, they seemed to have no interest in the boxes marked 'Child comes out as gay' and 'Child loses teenage lover in freak accident'.

It was a world away from her own parents' style of parenting. They had three daughters, although two of them were quite a bit older, married and safely out of parental control. Amy's sisters laughed at their afterthought sibling's complaints of parental fussing. In truth, Amy preferred the Crawfords' version of family life. None of the children ever had any doubts that they were the most important thing in their parents' world.

Whereas she knew that Jonny felt it was a toss-up between him, the boat, or the Le Creuset gratin dish. In fact, his mother always seemed at her happiest when she was cruising down the river or being congratulated on her Pommes Dauphinoise. He'd probably decided that he might not have made it onto the shortlist.

Amy shook her thoughts away and turned her attention back to Jonny. He'd retreated into himself while her mind had been wandering. He sat on the edge of the bed, blank eyes, and expressionless face. His body reminded Amy of a recently abandoned building. All the fixtures and fittings might still be in place, but they were no longer being used by anyone.

She was determined to shake that building back into life.

'So,' she said. 'Just six weeks to go until the big day. I've got a brilliant present planned for you.'

'Don't. Please.' The last thing Jonny wanted, was to be reminded about his eighteenth birthday. Jonny would never tell

Amy this, but anything wonderful she had planned to give him would just remind him of the one irreplaceable gift who wouldn't be there.

'Oh, come on sweetheart,' Amy paused. She was nearly certain that the next offer she made would be refused, but she was determined to pass the invitation on. More than anything she wanted Jonny to fully realise that her boyfriend was turning into a lovely man. 'Ben wants to have a joint party with you. Invite the whole year. Put the past month in the rubbish bin and start again.'

Jonny gave her no reaction at all. She had just decided that he hadn't heard her and was going to repeat herself when he spoke in the same emotionless tone.

'Will Tanner be there?'

Amy sighed gently. 'Yeah. Of course he will.' She tried to put an optimistic spin on the unwelcome words. 'But he's been better, hasn't he?'

Jonny didn't say anything. He didn't say that just before half term Tanner had followed him into the lavatories. They had been alone. Jonny had been heading towards the urinals when he heard the door closing. When he glanced behind him and had seen the identity of the new arrival, he changed his mind and decided to use one of the cubicles instead. There had been something about the vicious smile behind Tanner's eyes that had informed Jonny that the armistice was officially over.

Tanner hadn't done much. He had merely blocked Jonny's path to the safety of the cubicle, and then walked relentlessly forward. Jonny had had no option but to retreat. Tanner kept on walking until Jonny's bottom was pressed flat against the stainless-steel urinal just as the automatic flush was in the process of relieving itself. Tanner had kept a hand on his victim's chest until Jonny's trousers were soaked. Without saying a word, Tanner turned and went to relieve himself in the cubicle that was nearest to him.

Suddenly, Jonny hadn't wanted to use the toilet at all. He simply wanted to get as far away from his tormentor as possible. Without even pausing to dry his sodden trousers, he dripped his way out into the corridor.

The first person he saw in the corridor made him realise that the circle was nearly complete, and he was close to being back at the start once again.

Close to where he had been, before Will had arrived to save him.

Ben was leaning against the wall in the corridor.

He pretended not to see Jonny. Pretended not to notice the river that Jonny was leaving behind as he hurried down the corridor. Pretended that he was counting the number of ceiling tiles while he was waiting for his mate to finish off having a pee.

As fascinating as the ceiling tiles must have been, Jonny was turning the corridor into a replica of the River Hazel. Ben would have noticed.

Jonny guessed that Ben knew exactly what was going on. He simply wasn't brave enough to tell his best friend not to be such a moron.

And he never would be.

Jonny knew that it wouldn't be long before Ben left his sentry duty in the corridor and joined in with the action at the scene of the crime. He also knew that when that happened, it wouldn't simply be soggy trousers that Jonny would have to endure.

Jonny was saved from answering Amy's question by the sound of the doorbell ringing. Glad of the interruption, he left the room almost as quickly as he had dribbled his way down the corridor, a few days before.

The first hint of the latest horror was a tall silhouette that was visible through the frosted glass. As he opened the door, Jonny already had a question mark tattooed onto his face.

The young PC manoeuvred his features and followed the textbook instructions he had been taught at Police Training College.

He had bad news to break.

~ 26 ~
OBSESSION

Carmichaeltown: Fifteen Years Earlier

How to commit the perfect murder.

Ever since the day that Tanner had been on the receiving end of a human bungee rope, he had become obsessed with the topic.

What had been a bit of light-hearted banter, during the ice cream and sunscreen days of summer, had mutated into a worrying fixation as winter began to pull on its woolly jumper.

Because now, Tanner had a victim lined up.

Every time Ben saw his friend, he had another piece of research that he wanted to share. Another full-proof plan that would rid him once and for all of 'Gaylord'.

Just recently he had started to include Ben in the plans. Not just as a sounding board to evaluate his latest theory, but as a fellow perpetrator.

He reckoned they could be the Leopold and Loeb for the twenty-first century.

Ben didn't mention that Leopold and Loeb's plan to commit the perfect murder hadn't been a great success. They'd got caught.

He also thought it best not to mention that the two of them had been in a homosexual relationship.

Ben knew that Tanner was testing him. Still checking that with Ben, at least, he had control. Checking that he could still make Ben do exactly what he wanted him to do.

And Ben didn't know how to change it.

He knew he should try. Point out how he was coping with their new unwelcome status as whipping boys. Tanner would become incensed every time there were shouts of 'Hoots!' and the obligatory owl noises, whereas Ben would just grin along with his tormentors if they ever tried to tease him. They soon gave up and concentrated their efforts on Tanner, simply because Ben wasn't half as much fun to bait as his explosive friend.

Ben also considered saying something to someone, but didn't really know what, or to whom. If he asked at home, his dad would probably side with Tanner and tell Ben he should do more to support his friend. If he asked at school, he couldn't imagine any of the teachers being overly sympathetic to Tanner's plight.

So, Ben decided that it was safer to go along with it. Give Tanner a platform where he could air his most controversial plans.

People who talked about murder, very rarely committed it.

Did they?

~ 27 ~
THURSDAY EVENING

Carmichaeltown: Ben

It wasn't until Thursday evening that fate decided to kick me in the gonads once again.

Wednesday, and the first part of Thursday, had been uneventful. Mind you, when the yardstick I was using involved a knife fight with a psycho-teen and an argument with a man whose fists were the size of a small skip, that hadn't been too tricky to achieve. Everything is relative.

I was really enjoying working as part of a team. This was something I had never missed before because I'd never known it. It really hammered home how isolated I was in Westcastle. The company's mantra was: 'RD Eversen, we're one big happy family!' It was always being banged into our heads on those never-ending training days we reluctantly attended.

'Bollocks!' Tanner and I would snigger afterwards when we thought that no one else could hear us.

But here, it really was like that. And it was nothing to do with the company ethos. It was the people who worked there. People who really seemed to like each other, and Jonny in particular. Although he might have been treated as an easy target by idiots like Chance Bagley, at work it was different.

Colleagues who wouldn't have given me a grain of sugar from their mid-morning doughnut, bantered, bickered, and joked with him as old friends tended to do.

Nothing illustrated that difference more than Jonny's relationship with Kerie, from the next-door desk. When Gemma in reception had ignored my flirty grin, earlier in the week, I had mistakenly thought that people didn't expect Jonny to flirt. I was wrong. It was simply that Gemma was a player. She had got what she wanted from Jonny and couldn't spare him the effort of a smile afterwards.

But Kerie? She was on the outrageous side of dirty and I got the impression that Jonny could give as good as he got. Not the wet and wimpy nerd I remembered at all.

I loved to flirt. Nothing that had ever led to infidelity, just a good old-fashioned bit of flirting with someone who knew the score and was reading from the same page of results. Sadly, most people viewed me, and Tanner, as men you didn't flirt with.

But Jonny. Jonny was gay. Women could go as near to the knuckle as they liked without the fear that things might spiral out of control. They could swap innuendos, and trade compliments, which made them feel better about themselves. Then they could go back to their boyfriend or husband guilt-free. For the first time, I was jealous of a group of people I'd spent the whole of my adult life looking down on.

Lucky bastards.

The other exception to the rule was Cameron. He never seemed to be included in the happy family atmosphere. Everyone seemed to give him a wide berth because of the way he'd treated Jonny. He would camp about, laugh and joke, but no one would pay him much attention. He looked hurt every time one of his priceless quips were ignored, but the stupid bastard didn't seem to have a clue as to the reasons behind it.

Maybe it was because I was feeling guilty about my treatment of Jonny in the past, but I had a sudden urge to help the man whose body I was inhabiting. To leave him something. It was simple to do, and I didn't think it would make enough waves to bugger up our chances of getting back home.

I waylaid Cameron in the corridor and eased him into one of the meeting rooms. He was a little surprised. From the mutterings I'd overheard when people thought I wasn't listening, Jonny had barely spoken to Cameron lately. Apparently, he didn't want to pressurise him into to returning the money he'd borrowed.

Sadly, for Cameron, I didn't give a stuff about putting him under pressure.

'It bothers you, doesn't it?' I asked him when the door was closed, and I had his full attention. 'Everyone ignoring you. Not being the centre of attention anymore.'

He looked at me as if he couldn't believe what he was hearing. Couldn't believe that it was coming from the mouth of Jonny Vincent.

'It would all go back to normal, you know,' I continued. 'They're only giving you the cold shoulder because they're my friends, and they don't like the way you've treated me. Even if you only started to pay me back fifty pounds a month, they'd soon forgive and forget.'

A sly grin crossed over his adolescent baby face. He stretched out his arm and stroked a bit of my shirted chest between tie and tit. I tried not to show the flinch I was feeling. I must have been successful, because he continued to stroke and when he spoke, there was a definite flirty, wheedling tone to his voice.

'Or you could tell everyone that I'd paid the money back.'

I moved away, so that I was out of the reach of his teasing fingertips. I might have been getting used to an odd bit of gentle lip on lip action with Arnie, but this was outside my comfort zone. It also fitted in very well with what I wanted to say next.

'I could,' I said slowly, giving him another few seconds of hope before I rudely pissed on his parade. 'But I'm not going to.'

His nose twitched in surprise and displeasure. He had not been expecting that. He had expected Jonny to crumble, in the face of one bit of flirting, after months of being blanked.

Afraid not, sunshine. I thought.

'Come on,' I said reasonably. 'It's the price of one Urban Dross shirt a month. It's not going to kill you.'

Cameron looked horrified. It was as if he'd suddenly realised that the loan had actually been a loan, and not a gift from the bank of Jonny. On the other hand, it could have been the fact that Urban Dross was not the go-to uniform of young gay men in their late teens. He certainly looked as if I had asked him to dress in a suit made from pan scourers.

His expression changed to the wheedling look once again. 'Oh, come on Jonny! You never really expected me to pay it back, did you?' He moved forward towards me, and this time grabbed hold of my tie, reeling himself in like a suicidal trout. He eventually stopped a few centimetres away from me, and the look on his face made no mystery of what he was suggesting. 'My offer still stands, you know.'

Now, although I like a bit of flirting, there are limits.

I pushed him away, gently but firmly. I thought it was time to use the information I knew about his Westcastle alter ego to my advantage.

'I helped you when no one else gave a stuff.' I raised my voice slightly, but it was still well shy of a shout. 'You're the only one who knows what would have happened if I hadn't lent you that money, but I have a feeling you would have been in some pretty serious shit.'

The look on Cameron's face told me I hadn't used the language that Jonny would have used, but then, he was probably surprised by the whole conversation. One more shock wouldn't kill him. I decided to leave him a final message from Westcastle before I went back to my desk.

'I think you're aware that without my loan you could be running drugs to pay your debts. You might even be in jail by now.' I gave him a hard look and one more comment that he wouldn't have normally associated with Jonny.

'Don't take the piss.'

* * *

I was shattered by the time I got home. I threw my jacket onto the armchair, loosened my tie, and undid the top button of my shirt before flopping on to the sofa in front of the TV. I half watched a programme chocked with home videos of cute kids, cute dogs, and random people falling over. It occupied the same scheduling slot on TV at home. It was still crap.

At first, I mistook the look of surprise on Arnie's face when he arrived home half an hour later. I thought that it was probably out of character for Jonny to slop around in front of the telly without changing into his smoking jacket, lounge trousers, and comfy house shoes.

I soon found out that I was wrong.

'Come on lover. We'd better shift ourselves or we're going to be late.'

I looked at him blankly.

'It's the St Edmunds parent/teacher meeting tonight.' He explained patiently, a gentle look of amusement hovering around his eyes.

I couldn't understand why two childless homosexuals, who didn't work in education, would be going to such a meeting but didn't put my query into words. I must have still looked confused though, as he continued patiently.

'You know, St Edmunds, where JJ goes?'

I still had no idea why Jonny and Arnie would need to go to the meeting, unless they had adopted the boy overnight and no one had told me.

Arnie was now enjoying himself in the face of my continuing bemusement.

'You know? JJ? Child. About so high,' he held out a hand so that it was about three feet above the ground. 'Practically welds himself to you every time we go next door. You can't have missed him.'

I joined in with the bantering, mainly to hide my confusion. 'Yes, oh brilliant and wise oracle. I know who he is.'

Arnie pursed his lips, trying to stop the grin from reaching them and then rolled his hands around each other, as if he was encouraging me to work out a tricky conundrum. Eventually he gave up and told me the answer.

'Amy and Elliot go to the meeting, and we babysit for them.' He looked at me curiously. 'We do it every month.'

Luckily his last sentence gave me the information I needed to save a little face.

'Thank you, you sarky article. I am aware. I just can't believe that we're around to that Wednesday already. Where on earth is the time going?'

The night that followed was a repeat of the one before, except Amy's home-made chicken pie replaced the Hulk with anger issues. It was a definite improvement. Besides his hatred of fish, I had worked out that Jonny was a vague vegetarian who seemed to think that chicken didn't quite count. Before the last few days, I would have mocked him and said it was typical of the dweeb I used to know. But now? Now, I was beginning to like him. And not despite his daft quirks, but because of them.

I might have begun to like Jonny, but I was already beginning to fall in love with the Harper boys. They had the perfect combination of gutsy mischief and unquestioning respect. Arnie seemed to think that it was our duty, as uncles, to spoil them rotten. This meant that they could take advantage and wrap us around their little fingers if they wanted to. And they quite often did. But, as soon as their parents returned and a little bit of loving authority was restored, they pattered off to bed quite happily in a flurry of kisses and giggles.

Arnie and I didn't need too much persuading to stay for a drink once the lads were safely upstairs. At one point in the evening when Arnie and Amy were nattering in the kitchen, Elliot had been laughing with me about one of his fellow committee members. Elliot seemed to think he looked like Donald Duck and made me chuckle by repeating the poor man's words in a cartoon Disney voice. He stopped laughing suddenly and changed the subject.

'Amy says that Ben is back in town,' he paused. 'She says that he wants to meet up.'

I nodded and said that Amy had told me.

He frowned and said: 'I don't know what to do Jonny.'

I smiled encouragingly and he continued. 'After all, I waited until the guy was in jail and nicked his girlfriend. What if this is some sort of revenge? What if he wants to break me and Amy up?'

I thought about that damned email I'd sent.

I know Amy is keen to meet Ben as well.

Desperate not to give any hint of my own inner demons, I kept it simple. I touched him lightly on the shoulder and said, as encouragingly as I could, as encouragingly as I thought Jonny would have done. 'But you two are solid. He wouldn't stand a chance.'

He smiled at me gratefully, without being entirely convinced. 'With anyone else, I'd agree with you. I know that Amy loves me. No question. I know that with anyone else, she'd never cheat on me. But Ben was her first love...' He trailed off before suddenly staring me straight in the eyes. 'Would you go and see him Jonny? Would you find out what he wants?'

As I nodded my agreement, I felt a sense of relief that the meeting with Ben I had already arranged, would have happened anyway, even if Jonny had been here in my place.

If only I hadn't written that bloody PS.

Before Arnie and Amy had come back in with a round of liqueur coffees, I asked Elliot what he thought of Tanner now. I was still trying to find out what had happened to my mate and thought that if the old school crowd were ready to forgive Ben, the same might have been true about his sparring partner. Once again, I was left with the same impression. Not only did Tanner not exist, but also, he had never existed.

'I try not to think about him at all.' Elliot said, without any emotion.

* * *

I was feeling happier driving home on the Thursday afternoon than I had been for a long time, even long before my holiday in Carmichaeltown had started. I was enjoying my friendship with Elliot and Amy. I had, at last, managed to stuff my stupid competitiveness into a box. I was no longer thinking of Amy as 'my Amy' or Elliot as my love rival. They were more like completely different people who reminded me of friends that I used to know. I enjoyed their company.

I also admitted to myself that I was looking forward to spending an evening with Arnie on his own. I wasn't on the turn, I was still desperate to get back to my Amy, but I was enjoying the feeling of having a proper best mate. Not someone who seemed to control everything I did.

After my conversation with Elliot, I knew that I would have to tell Arnie about my meeting with Ben. So, I told him the truth. It was the best excuse available for abandoning him on Friday night, after all. I'd told him that I wanted to meet Ben, to finally exorcise the ghosts of my youth. I'd been chuffed with that one when I'd thought it up. It sounded well in line with the reasoning that had kept me out of his bed since Monday. Fair play to Arnie, he had completely respected my argument that I 'needed some space to come to terms with a lifetime of bullying'.

Last week, I would have laughed along with Tanner. 'Sucker!' We would have said.

It was completely different now.

Now, I simply thought that Arnie was a top bloke.

It was only an hour or so later when fate delivered that swift kick to my nuts.

I had changed into jeans and a sweatshirt before flopping onto the sofa. I'd checked with Arnie that we hadn't arranged to host a meeting of the United Nations in our lounge, and we weren't meant to be staging the World Cup in our garden.

Luckily, as it turned out, Arnie had gone upstairs to throw himself into the shower. So, it was me who reluctantly peeled himself from the sofa and went to answer the door when the bell had rung.

During my brief journey into the hallway, I was slightly concerned that I might find some more barking mad bruisers on the doorstep.

I certainly hadn't expected to find Cooper-Wilson there instead.

'Hello Jonny,' he said pleasantly enough, before the characteristic smirk took over his face. 'That is, if it is actually Jonny I'm talking to.'

Oh Shit! I thought, fighting a battle with my face to make sure I kept my expression as neutral as possible.

'It is, yes. We met on Tuesday.' I reminded him in as easy a manner as I could muster up under the circumstances. I carefully formed my features into an expression that implied I couldn't believe he'd forgotten our encounter.

'Well,' the pomposity had been turned up to level eleven and he paused to ensure I knew how clever he was being. I wanted to punch him, but I managed to control myself. I thought that the doorstep had seen enough violent intent over the course of the last forty-eight hours. And I didn't want to bring Elliot or Amy out of their house on this occasion.

After about ten seconds or so he spoke again. I think the intention had been to make me stew. It had worked. 'That's who you said you were.' He stared me straight in the eye. Hoping that I would blink, figuratively.

'Why would I say I was anyone else?' I said easily enough, hiding the fact that my stomach felt like I had overdosed on antacids.

'Because you are actually a "traveller".' There it was – the poker player had laid down a full house.

Actually, Cooper-Wilson would have been rubbish at playing poker.

I managed to laugh a disbelieving laugh. 'A traveller? Come on! I merely found the subject interesting and wanted to find out more.'

The poker player followed up the full house with four aces. 'When I asked you to join us for our meeting on Tuesday night, you said that you urgently needed to get back to Westcastle that evening.'

For a moment, I missed the significance. I started to say, 'Yes, I had an important...'

'Nobody has called it Westcastle for years,' he interrupted me rudely.

Shi-i-it! I thought and cursed my stupidity.

I manufactured a cough to play for time. I quickly thought of something that had come up in a conversation with Arnie. As easily as I could, I said: 'Oh that's because of my mum. They moved to Spain, just before the name was changed, and she still calls it that. I'd chatted to her on the phone on Monday night. Our conversation was still on my mind when I met you, I expect.'

He blinked and for a moment I thought I'd got away with it.

That moment lasted until he spoke again.

'You've behaved differently, in the last four days.'

'What on earth do you mean?' I said, in an irritated tone. 'How could you possibly know that? I'd never met you before Tuesday.'

The smug expression returned in full force and the poker player laid down a Royal flush. 'I've been talking to people – your colleagues. They tell me that Jonny Vincent has been a different man since Monday.'

'You've been talking to people at work?' I was horrified. For more than one reason.

He smiled in a placatory fashion. 'Oh, don't worry, I was very discreet. I just had a little chat with that lovely receptionist on the front desk. She seems to know everything that's going on.'

Bloody Gemma! I cursed inwardly. Luckily, I was able to hide behind a little bit of righteous indignation.

'How dare you check up on me?' I hissed. It was a small relief that I could hear water drumming on the shower tray from upstairs. I certainly didn't want Arnie joining in on this conversation. 'What on earth made you think you had the right?'

The very punchable face settled on an expression that was misleadingly calming. 'Oh, come, come.' His tongue appeared and briefly licked the edges of his shocking pink moustache. Like my faked coughing fit, he was using the action to get his thoughts into order. 'You got involved in a fight on Monday night, sticking up for your "boyfriend".' The emphasis on the final word was difficult to miss. 'My receptionist friend also told me that you asked the office junior to pay back the money he owed you.' Again, the emphasis was obvious. 'Very unlike Jonny Vincent, apparently. He, by all accounts, is very nice, if a bit wet.' Once again he stared at me, willing me to unburden myself and come clean. 'When I met you on Tuesday, you didn't strike me as wet in any shape or form.'

'Well thank-you for that,' I said sarcastically. 'But now I would like you to leave my house. Go and practise your delusional crap on someone else.'

Cooper-Wilson smiled as if he was completely exonerated. 'That's exactly what I mean. Not very Jonny Vincent-like at all, from what I've heard.' He practically tutted at the fact I was so rubbish at keeping in character. 'Let me go through what I've worked out.'

Like anyone could stop you. I thought viciously.

'Monday: Jonny doesn't come in to work. This is very unlike him. He has barely had a sick day the whole of the time he's worked at RD Eversen.'

'I felt ill for one day. Is that a crime?' I was trying desperately not to get angry. I knew that it would have been a complete giveaway.

He smiled like a barrister who had tricked a witness into revealing a vital fact. 'You were perfectly fine when I saw you on Tuesday.' He then returned to his invisible list. 'You and your boyfriend went out for a meal on Monday night. Apparently, Jonny Vincent wouldn't have done that on a day he'd been off sick.'

I said nothing, just fixed my face into a bored expression, as if it wasn't impressing me at all. Inside, my stomach was twisting and turning like a gymnast on the parallel bars. I was feeling that Jonny Vincent's imaginary illness could become real at any given moment.

Cooper-Wilson was unstoppable. 'You met me for lunch on Tuesday. I've been told that Jonny always has lunch with his boyfriend on a Tuesday. We could have met any day.'

'I'm beginning to wish we'd never met at all,' I said truthfully, while trying to keep the boredom in my voice.

He ignored me and tried peering around me, as if he was looking for someone else. 'In fact, I could ask your boyfriend if he's noticed anything different about you.' He smirked again. 'I wonder, are you straight, back in Westcastle?' He ramped up the taunting. I think he was hoping that I would lose my cool and blurt out something I would regret. 'How are you finding sleeping with men. Enjoying it?'

It nearly worked, but the rage I felt was over-shadowed by the horror of realising that the sound of running water had stopped. In minutes Arnie would come down the stairs to find out who I was talking to. I had no doubt that Cooper-Wilson would take great delight in asking him some very awkward questions. I had to get the idiot away from the house. Luckily, he had given me a reason to be justifiably angry.

'Right. That's it! I read your article. It interested me. I got in touch with you to find out more. End of story.' I got hold of him by the shoulder, twisted him around gently enough to avoid an assault charge, and propelled him a few steps down the pathway. Once again I spoke in a hissed whisper to avoid alerting the neighbours. 'I would like you to go now.'

For the first time that evening, Cooper-Wilson lost the attitude. He put a hand on my arm and pleaded in a way that was both a little bit pathetic and strangely charming. 'Take me with you. Please. I know you "travelled" on Monday morning. I know you did. Next Monday when you try to go back. Take me as well.'

Luckily, I realised how disastrous that scenario would be before his softer side had the chance to do me in. I took his hand from my arm but turned it into a sort of handshake to stop the gesture from coming across as rude.

'I honestly don't know what you're talking about.' I said, with a lot less aggression, before letting go of his hand – dismissing him. At first, I didn't think he'd go, but he obviously saw the determination on my face.

I watched him crawl snail-like down the street, pausing every few yards to look back at me, in the vague hope that I would change my mind and call out to him.

I didn't. I watched him disappearing into the amber-lit gloom, as I reversed back up the path to the front door. I was concentrating so hard on making sure my unwanted guest had disappeared, that I didn't realise that Arnie had come down the stairs. I was still peering around the door as I closed it, just to convince myself that he hadn't changed his mind and come back up the road after all.

Having decided finally that everything was Cooper-Wilson free, I closed the door and turned to go back into the lounge.

I walked straight into Arnie, enquiring look on his face, white towel wrapped around his waist, hair damp and roughly rubbed so that it was half dried. My hand, which had just let go of the front door latch was at exactly the right height to brush against Arnie's nipple as I turned.

It didn't take long for his genitalia to respond to the feel of my touch, and I tried not to overreact as his towel clad penis touched my denim covered one.

'Careful lover!' Arnie laughed. 'I'm trying to be good, but that sort of behaviour is liable to send me over the edge.'

I laughed, but it wasn't Arnie's rapidly responsive genitalia that was worrying me. I already trusted Arnie enough to know that he wouldn't do anything, unless he was sure that Jonny wanted it too.

No, what was worrying me was the fact that, for a brief second as his penis had touched mine, my body had threatened to react.

For a millisecond, I had wanted it too.

~ 28 ~
BEYOND THE BIRTHDAY PARTY

Carmichaeltown: Fifteen Years Earlier

Tanner's life was unravelling. The taunts, the hooting, the knowledge that he was no longer in control. Moreover, Mr Roots, the football coach had caught him smoking behind the bins at the back of the kitchens. He had stripped him of the captaincy and handed him a two-match ban.

It was the day of the party when the unravelling increased in speed, as if a kitten had grabbed hold of a ball of wool and danced the length of the garden with it. Jonny hadn't wanted to invite Tanner, but he was aware that it was also Ben's birthday and the Shawcrosses had opened their house for the occasion. To insist that a family friend was barred from the festivities seemed churlish.

In fact, Tanner caused no trouble. He spent the night hidden in a corner, morosely getting drunker and drunker. For most of the evening, the only person who spoke to him was Ben and that was only intermittently, when Amy allowed him to escape from the dance floor.

Later, Jonny would remember dancing with Will, whirling around and smiling towards Amy, both of them loved-up, drunk and happy.

It was all a bit of a blur, that evening. Looking back, Jonny would realise that it was one of the last times that he would be completely happy until Arnur Bjorn Pétursson came into his life, nearly ten years later. If he had known this at the time, he would have stored every moment to a DVD in his head. The name of the song that was playing when Will whispered into his ear: 'This will always remind me of you.' A joke they'd laughed at, which was hilarious at the time, but had got lost in the alcohol and the haze of so many other funny moments. The number of times that Will had told him he loved him.

But he hadn't, so he only remembered the evening as a vague montage of fun. Every now and then he would get a chance to grab a memory of one of the moments, but it was like a ball that had rolled down a drain in the street. He would try and grab hold of it, but just as his fingertips touched it, it would roll a half-turn further away from his grasp.

More than most of the people at the party, Ella Conway had very good reason to dislike Tanner. She had lost count of the times that she had suffered from his sharp tongue.

She had never known there could be so many ways to call someone a slapper.

Ella liked sex, in the same way her twin sister liked boy bands and netball. No one teased Chloe for that.

No one had teased Tanner either, or called him a hypocrite when he taunted Ella. And he'd bedded most of the female members of their school year, in the days before he became persona non grata. She didn't understand why a bloke was given knowing looks and congratulations in the shower room, but a girl was left with a reputation that was difficult to shift.

She decided not to bother trying to shift it, and simply enjoyed herself instead.

And, she thought, *although Tanner Hootley was an arrogant prick, he was also undeniably hot.*

Unfortunately, the alcohol that Tanner had turned to earlier in the evening as an alternative to company had consequences. It destroyed his chances of enjoying that company when it finally made an appearance.

In the early hours of Sunday morning, Ella was slightly irritated to be faced with a stubbornly flaccid penis. By the time she'd had a few hours' sleep, she decided that she could get almost as much entertainment by telling everyone about it.

After all the malicious comments that Tanner had hurled in her direction over the years, Ella thought it was the least she could do.

After the party, Amy had been allowed to stay over at Ben's house and they'd spent a very lazy Sunday getting over the amount of alcohol they'd thrown down their throats. They weren't aware of what was happening in the world around them.

With Ben's assistance, Amy had managed to stagger home on Sunday night but on Monday morning the hangover had mutated into a two-day affair. Her parents had rung the school with a tale of an unpleasant bug.

Ben had spent all morning with Tanner and was aware of a few whispered giggles. He knew they were aimed at his friend. Tanner wouldn't talk about Saturday night or share any details of what happened after he'd disappeared with Ella. This was unlike Tanner. Prior to the last couple of months, he would have bragged about any sexual conquest until Ben had feared his ears were going to bleed.

Will had decided to let Tanner sweat for the morning. He waited until just after lunch. Everyone had convened in the classroom for afternoon registration before they disappeared to various sports pitches for the rest of the school day.

Will considered it was the perfect time for an announcement.

He was once again leaning against the teacher's table when Tanner walked into the room. Ben had noticed that the arrogant swagger his friend had cultivated over the years had disappeared, and he shuffled into the classroom in the hope that no one would see him.

Will made sure that this ploy was doomed to fail.

'OK, OK! Quick impression.' He yelled to attract everyone's attention. Once he had achieved that, he held up one hand so that his fingertips were pointing at the ceiling. With an accompanying whistle, he gradually let his fingers fall so they eventually faced the floor.

The fact that they ended up mimicking a limp wrist, as well as a body part that was unable to perform, was no happy accident.

The ever-present cat calls of 'Hoots! Hoots!' made a brief appearance before Will quietened his disciples by raising his hand for a second time.

Once again, only Elliot and Steve seemed uninvolved with everything that was happening around them. They'd had a trial flight of their microlight aircraft, before the party on Saturday, which had raised some problems that needed to be solved. They were both hunched around a desk at the back of the room, much more concerned about an unresponsive wing than an unresponsive penis.

'No, No. Ladies and gentlemen, boys and girls. Be nice.' Will smiled with fake sympathy. 'Poor old Hoots is having a terrible time. He's been kicked off the football team for being a dope-head and now we have undisputed proof that he can't perform in the way a real man should. Have some sympathy.'

Ben knew he would have to say something. He wanted to say something to support his friend. He was just about to speak when Jonny spoke for the first time.

They say that timing is everything in good comedy. Into the void created by a brief hiatus between taunts, Jonny spoke gently but clearly.

'Roots boots Hoots oot for being in cahoots with cheroots.'

There was something about Jonny's delivery. Something about the fact that he didn't often joke. Something that affected Ben in the same way Jonny's 'Navbratalova' comment had done on that summer afternoon in the park. It made him laugh.

Even as he did so, he glanced over at Tanner and what he saw on his friend's face, sobered him immediately.

He saw anger. He saw a violent intent.

He also saw that Tanner was hurting.

It was a remark from one of Will's random disciples that mixed the anger, violence, and hurt, into an explosive cocktail.

'Ooh Tanner. What will your daddy say? I expect he'll give your arse a good tanning – eh, Tanner?'

It was a lame attempt to follow up Jonny's humour.

Harmless enough.

Unless you knew the history.

A couple of years before, Tanner's father had temporarily remembered that he had a son and returned home unexpectedly. Tanner and Ben had been smoking in the conservatory and although they managed to extinguish the cigarettes in time, they hadn't managed to clear the smell of smoke. To humiliate his son completely, Mr Hootley had told him to strip naked in full view of his friend. He had then ordered Tanner to hand him a trainer. He had beaten him with it as Ben had watched on, appalled, but completely helpless.

Afterwards, a defeated Tanner had pleaded with his friend not to tell anyone.

His plea had been unnecessary. Ben had no intention of sharing the horror.

Two years later, on that afternoon in December, Tanner saw Ben laughing. He heard the comment. He believed that Ben had been spreading his shameful secret. It served to confirm his greatest fear. Ever since the day of the race, Tanner had dreaded the thought of losing Ben's friendship. He now believed that he had lost it.

'Bastard!' He screamed.

The power of the one word was so visceral, the hatred so real, that on this occasion no one laughed or hooted as Tanner stormed out. Ben was the only person who moved. His one thought was to follow Tanner and talk to him.

'Let him go Ben.' The taunting tone had disappeared from Will's voice. He wasn't quite sure how, but he was aware that this time, things had gone too far. 'You'll see him at football practice. Give him a chance to cool down. You won't be able to talk any sense into him now.'

By the time Ben reached the changing room, fifteen minutes later, he felt like he was trying to crack the Enigma code in his head. Every time he thought about a way he could apologise to Tanner, he also thought of forty different directions that the conversation could take.

He desperately wanted to convince his friend that he hadn't told anyone what had occurred that summer afternoon, two years before. Not even Amy. He desperately wanted to convince Tanner that he would never betray his trust.

But Tanner wasn't there. Ben had been sure that he would be. He knew better than anyone how desperate Tanner was to regain his place in the team. Missing his first practice session after he'd been dropped, would be a sure way to anger Mr Roots and make a swift return unlikely.

Ben knew that he wouldn't be able to concentrate. He invented a tight hamstring and told the football coach that he wasn't sure he should risk a practise session. Because Ben had never tried to swerve training before, Mr Roots swallowed the lie. Ben headed back towards the main school building, hobbling at first. As soon as he had cleared the school grounds, he lost the hobble and increased his speed.

Tanner wasn't at his home when Ben arrived. Neither was he answering his phone, even though Ben tried to call him ten times. Tanner was angry with him in a way he had never been before. That much was obvious.

Ben thought he'd give it a couple of hours and hope that Tanner would calm down enough to answer his phone.

Ben decided to pop in and see Amy. If anyone could manage to soothe his addled brain and stop him from over-thinking the situation, it would be her. It was purely a misunderstanding. Tanner and him, they'd be able to fix it. And while they were at it, they might get around to the conversation they needed to have. He wanted to tell his mate about the way he was dealing with things in general, and Will in particular.

As he arrived at Amy's house, Ben hoped that she had stopped vomiting. He wasn't particularly good at dealing with sickness.

But Amy was no longer being sick. As Ben raised his hand to rap on the door. He heard something much worse than the sounds of an upset stomach.

Amy was screaming.

~ 29 ~
THE BROKEN DOOR

Carmichaeltown: Fifteen Years Earlier

Ben didn't spare a thought for the Crawfords' front door. He didn't stop to wonder if it was as easy to batter down a door as it looked on TV. He just went ahead and did it.

The scream had sounded as if it was coming from downstairs, so he rushed into the lounge.

He'd only been in the room on Friday evening. The Crawfords had returned from badminton, armed with a Chinese takeaway, and declared that Ben's birthday celebrations were underway. On the dot of midnight, they'd opened a bottle of champagne and Amy had appeared with the first of his presents.

It was hard to associate that scene of domestic happiness with the room that Ben saw in front of him.

It looked like a cross between a sick bay and a brothel.

Ben could see all the detritus from a day spent feeling poorly. A plastic bowl was tipped on its side near to the sofa, and a packet of aspirin was splayed across the carpet like a useless pack of cards. The blankets that had comforted Amy as she'd wallowed in a day of rom com DVDs, had also fallen to the floor.

The two people in the room could have been characters in a rom com. Ben's girlfriend and his best friend. However, the scene they were playing was far from funny.

Amy was putting up a fight. The screams that Ben had heard from outside had continued constantly while he'd battered his way into the building. She was by the side of the sofa, back pressed against the wall, her arms flailing towards the man in front of her.

It was like King Canute trying to stop the tide from coming in. Amy wasn't going to succeed either.

Tanner had decided that the best way to stop the hands from scratching his face was to grab hold of them. With a roar of his own, he pushed Amy's arms, so they were above her head. He then held them in place with one hand, while he ripped the tie from around his neck with the other. He looped it into a noose and dropped it over Amy's wrists, like a ring tossed over a goldfish bowl at the fair.

Neither of them were aware they had a visitor. Amy was enveloped by a man who meant to harm her. She was only aware of the threat Tanner posed and the fact that her last chance of defiance was now trapped by an item of his school uniform.

Tanner was lost in his thoughts, Amy's screams, and the excitement they gave him. He pressed into her, feeling her warmth, revelling in her fear, trapping her body so that she was unable to move. With both hands now free, he tightened the knot around her wrist.

When he'd stormed from the classroom earlier, all he could hear was that joke. Not Jonny Vincent's joke. The other one.

I expect he'll give your arse a good tanning – eh, Tanner?

As he escaped the school grounds, the joke blended with all the other humiliations he'd suffered since the day of the race. The hoots. The human bungee rope. The fact that on Saturday night, his dick hadn't reacted in the way that it should. And everyone knowing about it. He needed to feel that he was in control once again. Suddenly he'd known where he was heading.

He'd lusted after Amy for a long time and hated her for even longer.

But it wasn't even about her. Not really. More than anything, he needed to hurt Ben.

And this would hurt him.

Amy could feel Tanner's weight squashing her, restricting her opportunity to scream. She could feel her wrists rubbing against each other and could almost taste Tanner's breath as he breathed his excitement into her mouth.

For a few seconds Ben stood there, immobilised by horror, before his own mouth involuntarily released the only name that mattered to him at that moment.

'Amy!'

It wasn't a shout. He barely raised his voice, but something alerted Amy to the fact that he was in the room. She glanced towards him. Her face was a strange mixture of relief that he had come to save her, and terror that he hadn't.

Tanner followed her eyes and moved backwards immediately, releasing his pressure on her body. Amy didn't move, didn't even drop her arms, simply stayed in place, as if she had been super-glued to the wall.

Tanner spoke, his voice cracking with the adrenalin that was still rushing through his body.

'Hey, mate ... it's not what it looks like.'

He walked across the room towards Ben, arms outstretched in a gesture of innocence. He looked like a guilty child who had been caught nicking freshly baked cakes from the cooling rack, rather than a maniac who had been attacking his best friend's girlfriend. He even attempted a grin, but it was forced. *Later,* he thought, *I'll talk to Ben and pretend it was a terrible mistake. I'll make him feel guilty for being disloyal. I'll blame Amy.*

After a lifetime, Tanner knew which buttons to press. He was sure he'd be able to talk Ben round. But, for now, he decided that the best thing to do was to leave quickly.

Ben knew that he should punch him. He knew that any decent boyfriend would kick Tanner in the genitalia, squash his face into the carpet, grab him by the neck, and slam him against the wall.

Afterwards, when Tanner had darted through the broken front door with a hurried 'Catch you later' on his lips, Ben wondered why he hadn't done any of those things. He told himself it was because he didn't want the Crawfords to have to explain a blood stain on the carpet, or a Tanner shaped hole in the plasterboard. He reasoned that a vandalised entrance was enough damage to report to the council for one day.

Even as he was inventing excuses for himself, he knew that it was all rubbish. He knew the real reason.

The real reason was Tanner. His brother from another womb. His best friend since forever.

He didn't want to ... couldn't ... believe what his own eyes were telling him had happened.

He put all thoughts of Tanner into a box at the back of his brain and focussed his attention on Amy. He moved quickly towards her.

Amy had finally dropped her arms and was fighting to loosen the tie that was binding her. She had just managed to do so, and had shaken her polyester handcuff to the floor, when she was aware of someone rushing towards her.

It didn't register that this person was there to help, rather than harm. It didn't register who this person was, and that he loved her. She merely saw another shape, much like the last, and she simply wanted to stop it from hurting her.

Amy lashed out in the general direction of the shape and caught flesh with her fingernails. She gashed a rip across Ben's left cheek, like a kitchen knife cutting through pork rind.

Ben didn't let it deter him. He didn't care that Amy's hands were flailing, as uncoordinated as a drunken dad dancing. He didn't flinch when they scratched his neck. He moved inexorably towards her, determined to comfort her.

When her hands were squashed once again and no longer able to flail, she curled her fingers into a fist and attempted to punch against the chest that was succeeding in trapping her.

All the time, Ben spoke gently and reassuringly. But in the end, it wasn't his voice that succeeded in soothing her, nor was it the strength of his body that forced her into a surrender.

It was the smell of him.

Some part of her brain recognised his scent and it encouraged her to believe she would be safe. Slowly, she relaxed into his arms and Ben held on to her, continuing to comfort her with gentle words. As the need to fight disappeared, so did all the strength in her body and Ben eased her onto the sofa, so that she wouldn't fall onto the floor. He sat beside her, still talking, still stroking, until eventually her head nestled into his chest.

Ben had no idea how long they remained like that, how many words he spoke, or even what any of those words were. He knew that they didn't really need to make sense, they simply had to let her know that she wasn't alone, that she was being protected. She was loved.

Her ordeal was over.

'I didn't want him to do that. I didn't ask him to.'

Her first words for an hour nearly killed Ben. It was as if she was pleading with him to believe that she hadn't been cheating on him. That she wasn't to blame.

Ben knew that Amy wasn't to blame. Even if he hadn't seen the impromptu handcuff or noticed the abused rag doll look in her eyes. Even if he hadn't felt the tremors jitter through her body, as he'd held her for the past hour, he would have known that Amy wasn't to blame.

Because he knew Amy.

He took her hand. 'Don't be soft,' he said gently. 'I know you, don't I? I know you and I love you.'

But, he didn't want to believe that his friend was to blame either. As he continued to soothe Amy, he slowly unwrapped the Tanner-shaped box in his brain. Tanner would never do that to Amy. He would never do that to Ben.

But he did. You saw him.
But he wasn't in his right mind.
You saw him.

Ben thought back to earlier in the afternoon. Thought back to the time that Tanner had seen him laughing at Jonny's joke. Thought back to the feeble joke that had followed it. He remembered the word that Tanner had screamed and the look of betrayal on his face as he had screamed it. The look of betrayal and temporary insanity.

Tanner had not been in his right mind when he'd attacked Amy. He couldn't have been. Ben, his so-called best friend, had sent him to the point of madness.

Even as he blamed himself for another man's crime, Ben knew there was someone else he could blame as well. Someone safe. Someone that he didn't really care about. Someone he could honestly believe was the mastermind behind the madness.

Will.

Ever since Will had arrived in the town on his white charger, determined to rescue his dimwit in distress from the nasty bullies, he had set about dismantling Tanner's life. This afternoon he had succeeded.

And Amy had borne the brunt of it.

Ben stayed with Amy until Mrs Crawford arrived home, her face etched with the worry of being confronted with a battered daughter and a broken door. He told a vague story about Amy being attacked and left his girlfriend to fill in the details if she wanted to do so. He knew it was likely that Tanner could face some serious charges but didn't want to think about it any more deeply. At that moment, he was only interested in finding Tanner, and ensuring he didn't do any more damage.

There was a pub near to the back of the station. It had been a favourite haunt of theirs when they were still underage. The landlord didn't bother to ask any questions that would endanger a profit.

Ben knew exactly what his friend would do and where he would go to do it.

The landlord was looking a little edgy when Ben entered the pub. He nodded his head towards a back room and Ben followed his mute directions and found Tanner slumped against a table to one side of the skittle alley. The number of glasses that were littered around him, gave Ben a clue to his lack of sobriety, even before Tanner lifted his head at Ben's approach and started to cry.

'Mate! Mate! I'm so sorry ... I didn't do nothing ... wouldn't do nothing.'

Ben was torn once again. He hated the fact that Tanner was expecting Ben to dismiss the evidence his own eyes had seen, no more than two hours before. But he still felt a certain sense of responsibility, and a desire to keep his friend safe.

'Come on mate,' he pushed the table away and held his breath as one glass wobbled menacingly. It threatened to turn the table into a fragile replica of the alley in front of him, but luckily, it decided at the last minute to stay in place. He supported Tanner's body weight and eased him to his feet, before shuffling him back into the main bar, where they were hurried out of the front door by the landlord's scowl.

Once out in the cold December night, Tanner seemed to sober up a little. He unwrapped himself from Ben's grip and staggered backwards before waving a finger in the direction of Ben's face.

'It's that bastard's fault. That bastard. Will.' Tanner laughed nastily. 'Will E Muncher. Bastard.' Tanner was rambling. Ben realised that he had already moved from denying that the attack had happened to putting the blame on someone else. 'He pushed me into it with all his clever talk, all that hooting and shit.'

Ben made soothing noises and moved his mate towards the bridge that crossed the railway. Rush hour was fast approaching, and a wave of people descended the stairs, meaning that Ben had to hold on to Tanner to ensure that he didn't stumble into them. He edged his friend up one side of the staircase, allowing people to pass. A group of scantily clad angels on their way to an early office Christmas party ran past them. They had done the job properly with tinsel wings and cardboard harps. They giggled and waved their wands at the world; giddy happy that the festive season was nearly upon them.

'Girlies, let me play a tune on your gazongas!' Tanner shouted to their disappearing backs. One of them turned and frowned at him. Ben held up a hand in apology while using the other to stop Tanner from following her. He then continued to ease his friend up the steps while Tanner returned to his original theme, happy that he had his mate back on-side once more.

'We should have him Benjy. What do you say? You and me. The perfect murder.'

Ben looked at his friend. He saw the despair that was hidden behind his eyes, the fear of rejection that was written in bold capitals across his face.

He blocked his mind from thinking about what he had witnessed in Amy's lounge. And who was responsible for it.

He thought only about the look on Tanner's face when Ben had laughed at him in the classroom. The guilt he felt from that moment encouraged him to banter with his friend as he'd done in the old days.

More than anything, he wanted to prove to Tanner that he was still his friend. Sorting out the rest of the mess could wait.

Besides, people who talked about murder, very rarely committed it. Did they?

So, he joined in with Tanner's drunken ramblings about committing the perfect murder, and they started plotting the downfall of the hideous homo.

What harm could it do?

They had reached the top of the steps and he manoeuvred Tanner out of the path of an irritated businessman. He then turned him to the left, ready to cross the bridge.

Spurred on by Ben's encouragement, the latest plan for Will's demise fell from Tanner's mouth. They would go to Will's house, entice him to the water tower, push him to his death. No-one would ever know.

Ben smiled and nodded but said little. He didn't have to.

'Holy shit! Look at that Benj!' Tanner stopped dead, a malicious grin spreading across his face. 'There is a God – and for once he's on our side.'

Ben was recovering his balance after the shock of the heavy weight around his neck coming to a halt so suddenly. He glanced at his friend; a questioning look on his face.

'What on earth are you on about Tan?'

'There!' Tanner pointed towards the far end of the bridge. 'The Fairy King of the Faggots. Will.' His eyes glimmered with a vicious excitement. 'He's on the bridge Benj. He's walking straight towards us!'

Ben peered in the direction that Tanner's finger was signposting. He tried to look through the crowd of shoppers, businesspeople, school children, and college students.

And there, at the far end of the bridge, was Will.

'It must be fate.' Tanner said, before continuing in the tone of voice he used at City matches when he was urging the ball into the goal in front of them. 'Come on you bastard! Come to Mama!'

Suddenly, a tall man in a black overcoat, walked in front of Will and he was obscured from Ben's view.

Ben peered once more into the weaving, meandering, crowd. He spotted Will again. A little closer this time, but it was very brief, and he disappeared behind a crowd of schoolboys, barging their way across the bridge.

He looked at Tanner. He too was looking intently at the mass of people heading towards them.

'It's like that game Benj,' Tanner wobbled drunkenly on Ben's shoulder. 'You know, when some con-artist has a pack of cards, you're meant to find the Queen, but every time you think you've got her, the bitch disappears.' He stopped and then laughed as another thought occurred to him. 'Hey Benjy. Find the Queen ... eh...' He laughed at his own comic brilliance and peered at the oncoming crowd once again.

Ben spotted their quarry first. He was halfway across the bridge. Roughly about the same age, same height, and the coat he was wearing was a similar style to a coat that Will favoured.

But, with a sense of relief, Ben realised that it wasn't Will.

Drunk as he was, it took his friend a little longer. Eventually, as the lad who might have been Will reached the spot on the bridge, near to where they were standing, Tanner let out a grunt of disappointment.

'Bollocks!' He said angrily but then brightened immediately. 'Still, we can go back to Plan A. What do you say Benjy? Are you in?'

It took Ben a few seconds to remember what Plan A was. As he did so, he realised the insanity of what he was hearing. Focussing on looking for Will through a mass of people, seemed to have focussed Ben's mind as well. The plan was nonsensical, Tanner was incapable, and the woods by the water tower would be pitch black at five o'clock on a December evening.

And – Ben thought. *I have no intention of helping Tanner to murder Will – and never have.*

Even so, Ben was on the point of agreeing. His actual plan that night was to placate Tanner, get him home, wait for him to pass out so that Ben could hurry back to Amy.

Amy.

Who knows? When Tanner wakes up tomorrow, hungover, and sorry for himself, he might remember what he has done and feel ashamed.

A simple unguarded thought out of nowhere, and like pennies falling from a fruit machine, one thought followed the other...

I'm letting him get away with it. Once again, I'm letting him get away with it.

And then...

He's blaming Will for all the shit in his life. And I'm agreeing with him.

With a shock, Ben realised that Tanner's words were echoing Ben's own thoughts from earlier. On someone else's lips, he realised how stupid they sounded.

None of this is Will's fault. Not really. Tanner brought this all on himself and yet here I am babysitting the idiot, while my girlfriend is in bits.

Does he not care what he's done to Amy?

Ben realised that Tanner was waiting for his reply. He decided to give his friend an answer that he wasn't expecting.

'No Tan, I'm not.'

Tanner didn't even listen the first time. Typically, he heard what he wanted to hear and carried on in his own vengeance-soaked world.

'I'm not in.' Ben said it again, with a little more authority.

'You what?' Tanner stopped. This time Ben's words had hit their target and it was clear that the target didn't like them.

A woman squeezed through the space between them, focussing on peeling the lid from a takeaway coffee, ignoring the fact that she was momentarily blocking their conversation. It gave Ben time to collect his thoughts.

'All this perfect murder stuff. We're not fourteen anymore.' This time Ben had to move towards Tanner to allow a tiny elderly couple room to pass by. They walked past arm in arm, both carrying tubes of wrapping paper that were nearly as tall as they were. They shuffled along in a world that was moving too fast for them.

Ben waited for them to pass before he continued. 'So, you're either playing a game, which is pathetic at your age, or it's murder.' He paused to emphasise his words. 'There's nothing perfect about it.'

'Dick.' Tanner pouted. The sulk and the teenage insult merely served to prove Ben's point.

'You need to grow up mate. Will winds you up and you fall for it every time. Just laugh it off and he'll soon get bored.'

'Oh, like you do, I suppose.' The words could have sounded complimentary, but the tone Tanner used ensured that Ben knew it wasn't. Even so, Ben ignored the tone and took the words at face value.

'Yeah, I guess.'

'Do you know what a kick in the teeth that joint party on Saturday was...' Tanner changed tack slightly and stabbed his finger towards his own chest, '...to me?'

'Oh, come on mate. It was obvious. Jonny was eighteen, I was eighteen. Our social groups are the same...'

'You were cosying up to the faggot and his boyfriend, knowing all the time that they're bullying me.'

Ben managed to bury a laugh and said calmly: 'Yeah, well I don't think either of us could have much cause to gripe on that score, do you Tanner?'

'And now, today, I find out that you've told everyone about my father stripping me naked and beating me. The one secret you knew could kill me. And you told them.'

Once again, Ben heard the desolation behind the words and his irritation dissipated. He moved to soothe his friend.

'No Tanner, I didn't. That kid had a lucky guess. I would never do that to you.'

But Tanner wasn't listening.

'You think you're so effin' perfect, don't you?' He moved a pace away from the wooden wall and poked a finger towards Ben's face. 'Well, I tell you what mate, you've changed. Your pathetic bitch of a girlfriend has got you well under the thumb.'

It happened suddenly. One minute he'd felt sorry for Tanner. One minute he'd been desperate to make Tanner believe that he hadn't betrayed him.

And the next...

Ben rarely got enraged. The last time that he'd lost his cool was when a twelve-year-old with a snappy mouth had bitten his ear during a school football match. He could feel an odd rage building inside him, begging to be released.

He had never called Tanner by his hated nickname before, but if the man believed he was disloyal, it seemed churlish to disappoint him.

He suddenly had a desperate need to rile the drunken idiot.

'Careful Hoots.'

Tanner was riled.

'You know what Benjy? You should be thanking me for showing you how to treat a woman.' He laughed unpleasantly. 'She wasn't quite so gobby when I'd finished with her, was she?'

The rage was no longer building. It had engulfed Ben completely. It was like a feeling he'd never experienced before, and with it came a strange notion of being super-human. The lights from the railway below seemed brighter. The spider webs that encased the windows on the bridge seemed more defined. The breaths and fingertips that had glazed the glass became visible to him. The rumble of the trains increased in volume. He could hear a man on a mobile phone, ordering a taxi to an address Ben could still remember hours later. And all the while, in front of him, was that face. A face no longer etched with need. It was once again a face full of arrogance. Full of the complacent belief that his best friend would never seriously challenge him.

That look gave Ben licence to say exactly what he wanted to say.

'You raped her!' He sensed people turning to look and he corrected himself as if it were important for them that he got his facts right. 'You would have raped her if I hadn't stopped you.'

'Raped her?' The drunken mockery sounded more aggressive; more scorn laden. 'She should think herself lucky that I bothered to give her the attention. Frigid. Little. Bit...'

Ben hit him before he managed to finish the final word. He felt a sharp pain from the punch as if his fist was complaining against being used in that manner. Tanner staggered back and crashed against the wooden wall. The wood started to splinter and the window above it started to crack and shatter. Glass shards disappeared into the night sky like shavings from an ice carving. There was a blast of cold air as December invaded the walkway.

But Ben wasn't aware of the chill. He wasn't aware of the crowd or the fact they were standing on a bridge. Ben only felt the fury inside him.

It urged him to land a second blow. The rage had taken him over and he was ill-equipped to resist it.

Ben would never know if Tanner understood that he was falling to his death. However, the look he saw on Tanner's face would haunt his dreams for years to come.

Ben was aware of the screams of the crowd. He heard the shouts and the crying. He didn't really understand what it all meant, but he heard them.

They seemed to grow into a mind-numbing crescendo as Tanner's body fell irrevocably towards the fast train from London.

~ 30 ~
THE OTHER 'ME'

Carmichaeltown: Ben

Friday night. Just an ordinary Friday night. But this was anything but ordinary. I, Ben Shawcross, was standing in a town centre pub talking to – Ben Shawcross.

The pub we'd chosen was packed with attendees from the Alec Carmichael convention. We were squashed into a corner, our pint pots sharing a ledge that had only been designed to hold a couple of shot glasses. The pub itself had mirrors everywhere. Massive Baroque styled gilt framed mirrors. Interior design by the Hammer House of Horrors. Squashed in as we were, it was almost impossible to avoid looking at them.

When I spoke, I could see Jonny Vincent's mouth opening and closing. When Ben spoke, I could see my mouth opening and closing.

It was more than weird. It was on the completely bonkers side of barking mad.

After a friendly enough greeting, the conversation had become difficult. Ben seemed nervous. I was nervous. Out of desperation, I'd asked Ben what had happened to Tanner. I suppose, because nobody I'd met since Monday would even mention his name, it had become an itch I needed to scratch. I thought that if anyone would talk about him, Ben would.

At first, he looked at me with a strange look on his face. But he did answer me. By the time he'd finished his story of Tanner's downward spiral, the joint birthday party, the attempted rape, and the fight on the bridge, I understood his incredulous expression. *Surely, everyone in our year would have remembered that shitstorm of a story?*

I decided that I needed to address that fact, before he decided that Jonny Vincent had completely lost the plot.

'Sorry to put you through that,' I said. 'I really wanted to hear your side of the story. There are so many bits I don't know, and I don't like to ask Amy about it ... for obvious reasons.'

Thankfully, he smiled. 'I completely understand,' he said and I'd thought I'd got away with it, until he frowned suddenly. 'You did look a bit shell-shocked though. It was almost like you'd never heard any of it before.'

Well, I thought. *There's a pretty good reason for that.*

I thought it best if I didn't say that to Ben. Instead, I encouraged him to get back to telling me about the aftermath of that night on the bridge.

I'd used Elliot's request from Wednesday night as an excuse, when I told Arnie where I was going. I also added that I thought it would be good for me 'to get some closure'. That was a sentence I'd never thought I'd hear myself saying, but I merely told myself that I was channelling my inner Jonny Vincent and keeping in character.

Arnie had accepted it with the supportive good grace that I was coming to realise was typical of him. He'd offered to come with me, but I said bravely that it was something I needed to do on my own.

As Ben re-started his story, a few hours later, I took the opportunity to study his face more closely. If anything, he looked slightly older than the face I had last seen, in the mirror, on Monday morning. His eyes were slightly more wary, there were a few more wrinkles across his forehead and he had grey hairs on the side of his head, just above his ears. Amy was always moaning that Tanner and I were immature. This version of Ben wasn't. The way he spoke, the way he listened, the way he looked. It all spoke of a maturity beyond his years.

'At first I was numb.' He said, almost as if he was grateful for the chance to talk. I suddenly realised that he desperately needed to talk. *Well, go for your life,* I thought. *I certainly won't be interrupting or correcting you.* 'I had killed my best friend. I had also discovered that my best friend, someone I'd always thought of as a brother, had attempted to rape my girlfriend.'

I nodded encouragingly and Jonny Vincent in the mirror, nodded at the same time.

'There was never a question in my mind about denying it. I had done it. Loads of witnesses had seen me punch him. What was the point?'

It was a rhetorical question, so mirror Jonny and I simply nodded again.

'My Dad's solicitor, on the other hand, advised me to say as little as possible.'

I knew the score. I've seen all those police procedural dramas on TV.

'He wanted to argue that it at all been a horrible accident caused by inadequate maintenance and cost-cutting by National Rail.' Ben explained. 'But, as the evening wore on, I realised that I didn't want to get away with it. I had punched Tanner. That punch had led to his death. Despite all the solicitor's advice, I didn't want to wriggle out of any charges on a technicality.'

I nodded. For me it would have been a no-brainer as well.

'I think I just wanted all the questions to be over. Admit it. Receive my punishment. Move on. It seemed that simple.'

'But it wasn't?'

'No.' He smiled sadly. 'Things like that never are, are they?' Once again, he wasn't expecting a reply, so I just nodded sympathetically, and he carried on. 'Tanner's parents wouldn't have it. In their minds there was no way it could have been called an accident. Even manslaughter wasn't enough for them. They wanted me to be charged with murder.'

'Murder?'

Ben nodded. 'It was the second punch that was the crux of their argument. Why did I punch him again when it was clear that the wall was collapsing, and a second punch would result in Tanner's death? They argued that I went through with it to get my revenge.'

'For the attempted rape?' It seemed an obvious thing to say, but Ben shook his head vigorously.

'No. According to them, that didn't happen.' He stopped suddenly, as his surprise over my ignorance of the story made an abrupt return '...Amy never told you any of this at the time?'

I shook my head and remembered some words that Amy had said to me on the afternoon I had crash landed into her world, disguised as her best friend. 'Amy and I weren't particularly good friends to each other back then.'

Ben nodded. 'Yeah of course. She did tell me that during one of her visits, back in the day.' Thankfully, he then went straight back to his tale so I didn't need to elaborate.

'There was no rape,' he repeated. There was little attempt to keep the scorn out of his voice when he added: 'Because Tanner and Amy were having an affair.'

I didn't have to manufacture the look of surprise. I was gobsmacked.

'Their take on the story was simple. I'd found out about their relationship and charged around to Amy's house to confront her. The Hootleys passed their "concerns" on to the Police and from that point on, the questioning became a little more hostile.' He paused, and frowned at the memory of that awful night. 'The investigating officer then suggested that the broken-down door was proof of my anger and the scratches on my neck and face were proof that Amy and I had argued. After that, they suggested, I had tracked Tanner down with murderous thoughts on my mind.' He sighed. 'Suddenly the fact that I had been keen to admit to manslaughter, made them believe I was hiding something more sinister. They started to investigate more thoroughly. And it was that second punch that really interested them. They found several people who were willing to testify that there was plenty of time for me to realise that the wall was collapsing, and pull back.' He gave a sad little laugh. 'They even found a woman who was crossing the bridge at the time and remembered me mentioning the word "murder".'

'But surely there were people who had seen you helping him, just beforehand?' I argued.

He shrugged. 'You'd think so, wouldn't you?' He smiled sadly. 'But, when people are aware that someone died minutes afterwards, even the most innocent of acts appear suspicious. Then, if you add in the action of the Hootleys themselves...' He paused, before explaining himself '...at one point, a week or so after the event, they informed the police that Tanner had told them about the affair. Apparently, he was worried what I might do to him, when I found out.'

I couldn't quite believe what I was hearing. The Tanner Hootley I knew wouldn't have told his parents the contents of his weekly shopping list. He certainly wouldn't have cosied up to them with details of his love life.

'Yeah,' Ben smiled. My face had obviously given away my thoughts on the subject. If he was surprised that Jonny Vincent would be aware of the situation, he let it go. 'My guess has always been that the case hadn't been moving fast enough for them, so they started inventing things. They wanted to persuade the police, and the CPS, to charge me with Tanner's murder.' The smile disappeared quickly. 'I just wish they had spent as much energy fighting for Tanner when he was alive.' He paused. 'Remembering they had a younger son would have been a good start. Tanner might not have turned into the mess he was, had they been better parents.'

With that he made signals that he needed to go to the loo and began elbowing his way out of our corner of the bar. I was relieved. I needed a bit of time to recover from the car crash of events he had just described, as well as to prepare myself for more to come.

As I struggled to save the space that Ben had left from being invaded by the latest crowd of Alec Carmichael devotees, I smiled ruefully to myself. *Christ, this just gets weirder and weirder. I'm standing in a bar that's full of people from a convention. A sort of annual wake for an Olympian who, until Monday, hadn't even died as far as I was concerned. On top of that, I am having a conversation with myself, and I don't mean an "oh bugger me where have I put my mobile?" type of conversation. "I" have just told myself that "I" killed my best friend fifteen years ago, when in fact, I only saw him last Sunday ... alive and well.*

I thought it best not to dwell on all of that. I thought instead about Ben's opinion of Tanner's parents, and the story he had told me earlier about the gym-shoe beating in the conservatory. I remembered the occasion so well. I remembered plenty of other occasions too; when his father, mother, or both, had metaphorically shat on him in front of me.

I thought of one of the occasions. Tanner's eighteenth birthday.

Some kids are given cars for their eighteenth. Some are given signet rings or season tickets to watch the footie. Even parents who can't afford anything flashy make sure their kids know they are loved.

Tanner was given news for his eighteenth birthday. He was told that when he left school the following summer, there would no longer be a room for him at the Hootley family home. His parents expected him to find his own way in the world, and they thought that making him homeless was a good way to go about it.

Along with this news, they gave him a generic card with a picture of two cricketers, a pint of ale, a church, and 'Happy Birthday' printed in gold writing. Twenty pence from the bargain bucket card shop. Tops. If they had signed the inside from 'Mr and Mrs Hootley' it wouldn't have been a surprise. It was shabby and soulless. Even at the age of seventeen, it made me realise what a crap set of parents Tanner had been landed with.

Tanner's birthday is at the back end of September, so it was a couple of weeks before the great race at the water tower. Which meant it would have happened in this world as well. But I wasn't going to mention it. It was my story, and it was Ben's story. It wasn't a story that Jonny Vincent would tell.

It was around then that Tanner and my dad became close. I think Dad felt sorry for the way Tan had been treated by his own family and wanted to teach him the ways of the great Jack Shawcross. In the Westcastle world, this led to Jonny being conned out of his rightful inheritance six months later. It provided Tanner and me with a house each. When I thought about it now, it wasn't surprising that everyone was convinced I was in on the scam.

I looked up to see Ben easing his way through the crowd, back to our corner. His progress was impeded by a group of lads dressed only in speedos, swimming caps, goggles, flip-flops, and shocking pink feather boas. One of the group stood in front of Ben suggestively, and although the lad had his back to me, I could tell by the camp delight on his friends' faces that he was flirting. Outrageous, unsubtle, flirting.

Ben laughed, grabbed both hands of his human blockade, simulated a dance move that twirled the lad around and ensured that Ben was no longer imprisoned by a flock of feather boas. To the delight of his fan club, he left them with a suggestive wiggle of his backside and still laughing, made his way back to me.

'I think I've pulled,' he said, completely unperturbed, and raised his glass towards the group.

I suddenly remembered the Friday before. Similar pub, similar situation. A whole world away – literally. Tanner and I had been out on the town with our football club mates. A group of queeny youngsters were camped out on a neighbouring table and were also enjoying a Friday night on the town. OK, they were loud, but they weren't bothering our group at all.

Except for Tanner. They were offending him by existing.

'Lads! Lads!' Tanner had shouted. 'What is both a fruit and a vegetable?' He then flicked a finger in the direction of the group, to make sure they knew they were being talked about, before hitting all of us with the punch line. 'A homo in a coma!'

I had laughed.

I lurched back into the room when I realised that Ben was staring at me.

'I'm not that homophobic arsehole any more Jonny,' he said.

For a second, I panicked that he had been able to read my thoughts. Then I realised, I'd probably had a strange look on my face. Ben had obviously assumed that I was surprised to see him flirting with a group of people that he wouldn't have pissed on, the last time Jonny had seen him.

I didn't tell him that having a strange look on my face had been my default setting for the last four days.

'I was really pleased that it was you who got in touch,' he continued, '"I really wanted to apologise.'

I decided that the strange look wasn't going to go away anytime soon.

'Apologise?'

'I was such a shit to you.'

'It wasn't really you though, was it?' It was the same thing I'd said to myself on Monday night after Arnie's assassination of Ben's character. It still sounded naff.

Ben came up with the same answer as I had done.

'I was there, I could have stopped it any time I wanted.'

It seemed that although our journeys had been totally different, jail for one of us and reality travelling for the other, we were still the same person and we'd ended up in the same place with the same thoughts.

'I saw a lot of bullying when I was in jail, was on the receiving end of some of it. It was shit.' Ben looked at me apologetically. 'And yet, we did equally bad things to you for years.'

I didn't know what to say. Didn't know what Jonny would have said in the circumstances. I felt like I'd felt on Monday night, when I wished that Jonny had been there to hear Arnie's speech, rather than me. Because of this, I'd started recording a message to Jonny on his phone. I wanted him to know, if we ever managed to get out of this madness, exactly what had gone on in his absence. I especially wanted him to know how Arnie felt about him. I made a mental note to tell him about Ben's apology as well.

For the first time that evening, I wasn't continually playing catch-up with the conversation. I could have talked about the way Ben used to bully Jonny. Easily. The tricky bit was to remember whose side of the tale I was talking about.

I decided that it was better to return to a story where I knew I was all at sea, rather than one where I would have to remember whether I was on the beach or in the ocean.

I made a return trip to the Carmichaeltown of nearly fifteen years ago.

'Surely, the fact that Tanner's parents were inventing all those lies wouldn't have made much difference in the end,' I said reasonably. 'Amy would have backed up your version of events, say that she definitely wasn't having an affair with Tanner, explain how she came to give you the scratches. The Hootleys would need to perjure themselves in court and they still wouldn't have got the outcome they wanted.'

For a moment, the sunny, friendly man who had met me was gone. Ben had been left with scars from that day fifteen years ago, no question. When he spoke again, he talked so softly that his words were in danger of being drowned out by the good people of Carmichaeltown getting hammered on a Friday night.

'The Hootleys knew that too. I think they realised that the best way to persuade the authorities to pursue a murder charge was to paint Amy as a little slapper, who was two-timing her boyfriend with his best friend. They said she'd been playing one off against the other and then crying rape when she got caught out.'

He was getting stewed up talking about it and I wasn't sure it was a good idea to carry on. I said as much, but he shook his head and gave a little laugh.

'I've been counselled to within an inch of my life as you might imagine,' he said. 'But it's really nice to talk to someone who knows her. Knows the real Amy. Not the hard-faced two-timer that the Hootleys were talking about.'

He took a deep breath. 'I knew I had to prepare myself for the fact that the prosecution would give Amy a real grilling. I knew that I had to decide. Admit to murder, or risk seeing Amy destroyed in court.'

I managed some comforting claptrap and he nodded gratefully, then laughed at himself.

'God, I loved that girl.'

You still do, I thought, in a mild state of panic. I wasn't looking forward to the way the conversation might pan out later in the evening.

I know Amy is keen to meet Ben as well. Ten words, tagged on to an email.

Ten words that I wished I'd never written.

To put off the moment when the questions about present-day Amy would arrive, I suggested another drink and made my way to the bar to order them. I avoided the feather boas. Although living with Arnie had quelled some of my more rancid homophobia, I wasn't planning on cosying up with a *Queer as Folk* boxset at the earliest opportunity. I thought that flirting with a group of gay lads, the way Ben had done earlier, was still well beyond my capabilities.

Unfortunately, the thinking time I'd given him had allowed Ben a chance to hit me with an awkward question by the time I returned, drinks in hand.

'What do you remember about that day? The day I killed Tanner.' he asked me as soon as I got back to him. 'I'm not being funny Jonny, but you don't seem to remember much about it at all.'

I didn't answer him straight away. I realised I needed to be very careful. I thought of how they'd been, the Will and Jonny I remembered in Westcastle, before Will had fallen from the water tower.

'I remember it, of course I do, but Will and I were stupidly loved-up.' I argued and pushed my luck a little. 'Even one of our class-mates killing his best friend didn't manage to rock our cosy little world.'

He seemed to accept it, and I was just beginning to relax, when he spoke again. 'And what about afterwards? You don't remember a surprise witness coming forward a few weeks later?'

I had a horrible feeling I was being set up, like a liar in *Law and Order* whose wrongdoing was about to be exposed in court.

I shook my head, but as I did so, I had a nasty thought.

That surprise witness, it hadn't been Jonny, had it?

How the hell would I be able to explain that one away?

And...

If that was the case, what was Ben's motive in leading me on?

I was so busy trying to get my head around that little dilemma that I nearly missed the fact that Ben had started speaking again.

'So, I decided that I wasn't prepared to see Amy chewed up and spat out in court. After all, she was the victim in all of this. I had managed to prevent her being raped by Tanner; I wasn't going to allow her to be metaphorically raped by the prosecution instead. I also wanted to make it as easy as possible for my family. They were already trying to recover from the fact that my Mum's cousin had shot Alec Carmichael, and now they would have to cope with this.'

Ben had just confirmed the thoughts I'd had, after I'd seen Cooper-Wilson on Tuesday, about my mum's cousin Marty. In Westcastle he was the butt of my dad's jokes for being 'one of The Twins'. But here, in Carmichaeltown, he would always be known as the man who murdered Alec Carmichael.

Ben took a large swig from his fresh pint and continued his tale. 'But, on the day I decided to tell my solicitor that I wanted to plead guilty, they had news for me instead. A witness had come forward to back up our story.' Again, I got the impression that Ben was playing with me, especially when he repeated his question from earlier. 'Amy never told you any of this?'

I shook my head and he continued to look surprised. 'It's just … well … it was Elliot.' He paused to let that sink in before explaining his confusion. 'My Mum told me that he and Amy were living next door to you and your boyfriend,' he gave a self-mocking laugh. '. I suppose no one likes being forgotten so completely.'

Especially by Amy. I thought, *it seems to bug you that you've been forgotten by her.*

Rather than commenting on that, I decided to steer the story back to Elliot – the surprise witness.

'So, what had Elliot seen?'

Ben shrugged away the disappointment that he wasn't at the centre of his ex-girlfriend's thoughts, and answered me.

'Elliot had told the police that he had been off games that afternoon. After registration he'd gone to the library to study but found that he couldn't concentrate because he was concerned about Amy.' Ben paused once again. 'I mean that wasn't a surprise. In better days, Tanner and I laughed about the fact that Elliot was head over heels in love with her.'

I remember, I thought, *although Tanner certainly hadn't put it like that.* It hit me once again that Ben now talked like an adult, whereas the language that Tanner and I used hadn't really moved on from the playground.

'He thought that I'd be at football practice, and it would be a good chance to go around to Amy's and check she was OK. But, when he arrived at her house, he knew very quickly that something was wrong. He could hear someone shouting, he realised it was Tanner. Then, he heard Amy start to scream.'

It was beginning to merge into the story he'd told me earlier. The only thing I didn't know, was where Ben had been at this point. I was about to find out.

'Elliot told the police that he was just about to break into the house when he saw that I was coming down the road, so he ran away in the opposite direction.'

'But why didn't he stay to help if he thought that Amy was in trouble?'

'Apparently, he didn't want me to see him there and thought that I'd be the best person to deal with Tanner anyway. He came across as pathetic, but credible.'

I was surprised. OK the Elliot who I'd known in Westcastle might have run away to Australia when his dreams of a future with Amy had blown up in his face, but he'd never come across as pathetic. And the Elliot I'd met in Carmichaeltown had been worried about his wife's ex returning to town, but he hadn't struck me as pathetic either.

'Anyway, whatever his reasoning, it now meant there were three of us who were saying the same thing. Even better for my defence, was the fact that Elliot had no reason to lie. Quite the opposite, in fact. We weren't close friends and he would have had a better chance of a romance with Amy, if I had been arrested for murder. So, why would he say that if it wasn't true? All the evidence they had to support a murder prosecution was circumstantial at best, so they charged me with manslaughter.'

'I don't suppose the Hootleys liked that?' The Giles Hootley I had known hated to lose at anything. He would have been fuming.

'They were livid,' Ben agreed grimly. 'They caused a lot of hell for my parents, practically destroyed my dad's business.' I remembered the unimpressive website that I'd discovered while I was searching for Ben. It seemed that Giles Hootley had been successful. 'They haunted my parents for years,' he shrugged bitterly. 'All legally of course.'

Ben shrugged and gave the Hootleys the heave-ho. 'My sentence was reduced because of the guilty plea and at first I thought it would be manageable.' He shook his head. 'God! Was I wrong or what?' He then gave a strange snorting sound to emphasise the point. 'It took quite some time for Amy's first visiting order to come through. While I was waiting, thinking about Amy was the only thing that kept me halfway sane. I fantasised about the life we would have together once my visit to hell was over. Travelling first, then jobs, a house, a family.'

A thought from Monday afternoon, when I'd walked into Amy's house and pictures of her kids had battered me around the head, came to my mind again.

When we got married, I thought we would have children. I wanted them. I still wanted them. I think Amy wanted them. It's just that it had never happened.

If it all hadn't gone wrong between them, I was sure that this version of Ben would have been a father by now. So, what was my excuse?

I shrugged my own demons away as Ben continued with his tale.

'No one would ever be able to explain how difficult prison visits are, whichever side of the bars you are on.' He shrugged. 'I don't think either Amy or I could really cope with it.'

Although he had said earlier that he had been counselled to within an inch of his life, I wasn't in much doubt that he wanted to use this evening as a bit of a freebie therapy session. *Well,* I thought to myself. *You asked for this. Literally. Deal with it.*

'In spite of everything, she visited me every chance she got, for all the years I was inside,' Ben continued. 'Then, two weeks before I was due to be released, she came to see me as normal. Except it wasn't normal. She was different. Nervous. I knew straight away that something wasn't right. To start with I thought she'd been subjected to one of the occasional bouts of harassment that the Hootleys indulged in. But I was wrong.' He pulled a long gasp of air through his teeth. 'It was then that she told me she'd been having an affair with Elliot for nearly six months.' He gave me a funny little look. 'She said she hadn't told me before, because she didn't want to abandon me until there was a very definite light at the end of the tunnel. But she also didn't want me to leave prison thinking that there was still hope.' He put his glass down onto the scrawny excuse for a shelf and fixed me with a hard stare. 'She made it clear that there was no hope.'

In some ways it had shocked me that Amy could be so cold and clinical about the way she had gone about breaking Ben's heart. But then I remembered something Amy had said to me on Monday.

'Do you ever feel guilty about what we did to Ben later? I suppose that's unfair, it was all my decision, but you were very definite about your views on the subject.'

'I'm sorry.' It wasn't meant to be an apology, just a bit of sympathy for the situation in general, but Ben took it as one.

'Yes, she said that you were, shall we say ... encouraging?'

I knew that by this point in the story Amy and Jonny had been back to being best buddies again, so I couldn't hide behind vagueness. Even so, I didn't plan the next words that came out of my mouth.

'Well can you hardly blame me? You said it yourself earlier, you put me through a lot of shit. Was it a great surprise that I wasn't your biggest fan?'

Ben looked a bit surprised at that, but he wasn't the only one. It was the natural anger behind the words. *Where the hell had that come from?* I thought. Ben dropped his eyes and studied his nails as he spoke.

'No Jonny. No, it's not, and like I said before, I'm really sorry.' He then seemed to remember something else. 'I was also so sorry to hear about that horrible time you had ... you know ... Will and all that.'

Screw me, I thought. *My life is turning into a never-ending quiz show. As soon as I discover the answers to one set of questions, another mystery pops up to bite me on the bum.*

...Will and all that. What did that mean?

I knew there was no way I could get away with being ignorant about that particular tale. So, I simply gave Ben a grateful smile and encouraged him to get back to his own story.

'I was in such a state after Amy had gone. I didn't care what I did. At that moment I didn't mind if I was locked up for the rest of my life. Nothing seemed to have a point.' It sounded a bit over-dramatic in the comfortable setting of a town centre pub at the end of the working week. I had no doubt that in a prison cell, it had seemed like an understandable reaction.

'Billy, my cell-mate, had given me a hard time to start with.' Ben continued. 'But, over time he mellowed. I suppose I stuck up for myself when I needed to and answered the rest of his rubbish with a smile. Even so, I didn't realise what he really thought of me until those last two weeks. He formed an unholy alliance with a prison guard we called Tractor,' he grinned, 'they might have hated each other up to that point, but they joined forces to make sure that there wasn't an hour, night or day, when I could do something to muck up my future. They were good blokes, Billy and Tractor. I owe them a lot.'

I noticed his second pint was going down a lot quicker than the first. I hoped he was good at holding his ale. It would be better if he were sober when I finally got around to asking the question that I knew I had to ask and gave him the information I knew he needed to know.

'I came back to Carmichaeltown when I was first released but my parents decided, very quickly, that I would be better off out of the town. Mum and Dad weren't entirely sure what I'd do if I saw Amy, or Elliot, or even you for that matter.' He gave a funny little grunt, 'And then, there were the Hootleys, who were practically camping in our front garden. I have an aunt, who lives in the North Midlands, she offered to take me in. She and her husband were foster parents and they specialised in helping troubled teens. I was a little bit older than their normal guests, but I was certainly troubled.'

Aunty Nicola and Uncle Mac. Mum's sister and her husband. Doing what they'd always done, in both worlds, it seemed. Helping youngsters rebuild their lives. I was just about to say something about them, when I realised that Jonny wouldn't have had a clue who they were. We both took swigs from our drinks and Ben finished his story.

'Slowly and gradually, they helped me to rebuild my life.' He held out his arms in the style of a karaoke singer who had just finished murdering *I Will Survive.* 'And here I am.'

I decided it was now or never, I took a deep breathe, and launched right in.

'Amy and Elliot,' I said hesitantly. 'They're solid.'

At first, I couldn't quite make out the look on Ben's face. I thought it was anger or disappointment, or possibly confusion. It was only when the peculiar look turned into a belly laugh, that I became really baffled.

'Oh my God! You thought...' he must have then re-run the conversation we had just been having '...of course you did. Oh Jonny! No.'

'No?' I repeated stupidly.

'I've not come back to try and win Amy back, and I certainly don't want my revenge on anyone.'

'You don't?'

Smilingly he shook his head. 'I don't. I have the most fantastic woman in my life. Sarah. She would have come tonight, but she thought it probably better if we met up alone the first time.'

I grinned in relief. 'Mine thought the same.'

Mine?

Ben grinned too, but the grin disappeared quickly. 'You didn't see me when I was in jail. You don't know what I turned into. Amy did. As I said, I was angry at first and some sort of revenge might have been attractive. But, as I slowly adjusted to life as a free man, I began to see things from her point of view. I even reckoned I could pin-point the moment when she stopped loving me.'

By the time he'd explained himself, told me the words he'd said to Amy on an ill-fated visit about two years before the end of his sentence, I could understand it too. It had bothered me that Amy had dumped Ben when he was at his lowest point. A few short sentences had helped me realise how dangerous it was to jump to conclusions when you've only heard half the story.

'So why now? Why have you come back now?'

'Well, Sarah was offered a job in the area and when I checked with the prison service,' he shrugged light-heartedly and explained. 'It's a case of poacher turned gamekeeper. I deal with prisoner rehabilitation. Trying to ensure that young offenders have the best possible opportunities to get on with the rest of their lives. At first, I got into it as a kind of tribute to everyone who had helped me, and then I discovered I loved doing it. Anyway, I found out there were vacancies down here, and the whole idea began to take root.' He scrunched up his face suddenly before continuing. 'The only problem would have been the Hootleys. I didn't want to cause them any undue agony.'

I couldn't stop myself from scoffing. It probably wasn't very Jonny-like, but I couldn't help myself. 'I'm not sure they deserved that, after all they had put you and your family through.'

'But I had been responsible for killing their son. And they truly believed I hadn't been punished enough.' He looked at me and grinned at the look of disbelief on my face. He then held up his hands in submission, taking the mick out of himself. 'OK, I admit it. That wasn't the only reason.' He grinned self-deprecatingly. 'I was being a coward. I just couldn't face the proverbial crap they would be likely to throw my way, and I wasn't sure my parents could put up with any more of it either.'

'So, what changed your mind?'

'We found out that they'd moved to Cornwall, about six months ago. My Mum thought they'd been quiet for a while and, when she checked it out, she discovered they'd gone.'

In my world, the Hootleys had also retired to Cornwall. They'd wanted to be nearer their elder son, who was busy churning out a dynasty and needed help with childcare. But, it had happened ages ago. It had been positive proof, in Tanner's eyes, that he wasn't the favoured one. It seemed that, in Carmichaeltown, the Hootleys had missed over ten years of seeing their grandchildren growing up, simply to get revenge on the Shawcrosses.

It struck me as sad and pointless.

After this, Ben turned the conversation towards Jonny and what he'd been doing. This could well have been tricky, so I concentrated on things that I was confident about. For the first time I was glad that it'd been such an eventful week in Carmichaeltown as it gave me plenty of material. I also talked about my job, and Arnie.

'I'm so glad you found someone wonderful,' Ben said genuinely. It made me realise the amount of time I'd spent rattling on about Arnie's good points.

Steady. I told myself. *It almost sounds like you're falling for him yourself.*

That was a terrifying thought.

After we'd parted at the end of the night, I walked up the hill away from the town centre and realised how much I'd enjoyed the evening. I really liked the Ben Shawcross who'd emerged from the wreckage of that day in December, fifteen years ago. I admitted, to myself, that I liked him much better than the Ben Shawcross I'd left in Westcastle.

I hoped that if … when … Jonny returned, the crowd in Carmichaeltown would invite Ben and Sarah into their lives.

'I'd love to have a second chance with you and Steve … even Elliot,' Ben had laughed at one point towards the end of the evening. 'I buggered it up the first-time round by sticking to the gospel according to Tanner, even when I knew he was wrong. I'd like to have a chance to put it right.' He had sighed reflectively. 'Sarah says there is nothing like the friends that you have known since playschool. She still sees hers regularly, even though they're scattered around the country. I'd like to have a little bit of that for myself.'

He left a little pause to let it sink in. 'I always thought that Amy was the love of my life, but life has a habit of throwing you a curved ball. Now, I have no doubt that Sarah is my soulmate. But, there was always more to me and Amy, we weren't just a couple, we were bloody good friends as well. I'd love to be friends with her again.'

That made me wonder a bit about my own situation. Amy and I had drifted over the years. Was it possible that we were hanging on to something that no longer existed, simply because we were too stubborn to admit that somewhere down the line, we had mucked things up?

Even as the thought hit my brain, I knew it was bollocks. Well, for me at any rate. I'd known from the moment I'd sat in her lounge on Monday afternoon, how much I loved Amy. The world had taken a barmy turn for Ben, and it had led him to Sarah. For me, there was no Sarah, and I didn't want there to be one.

My thoughts turned to Tanner as I wandered back up to Chancelwood Road. I'd discovered what he could be like and what he was capable of. Ben had found it difficult to talk about him.

But, for whatever reason, those awful things hadn't happened back in Westcastle. I knew what a good friend Tanner could be. My relationship with him was going to have to change, it was time for us both to grow up, but I still wanted him in my life.

Finally, as I passed number 32, I thought about Elliot. Pathetic but credible Elliot. That was a load of gumf. I was sure of it. I didn't believe he would have run away because he was scared that Ben would see him. Not where Amy was concerned. He would have stayed and helped Ben. Also, the road where Amy lived was a cul-de-sac, there was no way Ben wouldn't have seen Elliot, not if Elliot had seen Ben. I had got the impression tonight, that Ben hadn't been too convinced by Elliot's story either.

The fact that he'd been in the school library at the time would have helped his lie. You could be in that room for hours at a time, studying in a corner, hidden away by shelf-loads of books. It would have been quite easy to invent an alternative version of the afternoon.

No, I believed that Elliot had heard about the lies the Hootleys were spreading around the town and decided to do something about it.

I could see Elliot's face, just three nights before.

'*I was blagging it, of course, but thankfully the brick shithouse didn't realise that.*'

Elliot Harper was more than happy to tell a pack of lies to help his best friends out of a tight corner, when they were facing Psycho Hulk.

I had no doubt that Elliot Harper would have been quite happy to tell a pack of lies, if it would save the girl he loved going through the trauma of a day in court.

~ 31 ~
JONNY

Westcastle: Fourteen Years Earlier

Jonny stood in the front room of his new home after Amy and her parents left. A suitcase, two holdalls, and a rucksack lay on the carpet, straggled around his feet. He had battered them up the staircase an hour earlier, and they remained there, looking like an entrant for a pretentious art competition.

Mrs Crawford had carried up tea making essentials, and her husband had followed on behind, with an insulated bag containing a vegetarian lasagne for Jonny's supper. Out of sight in the larger of the two bedrooms, Amy had left carrier bags that contained a pump and a blow-up bed. It would provide both Jonny's entertainment for the evening and a place to lay his head afterwards.

The Crawfords had tried to remain positive during the impromptu tea party, but Jonny knew that they were feeling guilty. He knew they wished they could have done more to help him hold on to his family home. He didn't want them to feel guilty. They had at least tried. His uncle had simply told him that he was eighteen now and problems like this were all part of being an adult. A few weeks later, the same man had complained bitterly for the whole of a twenty-five-minute phone call. Apparently, the two per-cent share he had been bequeathed in his brother's will hadn't reaped the financial benefits that he'd been expecting.

But Jonny didn't even blame his uncle for his predicament.

He blamed one person, and one person alone.

Since the day the Thames had been recreated during Jonny's walk of shame, Tanner had increased the pressure on his perennial victim. But it was subtle, more secretive than it had been before. Even Tanner had decided that most people would have baulked at physical violence, so soon after someone had lost their parents and their lover over the course of one horrible month.

However, jokes at Jonny's expense were a different matter. Even Ben had started to laugh at some of them.

Jonny tried to laugh at the jokes himself and told no one, not even Amy, about the campaign that was insidiously growing beyond the school walls.

One night he had woken from a fitful sleep. He could hear noises. It sounded as if huge hailstones were battering against the back door. But the night was clear and stormless. When he investigated, he found a mound of poo bags that had been relocated from the dog bins in Hazelmeare park. They were lying where they had fallen after bouncing against the building.

One morning he had picked up his rucksack. It was still where he had dropped it the night before. It looked exactly as it had the night before. Except, when he opened it to put his homework inside, he discovered his school jumper had been cut into slivers, like woollen spaghetti. How anyone had broken in without disturbing him, Jonny had no idea. It wasn't as if he was sleeping soundly.

A week later he began to worry about sleeping at all. He came downstairs to discover the fridge door open, and a two-litre carton of milk turned turtle on the floor. The cap had been removed so that a lake was created, shimmering white, already beginning to turn rancid on the kitchen linoleum.

During the summer of the untouchables, when it had seemed that everything Jonny wanted was his for the asking, Will had started to plan for Jonny's eighteenth birthday. Every few days there was another hint, another clue as to how Jonny would be made to feel like a Hollywood superstar. But when the December day arrived, there was no big reveal, no massive fuss. Because there was no Will.

When a solitary parcel arrived, along with a few cards from distant relatives, Jonny thought it was from Amy. He knew she was feeling guilty about abandoning him on his special day. He didn't want her to feel bad. He understood there was a birthday weekend for her boyfriend that needed arranging at the Shawcross's house. It was his own choice that he had refused every invitation to the party. Even though she had given him a sack full of presents the day before, he thought she had sent him something extra, just to ensure he knew she was thinking about him.

When he unwrapped the packaging, he was surprised to find a margarine container hidden beneath the wrapping. He should have realised that Amy would have never wrapped anything so shoddily, but almost without thinking, he shook the lid from the box.

It wasn't from Amy.

Lying on a bed of toilet paper, was a dead snake.

Back in primary school, Jonny had let it slip that he hated snakes. The morning afterwards *The Ladybird Book of Reptiles* had been left on his desk, opened at the page that described a boa constrictor. There was a full page colour photo on the opposite sheet. Jonny had screamed and burst into tears. Tanner had tormented him about snakes ever since.

A day of silence and a dead snake led to the night of vodka, razor blades and the wish he could have been braver.

The night-time visitations continued up until Christmas. He changed the locks on all the doors, and he barely slept, but he still came down to unpleasant presents and silent vandalism.

The Crawfords were determined that Jonny would have a family Christmas at least. They moved him in on Christmas Eve and ignored all his protests. He ended up staying the week. Amy's sisters and their families arrived and for a while Jonny was caught up in their mad good humour and was able to escape from his life. Even when Ben came around, after his own Christmas dinner at home, he was on his best behaviour. Jonny remembered the thoughtful, caring lad around the time of Will's funeral. He thought that if things had been different, had one person in Ben's life been different, they could have become friends.

But Christmas was merely an oasis of calm between two storms.

The texts started arriving on the second day of the new year.

What's the difference between a florist's ball of string and Will Flanagan?

One ties up a flower, the other flies from a tower.

A few days later.

What is the difference between Will Flanagan and a gay castaway shipwrecked with his straight mate?
One is fucked and the other ends up with a broken nose.
A day after that.
What is the difference between a cheque and Will Flanagan?
Cheques bounce.
Jonny changed his number. He only gave his new one to Amy on strict instructions that she wasn't to share it.

'I've been getting lots of unwanted cold calls,' was all he would tell her.

So, the letters started arriving. The 'jokes' were the same and occasionally there would be a suggestion that Jonny would be better off living somewhere else.

It was at that point a solicitor acting under instructions from Jack Shawcross started to make offers to buy both properties from Jonny.

Jonny was pretty sure that neither Mr Shawcross or the solicitor knew about the vandalism, the texts, or the letters. They were simply preying on a young innocent who'd had to grow up too fast and wasn't capable of doing so. When details of the sale and the properties involved became public knowledge, Amy asked her parents to speak to Jack Shawcross.

She might as well have asked an antelope to persuade a lion not to eat its babies.

Jonny didn't blame Jack Shawcross; he didn't blame the solicitor. Jonny had realised he was being conned, but he just wanted it all to be over. He knew that Tanner wouldn't stop until he had won.

So, Jonny let him win.

There was another overriding thought as well. Everything in the house shouted 'Will!' at him. When he looked at the sofa in the living room he could see Will. He was talking politics with Jonny's father or calmly not answering an embarrassing question about which member of Girls Aloud he fancied. All the while, Jonny could see that his face was alert, waiting for the moment that the Vincents would swan off down to the golf club and leave the two of them, alone in paradise.

Every time he went into the kitchen, he could see Will at the sink downing a glass full of water after jogging around to see Jonny. He used to slurp the drink so quickly that half of the liquid would miss his mouth and run down onto his T-shirt making it see through, accentuating his taut nipples. The cheeky grin on Will's face made sure that Jonny was aware that it wasn't entirely an accident.

Each time he went to climb the staircase he was reminded of the way Will would stop four steps from the bottom and launch his body downwards, landing on the carpet like a triple jumper landing in the sand pit.

And Jonny thought. *Please God, don't even let me think about upstairs.*

As he stood in the lounge area of his clean slate of a new start, he thought about the future for the first time in months. A house clearance and a few sales courtesy of the wanted ads in the local paper had given him enough money to start again. The white goods were coming the next day. The day after that the Crawfords were taking him to the nearest Swedish superstore, where he could acquire a future in flatpack.

Jonny stopped going to school.

Amy and he had worked at a bookshop every Saturday since they were sixteen. Jonny had managed to persuade the owners that they were in desperate need of a trainee manager. He started working there fulltime, the Monday after he'd moved into the flat.

He managed, mostly, to erase Tanner from his life. Although he could have easily found out Jonny's new address, Tanner didn't bother. He had got what he wanted and was more than happy to move on to another easy target to get his kicks. Occasionally, Jonny would bump into Tanner in town; he was normally with Ben. They would still make a puerile joke at Jonny's expense, but it no longer had the power to hurt him.

Jonny's life remained that way for the next fourteen years. He wasn't happy or unhappy. He enjoyed his job. He could talk to people about books all day. He could escape his own life to live vicariously through a hero in Times New Roman font.

He had a few love affairs, but at best they were just extenuated versions of one-night stands.

To a man, they were all lovely. There was only one thing that was truly wrong with any of them.

They weren't Will.

~ 32 ~
BUTTERFIES

Westcastle: Jonny

As I walked down into town, I felt a flutter of nerves. Ever since I'd met Arnie for lunch on the Wednesday before, I'd been working on my plan for the evening ahead. It had seemed obvious when I'd first thought of it, and I'd spent a lot of time imagining every eventuality. I just hoped it would turn out the way I wanted it to.

Amy had expected another weekend of neglect, so she'd made plans to have a night out on the town with Jonny on the Saturday night. She was going to cancel, but I managed to persuade her that it would be a good idea to go ahead with it. Five minutes after she had pulled on her longline padded coat and left the house, leaving a hint of Marc Jacobs' Daisy in the hallway, I had grabbed my own coat and followed her footsteps into town.

Things had settled down somewhat after the harem scarem of throwing my 'father' out of the house on Tuesday night. Tanner continued to seethe. He mainly seethed in the style of a stroppy teenager, but alternated it with warnings about what would happen if I continued to put 'dates before mates.' I veered between avoiding him as much as I could, setting my internal volume controls to zero when avoidance wasn't possible, and muttering vague placatory nothingness if things became desperate.

I didn't destroy their friendship irreparably, but the changes in the Hootley/Shawcross relationship had been noticed at the office. Tanner had made a lot of vulgar comments about it. People were talking to me, and I got the impression that it was an unusual occurrence. I was beginning to be included in little pieces of gossip that were floating around. It was during one such reveal that the good-looking secretary, who Arnie had taken to lunch, mentioned Cameron and his prison sentence for drug running.

It almost made me feel happy that he'd wheedled the thousand pounds out of me.

Without doubt the biggest change that had occurred, during the five days I'd been visiting Westcastle, was with Amy. My friend had been restored to her full, glorious, technicolour self. We hadn't done much. On Wednesday and Thursday, we'd stayed in and watched box sets. On Friday, we'd gone out for a few drinks and an Indian meal. But we'd laughed. We'd laughed so much that I had seen Amy transform into the girl I'd left in Carmichaeltown. The change was so acute that I worried I would suddenly start talking about Arnie, or Elliot, or ask her what nonsense one of the boys had been up to that day.

I saw Arnie as soon as I arrived at the pub. This was unusual. The Icelandic love of my life had never been known for his timekeeping. Did this mean he was keen, excited about the evening in store? I said another little prayer that the night would turn out the way I'd planned. I stood in the doorway for a second while I waited for a woman, with a feathered grey pixie haircut, to shrug on her coat. She was taking her time and her friends, who were already out on the street, were launching cheerful insults in her direction.

This gave me a chance to stare at Arnie, unobserved. I never got tired of looking at him. Even from my position in the doorway I could see his eyes darting this way and that, scanning the pub. Always alive for a quirky piece of information he would be able to exaggerate, later in the evening.

It was during the second scanning of the surrounding area that he noticed me, just as Pixie Cut had finally managed to sort herself out, and I was able to enter the pub. His face morphed into a genuine smile of welcome.

Oh my God! I loved him so much.

Amy and I had made love every night since Tuesday. The ease with which I'd fallen into Ben's role had made me question whether I was a gay man at all. The strange feelings I felt as I watched Arnie from the pub doorway; heart racing, legs shaking, breathlessness in my chest, and butterflies in my stomach. All those things told me the truth. The fact that Amy and I had always shared a special relationship had made the lie easy to live with. But it was a lie. I had no doubt that had I been straight, Amy would have been the woman I wanted to spend my life with. But I wasn't. For the hundredth time since Wednesday, I sent up a silent prayer that my plan would work. I pushed the door closed behind Pixie Cut and walked towards Arnie.

'I feel scammed!' he laughed as I went up to greet him. He nodded to a poster stuck on the wall behind the bar. 'No Dusty, she's not here until next Saturday.' He clutched his hand to his heart. 'I'm devastated. I'm not sure I'll get over it.'

He didn't look devastated.

I was a bit relieved. When I wafted the temptation of an evening with the Dusty tribute act under Arnie's eyes, it was out of desperation. I had no idea whether she existed in this world, let alone whether she was still doing evenings at the King John. To be honest, after the experience with the disappearing French café in the city, I wasn't even sure that the King John was still trading under that name. The fact that she was, it was, and I was only a week out with the dates, made the invitation seem more genuine.

I wasn't sure why that mattered so much.

We fell into conversation easily, as we had done on Wednesday lunch time. I became engrossed in a story about a one-night stand. It had happened in the last four years, so it wasn't a story I knew. Arnie was retelling the tale with his usual self-deprecation. I could also tell that he was changing some of the facts, slightly, so he could make them fit in with the punch line.

Truth is important in history books. A good story is important for a night out at the pub. It was one of his favourite sayings.

I was so caught up, listening to Arnie's tales, that I nearly missed the sounds emanating from a pocket in my jeans. I had a message.

'I'm sorry,' I held the offending phone in the air. 'Do you mind if I get this?' Almost at the same time as he started to shake his head, I began to back away. 'Don't go away, I'll be right back.'

I disappeared around the corner, into a quiet enclave at the back of the pub. I was very aware of how different it was to the corresponding Saturday night, back at home. The pub would be heaving. Alec Carmichael had had the good sense to have a birthday in the middle of January. This meant that when the hospitality trade invented a week in his honour, they could justifiably do it during one of their quietest periods. Without Alec Carmichael's unfortunate demise, the King John in Westcastle was in the middle of its post-festive season slump.

I squatted on a chair behind a pillar and stared at my phone; just in case Arnie could see me. I didn't need to look at the screen. I knew the message would be blank.

On cue, the door opened, and Amy entered the pub with Jonny a few paces behind. They made their way to the bar, on the other side of Arnie. Just as I could see that Jonny was offering Amy a drink, I pressed the icon on my phone that had Amy's face on it. My 'wife' answered her phone and made similar gestures to Jonny as I had made to Arnie, a few minutes before.

'OK Cupid,' I said as she joined me behind the pillar. 'Ready for the next part of the plan?'

Amy grinned wickedly and nodded. 'Uhh huh. I go back to Jonny and tell him that you've left your bank card at home. You want me to meet you at the bank, so you can withdraw some money on my card. I then ask the man next to him if he'd mind keeping my friend company for ten min...' She broke off as some movement at the bar distracted her '...strike that! We may not need your ridiculously contrived plan after all.'

I poked my tongue out at her but conceded that she may well be right. I had also seen the latest action at the bar. Jonny had been waiting patiently for a mini rush to die down and he was next in line to be served. In a reconstruction of the previous Sunday in Carmichaeltown, which was so accurate it took my breath away, a man with inflated self-esteem – and no visible manners – had barged his ego in front of Jonny. He was already holding up his hand in the direction of the next available server.

Predictably Jonny had done nothing to stop him. However, unlike the Sunday before, Arnie was in the perfect position to object on Jonny's behalf. I watched as he did so in his normal good-natured way. The Ego looked tempted to bully Arnie as well but decided, quite accurately, that Arnie was not a man to be bullied.

He backed down.

Now, I've never been any good at lip-reading, but it turned out that Amy could have worked for the secret services, and she kept me up to speed with a running commentary.

'Jonny's thanked him and offered him a drink.'

'They're talking about what they do for a living.'

'Your mate has just asked Jonny what has happened to the woman he came in with.'

And then.

'Ooh 'er, we've been rumbled. Jonny has mentioned my name and your mate Arnie has mentioned you.' She then grinned delightedly. 'Jonny's just said: "I think we've been set up" and explained why.'

'And...?' I started to prompt her in false irritation, but stopped almost immediately, as the two men clinked glasses and laughed.

Even I could work out that it was going well.

Not that I had ever doubted it. After all, the combination had been tried and tested in another reality.

It had only taken about fifteen minutes, after my lunch date on Wednesday, for me to work out that my original plan was never going to work. For a start, I knew Arnie's views on extra-marital relationships were inflexible and he wasn't the type of man you could coerce into doing something out of character. Also, I knew I couldn't do it to Amy. I had criticised Ben all week for neglecting her and yet I was contemplating a homosexual affair with Arnie, while pretending to be her husband. It certainly wouldn't qualify as the unconditional love that I knew she deserved. No, the thing I wanted to do was get back to my Arnie. However, I couldn't ignore the chance of making sure that Arnie and Jonny met in this world as well. No one knew better than me, now, that they were made for each other. I'd been sure that all I needed to do was make sure they met. That couldn't be called messing about with history. They may well have met anyway. I was simply making sure of it. Wasn't I?

I would have been happy to leave at that moment. I didn't want to risk meeting my alter ego. I still hadn't found out any information to let me know whether that was a good idea or not. However, Amy, bless her gorgeous soul, wanted to make sure that her friend was alright. So, we loitered behind the pillar for another half an hour until she was satisfied.

Have you ever seen yourself on film? Everyone always says it's a weird experience. Well, seeing your alter-ego in real life is one step stranger still. For a start, Jonny was better looking than I'd ever believed myself to be. Also, I always expected people to find me weedy and pathetic, a bit of a soft touch. Looking at Jonny chatting to Arnie, laughing and flirting in a strangely genuine way, I saw the man that my best friends saw. The man they were always encouraging me to see.

I knew I had to harden my heart a little against the people who still took advantage, or called me 'Rubber Jonny' and teased me for being the easy target that I was. The people who didn't know the real Jonny Vincent. But spending five days in another man's skin had taught me something. I had seen how the people at work treated Tanner and Ben, compared to how they treated me. It encouraged me to believe that I was all right. And possibly that was the only lesson I really needed to learn.

'Well, little Mr Matchmaker,' Amy teased after we'd escaped from the pub without being seen. We headed back up the hill towards Chancelwood Road. She linked her arm with mine and lent on my shoulder, gazing up at me fondly. 'When the hell did you turn into a one-man lonely-hearts club agency? How did you know they would get on so well?'

'Oh, they reminded me of two people I used to know...'

'Not from the football club surely? Tanner would go into anaphylactic shock if he thought there were two homosexuals on his team.'

I laughed back at her and shook my head. 'No.' Then, as had been happening quite a lot this week, I said something that hadn't occurred to me before. However, this time I didn't think that Ben had anything to do with it.

'Arnie reminds me of Will.'

Amy looked at me strangely. It could have been that Amy didn't expect Ben to talk about Will like that, after all they had never been particularly close friends. Or it could have been that she didn't expect her husband to be quite so intuitive.

But, I suddenly realised, it was true. He had the same cocktail of self-deprecation and swagger, the same wicked sense of humour, the same brave heart and unswerving loyalty towards lovers and friends.

There was only one difference. Arnie had never, in the four years I'd known him, been cruel. And Will, at times, had been.

I remembered Arnie saying to me one night, when we were talking about what had happened in the dreadful months after Tanner's death.

'What Will did to you. That was cruel.'

~ 33 ~
A NON-LEAVING LEAVING DO

Carmichaeltown Ben

It had been after I'd said goodnight to Kerie, in the office on Friday evening, that I'd first had the idea. It was the realisation that although she thought she was saying goodbye to me for the weekend, it was my intention that I would never see her again.

And I liked her.

I should have organised a leaving party, I thought, then taunted myself. *I mean, you can't have a leaving party for someone who isn't leaving, can you?*

Nobhead.

But, I would have liked it.

The thought was wiped from my brain by Cameron arriving at my desk. I hadn't said a word to him since I'd left him shell-shocked, with his gob wide open, in the meeting room the day before.

'How did you know?' His manner was both flirtatious and surprised, as if he was amazed that Jonny Vincent would have the nous to work it out.

'What?' I asked. 'About your situation, you mean?'

He nodded. 'I've been thinking. You were right; you saved me from a bag load of shite.' He lowered his eyelashes in a way that he hoped was alluring.

Wrong sucker sunshine.

But it seemed that for once, he wasn't trying to flirt his way out of trouble.

'I've been a bit of a douchebag to you ... and ... well...'

Elton John obviously wasn't the only person who found that sorry was the hardest word to say.

Instead of putting himself through the trauma of an apology, he cut straight to the explanation. 'I've transferred some money into your bank account, fifty a month OK?'

I nodded and managed to mumble an agreement. 'Fifty a month.'

'You were also right about the fact that I can forego one shirt a month without it killing me.' He then wrinkled his nose in distaste. 'But please Jonny; get that lovely boyfriend of yours to treat you to some lessons in twenty-first century fashion.' He then snorted his exit line as he flounced away. 'Urban Dross indeed.'

I was so flushed with my success that, as I took the lift down to the reception area, I set my sights on the other member of RD Eversen's staff who had been taking liberties with Jonny's good nature. It didn't hurt that I was narked with her on my own behalf as well. After all, Gemma's gossiping had been responsible for sending Cooper-Wilson around to my door on Thursday night.

'Thanks for that Gemma.' I had caught up with her in the atrium as she was intent on making her normal speedy exit.

She blinked her beautifully applied eye lash extensions at me.

'Excuse me?' she said, as if she couldn't believe that I was talking to her.

'For sending that idiot around to my door last night.' She still looked surprised, although it might have been the amount of foundation she'd applied. Her features seemed to have been trapped in a cosmetic prison. 'I really don't appreciate being gossiped about to strangers.'

Now she was genuinely surprised, and it was nothing to do with any beauty treatment. Her look of shock practically screamed: 'Jonny Vincent does not talk to me like that.'

Well, sorry love – this one does. And I hadn't finished.

'It would be a real shame if the CEO got to hear that one of his candidates for the personal secretary vacancy borrows money she can't be bothered to pay back.' I looked at her knowingly. 'Especially when you're so close to being offered it.'

Now you can really tell people that Jonny Vincent has had a character transformation. I thought.

I realised that I was being hypocritical. Attacking Gemma for gossiping about me and then using rumours I'd heard, about her, to ram my point home. I guessed there were just some aspects of office gossip that I quite liked.

As much as Gemma might have been staggered by the character transformation in Jonny Vincent, I thought that it was a little bit of a character transformation for Ben Shawcross as well. I thought back to earlier in the week. I had arrived in Carmichaeltown and mocked Jonny for being wet and a bit pathetic. What about myself? I had let Tanner, and my dad, control my every move lately. I'd allowed them to let me think that my wife was no longer important.

And that was unforgivable.

It seemed that sorting out someone else's life, was so much easier than sorting out your own.

It wasn't until I was lying in bed, on Saturday morning, that I thought about the idea of a leaving party again. It was something that Ben had said, the night before, about the aftermath of the shit show of their youth.

'That horrible time you had ... you know ... Will and all that.'

What had happened to the Carmichaeltown version of Will? If I didn't find out about it this weekend, then I wouldn't ever know. And I wanted to know. I thought that a dinner party might be a good way to get people to talk at last.

I didn't invite Kerie and her husband – it wasn't that I didn't want them there – it was more for them, to be honest. There are few things worse at a dinner party, than to be stuck with a crowd of people who have a shared history and won't stop banging on about it. And it was the shared history that I wanted everyone to bang on about.

Two quick texts and fifteen minutes for both households to sort out last minute babysitters, and it was sorted.

It was then that I had a horrible thought. At some point during the week, I'd found out that Arnie was quite happy to do the day-to-day cooking if Jonny dealt with all the 'poncy stuff'.

That's OK, I'd thought at the time. *We won't be having any poncy stuff this week.*

I'd just invited Amy, Elliot, Steve, and Lottie to a dinner party.

With Jonny's reputation, they would be expecting poncy stuff.

I didn't cook. No. That makes it sound like I had a choice. I can't cook. I once redecorated the microwave because I failed to read the instructions on how to reheat a supermarket meal for one.

I decided that an Indian takeaway would be the safest option. It wasn't very Jonny-like but it was better than a Sunday morning visit to A&E for everyone.

As it happened, no one was bothered about the lack of showstopper delights. My dad would have gone loopy if he thought that someone was cutting corners after inviting him to dinner. Jonny's friends, my friends, didn't care.

When I'd first invited them, I wondered if they'd be surprised that I'd suggested another party. After all, they'd only met up the week before at Amy and Elliot's. As soon as they'd arrived and I'd offered them drinks, poppadoms and chutneys, I realised why that wasn't the case. They were dying to hear about my night out with Ben, and had assumed that I was dying to tell them.

Elliot was hiding it well, but I could almost read the question that was banging at his brain. Was Ben intent on making trouble for him? When I reached the part of the story where Ben's wife Sarah was mentioned, I could almost see the breath of relief escaping from his mouth.

And Amy? She looked pleased, genuinely pleased, that her ex had managed to find himself a new life. I studied her face. There was no jealousy, and no what ifs. She knew that she was spending her life with the man she loved.

I wasn't quite sure how I felt about that. I just knew that I had to get back to Westcastle and prove to the Amy that lived there, that Ben Shawcross was the right man for her.

The debris of the Indian dinner was spread around the table. Empty bottles fought beer cans for a spare space, and I could imagine my neat-freak alter-ego feeling the need to rush and find a bin bag. In fact, I felt uncharacteristically in the need of a tidy up myself. So, with my ears ringing to the sound of good-natured teasing, I went to do just that.

By the time I'd returned to the party, everyone was involved in Arnie's deliberately exaggerated retelling of his fight in the back alley with Chance's mates. The atmosphere was relaxed and amused. The room was alive with friendly banter. I decided that it was a good time to try and uncover the truth about Will.

I used the things that I'd learnt since I landed in Carmichaeltown, combined with one or two guesses. I just hoped that it sounded as believable in reality, as it had done in my head.

'Talking to Ben last night got me thinking,' I began, 'I know that we never talk about what happened to Will,' I kept my wording vague. This was mainly because I didn't have a scooby what I was talking about, and I was trying to prove to my guests that I did. 'I know you're all trying to protect me, but ... I'm a big boy now...' I grinned. 'I want to know. How did you all feel about Will at the time?'

There was only a slight pause before Amy said, in a tone that made me think she had thought about this a lot over the years, 'I was furious with him.' She shook her head and tore off a stray bit of naan before wiping it around her plate absent-mindedly. I got the impression that there was something she wasn't saying.

'I think it was different for me,' Lottie said. 'I was a year younger, and you lot seemed especially exotic at the time.' She laughed. 'My friends were so impressed that I'd managed to grab myself an older man,' she squeezed Steve's hand affectionately, 'but I didn't feel quite so involved.'

'I was relieved when Will first arrived.' Steve said suddenly. 'I know that both Elliot and I felt a little guilty over the way we'd treated you,' he looked across at me apologetically and Elliot nodded his agreement. 'You were our friend. We were quite aware of how that little termite was torturing you, but we did nothing. Then Will took you under his wing.' He sighed sadly. 'It was the perfect get-out clause for us.'

Elliot nodded in agreement. 'Then, after that stupid race,' he added – taking over the commentary duties from his best mate – 'Steve and I concentrated on our microlight 'plane and kept our heads down.'

'You never got that thing to fly, did you?' Lottie teased her husband.

'We did!' Steve replied in good natured outrage before admitting sheepishly, 'well, for about fifteen seconds anyway.'

I was just wondering how to get the subject back on track without sounding too obvious, when Lottie did it for me.

'I remember all the girls in my year thought that Will was wonderful.' Again, there was a tone of good-natured taunting in her voice. Both Elliot and her husband gurned rudely in her direction. She gleefully ignored them. 'For a start he was gorgeous, and of course, completely unattainable. We'd never met anyone like him before.'

'Do you mind?' Arnie laughed supportively. 'I've seen photographs. Jonny was gorgeous and unattainable as well.'

'Yes, he was,' Lottie said slowly, 'but he was also...' she glanced over at me, '...I'm sorry Jonny, but you always seemed embarrassed to be gay. We all thought you were a bit of a saddo...' I nodded to say there was no offence taken. Lottie smiled in relief and continued. 'Will was different. He loved being gay. He didn't just accept it. He was proud of it. To us, he was sex on legs anyway. That confidence and the unattainable thing made him about ten times more attractive.'

It was all interesting but not going in the direction I wanted. I'd just decided that I wasn't going to find out what had happened to Will, when Amy spoke.

'I'd screamed at Will, the day before it happened.'

Nobody spoke. But everybody looked at Amy except for Elliot. He brushed his hand down her arm as a gesture of support. He knew what she was going to say.

'I know we've never spoken about this, and I've always assumed that Will hadn't told you about it, because you've never once brought it up.' A few years ago, when my wife was still bothered about me, I reckoned Amy could get me to admit anything with just a stare. She fixed those eyes on me at that moment. They still had the same effect. The only problem was, I didn't have a clue what the truth was. I decided to smile at her gently, in the hope that it would encourage her to continue.

Luckily, it did.

'Tanner Hootley was evil.' Amy changed track slightly and I suddenly realised why I hadn't heard my old friend mentioned by name during the whole of my visit to Carmichaeltown. The warm atmosphere around the table plunged somewhere towards the Arctic. Everyone visibly stiffened, just at the mention of his name. I had a brief splurge of sympathy towards him. Then immediately remembered what he had done to deserve this reception. He might have died, but in everyone's opinion, he died as a rapist. There was no sympathy for him here.

I zoned back into the familiar sound of Amy's voice. 'I never liked him. I hated the way he treated you,' she glanced towards me and smiled. 'Well, you know that. Do you remember all the arguments I had with Ben about Tanner?' I nodded. 'It was about the only time we disagreed.' It might have only been faint, but I was sure I saw Elliot stiffen slightly. *Elliot will always feel slightly on edge whenever Ben's mentioned, especially now, when he's likely to be around more often,* I thought.

'When Will arrived, fell in love with you and stood up to Tanner, it was as much as I could do to stop myself from standing up and cheering. I thought he was wonderful too.' Amy glanced over towards Lottie, who smiled back at her. 'But then, he and Tanner had that stupid race at the water tower and Will won.' She stopped suddenly, which put an emphasis on the words that followed. 'That should have been enough. Tanner's influence was over. No one was following him anymore. I could tell that even Ben was becoming a bit embarrassed by him. We could have had a wonderful final year at school. But Will couldn't stop, could he?'

'He was doing it for me.' Once again, I had that strange feeling that Jonny was speaking for me.

Amy sighed. 'I know lovely boy. But he didn't need to, did he? You wouldn't have cared if Will had ignored Tanner for the rest of his life.' She smiled knowingly. 'You wouldn't have cared if Will had ignored everybody for the rest of his life. Just so long as he hadn't ignored you.'

I glanced towards Arnie, who reached out to hold my hand. I let him. Unlike Elliot, there was no tension on his face when a previous lover was mentioned. He simply wanted to support Jonny. He wasn't scared by all the talk of an ex.

'What he did to Tanner afterwards,' Once again she paused to give more power to the words that followed. 'That was bullying too. I know everyone thought that it was justified, but it was still bullying.'

'You're right,' Steve agreed, 'I know that's why Elliot and I kept out of it.' He looked at his friend who nodded. 'Tanner was an arrogant twat, who was also a trainee sociopath. There was no way he was going to accept what was going on, but he didn't have the intelligence or maturity to know how to deal with it.'

'And we all know how he chose to deal with it.' Elliot glanced at his wife and a sympathetic murmur rumbled around the table.

Amy shrugged to say that it was in the past. That might well have been true, but I could tell that it would never go away completely.

'I was so busy supporting Ben that I didn't see much of you, or Will, in the year after it happened. I was cross with the both of you, if I'm honest.' She smiled sadly at me before continuing. 'Then, one day I bumped into Will in the street. For once you weren't joined at the hip. I think you might have been having a tricky phone call to your parents in Spain...'

Amy paused and re-tracked slightly. 'The day before, I'd been to see Ben in jail. It was the first visiting order I'd managed to wangle, and I'd been so looking forward to seeing him.' She sighed. 'The whole meeting turned into a nightmare. Ben was having a lot of difficulties adjusting to life inside. I saw bruises on the inside of his arm, and it was obvious from the way he was moving that there were injuries I couldn't see.'

There was complete silence in the room. The play-list that Arnie had set up on the computer had reached its end, but no one was thinking about listening to music.

'It was the look on his face that really shocked me. Ben had always been very anti-drugs, but I could almost believe he had started taking them. He looked completely spaced out. And his attitude,' she paused to take a sip of wine, 'The Ben I remembered was positive, always looking on the bright side. That day, the bright side seemed to have been beaten out of him.'

'That must have been rough.' Arnie said sympathetically.

Amy nodded. 'So, when I saw Will the next day, I couldn't stop myself. I was screaming random stuff at him, I have no idea exactly what I said but I do remember saying before I stormed off: "One lad is dead, and another is in bits. How can you live with yourself?"'

Amy looked at me again. This time her eyes were full of sadness.

'I never saw him again.'

~ 34 ~
AFTER THE MIDNIGHT DANCES

Carmichaeltown: Fourteen Years Earlier

As Jonny followed Will up the track to the water tower, his brain was tormenting him with a playlist of happy memories. The torchlit summer nights. The victory parade on that October day when everything had seemed possible. The autumn walks that followed, their bodies now encased in thick jumpers and sensible shoes, wrapping their hands around each other for warmth in preference to an antisocial glove. 'The King is dead! Love live the King!' Will had shouted every time they passed the scene of his triumph.

It had all started to change on that anonymous Monday in December.

Jonny hadn't noticed it at first. He couldn't be hypocritical enough to grieve for Tanner. He had some sympathy for Ben, but his skin still remembered the bruises and the burns. It was difficult to feel more than a passing wave of sadness.

His heart hadn't even ached for Amy at first. He had just felt relief. The King really was dead. His thoughts were so full of Will, he was unable to find space for her in his brain.

For years afterwards, his forehead would furrow into an automatic frown every time he thought of the way he'd abandoned her. Amy, who had stuck by him for the entirety of his life, had been attacked. Her boyfriend, almost certainly, would be sent away from her. For the first time in their lives, she needed Jonny to be the strong one; she needed a best friend to turn to and he had turned away.

When he finally thought about her, when his heart finally ached for her – she wasn't interested. Too little, too late. That was what her disappearing back seemed to be telling him. He had tried to approach her one day after the Silent Nights and Auld Lang

Synes had faded for another year. She pretended she hadn't heard him calling her name in the corridor.

School became a necessary torture for Amy. She attended the classes. She handed in her work. She did not socialise. She did not volunteer. Her teachers would sigh at one another when her name was mentioned in the staffroom. They offered support but weren't overly surprised when it was met with a polite refusal. Amy dealt with it in her own way.

She disappeared from Jonny's life.

Later, when the newly named Carmichaeltown was experiencing the false dawn of a warm April, Jonny discovered the truth about Will. His wonderful, strong, charismatic boyfriend was hiding a secret.

Jonny's driving lesson had been cancelled because his instructor had been suffering from the unseasonable weather. The man's hay fever had arrived before he'd stocked up with antihistamines. He felt he couldn't control his sneezing and the dual control pedal, at the same time.

Jonny did what Jonny always did when he had a free moment. He popped around to see Will. Mrs Flanagan was on the way out when she answered the ring of the doorbell. She smiled at Jonny and said over her shoulder as she disappeared down the garden path: 'Go straight up love, I haven't seen the hermit yet today. Force him out of bed if you have to.'

At first, Jonny thought that Mrs Flanagan was right and Will was having an uncharacteristically long lie in. The curtains were closed, and the lump covered by a summer duvet wasn't moving. Jonny was just about to dive onto the bed and wake his boyfriend with kisses, when he heard the most unexpected sound.

Will was crying.

'Oh my God, Will, what's the matter?'

The figure in the bed, moved suddenly and sat up. He searched his brain for an excuse, and he arrived at an unexpected realisation. He didn't want to find one. He wanted Jonny to know.

'Oh J. What have I done?'

For a moment Jonny thought that Will was just about to admit to having had an affair. With the onset of an early summer, Jonny had wanted to start their midnight dances again, but Will had put him off on several occasions. Was he about to be told of a secret lover?

But Jonny didn't have a love rival.

'Amy nearly got raped because of me. Ben will go to jail, because of me.' The words were flat and monotone, devoid of any expression. Devoid of anything that Jonny associated with his much-loved friend. 'Tanner is dead because of me.'

'Don't be daft...'

'It's not daft. It's the truth.'

'Well even if it is, Tanner's not much of a loss to humanity, is he?' Jonny regretted the words as soon as he'd said them. But it didn't matter. Will wasn't listening.

'I could have left well alone J.' Jonny had been hurt many times before. The look in Will's eyes on that April morning injured him more than any beating that Tanner had given him. 'Why didn't I let him get on with his pathetic little life?'

Jonny didn't know what to say, but he did know that it was time for him to step up. Brave, adorable Will was struggling. Like Amy he'd always been the strong one in their relationship. He'd been there at one of the lowest moments in Jonny's life. Jonny had let Amy down; he realised that now. He didn't want to let Will down as well. He wanted to be there for him.

He tried. For three months of a summer that had faded into a dreary anti-climax, once the early promise of April had melted into a miserable May, he tried every method at his disposal. By turns, he listened, cajoled, sympathised, and listened some more. There were times he simply held Will in the hope that he could squeeze the hurt away.

No one else knew about the struggles that Will was going through. His brave face fooled everyone. His family, friends, and the teachers at school knew nothing of his inner torment. Jonny knew that he should get help. He might have approached someone to get it, but for two things. First, Will made him swear that he would keep it between the two of them and second, Jonny liked the fact that it was just between the two of them.

However, on the muggy and murky August morning when he was following Will up to the water tower, Jonny was regretting that decision.

When he had met up with Will the night before, Jonny's head had been swimming from a particularly arduous phone call to his parents in Spain. They hadn't been the least bit worried that they'd abandoned him for a new life in the sun without leaving the smallest hint on maintenance issues in two houses. They had left no numbers, no contacts, and didn't seem to care that the bulb in the hallway blew every time he switched on the light in the bathroom. They were full of much more important news; they had found a 'darling' local bar that served jugs of sangria for two euros each.

The look on Will's face dismissed the memory of the conversation from his mind.

'What is it Will?' He asked.

Will didn't answer him directly. He asked Jonny a question instead.

'Would you come flying with me J?'

The question sounded innocuous enough. He could have been inviting Jonny on a romantic weekend in Paris, a city break to Budapest, or a four-day trance-fest around the Ibizan nightlife.

But Jonny knew that there was no airport involved in the flight that Will was talking about.

And there was no return ticket either.

By the time Jonny had thought through the last few months of memories, they had reached the water tower. Jonny knew he had less than ten minutes, maybe less than five, to persuade Will to change his mind.

He had no idea how to do it.

A sudden thought hit him. *If I don't succeed, this could be the last ten minutes of my life. Of our lives.*

He tried. 'I couldn't live without you Will.' It wasn't the best choice of words. It only seemed to convince his boyfriend that they had no other alternative.

'I know J,' he said gently. 'I don't want to leave you behind either. That's why it's best if you fly with me.'

It doesn't matter how he tries to wrap it up, Jonny thought. *He's still talking about killing ourselves. He's talking about a suicide pact.*

Afterwards, he would think about all the things he should have said. He should have told him how many lives he would destroy, his family, his friends. He should have encouraged him to search for help to rid him of his demons.

He should have also told him one simple truth.

They crawled through the same hole in the fence that had been Will's designated entry to the race back in October. Jonny prayed that Will would become caught on the barbed wire and be unable to free himself. He prayed that the imprisonment would bring him to his senses.

Will slid through the gap with his accustomed ease.

As they walked towards the staircase, rusted and abandoned, Jonny felt a certain sense of irony. The staircase, even though it was uncared for, could sit at the top of the woods for many years to come. Whereas Jonny, because he was cared for too much, might not be here in a matter of minutes.

As Will trod on the first step of the staircase, Jonny reached out for his hand and took it. He pulled at his boyfriend's arm, which forced Will's head around so that he was looking at Jonny.

But still, the right words would not come to him. No words came to him at all, and in the end, it was Will who broke the silence.

'How can I live with myself, J?'

He pulled away from Jonny, firmly but gently, and then started to climb the tower in a determined fashion. Realising that he had failed, for possibly the last time in his life, Jonny followed him.

Neither of them spoke again until they reached the sixth flight of the staircase. The one without a handrail. Will set foot on the top step, which was wider than the rest. He turned towards the edge and waited for Jonny to join him.

Jonny could see the walkway behind Will, leading to the other side of the tower and relative safety. He remembered the euphoria he had felt, when he had seen Will running across the walkway, the last time his boyfriend had been at the top of the tower. Race over. Victory within his grasp.

But this time? This time, Will had no intention of crossing the walkway. The toes of his trainers were already balanced over the edge as he held out his hand to Jonny.

Jonny took it.

Will looked at him. 'I've been having dreams lately.' He paused and glanced away from Jonny, looking down onto the clearing in the woods that held so many happy memories. Jonny fought every instinct that was forcing him to follow his boyfriend's stare. Knowing what Will was planning, he had no desire to see the distance they would fall, or to guess which patch of grass they would land on. Jonny had just decided that Will wasn't going to explain himself when he spoke again.

'I think I was meant to die that day. The day of the race.' He blinked, trying to rid himself of an unwelcome tear. When he spoke again, his voice was full of self-hatred. 'If only I had, so much shit could have been avoided,' He turned to Jonny once again. 'I need to put that right.'

No! Will, you're talking nonsense; none of this is your fault; we'll get through this; I'll get you help. So many things that Jonny wanted to say. Many variations on the same theme rolled around his head. However, he was distracted by the broken railing and the fact that Will's trainers seemed to be inching closer to the edge. In the end he didn't say anything.

'I just want you to know that I love you so much,' Will continued. He rubbed Jonny's hand and repeated his plea from earlier. 'Fly with me. I don't ever want to be parted from you Jonny Vincent. I love you.'

Once again, Will turned his head way from Jonny so that he was looking in front of him. One step away from ending his pain.

This time Jonny couldn't prevent himself from following Will's gaze. A wave of dizziness swept over him so that he almost felt like he was already flying. He could see the tops of the trees, heavy with leaves and just a month away from the day they'd start to lose them. He could see segments of the track they'd walked up, as it wound its way down to the spot where the woods ended and the town began. He could feel the warm, dank air on his face.

His heart was pounding, his legs were numb. His stomach felt like a lump of dough on the receiving end of a baker's fist.

Will never said another word. He simply took a deep breath and took a large step forward. Jonny could feel the pressure on his arm, pulling him forward, urging him to follow. Suddenly, a notion that had been lurking on the outskirts of his thoughts since the moment they crawled through the hole in the fence exploded into one simple truth.

Jonny didn't want to die.

Self-preservation took over and just before a change of heart would be impossible, he disentangled his hand from Will's and threw himself backwards on to the walkway.

Whether it was a case of distance, whether it was the sounds that Jonny made as he crashed onto the rusted metal walkway, or whether he automatically shut his ears to block out the sound of his lover landing in the clearing below him. Whatever it was, Jonny heard nothing. However, as he looked behind him to the empty spot where Will had recently been standing, Jonny was aware of the horrifying truth. Gravity doesn't have too many tricks to play.

He turned his head back towards the walkway and sunk it into the muck and the rust. He knew he would have to pick himself up, climb down the tower and face the horror on the grass. But, for a few precious seconds more, Jonny wanted to hold on to the hope that Will might still be alive. His desperate action had failed.

However.

Jonny didn't really believe that Will would fail. He had never seen Will fail at anything since he had known him. He wasn't expecting him to start that day.

He knew that once he had confirmed the obvious, he would have to call the emergency services and face the many 'why didn't you' and 'you should have done' comments that would be thrown in his direction. But, more than anything, Jonny wanted to delay the moment when he would see the betrayal written on his lover's face.

As he lay there with the galvanised metal acting as an uncomfortable pillow, there was one thought in Jonny's head and it formed many different strands, like a spider's web encasing him, trapping him.

As Will had fallen from the tower, had he realised that Jonny had abandoned him? Had he felt the empty space in his hand where Jonny's hand should have been?

And, had he realised that he would die alone?

Jonny let out a low guttural moan as a question formed in his brain.

Why couldn't I have been brave enough?

~ 35 ~
REVELATIONS

Carmichaeltown: Ben

After Amy had finished telling us all about her meeting with Will, the day before he died, all eyes turned in my direction. They wanted to know details they'd not heard before. What demons had led Will to do what he had done? And, what had happened on that August day at the water tower?

This, obviously, was a slight problem for me.

I looked over at Arnie. He was looking worried, sympathetic, and as supportive as ever. It gave me an idea.

If Jonny had shared his thoughts about that day with anyone, it would be Arnie. I had no other chance, so I decided it was worth a shot.

'Would you mind?' I asked. 'I think it's time everyone knew the truth. I'm just not sure I can get through the story without making an idiot of myself.'

Arnie nodded in agreement. He then told everyone what happened fourteen years before.

I listened in stunned silence, but apart from Arnie, no one was looking at me. He would glance over occasionally, just to check that I wasn't heading for a full meltdown.

By the time he'd finished his tale, the room was as quiet as a monastery during silent meditation. I couldn't believe that I'd been mocking Jonny all week, for being a pathetic wimp. He had seen his boyfriend die in front of him, had experienced guilt and anguish because he hadn't joined him, and had faced the aftermath of Will's actions alone.

I wasn't sure I would have coped so well. In fact, I knew I wouldn't have done. Last night I'd been told exactly how the eighteen-year-old Ben Shawcross had dealt with disaster. From what Ben had told me, it hadn't been pretty.

That thought led very quickly on to another. Jonny Vincent had seen his boyfriend die in Westcastle as well. He had also lost his parents in an exploding boat, not long afterwards, and then gone through the hell of losing his home.

Yet Tanner and I had always taunted Amy. We'd call Jonny her 'girlfriend' or 'her husband without the shagging rights'. We'd always baited Jonny whenever we saw him. We'd always felt superior to him.

Christ, I'd been an arsehole.

I had seen Arnie wince slightly when relating Will's words on the tower. *'How can I live with myself, J?'* He moved on swiftly as if he wished he could press an invisible edit button. I glanced over at Amy, who gave me a watery smile in return. I suddenly understood. Since that day, Amy must have always feared that her words were on Will's mind when he decided to take his final flight.

At the end of the story, Arnie had repeated his view that Will had been cruel, in doing what he'd done. It was the only thing Arnie had said, during the whole week, that I didn't agree with.

It made me realise, for the first time in my life, how scary and unpredictable the subject of mental health was.

Amy glanced over at me again. 'The only – the one and only – good thing that happened because of Will's death, is that we got over our silliness, and started to talk again.'

'We should never have stopped Ames,' I smiled gently. I didn't think I was going too far out on a limb with that point of view.

'Christ! What a bloody year that was.' Steve swore gently, shaking his head. 'First the crap with Tanner and Ben – and then Will. I think it was the first time I'd heard of group counselling for trauma, but we needed it. Lots of our group deferred their university places for a year after Will died,' he looked around the table. 'Do you remember?'

Elliot nodded, then chuckled ironically. 'Except Kyle Hammond, of course. Nothing was going to stop him going to Oxford.'

'Where is he now?' I asked. Back in Westcastle, he was an MP for a constituency in Hampshire and one of the Tories' brightest stars.

'He's an MP down in Hampshire.' Elliot said. 'One of the Guardian's top ten politicians of the future.' He grinned. 'As if that's any surprise.'

It seemed that, whatever reality you were living in, nothing would be stopping Kyle Hammond any time soon.

'And what about that girl he used to go out with?' Steve asked. 'Dakota something, or other.'

I remembered the woman. Crying fake tears for a boy she barely knew at the version of Will's funeral that I'd gone to.

'Oh God no! The fact that she was a good-looking older girl was perfect for his street cred in sixth form,' Elliot laughed, 'but as soon as he got to uni, he dumped her for a politics major from the home counties. Much more suitable for our Kyle.'

'You bitches!' laughed Arnie, 'I thought Jonny and I were meant to be the catty gay boys around here.'

'You ... definitely,' taunted Elliot before standing up, walking behind me, and mussing up my hair affectionately. 'But our Jonny? Never...'

'You don't know what he puts me through...' Arnie hammed it up in the style of an actor in a bad soap opera.

'I don't know what I would have done without Jonny, when it all started to go pear-shaped with Ben.' Amy was carrying on as if no one had spoken. She looked at me. 'I know you have always said how much I helped you after Will's death,' she paused and then fixed me with those eyes once again. 'Well, I know I've told you this before, but I always get the feeling you don't quite believe me...' She reached across and grabbed my hand, which sent shockwaves all the way up to my brain. 'Believe it Jonny. You got me through a very dark passage of my life.'

Elliot nodded and turned to me as well. 'I've never properly thanked you either.' He then looked around the table. 'Jonny persuaded me that Amy needed all her friends around her. I had long since given up the idea of Amy romantically. But I suddenly realised that Jonny was right, just because I couldn't have the relationship I wanted with Amy, shouldn't mean that I couldn't be her friend.'

Amy glanced at Lottie and Steve, 'I'm not sure how much you two knew about my visits to see Ben...' Lottie gave her a little look as if to say: *It doesn't matter. You need to talk. Talk.* Amy looked at her gratefully and continued '...It was awful. He wasn't coping with prison, and I wasn't coping either. It was horrible seeing this lad I'd loved – put on a pedestal really – disintegrate before my eyes. To start with, I'd looked forward to the visits, I'd counted off the seconds until I could see him again. It didn't take long before I began to dread them.'

She was still gripping on to my hand tightly. It was beginning to go a little numb, but there was no way I was going to ask her to let it go.

'A lot of people were shocked when I broke up with Ben so close to his release date,' she gave a small snort of irritation, 'a few of them decided I should be told what a bitch I was.' She dropped her eyes towards the table as she muttered: 'None of them had a clue what it was like...'

'And you're still not going to tell us, are you?' Eyes turned in my direction and I glanced at Amy sympathetically as I explained. 'Ben told me last night.' There was a mumble of questions, but I ignored them. 'He knows exactly when you finally stopped loving him. And he doesn't blame you.' The glance turned into a supportive stare. 'In fact, he wanted me to tell you how sorry he was.'

Amy was expressionless. It was a bit of a risk, pretending that Jonny had only found out about it the night before. Amy might have already opened her heart to him at some point in their past, but somewhere deep inside me, I knew she hadn't.

I continued. 'Ben told me that he became more and more vicious towards Amy when she visited. He doesn't know why. His counsellors have since told him that it was probably a form of release.' I looked around the table. Amy had pulled her hand away from mine and she seemed to be in a trance-like state; she wasn't even twisting her ring around her finger. Elliot was watching her carefully. Everyone else seemed to have forgotten how to breathe. 'Before every visit he would swear to himself that, this time, he would tell her how much he loved her, how much he was looking forward to his release date, and how much he wanted to plan their future together.' I paused. 'He never did.'

I remembered the look on Ben's face, the night before, when he had reached that part of the story. The pain had been heartbreaking. His voice had broken on a couple of occasions, and he found it difficult to swallow. I offered him a way out, but he'd refused it.

'If I'm going to meet everyone again, be accepted back into the group, they need to know the truth,' he'd said. 'Make sure you tell everyone Jonny. I'm sure that Amy won't have said a word.'

Twenty-four hours later, I was having a similar problem. Like Ben last night, I seemed to have a lump in my throat that wasn't easy to shift.

After one false start, I cleared my throat and tried again. 'One day, when he was a fair way through his sentence, they had a particularly difficult visit. Despite all his good intentions – all the times he swore to himself that he would try to be strong – he could feel the viciousness building up inside him once again. As soon as he saw her, he wanted to lash out. To hurt someone. He wanted to hurt Amy.'

Last night, Ben had closed his eyes at that point. He'd been silent for so long that for a moment I'd thought he'd decided not to tell me after all. The night afterwards I was silent for so long that the crowd around the table must have thought the same thing.

I shouldn't feel like this. I thought. This time last week I would have laughed at myself for being so wet. It wasn't even my story.

And yet, in some way, I felt it was.

In the end I wasn't the one who finished the story. Amy must have felt that Ben had given her an open invitation to exorcise her ghosts.

She accepted it.

When she spoke, her voice was low and slow. And clear as a moonlit winter night.

'Ben said: "Why do you bother coming? Guilt is it? Knowing that you're the reason I'm here in the first place".'

There was shocked silence around the table. After speaking, Amy just sat there with a glazed expression on her face.

I took over quickly, forcing people's attention away from her. 'Ben said it shocked him too. When Amy had gone and he was back in his cell, he knew that he had to change. From that point on he resolved to toughen up and he started studying again.' I shrugged, 'before that he couldn't be bothered. Every time he felt the anger building, he forced himself to remember the look on Amy's face at that moment. The horror of the memory always smothered his rage immediately. He said it was better than any of the exercises his therapist had suggested.' I took a breath and summed up the story. 'He knew the old Ben had gone forever, but suddenly realised that he should try and find a better Ben...'

'It was too late for me.' Once again Amy's voice seemed to surprise everyone. 'Ben's right, I think I finally stopped loving him the moment he snapped those words at me. I carried on visiting him, more out of duty than anything else...' She paused and lowered her voice so that the next words she said were nearly lost. 'Because, deep down, I agreed with him.'

There were mumbles of support and disagreement, but Amy ignored them.

'Elliot turned up for one of his regular visits the night that Ben had...' Even now she was finding it difficult to describe '...said those things.' She smiled at her husband gratefully. 'He was the only person I ever told.'

Elliot wrapped his arm around Amy protectively and she patted it gratefully. 'The more I dreaded my visits to see Ben, the more I found I was looking forward to my evenings with Elliot.' She smiled at her husband. 'Then one day, a little later, I realised I'd fallen in love with him.'

There was silence around the table. Arnie broke it.

'I saw your face,' he nodded across the table to Amy. 'When I talked about Will's suicide.' He sighed and said the next words carefully. 'You didn't cause Will to take his own life, Amy.' A murmur of agreement rumbled around the table. 'What Ben said to you when he was in jail; that was more vicious, much crueller. It might have led to your relationship being destroyed, but it didn't destroy you. What you said to Will, that was only a tiny piece of the hell he was going through.'

'It didn't exactly help though, did it?' Amy argued.

'If we had the chance to rephrase everything we've said, like authors do with a passage in a book that they're not happy with, don't you think we'd change about fifty per cent of what we say every day?' Arnie countered reasonably. 'No one will ever know what demons led Will to kill himself, but they were his demons. They were nothing to do with anything you might have said to him. It might as well have been written in the stars.'

It might as well have been written in the stars.

When I'd met him the other day, Cooper-Wilson had been banging on about pre-requisites and how certain things must happen, whether it be at the same time, or thirty years later.

I, of course, had mocked him royally.

But now?

In one reality Will Flanagan had fallen from the water tower in the woods during a race.

In another reality Will Flanagan had not fallen from the tower and had gone on to win the race. But, a year later, he had jumped from the same water tower in the woods.

Written in the stars?

~ 36 ~
A TALENT FOR NONSENSE

Carmichaeltown: Ben

It was freaky. One minute we were all mega-stressed, as if we were trapped in a never-ending episode of *Casualty*. The next, we were laughing, joking, and taking the piss.

They were life-long friends. Any one of them could have had a meltdown and no one would have thought less of them. Amy had been visibly upset and everyone had been supportive. But, once the moment was over, it was over. The party could start again.

This was mainly down to Arnie. As I'd discovered during the week, he had a medal winning talent for nonsense. He eased us into his world with tale about a friend, of a friend, who he refused to name. Her Friday night fun had been scuppered by a dud battery in her vibrator. Refusing to be beaten, she had crept into her teenage son's bedroom and nicked a replacement from his alarm clock. This caused the poor lad problems when he woke up the next day and found out he was late for his Saturday job. OK, he had an explanation, but as Arnie put it, he would probably have juggled with cowpats, rather than use it. The twinkle around his eyes let us all know that he'd probably made the whole story up, but it did the trick.

Within minutes, the tension around the table had gone and the laughter had started.

Will's death was mentioned once more that evening. I'd gone to get another bottle of wine from the fridge and Amy had followed me.

'Are we all right Jonny?' She asked quietly.

I put the bottle of wine on the nearest work surface and held her hand. 'Of course we are. I'm with Arnie. We will never know what caused Will to jump.' I brushed a stray strand of hair away from her eyes and looked into them, urging her to forgive herself at last. 'It's time to stop punishing yourself.'

For once, I hadn't had to second-guess the answer that Jonny would have given. He was the forgiver-in-chief after all. I thought I was on very safe ground.

She put one arm around my neck gratefully and brushed my cheek with her lips. It was strange. When I had gone into her house on Monday, I'd been as horny as a teenager in a brothel every time she had come near to me. Tonight, she looked the same. Her scent was the same, the sound of her voice, the gentle buffets of her breath on my face. None of that had changed in the last five days. The only thing that had changed was me. She felt more like a much-loved sister, than my wife.

And the most worrying thing, was the fact that I wasn't worried at all.

I picked up the bottle with one hand and wrapped the other around Amy's waist as we went back to re-join the party. Arnie was in the middle of performing his own version of *Titanic*, where he played Jack, Rose, and the iceberg, all at the same time. The table was rocking with laughter, and we carried on laughing until the witching hour of twelve o'clock approached.

Lottie said that, as with Cinderella, everything in the world of babysitting changes at midnight. 'OK,' she said, 'you don't have glass coaches turning back into pumpkins, but placid sixteen-year-olds start having teenage tantrums and their lovely amenable parents turn feral.'

Once coats had been found, an argument about City's back four had been interrupted, and Lottie and Steve had sent a precautionary text to say they were on their way home, we bundled our way out into the hallway. Arnie and I then waved our guests goodbye.

I watched Arnie out of the corner of my eye as we gave our friends one final wave and closed the door behind us. His eyes twinkled. A mixture of happiness and one glass of bargain buy Malbec too many.

'I love our friends,' he said happily.

I kissed him.

It wasn't an accident. His head didn't move at the wrong time so that our lips bumped each other.

And it wasn't a case of him kissing me.

No, I kissed him. A full-on snog, with a promise of a lot more to come.

In the same way, no one was holding a gun to my head when I stripped him, item by item, which was quite a feat in the small hallway at the bottom of the stairs.

Leaving his clothes in an untidy pile just inside the door, I took his hand and started to lead him into the lounge. My doppelganger, the real Jonny Vincent, Mr Neat Freak himself – would have been appalled. Arnie laughingly mentioned the fact.

'What's with you Jonny?' he mocked. 'No coat hangers?'

'Oh! Shut up and come here,' I said with mock irritation. I pulled him towards me. His naked body felt strange in my arms, but as I ran a finger down his torso, between his pecs and on towards his belly button and beyond, I forgot about the fact that I wasn't gay, and that I had a wife who I loved to bits, somewhere in the sanity of another reality.

I didn't feel like Ben Shawcross, trapped reluctantly in Jonny Vincent's body

I felt like Jonny Vincent.

And it felt right.

~ 37 ~
THE SUNDAY VISIT

Westcastle: Jonny

'Ben, can I talk to you?'

There was an edge of anxiety in Amy's voice, but there was something else too. There was a hope that whatever she wanted to say, it wouldn't go half as badly as she had always feared.

She was leaning against the sink, pecking at her glass of orange juice like a starling at a bird bath. I was sitting at the breakfast bar, eating a croissant, and trying not to get jealous at the thought of what Arnie and Jonny might be doing on the first Sunday morning of their relationship.

It was ridiculous. After our foray into the world of *Blind Date,* Amy and I had fallen into bed the previous evening. To start with I'd felt guilty, remembering the intense longing I'd experienced, when I'd seen Arnie standing at the bar. Then I realised that I no longer felt like Jonny Vincent, playing the part of Ben Shawcross making love to his wife.

I felt like Ben himself.

And yet, here I was, feeling jealous of the fact that the Jonny Vincent of this world had at last found his soulmate.

I clicked myself away from primary school jealousies and answered my wife's question instead.

'Of course,' I smiled encouragingly. 'Always.'

I have questioned those moments in a film when the phone begins to ring just as the heroine was about to say something important to the hero. The audience is left cringing in frustration, knowing they'll have to wait another half an hour for the denouement. It has always felt contrived and convenient.

The phone started to ring.

It was Jack Shawcross. 'Just checking that you're not going to bail on me son. The poor old girl is in a very bad way, and you know how she looks forward to our visits.'

I glanced across at Amy. Jack Shawcross's voice carried like a foghorn across an empty ocean, and she'd heard every word. Although her face wasn't giving anything away, I was sure there was something behind the neutral countenance that I shouldn't have been ignoring.

On a whim I asked if Amy could come with us. 'She'd like to see Gran too,' I added. I looked across and I was sure I could see gratitude in the smile she gave me.

There was a definite pause while Jack gave himself thinking time. It was obvious he wasn't dancing a tarantella at the thought of his daughter-in-law's company, and I couldn't understand why.

'I think three of us will be too much for the old girl,' he said meaningfully. He obviously realised that Amy was in the room, and he was trying to tell me something that he didn't want her to hear. I had absolutely no idea what it was.

I looked across at Amy and she shrugged her acceptance. However, there was something about the shrug. I could tell she wasn't happy, but equally, she knew there was nothing we could do about it.

I felt as if I was trying to umpire a game of tennis with a blindfold on. I could hear noises from both sides, but I didn't have the slightest idea what was happening.

I understood even less, a few hours later, when I was standing with Jack looking at his rapidly declining mother. Except she wasn't. She was strangely perky, for a woman who was meant to be close to death.

To be fair to Jack, Mrs Shawcross senior didn't seem too bothered that we were there. She treated us as if we were two members of the paparazzi, who were writing an expose on her nursing home. She answered our questions politely but gave very little away. She seemed much more interested in looking at photographs of one of her carers' grandchildren.

After twenty-five minutes she caught Jack trying to steal a crafty glance at his watch.

'It's alright Jack,' she said, eyes gleaming with mischief. 'Five minutes more and you've done your half an hour. You can run away, without worrying what the staff will be thinking of you.'

The bafflement increased, as far as I was concerned. I had assumed, from what Amy had told me, that the visit would last all afternoon. I finally discovered the truth, when Ben's grandmother had marched off to enjoy her Sunday afternoon game of Bridge, leaving Jack and I to return to the car.

'Right Son!' Jack said happily, pulling the seat belt across his ample frame. 'Next stop my office and we can pick up the golf clubs. We can fit in a quick nine holes before dark.'

It all became clear. Once a month, armed with the alibi that they were visiting Mrs Shawcross the elder, Ben and Jack kept that visit as short as possible and sneaked off for crafty game of golf. Jack had two sets of clubs at his office for such occasions. I found it quite bizarre that anyone would want to chase a little white ball across a fairway. Especially when he could be spending an afternoon with a woman who had a sharp intellect, a waspish sense of fun, and a lifetime of stories to tell.

Was it endearing that Jack took part in such a charade, simply to spend more time with his son? Or, was it more evidence of his need for control? I couldn't really imagine that the mighty Jack Shawcross needed his wife's permission to do anything, so the latter was probably the more likely. Whatever the truth was, I realised what I had to do.

After the phone had interrupted her earlier, I'd tried to get Amy to return to the conversation she'd been wanting to have. However, she had just muttered that we'd talk about it later and I'd not been able to get anything more out of her.

I desperately wanted to get back to her and re-start the conversation.

Also, I didn't want to play golf. No. That's not quite right. I couldn't play golf. Years ago, I had played pitch and putt with a seven-year-old friend of the family. Eventually he patiently agreed to give me a few tips as I'd barely managed to launch the ball from the ground, and he was getting bored by the lack of competition.

I'd been twenty-four at the time.

If I'd wanted to make Jack suspicious that there was something wrong with his son, playing a round of golf with him was a sure-fire way of doing so.

Jack wasn't happy when I said that I wanted to spend the afternoon with Amy instead. However, he was simply angry at not getting his own way. It was preferable to him being convinced that the real Ben Shawcross had been whisked away by aliens. I was subjected to a moody silence, for the rest of the journey, only interrupted by thinly veiled suggestions that I was becoming henpecked. It was very similar to my last few journeys to and from work with Tanner.

After I'd dropped Jack off, outside the gateway of his house, I breathed a sigh of relief and headed back to Chancelwood Road.

As I opened the front door, I heard raised voices coming from the lounge. Thinking that Amy had settled herself in front of an omnibus of her favourite soap for the afternoon, I thought it best not to disturb her. I decided to take myself upstairs. I had been writing notes to Ben all week and had a few more things to add. My plan was to come down, as soon as I heard the closing theme tune, and have the conversation that I wanted to have.

I was just about to close the front door when a random thought entered my head. *That angry actress doesn't half sound like Amy.*

With one hand still resting on the open door, I listened more carefully.

The actress who sounded like Amy was continuing to speak, but softer now, and I had to strain in order catch the words.

'...It's just that this week he seems more like the boy I fell in love with. I think he might believe me.'

It was when a man answered her that I finally realised. Amy wasn't watching a soap.

There was no mistaking the arrogant drawl.

Tanner.

'We've talked about this before. Ben does nothing without checking with either me or his dad first. Never has and never will. If you tried to disrespect me, he wouldn't believe you.' He paused and I could almost see the sneer on his face. 'I'm sure it gets on your tits, but face it sweetheart, your husband and I are solid. It would be a very stupid woman who tried to come between us.'

However, Amy wasn't giving up. She replied with a taunting air of her own.

'Oh, come on Tanner. Even you must have noticed that he's changed this week. I have no idea why.' I could imagine the quirky grin on her face as she continued to taunt him. 'Perhaps the bang on the head he received on Monday morning made him realise that his best friend was an arsehole.'

I hadn't spoken about my semi-fictitious crash to Tanner, but he ignored Amy's mention of it and concentrated on dealing with her insult instead.

'Steady sweet cheeks, you know how it turns me on when you get all feisty. You haven't been like that for a while, and I've missed it.' Then his tone turned harder. There was still the air of mockery behind it, but there was also an underlying sense of a threat. 'I might have to stuff something into that pretty mouth of yours and shut you up.'

Amy was not going to back down. 'Yeah, remember what happened the first time you did that.'

Tanner snorted. 'But you never did that again, did you? Not after I'd persuaded you it was a bad idea.'

I hated the violence in his voice. I hated his sense of ownership. I hated what I thought his words meant.

'I'm going to tell him as soon as he gets home from seeing his gran,' Amy countered. 'I'm going to stop being the stupid pawn in your warped little game.' I could hear the determination in her voice. 'I'm sick to death of being a pathetic victim and I'm going to tell him exactly what his 'rock' has been doing to me every fourth Sunday, when he's on a family visit.' She rapped out her belief in a sharp staccato. 'At last, I trust my husband again. I trust him to believe me.'

Tanner didn't say a word, but the muffled sound of him moving across the room was the only cue I needed.

Without pausing to shut the front door, I opened the lounge door and charged in. Even then, I wasn't quite quick enough.

Tanner had already managed to grab hold of Amy by the arms, and he'd pushed her against the wall. He was holding her wrists above her head and pressing his body against her legs, preventing her from launching any form of attack. His face was centimetres from hers, twisted into a vicious mask, Desire, hatred, and arrogance fought for control. But the thing that scared me most was the twisted excitement he seemed to be getting from the situation.

I froze. My experience of fighting for myself, or my loved ones, was limited and that was being kind.

Both Tanner and Amy had become aware that I'd entered the room. Amy had a strange look on her face. Hope, mixed with an acceptance that she might be disappointed.

Tanner jumped back and raised his arms in an expression of innocence.

'Hey Benjy ... it's not what it looks like.'

I stood rooted to the spot, just inside the door of the lounge. My apparent lack of anger seemed to encourage Tanner to continue.

'I'm sure you know that your wife likes it a bit rough...' He then addressed the fact that even if you took the violence away, I had still walked in on him making a move on my wife. 'Hey, we're brothers, right?' He actually gave a little smirk. 'Mates before dates?'

And still, I couldn't move.

Encouraged further by my lack of reaction, Tanner's natural arrogance continued to return. He moved towards me and contorted his face into a conspiratorial smile. 'You've always said what's yours is mine.'

He was talking about Amy as if she was a pair of jeans he'd borrowed from my wardrobe.

I hit him.

I've never hit anybody before. The overriding feeling was surprise.

The most useful thing about being trapped in a body that was more muscular than my own, was the power that I suddenly possessed. Had I hit someone with Jonny Vincent's fist, I'm not even sure that the person on the receiving end would have noticed.

Tanner noticed. He fell to the floor with a surprised groan.

It was then that I became aware of the second thing about hitting someone. It hurt.

However, the pain that shot through my hand and up my arm wasn't enough to override the adrenalin that had been released.

And with that adrenalin, came a sudden avalanche of memories: Tanner, launching me – the Jonny Vincent version – into the bins. Tanner. laughing as he forced bite sized pieces of breaded fish down my throat. Tanner, hand around my neck as he lifted my feet from the ground.

These memories led me to a much more recent one. Tanner, hand around Amy's neck as he imprisoned her against the wall.

As he began to recover from the unexpected attack, Tanner rose to a kneeling position. He crawled along the floor, so that he was by the side of the coffee table. He put his hand out to use the table to help him stand up.

I stared at him. He looked astonished that his best friend would hit him.

I suddenly had the most intense feeling of hatred for what he'd done to Jonny Vincent in the past and what he was doing to Amy in the present. I even hated him for the way he was treating Ben.

I wanted to hit him again.

I didn't give a thought to the fact that I would be inflicting more pain on my hand, which was still feeling the effects of its previous connection with Tanner's cheekbone.

I simply wanted to hit him.

I'm not sure if I was aware of the geography of the contents in the room. Did I realise that if I was to hit him, the natural angle of the punch would send Tanner's head smashing towards the corner of the coffee table with the wonky leg?

I have no idea.

And the fact that this would, probably, be enough to kill him.

In that split second, I didn't care.

I think I wanted him to die.

~ 38 ~
AMY IN MONOCHROME

Westcastle: Jonny

'Ben!'

The sharp tone of panic in Amy's voice brought me out of the weird and violent trance that I'd found myself locked into.

'Don't.' She said soothingly. 'You could kill him.' She paused before muttering softly, 'trust me, he's not worth going to jail for.'

I was aware of the figure kneeling below me and I steeled myself to stop the anger from returning when I looked at his face. In the end it was surprisingly easy.

He looked pathetic.

Tanner flinched as I took his hand from the coffee table, to pull him up. He relaxed a little when he realised that I wasn't about to punch him again, and allowed himself to be pulled to a standing position.

I wasn't being helpful. I simply wanted him out of the house, as quickly as possible. I knew that my rage could return at any minute. I had never felt anything like it before. I had finally let it out. I wasn't confident that even Amy's wise words would be able to contain it again.

'Go home Tanner.' Once he was standing, I pulled my hand away from his. I didn't want him to mistake the gesture for a sign of friendliness.

He walked past me, then stopped and looked back. The sense of entitlement, and the swagger, were beginning to return. He appeared to be on the cusp of saying something. Whatever he saw on my face, stopped him, and he walked quickly from the lounge and out of the front door.

I followed him out and closed the door firmly. Then a bizarre mixture of shock, panic, and relief hit me. I realised that my aching hand was shaking, my heart was pounding, and I was aware of an intense wave of nausea. I turned and leant against the door. I took deep breaths and persuaded myself that an emergency call to the paramedics would not be necessary.

More than anything, I needed to think. I needed to think about exactly what I'd interrupted, and what it meant, before I talked to Amy.

I'm going to stop being the stupid pawn in your warped little game.

I'm sick to death of being a pathetic victim.

I'm going to tell him exactly what his 'rock' has been doing to me every fourth Sunday when he's visiting his gran.

One thing was certain. Amy was not talking about an affair.

I also remembered the conversation Tanner and I had had on Wednesday morning.

Make sure you don't bail on your old man on Sunday. You take him to see your grandma, no matter what sad sort of second honeymoon you seem to think you're going on.

It had surprised me at the time. I thought it had showed a rarely seen side to Tanner.

I'd thought it was almost endearing.

I should have known better. Tanner was only thinking about Tanner, as per norm.

He wanted to make sure that Ben was out of the way, so he could rape his wife.

The thought didn't help me regain my equilibrium. It took a minute, but eventually my heart rate settled, my hand lost the violent tremors and the very real need to find a bucket receded. It would be a lie to say that I'd got my head straight, but I felt I could just about cope with the horrible truth. One thing was sure, Amy needed her husband to be strong. If I'd understood correctly, she had needed her husband to be strong for a very long time. I was determined not to let her down.

I now realised why, when I'd seen her last Monday, she had seemed like a monochrome version of the girl I knew in Carmichaeltown. Why she had reminded me of a butterfly pinned to a cork board.

I realised I was still wearing Ben's Berghaus padded jacket. I took it off and walked back into the lounge to check that Amy was all right and discovered that she, very definitely, wasn't.

She was hunched on the sofa; the palms of her hands were boring into her eyes and her shoulders were rising and falling as she sobbed uncontrollably.

I eased myself onto the sofa beside her and gently put my left arm around her shoulder. She took her hands away from her face and turned towards me, burrowing it into my polo shirt.

I have no idea how long we were sitting there. I didn't care. I would have stayed until the next square moon had risen, if I'd thought it would help her.

Eventually the weak winter sun had lost its battle with the night, and I mentioned softly that I should probably put a light on. She lifted her head, allowing me to do so.

'I was so sure that you wouldn't believe me.' She blinked. 'Until this week, I was so sure.'

You stupid git Ben, I thought, not for the first time that week. *Where the hell have you been when your wife needed you?*

'Do you want to talk about it?'

She nodded. 'Yes.' Then shook her head. 'No.' Then shrugged. 'I don't know, I just don't ... know...' She smiled sadly. 'But probably yes.'

'Take your time,' I said encouragingly. 'Stop anytime you feel it's getting too much.'

She nodded once more. 'It first started last year,' she began tentatively. 'Do you remember the Sunday afternoon you came home from seeing your nan and I told you that Tanner had been around?'

I nodded vaguely and Amy continued. 'It was a bit of a surprise. I mean, he knew you wouldn't be home. It normally takes him all his time to grunt in my direction, let alone visit me when you weren't here.' She twisted her ring around her finger absent-mindedly. 'He talked non-stop for about half an hour. The normal arrogant misogynistic rubbish he always bangs on about. I remember cursing myself for offering him a cup of tea, because it prolonged the visit. When he'd gone, I wondered why he'd even come.' She looked at me meaningfully. 'You were going to ask him, but you never told me if you did, and I don't think that I asked again.'

'I don't remember.' I said with complete honesty.

Amy shrugged to imply that it didn't matter. 'The next month, he arrived again. I swore to myself that I wouldn't make the same mistake but after five minutes I offered him a drink, just to shut him up.'

She stopped suddenly. From outside I could hear the sounds of a normal Sunday evening. Someone, possibly Greg, was wheeling their bin to the edge of the pavement and shouting a greeting to a neighbour. I could hear the shriek of an urban fox and the metallic thrum of a car, which was driving carefully down Chancelwood Road. However, inside number thirty-four, all was not normal. Amy was desperately trying to prevent herself from falling apart.

Eventually she continued. Her breathing was sharp and ragged as she struggled to control herself. Her words were barely audible and yet, I heard every syllable.

'I had just filled the kettle from the sink and turned it on, when suddenly Tanner put his arms around my waist and nuzzled into me.' Her eyes latched on to mine as if pleading with me to believe her. 'I told him to stop.' She twisted the ring once again. 'I told him to stop.'

There was no need for her to try and convince me with her eyes. There was no need for her to repeat her words. I believed every one of them.

'He laughed at me. He said: "Come on sweetheart. Think of it as a treat. A chance to have a real man, for once, instead of that nice but pathetic streak of piss you call a husband."'

I was staggered. For as much as my week in Westcastle had re-affirmed my dislike for the man, I would have named his loyalty to Ben as his one redeeming feature – until now.

'I told him to get out.' Again, the fact that she checked my face to see if I believed her; broke my heart. 'But he just laughed and said how he loved it when I got feisty. The sort of thing he says every time.' She paused. 'He said it today as well.'

I nodded. 'I heard him.'

She nodded also. She was slowly coming to terms with the fact that I believed her, and with the fact that I was taking her side against my so-called best friend.

'Without seeming to use any power, he managed to turn me around. He pushed me against the table and then onto it.' Amy then seemed to change tack. 'Do you remember the day you came back from your nan's and your favourite mug had been smashed?

I had no idea if Ben would have remembered that or not, so I simply nodded and gave as little information as I dared.

'I didn't break it while taking it out of the dishwasher, as I told you. It got knocked off the table when I was pushed onto it.'

'Why didn't you tell me the truth?' I asked, although I thought I could guess the answer.

Amy didn't reply. She simply continued with her story.

'I tried to fight.' Again, she gave me a little glance. 'I did. I tried to gouge his eyes, kick him in the goolies – anything.' She gave a defeated sigh. 'He was stronger.' She fixed her gaze just above the mantelpiece, concentrating on one spot on the wall, hoping that it would help her get through the rest of the story.

'While he was...' She couldn't say the word and I nodded quickly to let her know that I understood. 'I closed my eyes. I closed my eyes and hoped it would be over quickly.' She took her gaze from the wall and her eyes blazed suddenly. 'Hoped he would get his rocks off and just fuck off.' The sudden anger was stilled almost immediately. 'I got myself into a sort of trance and, thankfully, I remember very little of it.'

'Why didn't you tell me?' I asked again.

Amy sighed, but this time she answered my question. 'What has our marriage been like in the last couple of years Ben?' She asked. 'Have you been my best friend? Have you even realised I existed for the most part? We've spoken more in the last six days than we have in the previous six hundred.' There was the smallest hesitation before Amy continued. 'I hate to say it, but Tanner was right. You would never have believed me.'

'Oh my God, Amy...'

Amy didn't let me finish Ben's apology. She moved swiftly onwards. 'As you now know, I've dreaded the Tuesday night suppers for a long time. But that week! The thought of seeing Tanner again – let alone spending a night in his company – filled me with dread, hate, anguish. Delete as applicable.' She smiled, but there was no mistaking the anger inside that smile. 'And suddenly there he was, waltzing into our house, as innocent as Bambi.' She stopped suddenly, before continuing bitterly. 'Laughing at me,' she then nodded towards me, 'and laughing at you.'

I didn't know what to say. I settled on looking sympathetically appalled, which wasn't difficult, and allowed her to finally get the whole horrible story off her chest.

'There were times, in the weeks that followed, that I actually believed the whole thing was a nightmare and I'd dreamt it all up. It was as if I was looking at a different world to everyone else.'

Now that was something I could relate to.

'Even so, the next time the monthly visit came around; I arranged to go out to lunch with Jonny. I figured the best tactic was avoidance. Tanner would never do anything while you were around; all I had to do was keep out of his way for four hours a month. It seemed simple.'

'I guess it didn't work?' Given what I'd just witnessed, it seemed an obvious question to ask, but why?

'Tanner was early that week. Almost as soon as your car had driven off, he arrived. I can't tell you how smug he looked. I guess he knew what I would try to do, and he was happy to let me know why it wasn't a good idea to avoid him.'

'Why?' I asked stupidly.

Amy turned away from me slightly and her wedding ring was rotating around her finger like a gymnast on the asymmetric bars.

'He had a video.' Her tone was flat – emotionless – the ring twisting stopped suddenly and she turned back to look at me. 'While I had zoned out during the...'

She tailed off and I was aware, once again, how difficult she was finding it to give the attack its proper title.

'He'd filmed the whole thing on his phone.' She paused. 'Don't ever tell me that men can't multi-task.' Her face twisted into a grin, but there wasn't a shred of humour there. 'Later, he'd edited it. You know the saying: *The camera never lies*?' It was a rhetorical question, so I didn't answer. 'Well,' she shrugged. 'It does. The fact that I was lying there with my eyes shut – just praying for him to stop – looked like I was lying there compliantly, enjoying every moment.'

'Oh, my God, Amy.' I said horrified.

'When he had...'

'Raped you, for the second time.' Although I said it gently, I worried as soon as the words fell from my mouth. She couldn't bring herself to say the word. How would she cope with hearing it?

However, she didn't fall apart. She simply looked at me with a confused expression on her face. 'Was that really what it was?' She asked.

I nodded briefly and held her gaze. 'He had sex with you without your agreement. He then blackmailed you into silence. That's rape Amy.' I glanced in the direction of the house next door, as if I was talking to the man who lived there. 'It's vile. It's so many types of vile.'

'He made me feel like I wanted it.' Her tone was so unemotional, so calm.

It broke my heart.

I gently took hold of her hand, massaging my thumb around her palm in what I hoped was a comforting motion. 'This is not your fault, Amy.' I said, silently urging her to believe me.

She gave a brief nod and continued speaking in the same rational monotone. 'Once he had finished that second time, he simply tapped his phone and said: "same time – same place – next month" and walked out. Over the year, I've tried everything. After being submissive and zoning out until it was over, I tried being aggressive. I then tried being sarcastic – funny. I tried to make him think I didn't care – that it didn't bother me.' She looked up at me in confusion again and repeated her words from earlier. 'I never thought you'd believe me.'

'We should report this,' I said, battling with the guilt I was feeling on Ben's behalf.

Amy shook her head. 'After more than twelve months? As much as I would like to see Tanner answer for the things he's done to me, I think you and I would end up losing more than him. The case would probably never come to court, while we would be on trial by social media. I haven't got the stomach for the fight.' She smiled, the first hint of warmth I'd seen for a while. 'You believe me. Let's leave it at that.'

'Did you tell no one?' I had a horrible feeling I knew the answer to this, but I had a masochistic need to know for sure.

'Jonny.' She looked at me sharply, accurately reading my unspoken thoughts. 'Don't you dare criticise him, Ben. He's been wonderful, supportive, and loving.' For a few seconds there was a brief glimpse of the warrior I knew her to be, as she defended her friend.

He might have been all of those things, I thought. *But he was no help at all when it came to preventing it from continuing.* It seemed that Jonny couldn't even fight for his friend, when she needed him most. No wonder I drove poor Arnie to the edge sometimes.

Just get me home and I will change.

Amy looked shattered. I suggested that a proper lie down might help. I helped her up to bed and held her hand until she dozed off. Then, I went into the office and collected the notebook I'd been using to write my messages to Ben. I returned to the bedroom. The disturbance I made, climbing onto the bed, caused Amy to turn towards me and cuddle into me as she slept. Propped up on my pillow, I wrote a verbatim account of everything she had just told me.

Once I had finished, I lay there stroking her hair, contemplating yet another problem. It could mean that everything I'd just written would never be read.

How could I leave her now?

~ 39 ~
GUILT AND GOOD FORTUNE

Carmichaeltown: Ben.

When I woke up on Sunday morning, I felt like shit.

Surprisingly enough, having had gay sex the night before wasn't really bothering me. It would have done. Before I'd spent this week in Carmichaeltown, my poor homophobic brain wouldn't have been able to cope with the fact that I found a man attractive. Now, I could admit it. I fancied Arnie, I had even started to love him; the fact that he was a man, and not a woman, made no difference at all.

It seems the posters were right after all.

Love is love.

Spending a week in another man's shoes had changed me. The fact that I was living a different man's life had made me a different man.

The problem was – I was suffering from guilt. I might have been a different man, but I was still a married one. The only thing I could say. in defence of the way I'd been treating Amy over the last couple of years, was that I'd never cheated on her. I'd abandoned her, taken her for granted, not supported her. But, I'd always been faithful, until now.

I tried to tell myself that it wasn't really cheating. I was more like an actor, playing a different role. No actor would refuse a part just because the love interest didn't happen to be played by his wife, or husband, would he? The thought made me feel better for a millisecond, until I realised that the two actors probably wouldn't have had actual sex...

I tried another train of thought instead. I had noticed that I was beginning to think more like Jonny. Fully formed sentences had come out of my mouth that were much more Jonny, than Ben. I was living in his body, perhaps I'd also got a little bit of his brain as well. A kind of time-share agreement where the renting agency had cocked up.

Yeah, save that one for the judge.

I looked across at Arnie, just as he stirred, stretched, and sat up. He glanced over at me and gave me the grin that had done me in the night before.

'Hello lover,' he said.

'Hello yourself,' I grinned in return.

We spent the morning switching and swapping between cuddling, snoozing, and suitably gentle Sunday morning loving. The latter didn't do a lot for my feelings of guilt but I told myself that trying to put the horse back in the stable, when he was halfway down the final furlong, would have looked mighty strange.

After we'd had breakfast and shared a shower, Arnie got on with preparing a roast while I added a rather tricky codicil to the messages that I'd been leaving Jonny on his phone.

Once everything was in the oven, and slowly roasting away, we headed down to the Chancelwood Arms for a swift pint before dinner. I insisted on buying the round and went up to the bar to get them. There was a late afternoon rush, and the barman was just getting around to taking my order, when Tonker – a bloke I knew from the football club – crashed his way to the front of the queue. He was famous amongst my friends in Westcastle for having had an unfortunate experience on a bowling green at my stag night. That Sunday, in Carmichaeltown, he was only interested in taking the barman's attention away from me.

'Six pints of lager, bar keep!' He hollered in his normal style.

'Excuse me,' I said, as politely as I could manage. 'I think I was first.'

'Hey!' He said, recognising me. 'It's my old mate from last week.' I had no idea how he would have known Jonny. I didn't think that Jonny would have spent much time at the football club, and the Tonker I knew was rarely anywhere else. Apart from on a Sunday afternoon, apparently. 'You don't mind if I go first do you mate? We're gagging here.'

'I do actually,' I said and turning to the barman, ordered my drinks. I noticed that he had a little grin to himself as he started pouring my pints.

Right on cue I heard Tonker say 'Wanker' under his breath, but I knew he wouldn't do any more than that. He had a very large mouth, but very small bollocks.

'Bloody hell Jonny,' Arnie smiled when I returned to our table. 'I am so proud of you.'

The various reactions made me think that something must have happened in the pub recently. I guessed it would have had something to do with poor old Jonny being poor old Jonny.

I was being a bit of a shit. As I'd realised the night before, Jonny had dealt with lots of rubbish over the years. He'd just done it internally. He had strength there; he just didn't show it to the people who needed telling. Maybe seeing himself from another man's eyes might have changed him, like it had changed me.

The rest of the day was, in fact, typical of the Sundays I used to have with Amy when she still liked me. I had dinner with Arnie, followed by cuddly, cosy Sunday night TV. We then got ourselves ready for the working week. Arnie made no offer to iron my shirts as Amy would have done, which was a bit of a challenge. I managed to complete it without burning the house down. I felt it was a bit of a win.

* * *

When I woke up on the Monday morning, I was a bag of nerves. In less than a couple of hours, I'd know if I would be going home to Amy. Despite my feelings for Arnie, I knew that I really wanted to go home and put everything right with her. Be the husband she deserved.

Arnie was still sleeping when I came out of the bathroom, washed, dressed, and ready to go. He had an office day on Mondays and was taking the train. It was daft, but I didn't want to leave him without saying goodbye.

If I got back to Westcastle, I would only see him from a distance, when he came in to have a meeting with Tanner.

I knelt by his side of the bed and gently kissed his cheek. 'Thank you,' I whispered. 'Thanks for managing to do the impossible without even knowing it.'

I hadn't meant to wake him, but he stirred sleepily as I started to stand up. He clumsily grabbed my face with both hands and kissed me on the lips.

'You're gorgeous,' he smiled happily.

'So are you,' I whispered.

I looked at the sunny photos, from Sitges and beyond, as I walked down the stairs. The photos that had bothered me so much when I'd arrived – they didn't bother me now.

I realised that the next time I'd see this staircase, it could be stripped naked, except for a couple of wedding photographs and a picture of Mum and Dad on their twenty-fifth anniversary.

I wandered through to the kitchen and had a quick breakfast before making sure I'd packed everything that Jonny would need for a working day. I patted my jacket. This Monday it was more important than ever that I remembered to take my wallet, and vital that I took my phone. I checked that I'd left the link to my messages for Jonny open on the screen, I wanted it to be the first thing he'd see when he slotted his finger into the scanner.

I looked around the lounge, turned the light off, and left the *Maison de Gay* for what might have been the last time.

I shuddered. What an idiot I'd been when I named it that.

As I locked the door my mind was going bonkers, just thinking of the various ways this day could pan out. I had no idea what to expect.

What I hadn't expected, was to see a figure hovering by my car. It was just a shadow in the darkness when I first saw it. I walked onto the street and the lights gave the shadow a name.

'Cooper-Wilson,' I tried to sound surprised, rather than horrified.

Not an easy task.

'Take me with you.'

No 'good morning' – no 'how do you do' – just a blunt and slightly aggressive request. I appreciated his directness, if nothing else.

I let out an exaggerated sigh.

'For God's sake!' I didn't have to manufacture my irritation. The man was doing my head in. 'I thought we'd sorted this out the other night.' I deliberately slowed the speed of my speech and pronounced every word carefully, as if he was lacking in the intelligence department. In fairness, it was exactly what he'd done to me during our lunch in the city, so I was only returning the favour. 'I am not one of your travellers. I had never even heard the term until I met you...' I dodged him and walked around to the driver's door of my car. '...and to be fair, I would be very happy if I never heard the term again.'

He glanced up to the bedroom window of number 34. Arnie had turned the light on after we had said our goodbyes, so it would have been hard to argue that he was still asleep.

'What about Arnur?' he taunted nastily. 'I'd be quite interested to talk to him.'

It was the same threat he'd made on Thursday evening, but it held less power now that I was on the verge of going home. I had a feeling that Arnie's reaction would be: 'Yes he's toughened up a little, but he's still my Jonny.' He would take Cooper-Wilson's tales of gateways, and alternative realities, with a pinch of salt. He would probably, very politely, take the piss a little.

It was only when I ignored Cooper-Wilson, and clicked the button on my key, that I realised how desperate he was. Before I had the chance to stop him, he'd opened the passenger door and hopped inside.

'What are you doing?' I opened the driver's side door and snapped the question at the lump who'd invaded my passenger seat.

'Jonny wouldn't be irritated.' As he had done on Thursday night, he rubbished my attempts of playing Jonny Vincent. 'The real Jonny Vincent would have rolled over and given way.'

'Get out of my car,' I ignored the taunt.

'What's the time?' He asked, ignoring me, ignoring him.

I turned the key, and the digital clock was illuminated. It read 6:35.

'You'd better get a move on then,' he said. 'Your only chance of getting home will be gone if you don't get to Sandelwood at exactly the right time.'

'Oh yes.' I said with a sense of ease that I wasn't feeling. 'And what time is that exactly?'

He wrinkled his moustache, '7:05, as you well know.'

'Get out of my car.' I said again, more forcefully this time. I didn't care if my Jonny impression was crap. I was trying to bully him out of my car because, as much as I hated to admit it, he was right. I needed to get to Sandelwood for five past seven.

He ignored me. I swear he was gripping the sides of the seat, just in case I got back out of the car and tried to pull him from it. It could end up like a warped version of tug of war, with him playing the part of the rope.

I glanced at the clock. It had flicked over by a minute, since I last looked.

It was then that a sudden, and slightly desperate, plan exploded in my brain. I sighed and turned the radio off.

'OK,' I said, with forced reluctance. 'You win.' I sighed again. 'I'll take you to Sandelwood...'

His excitement, when he spoke again, was kind of touching and kind of irritating.

'So, you admit it? You did *travel*.'

I shook my head. 'Absolutely not – but I'm obviously not going to get you out of the car without the help of a JCB.' I looked at him. 'Unfortunately, the only way I'm going to convince you that you're barking...' I was going to add 'up the wrong tree' before deciding the shorter sentence was closer to the truth '...is to take you to Sandelwood and show you that your bloody gateway doesn't exist.'

'You are definitely not Jonny Vincent.'

'Yeah, yeah,' I said in the tone of someone who'd heard it all before. 'We'll see in Sandelwood, won't we?'

My lack of enthusiasm did nothing to curb Cooper-Wilson. He looked like a man who had won a million pounds on Groundhog Day. As I headed the car out of Carmichaeltown he wittered on excitedly. 'Just think, I'll be responsible for the most important development in alternate reality research there has ever been.'

Of all the things I would have called him; a shrinking violet was not on the list.

When Carmichaeltown had receded in the rear-view mirror and I was on the A road that headed southward from the town, I managed to zone out from Cooper-Wilson's ramblings. I thought through my plan, to check that it was possible, and then thought through it again to make sure. I glanced at the clock and risked a little bit of illegal acceleration as I headed towards the long, straight, downhill stretch that ended at the turn off to Sandelwood.

By the time I made that turn, Cooper-Wilson had stopped talking. He'd either managed to bore himself to silence, or become so excited that he'd lost the power of speech.

I was so wrapped up in my own plans that I nearly forgot one very important factor.

If I knew nothing about the Sandelwood gateway, I wouldn't know where it was.

It was just as I was passing the 'Welcome to Sandelwood' sign that I remembered this fact.

'So, where is this gateway then?' I asked, trying to sound as if I was humouring him.

'My calculations and the evidence I have calibrated from my 'travellers', which I have transcribed onto ordnance survey maps and then verified...' He sounded like a presenter on a TV talent show trying to tease out the tension, while the whole audience was inwardly screaming: 'Get on with it!'

I was inwardly screaming.

'...has determined that the most likely site is...' he smiled his most aggravating smile and slapped his hand down on the dashboard like a demented driving test examiner '...here!'

I gained four faults for refusing the emergency stop and travelled a little further before I stopped safely. Cooper-Wilson tutted at that and flicked his fingers over his shoulder to indicate that I should reverse. I rammed the gearstick into the 'R' position and went backwards until he was happy.

'The Sandelwood gateway,' he said happily and then told me off in a good-natured fashion. 'But you knew that,' he beamed in a 'no one gets the better of me' kind of way, 'it's where you had your incident almost exactly a week ago.'

I ignored him and looked at the clock.

7:03

'So where do I park? Just on the grass here?'

He gave me the same look, as if he was humouring me. 'Park in the middle of the road, of course. I believe that is where the 'point de transition' actually is.'

Holy cow! I thought. *And I'd reckoned it was impossible for him to get any more pretentious.*

Although the road wasn't the busiest one in the world, at that time on a Monday morning, I wasn't the only person who used it as a short cut. It also wasn't the widest of the county's highways. I nearly got rear-ended by a car whose driver was surprised to find us using the Sandelwood Road as a parking lot. He came to a stop behind me, flashing his headlights into my eyes. Then, horn blaring, he used a grassy patch on the opposite side of the road to get past me. It was far too dark to see the V sign he flicked in my general direction, but I was sure he must have used one.

'Idiot.' Cooper-Wilson was not impressed. I didn't bother to mention that I thought the driver had a point.

As the clock flicked over to 7:05, Cooper-Wilson became more and more animated.

At first, nothing happened.

Then, a car appeared from the direction of the city and Cooper-Wilson braced himself for the collision to come. The driver of the car saw me, with plenty of time to spare, slowed down and used the same avoidance tactic that the horn-blarer had used a couple of minutes before.

7:05 became 7:06.

'Well, I couldn't be absolutely exact.' Cooper-Wilson was becoming irritable. 'My calculations may need a little leeway. It may be 7:06 or maybe even 7:07.'

This became 7:08 or 7:09. Finally, at 7:12, after being avoided by several vehicles but not swapping places with any, I decided that I might stand a chance of evicting him from the car.

'Look, I've given you seven minutes, which will probably mean I'll be late for work. I'm not prepared to give you any longer.'

For the second time that day, Cooper-Wilson was silent.

'I will say this once more. I am not a traveller. I am an ordinary man who lives with an extraordinary boyfriend. I cannot help you.'

The passion behind the words surprised me. I really meant them.

'If you walk back to the main road, there's a two-hourly bus, it will take you to Carmichaeltown.' I put an emphasis on the town name, a direct reference to the cock-up I'd made on Tuesday lunchtime.

He moved slowly and reluctantly, but eventually Cooper-Wilson got out of the car. He paused before he closed the door, as if he was trying to think of a last-minute argument to prevent the inevitable. I said a very firm 'Goodbye', lent over, closed the passenger door, got myself settled, and then pulled away.

I watched him in the rear-view mirror. He turned slowly and trudged back the way we had just driven, when his hopes were high of meeting another version of himself in a different reality.

If I'd wanted to, I could have told him that such meetings were not as straightforward as Cooper-Wilson might have hoped.

I felt a little bit sorry for the daft old duffer, but I couldn't take him back to Westcastle. It could have opened nine doors of shit and I certainly wouldn't have wanted that on my conscience.

I really hoped that the bus I had told him about existed in this reality. It would be the definition of sod's law, if it didn't.

I drove around the corner and pulled in, just before the telephone box library. I took the mobile phone from my pocket and placed it on the passenger seat so that Jonny couldn't miss it.

The road was wider and straighter here. Any passing traffic would be much less likely to hit me. I knew that the car I was looking for would appear at the last minute. Any car headlights, which I could see from a distance away, would not belong to the vehicle I was waiting for.

If I tried to crash into them, it would not end well.

I looked at the clock.

7:14.

This meant that the time was 7:04. I thanked my lucky stars for three things: Jonny's clock was ten minutes fast and I hadn't bothered to change it, Cooper-Wilson wasn't wearing a watch, and I'd turned the radio off as soon as I'd had the first glimmer of a plan.

As I prepared myself for the clock to click over to 7:15, I thought about my other lucky break. The one I hadn't planned for.

Cooper-Wilson had got so much right about the Sandelwood gateway, but even with all his calculations, calibrations, and verifications.

He'd got the bloody location wrong.

~ 40 ~
AN ORDINARY MONDAY

Westcastle: Jonny

There was a car heading towards me. I could see that Arnie was in the driver's seat. All I had to do was crash into the car and I'd be reunited with him. The cars got closer and closer until, suddenly, the other car had gone. Arnie had gone.

I woke up. I had lost count of the number of times I'd dropped into a doze, only to wake up and find that a mere ten minutes had passed.

Amy was still cuddling into me. I'm not sure how much she had slept, but she hadn't strayed more than a centimetre from my side all night.

She'd seemed a little brighter on waking up from her nap the night before. I'd just finished writing a long missive to Ben; ensuring he knew everything that Amy had gone through during the previous year. After she'd woken, I offered to make her a boiled egg with toasted soldiers. A little bit of comfort food.

Amy managed a gentle grin, and I remembered her comment from Tuesday night. It seemed that Ben really was a man who could burn water.

We chatted for a long time that night. I'd become quite good over the last week at adding to conversations about their lives, without giving any definite details. Last night she had needed a friend much more than she needed a lover. It had been an easy role to fill.

How could I leave her? The same question seemed to have been stuck on repeat all night. It was only when I awoke to the sounds of the early morning DJ that an obvious thought had, at last, occurred to me.

I had changed over the course of the last week. I'd stuck up for Amy, in a way that I'd never stuck up for myself, or even Arnie. You could argue that Arnie was more than capable of sticking up for himself, but even then, there were a couple of times when he'd needed me and I'd been found wanting.

What if Ben had changed?

I thought through the most likely scenarios.

Either, he'd coped with being trapped in the body of a gay man, or he'd lost his mind. If he'd coped, then he'd probably be at the Sandelwood gateway at 7:05 today. If he'd lost his mind, he wouldn't be there.

Therefore, if he was at the gateway, it was likely he'd changed as I'd changed. This would mean that he'd support Amy, instead of being Tanner's stooge. When he read my pages of notes, he'd believe them. And he'd become the husband that Amy deserved.

If he wasn't at the Sandelwood gateway ... I didn't want to think about it, but it wouldn't go away. The last time I had thought of Ben Shawcross, before I became him, was when he'd been sentenced for manslaughter. Under extreme provocation maybe, but ... he had killed someone.

Also, if he wasn't at the gateway. I wouldn't be able to go home.

I would live here, in Westcastle, with Amy. I'd think of a way to rid ourselves from Tanner's grip. Jonny and Arnie would become my friends. I'd have a decent life.

However, my Arnie was in Carmichaeltown, and I wouldn't even know if he was alive. That thought made up my mind.

I had to try and get home.

I disentangled myself from Amy and eased my body out of the bed. Now that I'd decided, there seemed to be little point in hanging around. I would rather get to Sandelwood early, and have to wait, than rush there at the last minute.

After I'd washed and dressed, I made sure I took the notebook from the bed side table, kissed Amy gently on the cheek and left the room. As I walked down the stairs, I muttered a silent prayer that she would be all right, and looked around me. I wondered if there would be sunny holiday pictures on the wall, the next time I saw this staircase.

I grabbed a bottle of water from the fridge and thought about making a piece of toast. But I was too tense to worry about having breakfast. I closed the door of the lounge and went through the checklist in my mind, one final time, to ensure I hadn't forgotten anything.

'Hi.' Amy was coming downstairs in her dressing gown. 'You're early.'

'Yes, I need to be at work by seven this morning, didn't I say?' I was beginning to find it disturbingly easy to tell a lie. 'Why don't you go back to bed? You don't have to be in until ten, do you?'

She nodded. 'I don't. Jonny's doing the breakfast shift with Miriam this morning.' She shrugged. 'I think I'll stay up though,' she smiled. 'That bed's too big without you.'

I gave her another kiss and then, on an impulse, gave her a huge cuddle.

'You're sure you're OK?' I asked. I wasn't quite sure what I'd do if she wasn't. However, she smiled a genuine Amy smile. 'I feel so much better today. I really believe that it might be over.'

A wave of guilt washed over me. *If he's there, it will be all right and if he's not, I'll come back here, and Amy will be all right.*

I gave her a supportive smile, blew a kiss, and opened the door.

The morning was just an ordinary Monday. A dark and slightly damp January day. Most of the people who lived in the road would either be sleeping or readying themselves for the start of the working week. I looked down the road; Malc's wife was one of the exceptions. She was heading quickly up their path, having returned from a night shift, ready for her bed.

Just an ordinary day, but in about an hour, something extraordinary could occur – and none of them would know anything about it.

I got in the car and put the notebook on the passenger seat so that Ben couldn't miss it. I turned the engine on and, while I waited for the windscreen to clear, took a swig of water.

I was just about to put the gear stick into first, when there was an almighty bang on the boot of the car, making me jump so badly that I almost head-butted the steering wheel. I looked in the rear-view mirror to see if I could work out what had hit me.

Tanner stood there, gesticulating wildly.

I sighed, turned off the ignition, and got out of the car,

'What the hell are you doing?' I asked angrily.

Tanner looked at me as if I was an idiot. 'Aren't you forgetting something?' He said while pointing at himself to give me a clue.

I looked at him, his shirt was unbuttoned, a tie had been flung around his neck, and he was holding his jacket. He hadn't even managed to slip his feet into his shoes properly. It was safe to say that I'd nearly got away with it. Nearly, but not quite.

'Sod off Tanner.' I said clearly. 'You can get the train today.'

He looked more than a little surprised. Then, seeing the determination on my face, said peevishly: 'Fuck that. I'm taking a sickie.' He seemed completely unaware of how angry I was with him. He was so unaware that he expected another favour. 'Make an excuse up for me.'

'No, I won't.' He was confused by that and scowled unpleasantly, so I thought I'd spell it out for him. 'I won't make an excuse up for you, I will not be giving you a lift and, quite frankly, I'd be happy if I never saw you again.'

He spread his arms in a placatory gesture. 'Oh man! You're not still pissed, are you?' He made me sound unreasonable. 'We were just having a little bit of fun while you weren't around. It was nothing serious.'

I walked around to the back of the car and forced him against the boot, crowding him for room. Over the last week, there had been a couple of times when I'd realised how useful it was to be slightly larger and this was another of them.

'You raped her, you arsehole. You've been raping her for about a year.'

Tanner blew out an argumentative snort. 'Ah. So that's the way she's playing it, is it? Poor little Amy. Butter wouldn't melt ... and you fell for it.' He taunted me with a nasty smirk.

Although Tanner was slightly taller; I, or more accurately, Ben, was in good shape and matched him in every other way. I grabbed him by the collar of his unbuttoned shirt, which meant his torso was exposed. It also caused his jacket to fall from his hand, and his tie to slip from his neck into the gutter. I then manhandled him back to his gate. 'You're bloody lucky that she doesn't want to press charges but, you never know, that might change.' If I came back, I decided, I would try and persuade Amy to report him to the police. However, I had no idea how Ben would react. If nothing else, I wanted to leave Tanner with the threat of it.

I had just turned to walk back to the car when he said quietly, menacingly.

'You're not going to leave her are you? Not with that horrible "rapist" next door.' The threat was definite, and he left me with it as he picked up the discarded clothes and stormed back into his house.

The short answer to his question was: 'No.' I locked the car and headed back to number thirty-four. I opened the door and called Amy's name. After a few seconds, I heard the bathroom door open and Amy, clad head to toe in towelling, appeared at the top of the stairs.

'Oh, hi love,' she said, 'forgotten something?'

'What time does Jonny get into work?' I asked, trying to hide the sense of urgency I felt.

Amy smiled. 'Oh, you know him. If he's on with Miriam he has to go in at stupid o'clock just to make sure he's ready.'

I nodded. 'When could you be ready?'

Amy frowned and came halfway down the stairs to get a better look at my face. What she saw there, made up her mind, without her needing to ask for details.

'Give me five minutes and I'll be with you.' She was already at the top of stairs before she'd finished the sentence.

Once she'd disappeared, I looked at my watch. 6:15. I thought, *If I'm lucky, that should give me enough time to take her into town, drop her off, and still make Sandelwood by 7:05.* I hoped against hope that I would be lucky.

Amy was as good as her word and within five minutes we were heading for the car. I took a quick look around to check for unpleasant invaders. The light was on in Tanner's lounge but, of the man himself, there was mercifully no sign.

Amy saw my glance. This distracted her enough for me to put the notebook, from the passenger seat, into my jacket pocket without her seeing. Once we were both in the car and moving swiftly down Chancelwood Road she said: 'Tanner?'

I nodded. 'Stay at the shop with Jonny. I'll pick you up when I've finished work. And if Tanner turns up...'

'He won't turn up.' Amy said with an assurance that I didn't feel myself. 'I'm not sure he even knows where the book shop is.'

I looked at her and she explained. 'Not interested, is he? And when Tanner's not interested, he doesn't listen.'

I realised that Amy was right, but still worried that if he was determined enough to cause trouble, he would find the only independent bookshop in town.

I didn't say that to Amy, I simply nodded and carried on driving.

At just before 6:30 in the morning, there was a parking space right outside the shop. Jonny had just arrived and was unlocking the shutters.

'Amy!' He noticed her as soon as she opened the car door. 'You are a sneaky, wonderful, lovely, cow!' He grinned the last word affectionately. 'Arnie is absolutely gorgeous...' Jonny stopped suddenly. 'Just a minute. Aren't I meant to be on with Miriam? Is she alright?'

It was at that point he noticed me in the car. He was about to turn away from me when he mellowed and came around to the driver's door. 'Hi Ben.' He smiled. 'I know about your involvement too.' A definite truce was on offer. 'Thank you.'

I'd not uncovered any evidence, in the last week, that meeting my doppelganger would unleash the hounds of hell. I just had to hope that it wouldn't.

'You're welcome,' I said. I could tell that he was dying to get back to Amy and tell her all the gossip from the weekend, so I let him go. Amy would tell him as much, or as little, as she wanted about the reasoning behind her very early arrival.

I was pretty sure that she would tell him everything and despite some of his/my rather pathetic characteristics, I was equally sure he wouldn't let her out of his sight until Ben arrived to take her home. I didn't have to ask him.

I scribbled the latest information in Ben's notebook and put it back on the passenger seat. I was hoping that I'd written enough to persuade him the real threat that Tanner posed to Amy. Ben needed to get Tanner out of their lives.

I glanced at the clock as I pulled away from the parking space. 6:29. As I'd done all week I automatically took ten minutes off, then realised once again that the clock in this car was not ten minutes fast. 6:29 was 6:29. I wouldn't have the huge amount of time I banked on, but I reckoned I should be alright.

It wasn't until I headed into Station Road that I started to worry. They were carrying out improvements, which involved three different sets of temporary traffic lights. There weren't too many cars around at that hour of the morning, but I got caught at the first set, so my progress stuttered to an inglorious stop.

6:31 became 6:32.

I drummed my fingers on the steering wheel. As Jonny Vincent, I had always been a very careful, patient driver. *Hold-ups like this happen*, I always told myself. *There's no point in getting stressed about it.*

Today, I was stressed. Just thinking about my own platitude made me irritable. I breathed out a sigh of relief when the lights changed and I headed the car towards the next set. I was about fifty feet away, when they also changed to red, and the car in front of me slowed to a halt.

Come on! I thought. *Don't do this to me.*

6:33 became 6:34.

I turned the radio on. I needed something to take my attention away from the fact that the clock seemed to be on steroids. It didn't help. The DJ was playing Geri Halliwell singing *Scream if you wanna go faster.*

Another age seemed to pass before the lights changed again. I headed towards the third set of traffic lights. They were green. I headed forward, daring them to change.

They accepted the dare, just as I was sure I was going to get through.

Sod it! I thought. *I can make it across before they change from amber.*

That may have well been the case, but I never found out.

The car in front of me decided to stop.

Andy Paulcroft

Brake lights pierced the darkness. I slammed down on my own brakes, and then watched in horror as I lost all control and the car slid inexorably towards a Monday morning disaster.

~ 41 ~
DARING TO BLINK

Carmichaeltown: Ben

The clock ticked around to 7:15 which meant it should be collision time, in old money. I peered through the gloom, but there was nothing to see. *It will appear at the last minute,* I told myself. I hardly dared to blink in case I missed the second when happened.

7:15 became 7:16.

I was surprised. From all I'd heard from Arnie, out of the two of us, I was sure that Jonny would have been on time.

I stared at the gloom and saw a set of headlights. They were too far away. I was sure that this was not how it happened last week. I would have seen them easily and I didn't see them until the last minute.

Even so, as the car passed, I started to wonder if that had been my chance and I'd missed it.

I found myself getting as desperate as Cooper-Wilson had been. I told myself that I'd got the time of the collision wrong.

I then had another spine-tingling thought.

What if Cooper-Wilson hadn't headed back to the main road to get the Carmichaeltown bus? What if he had realised that I was lying to him the moment after I'd gone? What if he was prowling around Sandelwood looking for a dark car, parked on a grass verge?

7:19 became 7:20.

~ 42 ~
ROADWORKS

Westcastle: Jonny

It's a terrifying feeling when you can see yourself heading for the back of another vehicle, and you know there is nothing you can do about it. My car was slowing down, but there wasn't enough room for it to stop completely. I waited once again for the crunch of metal on metal. I had a random thought. It was ironic really. Here I was heading towards a voluntary car crash, only to have an accident on the way.

I didn't know the owner of the car in front. I would never know them. I would never be able to thank them for giving me a chance of making my rendezvous. What they did next, gave me that chance.

They would have seen me careering towards them. The glare of my headlights, in their rear-view mirror, must have been blinding them. Luckily, they had the forethought to jump the red lights slightly. Not enough to be a danger to on-coming traffic, but just enough for me to slide up to the set of traffic lights, rather than into the back of their car.

I felt sick.

The owner of the car flashed their rear fog lights three times to ensure that I knew they weren't happy. I felt that was the least I deserved. My face was burning hot with fear and embarrassment. I rather stupidly held up a hand in apology.

After leaving the roadworks behind, I was relieved when the car turned right at the next roundabout. It meant that I didn't have to follow it all the way to the Sandelwood and could accelerate.

I was running short of time.

6:40 became 6:41.

I had less than twenty-five minutes to complete a journey that normally took just over thirty.

The probability of arriving at the gateway too late made me realise how much I wanted to get home. *I shouldn't be here*, I thought. *I feel like an imposter. Ben should be fighting for his wife. His friend was his problem, and he should sort it out. I should be at home with Arnie, my soul mate. Amy should be my best friend, not my wife.* With every passing minute that outcome looked less likely to occur and I became more and more disheartened.

My foot became heavier on the throttle. Speeding had never been a guilty pleasure before, but that morning I sped. I saw the needle hovering around the ninety miles per hour mark. I had a strange feeling in my stomach, a cross between excitement and fear. I knew I was being reckless, but I didn't dare stop.

I had read many newspaper reports where people had been convicted of doing something stupid while driving: answering their mobile phone, falling asleep at the wheel – and – speeding. It seemed there was a very thin line between selfishness and desperation.

Desperation became most prevalent when I had to pass slower moving vehicles. A couple of manoeuvres I executed could have been described as risky. I could imagine the drivers tutting and chuntering, as I had tutted and chuntered in the past. I didn't care what they thought of me. I only cared about the number of the miles to Sandelwood and my need to make them disappear as quickly as possible.

The jingle that signified the start of the seven o'clock news played as I was starting to descend the long hill that led to the Sandelwood turn off. For the first time, since I left Westcastle, I believed I would make my deadline.

I took a deep breath as I turned off the main road and forced myself to slow down. I had made up the time and there was no need to take any more stupid risks. It was just as well I was travelling at a more conservative speed because, when I turned the first of the three sharp bends that would take me to the edge of Sandelwood, my headlights lit up a problem.

A lad of about nineteen stood in the middle of the road. A man came out of a farm entrance and from the body language and gesticulations, I could tell he was not best pleased. I didn't need to guess what they were discussing. On the other side of the teenager, was a Land Rover with trailer attached. Attached, but jack-knifed, right in the middle of the road.

I was on the verge of tears. I felt wretched. All that risk for nothing. I wanted to get out of my car and scream at the young man, but luckily I realised that would be both futile and unfair. He hadn't meant to do it, a point he was trying to make to his equally unimpressed father. Eventually the older man climbed into the Land Rover and successfully rectified his son's mistake. But it took time. I closed my eyes and tried to keep myself calm, and sane, to prevent me from seeing the painfully slow manoeuvre that was being played out in front of me. Eventually, a car behind me hooted and I opened my eyes to see that the road was clear. As I passed the entrance to the farm, the man had climbed out of the Land Rover and was continuing to lecture his son.

I pulled in to let the car behind me pass. It was seven fifteen, so I thought it unlikely that Ben would still be at the gateway, or that the gateway would even be open anymore. Even so, I didn't want a car directly behind me as I reached it, just in case the driver was sucked into the Carmichaeltown reality with me.

As I drove, I kept repeating to myself: 'Let him be there, let the gateway be open,' as if such a mantra would make any difference in the scheme of things. I passed the Sandelwood sign and drove around the corner, which led to the long straight stretch of road that ran through the village. I saw the phone box in the distance and hoped, against hope, that a car would appear in front of me.

The phone box became nearer and nearer. Daylight was reluctantly starting to swap shifts with the night, and I could see the road ahead without any problem at all.

It was completely clear of cars.

That didn't stop me from straining every nerve, as I passed through the village, trying to summon up a vehicle out of nowhere.

Nothing happened.

~ 43 ~
THE GATEWAY

Ben

7:25 on the clock. 7:15 in reality.

Where was he?

I was gripping the steering wheel so tightly, my knuckles threatened to lock together. *Bloody stupid!* I mocked myself savagely.

The car wasn't even moving.

I had nothing else to do but wait, hope, and think. My mind was twisting and turning like a Morris dancer on Speed.

All week I'd relied on Cooper-Wilson's information and the hope that Jonny would find out about it as well. But I had never really thought that he wouldn't. I had always believed it would work. Now that it was beginning to look less likely, I suddenly realised something.

I wanted to get home.

I wasn't a gay man. I had, at last, realised that there was nothing wrong about being gay. You weren't a lesser person, your relationships weren't less important, and you didn't feel the need to sing *I am what I am,* at any given moment. And, if you did, then go for it, why the hell not?

Except, it wasn't me. I'd had a teenage sexual experiment about fifteen years late and I'd enjoyed it. Massively. But one sunny day doesn't always lead to a heatwave.

With every minute that clicked over, I got more depressed. I would never get the chance to put things right with Amy, tell her how much I loved her, and put Tanner and my dad back in their box. I'd have to hope that Jonny Vincent could do that for me. The irony of that, considering the way I'd treated him, wasn't lost on me.

Then suddenly, I was sure I could hear a car.

A flicker of light, like a half-hearted flash of sheet lightning, briefly caught my eye.

Then nothing. I looked both ways, but there weren't any cars coming from either direction.

Had that been my chance?

I felt deflated as my brief excitement disappeared. To be fair, the half-hearted lightning had been nothing like my non-crash of last week but even so...

I waited a couple of minutes more, and then decided I might as well go to work. Arnie wouldn't be at home, and neither would Amy or Elliot. There was no point stuffing up my new life by taking another sickie.

I sighed, put the car in gear, and pulled out onto the road.

Jonny

I had failed. Either what I'd read about the gateway re-opening was wrong, or I'd missed it by minutes.

I continued to drive in the direction of the city, before realising that I couldn't bear the thought of going to work. I decided to return to Westcastle instead. I could check that Amy was OK and work out what we were going to do about the arsehole next door.

I wasn't going to give up searching for a way to get home. However, I had no one to swap realities with, and I had no knowledge of how to open the gateway. I didn't fancy my chances.

It was only when I found a layby, which I could use to turn the car around, that I had the most obvious of thoughts.

I'd been coming from the wrong direction. I had been where Jonny Vincent had been last week. But, at this moment, I was Ben Shawcross. He had been heading back to Westcastle to retrieve his wallet.

It's probably too late, I told myself. *The gateway would have closed or Ben, if he was ever there, would have lost hope and left.*

Don't be an idiot, my new-found, more gung-ho spirit replied. *It's got to be worth a chance.*

With little optimism, and a lot of desperation, I turned the car around and headed back to Sandelwood. By the time I'd reached the telephone box, in the middle of the village, the optimism had faded further.

Then, as if from nowhere, there was a car in front of me. Its headlights were blazing, even though the natural light was beginning to render them superfluous.

There was no way I could stop in time.

I held my breath as the car came closer.

Ben

The first time in fifteen minutes that I hadn't consciously been looking for another car, it arrived.

I had just eased my own car onto the road, when it came from out of nowhere.

Although I had gone through it before, it still came as a shock when I crashed into another vehicle, only for it to disappear as quickly as it had come.

I took several deep breaths before I dared to look around me.

First, I wasn't heading in the direction of the city anymore.

Second, there was a notebook and pen on the passenger seat, where I had put a mobile phone.

I was back in the world where there was still a town called Westcastle.

Jonny

The notebook had disappeared, a mobile phone had appeared, and the car was a mess.

I couldn't have been happier.

I was back to where I wanted to be.

I stopped the car, picked up the phone, and slid my finger into the slot at the back. There was something I needed to sort out. There was someone I was desperate to see. However, the picture of Arnie and me that I used as background wallpaper didn't greet me. Ben had left a play list to several recorded messages and the phone opened directly onto that. This was a good sign, as long as the first message didn't open with the words: 'Sorry Jonny, I've battered your boyfriend...'

However, I thought that the messages could wait for a moment. The 'something' I wanted to sort out was more urgent. I scrolled down my list of contacts and rang my line manager who was slightly surprised that I was going to be off for the second Monday in a row.

'Something has come up.' It wasn't a complete lie, but neither was it the complete truth. 'I just need today to sort it if that's OK. Can I take it as a day's holiday?'

I rarely took sick days. I had never taken holidays that hadn't been booked months in advance before. He couldn't really complain, and to be fair to him, he didn't.

Once that was sorted, I touched 'play' on the mobile phone, and turned the car around. As I reached the junction to the main road, I pulled out quickly, so I could avoid being stuck behind the Carmichaeltown bus. Almost as soon as I'd done so, I realised that it wouldn't have been necessary. There was a man waiting at the bus stop, so the bus would have pulled into the lay-by anyway.

He was a funny looking man with a brightly coloured handlebar moustache. He was busy making sure that the bus was going to stop for him and was ignoring everything else. He didn't see me.

He looked vaguely familiar. I realised that I had seen his doppelganger on the TV programme about alternate realities, when I was surfing the internet, that night back in Westcastle.

However, I forgot him almost immediately. I became engrossed in listening to my own voice telling me a story. It was a story that I'd never heard before, which was strange for a start. But it was nothing when compared to the contents of the tale itself.

I could feel my mouth stretch wider and wider, in disbelief, the longer the tale wore on. By the time I reached the much-missed Carmichaeltown sign, I had practically dislocated my jaw.

At least there was one thing I could feel relieved about.

Ben had *not* murdered my boyfriend.

Ben

Holy Cow! I picked up the notebook and saw pages and pages of writing. I liked and respected Jonny a lot more now, but he was still a long-winded sod. I had to admit, though, it grabbed me from the first sentence. I had flicked over to the next page, before realising that it might not have been my best idea.

I was still sitting in the middle of the Sandelwood gateway.

After all I'd gone through to get home, I didn't want to be bounced straight back into Carmichaeltown.

I drove a little further on down the road and turned into the car park of the Sandelwood Arms, completely empty at that time on a Monday morning. I was pretty sure that I was out of range of cars sweeping through the Carmichaeltown side of the gateway.

I thought that I'd better ring Tanner and ask him to invent a sick day story for me. I'm not sure what it was, but something stopped me. I was gagging to read what Jonny had to tell me, however long-winded it was. I decided I would ring my boss with some excuse later.

I picked the notebook back up, from the passenger seat, and turned to the second page.

By the time I had finished the whole notebook, I was hurt, horrified, and very, very angry.

I changed my mind. I would go into work. Admittedly I'd be very late, but there was something I needed to do there. I trusted that Jonny would keep Amy safe until I could get back to the Westcastle bookshop.

As I drove towards Sandelwood, I realised that I would always be a little nervous about driving through it in the future. I thought about the gateway. What caused it to open? Was it just a random lottery for which Jonny and I had managed to grab the winning ticket? Or was there more to it? In Carmichaeltown, apart from a different partner, Jonny had my life. Also, Jonny and I shared a birthday. Did that create a link that made us more susceptible to the power of the gateway?

I thought about the only other reality swap that I knew about: Vince Garrity and Marty Wilding. Marty was my mum's cousin. Did the link have anything to do with my family? And poor old Jonny – had he just got swept along for the ride?

It was then that I noticed the car interior. Really noticed it. Apart from being cleaner than it had been when I'd last driven it a week ago, in every other way, it was the same as the car I'd been driving an hour or so before. I remembered something that Cooper-Wilson had said about Garrity and Wilding.

...both men owned pick-up trucks. The only difference between the two vehicles was that Marty Wilding kept a gun in his.

What if the original opening of the gateway wasn't random at all? Cooper-Wilson's belief that once the gateway had been opened, it would re-open a week later to the exact minute, was wrong. I knew that now. And as soon as I'd accepted it was wrong, I realised how stupid it sounded.

But even though that had been a load of crap, I realised that I owed a rather large debt of gratitude to the poor old bugger with the daft moustache and over-bearing manner. In typical Cooper-Wilson fashion he had got most of his facts right, but one big important fact wrong. And because of that big important fact he got wrong, I was where I needed to be, when I needed to be there.

It hadn't been about the time – not in that way.

I didn't really think that it was about sharing a birthday, or a family connection.

It was all about two cars, or two pick-up trucks, the same size and shape, at either side of the gateway. Obviously, they had to be there at exactly the same time.

But, apart from that, it was all about the vehicle.

~ 44 ~
THE STATION

Jonny

The Monday after Carmichael Week was always quiet in Carmichaeltown, and that day was no exception. I eased the car into the station car park, happy that I hadn't encountered the roadworks they were suffering in Westcastle.

I was still stunned by the story I'd been listening to. Ben Shawcross, the proud homophobe, had finally discovered the twenty-first century. Not only discovered it. He'd moved there, built a house, and decorated it with pink triangles and rainbow flags.

It was only after I'd parked the car by the station entrance, and bought the cheapest ticket to access the platforms, that I started to worry. Perhaps the tale on my phone had all been some sick sort of joke. Perhaps Ben *had* killed Arnie. After all, was there a better way of escaping justice than disappearing into another reality? He could then leave some sort of convoluted fairy story on my phone, which would encourage me to head home. Straight into the arms of the police.

There were two footbridges in the Carmichaeltown station. The one that Tanner had fallen from, which was the quickest way from Back Street around to the station entrance, or the internal footbridge I was walking over. I had a clear view of platform four, from where I was on this bridge. I knew exactly where Arnie would be standing. With typical meticulous Icelandic planning, he had worked out his positioning perfectly. If you got onto the train by the bottom of the footbridge in Carmichaeltown, it would stop right outside the exit gate when it reached the city.

I knew the best way to calm my ridiculous worries. All I had to do was to look and see him standing there. Then I'd know that everything was alright.

I looked. He wasn't there.

Stupidly I looked at my own watch. Monday, at this time he would be waiting for the 8:30 train to the city.

Why wasn't he there?

I suddenly realised I could contact him by phone for the first time in a week and was just reaching for my mobile, when I looked again. A large man in front of the stairs, folded his newspaper and moved one step to his left.

Arnie was there! I could see him nonchalantly leaning against the stair rail. He was happily mouthing the words to the song he was listening to on his phone.

I didn't want to waste any more time. I ran along the bridge and down the stairs. I was at risk of losing my footing and rolling like a dropped squash ball, all the way to the bottom. Arnie must have been aware of something moving speedily behind him. As I reached the platform, miraculously in one piece, he turned to find out what was happening and saw me.

'Jonny,' he smiled delightedly before a slight worry furrowed his brow. 'Is everything OK? It's not one of the boys? Amy? Elliot?'

'Everyone's fine,' I reassured him before adding with an unfamiliar air of recklessness. 'I just want you to come home and make love to me.' I smiled impishly. 'Do you think you might be able to move a few meetings?'

'On a Monday?' He pretended to be outraged at the thought, then laughed delightedly. 'Hell yes, I've already moved them.'

I pulled him towards me and kissed him on the lips. Public shows of affection were not the norm for me, so he hesitated for a millisecond before responding.

'My God Jonny,' he said when we briefly came up for air. 'I thought the weekend was fantastic, now this...'

I kissed him again. I suddenly felt a little jealous. Stupidly jealous. It almost felt as if Arnie had been unfaithful. Luckily, I realised how ridiculous that sounded. If you think you're making love to your own boyfriend, it's not normally known as infidelity.

'Excuse me.'

We hadn't noticed, we were a bit busy, but it seemed the man with the newspaper had had enough. 'Do we have to suffer one man kissing another, at this time on a Monday morning?'

I was going to ignore it, as I always used to do. Arnie seemed to be dying to say something, but was being careful not to upset me, as he always used to do. In the end, I decided it was a shame to go as far as I had gone and not learn anything from the experience.

I turned towards the man. 'I wouldn't complain if you wanted to kiss your wife or girlfriend in front of me,' I said reasonably. 'I really can't see the difference.' I smiled pleasantly. 'After all, it has been legal to be gay since 1967.'

The man didn't really have an answer to that, and I was being far too polite for him to complain about it. He blustered and growled and in desperation indicated a woman to his right. Her hair had been pulled back from her forehead into a ponytail, which exaggerated the rather pinched features of her face. She appeared to be harassed by the two over-active under-fives that were with her.

'This lady does not want her children to see that sort of behaviour.' He barked out eventually.

I looked at the lady in question. She still looked aggravated. I wasn't hopeful.

'I'm sorry,' she said, and I waited for another opinion on our outrageous behaviour. However, it was the man with the paper she was addressing her remark to. She turned to him. 'I would be grateful if you didn't speak for me when you don't know me.' She smiled, which completely transformed her rather harsh features. 'I was just thinking it was rather lovely. I've been in a rare old strop with these two all morning,' she indicated her boys. 'Seeing a couple who obviously love each other, and don't care who knows it, has made my day.' She addressed her children. The older boy was trying to wrestle a plastic Zog, from his younger brother's hands. 'D'you see boys. Make love, not war. It's the best lesson you could learn.'

Sometimes, I loved it when I was proven to be wrong.

The man decided that he didn't want to share a carriage with any of us, so moved away down the platform. We smiled gratefully at the mother, and then I started to push Arnie towards the stairway.

'Come on you,' I said, 'I need to get you home very quickly.'

Arnie stopped and dramatically looked to the heavens. 'Who is this and what have you done with the Jonny Vincent I used to know?' He said, before adding, 'don't worry, I rather like this new version.'

I smiled, gave him a friendly punch, and didn't say a word.

~ 45 ~
FIVE MONTHS LATER

Ben

I paused on the steps of Westcastle hospital and smiled at Amy.

'A boy,' I looked at her. 'Are you happy?'

She smiled her crooked smile. 'No, I'm as miserable as sin. You?'

I beamed back at her. 'Absolutely devastated.'

I hadn't been too worried about finding out about the sex of our baby, but Amy had wanted to know. She said that it made it easier to organise everything. I joked that it was only because she was a control freak.

I would never know who the baby's father was. I knew that. We'd made love, a lot, the week after I'd returned. But. as I was staggered to discover, Jonny and Amy had been active the week before. I'd gone through a bit of a moment when it really worried me, but I'd got over it. I had so much to thank Jonny for. I wasn't at all sure I would be about to become a father, had it not been for him, and I'm not talking about whether he donated the sperm or not.

The Jonny from my own world moved in next door, when it became vacant, and it didn't take too long before Arnie moved in with him. I'd had a word with my dad. I'd told him that what he'd done to Jonny when he was at his most vulnerable, was unethical, and more than a bit shit. He hadn't liked it and grumbled that I'd been quite happy about it fifteen years before, but he knew that I was right. He signed number thirty-two back over to Jonny. I did some digging and discovered the market value for our house when my dad had 'obtained' it. I offered to pay Jonny the difference. He refused. He argued that he still had the flat he could rent out, and having decent neighbours was worth its weight in gold.

He told me how happy he was.

After that, my relationship with my dad improved. Sometimes he just needs someone to tell him when he's being a twat. Even Mum isn't quite the doormat she used to be. I've never seen her looking so happy. Every week she appears with another knitted creation. They will probably only be seen on the baby at family get togethers, but she is so stoked at becoming a grandma, neither Amy nor I are going to ruin it for her.

Another person who I see a lot more of now, is my own grandma. I don't use her as an excuse to play golf anymore. Amy and I go to see her regularly once or twice a week. She has banned us from using the term 'Great-Grandma' when the new baby appears. Apparently, she has always told her friends at the retirement home that my dad is her husband and I'm her son. She must have had a hard time explaining my mum away, since she's taken my place on the Sunday afternoon visits. But, knowing my gran, I'm sure she had an answer ready.

I was worried when Arnie moved in with Jonny. It would have been tricky if I'd had a raging boner every time I saw him. But I've had no problems in that department. I like him. Massively. He's become my best mate. He and I go to watch City with the rest of the football club lads. They love Arnie, and don't give a stuff when he flirts outrageously. I think that all of us have become better friends since he's been around.

I can still tell that he's an attractive man, but I can honestly say that he does nothing for me sexually. Even when we leap up and down in each other's arms to celebrate a City goal.

I'm sure Jonny was influencing me, during my holiday in Carmichaeltown, just as I like to think I was influencing him. And it's not that I need to believe that to keep me sane or anything, I just figure it makes sense. I would have been worried if I still had the hots for Arnie, but not because he was a man.

I don't ever want to be unfaithful to Amy again, and Arnie would have been the only person who could have tempted me.

One thing is for sure. The feeling I had in Jonny's kitchen, during the dinner party, when Amy felt more like a sister than a wife … that has gone.

So, although I still go and support City, I no longer stay out all night afterwards. Arnie and I will have a quick drink, with the lads, then go home to join Jonny and Amy who have spent a mad day being 'ladies who lunch' and shopping for baby clothes.

Even that's going to change when our son arrives, it's bound to, we don't exactly know how; but it's all part of the excitement.

When Tanner's job was advertised, I noticed that one of the applicants was a lady called Kerie. It didn't surprise me when she got the job. She was perfect for it. The four of us in Chancelwood Road, along with Steve and Lottie, have formed a bit of a friendship group with Kerie and her husband. We often do Friday night suppers at each other's houses.

I almost act like a grown-up now.

'Do you know how much I love you?' I asked, as we walked towards the hospital car park.

'Enough to do night feeds and dirty nappies?'

'God no,' I laughed. 'Not that much.'

She laughed, dug me in the ribs, then turned and kissed me. The feel of her lips on mine. That *was* temptation. And I told her so.

'Probably best not to make love in the middle of the car park,' Amy said deadpan, as if I'd suggested it. 'Someone would only moan.'

'Spoilsports,' I laughed.

Amy grinned and changed the subject. 'I know your dad keeps going on about calling our baby Jack, if it's a boy, and Jacqueline if it's a girl.' She paused before diving back in. 'Well now we know that Bumpchild is going to be a boy,' she smiled at me. 'Could we call him Jonny?'

It was perfect. I felt as if the two worlds were beginning to realign. The four of us living in Chancelwood Road. Working alongside Kerie, being friendly with Steve. We'd even started regular video calls with Elliot, and his family, who are still enjoying life down under. And now, Amy would have a son called Jonny. Just the two more to go...

'I can't believe how miserable my life was at Christmas,' Amy said suddenly. 'And now,' she breathed in sharply. 'I love you so much.' Her face suddenly darkened, and she became serious. 'Please don't drift away from me.'

I took her face in my hands and looked at her. 'I will never do that again.' Her face relaxed into a smile, and I kissed her once more.

'I'm a different man now.'

~ 46 ~
SIX MONTHS LATER

Jonny

I shouted up the stairs. 'Come on Arnie, we're meant to be there in ten minutes. Don't forget we've got the Carmichaeltown traffic to contend with!'

There was a shout and a swear word. Arnie appeared at the top of the stairs, with a smile on his face and not a lot else.

'Shall I go like this?' He asked.

'Not again,' I flicked my eyes skyward. 'You wore that last time...'

'*Gleðispillir!*' He turned, wiggled his behind in my direction and disappeared. I resisted the temptation to follow him up to the bedroom. I told myself there was plenty of time for that later, tomorrow, and the rest of our lives.

Within minutes Arnie reappeared, looking far more suitably attired for a night out with friends. We walked down one footpath, back up another, and arrived at our destination within a minute.

'How was the journey?' Elliot asked with a smirk as he opened the door.

'Absolute hell!' Arnie said. 'We got caught in a tailback.' He grinned. 'Greg's two tabbies were blocking off the garden gate.'

Elliot laughed, gave us both a hug, and led us through to the lounge. The boys had been allowed to stay up to see their guests, and Jonny jumped onto my lap as soon as I'd sat down.

'We're allowed to stay until the food's ready,' he said to me conspiratorially. 'And then it's...' He dramatically drew his finger along the bottom of his neck.

'JJ, sweetheart.' I said, giving him a big affectionate cuddle. 'I think you're going to bed. I don't think you're going to be beheaded.'

'Oh, hiya you two,' Amy had emerged from the kitchen. 'I heard from Lottie, they all got there OK.'

Lottie and Steve, along with Kerie and her husband, were spending the weekend at a gaming convention. We'd all been invited, but Elliot said he'd rather eat his own eyelids. We jokingly accused him of being a luddite, but no one else rushed to book a ticket.

At that moment the doorbell rang. Jonny jumped from my lap and went to open the door before Elliot had the chance to beat him to it.

'It's Uncle Ben and Aunty Sarah,' he cried excitedly, did a little dance, then ran back to my lap.

I'd taken the suggestion, from the message on my phone, and got in touch with Ben. He, of course, thought we'd already met. I had to be a bit careful. But, after all the practice I'd had during my week away, it came quite naturally.

I liked him.

When I thought about it afterwards, I realised that there had been occasions when we might have forged a friendship before. A little help from Ben, when he was living in my body, was all we needed.

Elliot had been slightly prickly to start with. He'd just been worried, but he soon realised that he had nothing to be worried about. Amy loved him, and only him. Once he had worked that out, any tension between him and Ben disappeared.

'So how is my football husband tonight?' Ben had come through to the lounge and after saying hello to everyone else, gave Arnie his customary greeting and kissed him on the cheek.

It's brilliant for me. Ben fills the one void in our relationship that I can't cope with. It means that I don't have to pretend to listen when Arnie witters on about City's latest signings, and he has a receptive audience who doesn't think that a flat back four is something you buy from Ikea.

During the football season they started to go to see City. After a while, Elliot, Steve, and Lottie, who had always been part-time football fans, joined them. Meanwhile, Amy, Sarah and I looked after the children. Mind you, sometimes we wondered who was looking after who. One spring day, when we were having a picnic in the park, Sarah had said something typically caustic and hilarious. Amy and I were falling about laughing when JJ interrupted us by saying in his big brother voice. 'Mummy, Uncle Jonny, Aunty Sarah – please – you're showing us up...'

It didn't help much.

I have changed, since that week in January. Ben told me a lot of things in his voice messages. He mainly told me that he was sorry for everything he'd done to me, and that I had more strength than I would ever know. He told me that Arnie loved me. His messages ended with three simple words.

'Believe in yourself.'

It was a bit of a shock, once I'd returned home, to discover that both Gemma and Cameron had started paying off the money they owed me. They also began treating me with a lot more respect. They were then pleasantly surprised that other people started treating them with more warmth because of it.

I decided not to waste the helping hand that Ben had given me and became a little more assertive. The other day, I'd been tasked with explaining the multitudinous rules and regulations of RD Eversen to a new trainee. Afterwards, I overheard her talking about me to another lady who'd been with the company for years.

'Jonny's lovely, isn't he?' The trainee said,

'He is,' came the reply. 'As long as you don't take the mick. He won't be treated like an idiot.'

She didn't say 'anymore', but I could hear it on the edge of her voice.

I silently thanked Ben and thought I'd probably got it about right at last.

I saw an article about the Sandelwood gateway in the local paper a few weeks ago. It was one of those articles that gets updated and rehashed every couple of years, mainly during the summer, when there's not much news about.

One of the chief contributors was a man called Hadley Cooper-Wilson. There was a photo. He was the man I'd seen boarding the bus on the main road outside Sandelwood on the day I'd returned. He offered a lot of theories; some he had got right, but many didn't tie in with my experience.

It was only when I was thinking about it later that a thought occurred to me. *He doesn't really believe in the gateway. He's quite happy in his own invented world, playing the loveable eccentric for all to see. He might potter and probe into people's lives, hoping to find the link that proved the gateway did exist. But I'm not quite sure what he would do if he found it.*

I thought that it was all better left alone. I had seen what had happened when you 'travelled', as Cooper-Wilson liked to call it. It had turned out perfectly for me, but it could have been a different story.

When we got home after the dinner party, it was very late. We had taken advantage of the fact that, tonight, no one needed childcare. It will probably be the last time for a while.

Sarah and Ben will soon be joining all the others in the 'search for a babysitter dance' that normally occurs when we get together.

It hadn't taken long for us to work it out. They had both been beaming, even more than usual. They both seemed excited, and the killer clue was Sarah asking for a lime and soda. This was not a normal occurrence.

'That's so lovely for Ben and Sarah,' Arnie said happily, as he undressed.

'It is,' I agreed, then teased him. 'Mind you. I'm not sure I could cope with it. I have enough trouble clearing up after the child I've already got...'

He shut me up by kissing me. I didn't put up much of a fight.

'Love you,' I said.

'Love you more,' he countered.

I've often wondered what stopped Ben from walking out, that first night, when he realised he was in the body of a gay man. As I kissed my boyfriend, I was sure I knew.

Arnie.

There's something about the man.

And he chose me.

I think about them sometimes. The Ben and Amy who live in that other reality. The voice messages he'd left me showed that he had been changed, as I had done, by living in another man's shoes. I was confident that Ben would have been appalled when he discovered the things that Tanner had done to Amy. I was sure that Tanner had no power to hurt her anymore.

There was one thing that worried me. Here in Carmichaeltown, when Ben discovered that Tanner had raped Amy, he had killed him.

I hoped that Ben had learned from meeting his double.

I hoped that he hadn't done anything stupid.

~ 47 ~
THE WHOLE TRUTH

Ben

I stood and looked at the wall in the spare bedroom of our house in Westcastle. It was three months until baby Jonny was due. I'd decided that I should get my sad behind into gear, and deliver on the promise of providing him with a nicely decorated nursery.

Amy was aware of my expertise, but she'd been put on a decorating ban by the lads, my parents, and anyone else who knew us. She stood up, a little too quickly to be polite, and announced that she thought she might pop next door for coffee.

'Fair play,' I laughed. 'Don't blame you.'

I'd been standing there looking, but not really getting anywhere, for about five minutes when the doorbell chimed. I went to answer it and discovered Arnie at the door.

'Thought you might need a little help,' he grinned. 'Our beloveds are happy discussing birth plans, breast feeding, and early signs of urinary tract infections.' He flexed his muscles. 'I thought I'd come and do big, butch, manly things.'

'Come in you idiot,' I chuckled, leading the way upstairs. 'You might be able to tell me where the hell we start.'

We found it when we were moving the furniture. Amy and I kept some photographs, in an album, on top of the chest of drawers. I'd thrown a few of them out when I came back from Carmichaeltown. This one must have fallen down the back, without me knowing.

Arnie saw me staring at it and came behind me to grab a look over my shoulder.

'Oh, him.' He said without emotion. He'd only known him as a bloke he'd had to meet through his work, but he'd heard all about Tanner since. None of it good as the joke goes. But in this case it wasn't a joke. None of it had been good.

There was one thing Arnie didn't know, nobody knew, not even Amy.

The whole truth.

* * *

The Monday morning that I arrived back, I left Sandelwood and headed for the office.

I noticed that everyone was more friendly towards me than they had been the last time I'd seen them. I guessed that must have been the Jonny factor. They'd not been at all bothered by Tanner's absence. I told them he wasn't feeling well and left it at that.

It was more for my benefit than his.

When I'd done what I needed to, I asked the boss if I could have an afternoon off. I received a lecture about being late, wanting to go early, and my sickness record in general. But, he said that I could take the time off as holiday, if I had to.

I said that I did.

I drove to the book shop. The most important thing was to check that Amy was OK. During the drive I kept the radio off. I wanted to think. Mostly I thought about what an idiot I'd been, so it probably wasn't a good idea. I thought back to a week before. I had set off to work with no thoughts of parallel universes, gateways, and travellers. I had glanced up at Tanner's house and wondered about the girl he saw every fourth Sunday. The one I'd hoped might become a regular girlfriend for him.

The one he wouldn't tell me anything about.

Jonny saw me as soon as I arrived at the shop, and after a swift glance in the direction of the backroom, he moved towards me to have a word. 'You've finally woken up then?' he asked, not unpleasantly. 'You've worked out the type of man your lovely friend is.'

'You could have told me about what he was doing to Amy,' I said.

I knew exactly what his answer would be, and he was right. I wouldn't have listened.

'I will sort it,' I promised him.

I took Amy home and we chatted. I'd read Jonny's version of 'War and Peace' thoroughly, so I was able to talk to her as if I'd been there for the last week. It was the first time I'd talked to her like that for an age, and it was wonderful, even if most of the stuff we were talking about wasn't. I waited until she gave her first yawn and suggested she could do with a nap. She agreed gratefully and went upstairs.

When she had nodded off, I left her and went to knock at the house next door.

'We need to talk.' I told my ex-best friend as he opened the door. 'Shall we walk at the same time?'

I didn't give him chance to argue. I was already back on the street by the time he'd grabbed his coat and joined me on the pavement.

We walked down into town in silence, until eventually he'd had enough.

'So, is this going to be more of the crap you were ranting on about this morning?' he asked aggressively.

'Don't piss me about Tanner. I know what you did. You know what you did.' I turned to look at him. 'It's where we go from here. That's what we need to discuss.'

'And where do you think that might be?'

'Well, I know where you're going.' I said with a calmness I didn't feel. 'You're going to see your parents.'

'I don't think so,' he argued. 'I like it here.'

'You're going to see your parents,' I repeated. 'And you're not coming back. I will send all your stuff down to Cornwall, as soon as I can organise it. We will never see each other again.'

'Your dad and I had an agreement,' Tanner said confidently. 'Pay him back interest-free, and he'd sign the house over to me.'

I couldn't resist a smirk of my own. 'A verbal agreement, was it?'

He gave me a sharp glance.

'Why are you so pissed off?' He actually managed to make me sound unreasonable. 'Because I was having an affair with your wife? Well, I'm sorry, but not sorry enough to lose my house over it.'

'You weren't having an affair.'

'Oh, of course – that's what Saint Amy says – so it must be true.' He stopped suddenly. 'If I raped her, where were the bruises? Was there any proof of intercourse? Where is your evidence?'

I felt a sharp stab of guilt. There had been bruises. I'd seen them over the last year. I just thought she was getting clumsy. I'd never even asked her about them.

He was so smug, so bloody pleased with himself, I could have punched him. It took an effort, but I kept myself calm and set about destroying him.

'I used your computer today.' I said mildly. I started walking again, forcing him to follow. 'I told everyone that you'd asked me to take some work home for you, what with you being so poorly and all.' I gave him a sarcastic grin. 'They were amazed by that. I can't think why. But they let it go.'

I had managed to surprise him, and I intended to surprise him a little bit more.

'You really shouldn't have told me all your passwords,' I tutted. 'It's very bad security on your part. Especially the one for the encrypted file named Marshmallow.'

That had got him worried.

'You're bluffing.' He said, but he didn't believe it.

I pulled some pages that I'd printed off, from my jacket pocket. I handed them to him. 'They're only copies of course,' I said. 'There's no point tearing them up.' He looked through them, becoming less cocky by the minute. I took them back from him without a word, and stuffed them inside my jacket.

'And you still think I'll run away, do you?' He asked. He was trying to sound casual. But I knew Tanner. He was beginning to become desperate. 'I'll just say you were in on it. If I'm going down, I will drag you down as well.'

'There is nothing to link me to anything you've done,' I countered. 'Where is your evidence? Where is your proof?' I loved using his own words to make him realise he was well and truly stuffed. 'Now, your train is due. The offer only lasts until it leaves the station. You can go and start a new life in Cornwall, or you can stay and start a new life on trial for fraud. Your choice.'

Tanner's face twisted into an expression I'd never seen before. It was pure hate.

'I'd be careful if I were you.' He looked at me. 'I will go. But one day, when you least expect it...' He left the rest of it unsaid. Instead, he asked unexpectedly. 'Show me your mobile phone.'

I wasn't sure where he was going with this, but was curious enough to do as he asked. I kept a firm grip on it to prevent him wrenching it from my grasp. I could imagine him stamping on it, in some daft show of revenge.

He didn't do that. He looked at it carefully and then said: 'Good. Now put it back in your pocket.' I did as he asked. 'OK, I just wanted to make sure you're not recording this, so keep your hands away from your pockets.'

Stupidly, I hadn't even thought about doing that. I'd been so sure I was in control. I wasn't so sure now, but I was gagging to hear what he seemed so desperate to tell me.

'Just so you know that I don't make idle threats, I'm going to tell you something.' He paused, then said suddenly: 'Do you remember Will, at school? Had an accident. Fell from a tower. Died. No more Will.'

I nodded.

'Do you remember when I asked you to run up the tower during my practice sessions for that stupid race?' He affected a pathetic whine. 'Oh, please Ben, you're a much cleverer runner than me. Run up the tower for me. I want to see the best racing line to take. Ooh, thank you. Again, again,' he laughed but without humour. 'I must have sounded like some sort of Teletubby retard.'

I remembered it well. I just didn't have a clue what he was trying to tell me.

'I didn't want your wonderful expertise,' he scoffed sarcastically. 'I wanted to find the exact point on the tower where no one in the clearing could see what I was going to do.'

I couldn't believe it. And yet, in some way, I did.

He laughed. I think he'd been wanting to tell someone for years. And now, there was a bonus. He could use it as a threat. Hence the check of my phone to make sure I wasn't recording. Apart from that, I would have no proof that he'd told me anything. He wanted to scare me.

'Do you remember what Will said as he lay there after he'd fallen?' I must have looked blank. 'You must remember. Everyone was saying: "Oh that's so typical of Will, making a joke when he's dying."'

I remembered. His impression of some of the people in our school year was viciously accurate.

I remembered the shock I felt as I saw Will's body fall. I remembered the terrible sound that came from his throat as he lay there dying. A sort of death rattle. And before that, I remembered the word he said.

'Whoops.'

'And what did the sad bastard call me?'

I tried not to gasp out loud. I didn't want to give Tanner the satisfaction.

'Hoots.' I said without emotion.

Tanner laughed gleefully. 'Hoots! The sad fuck was trying to tell you that I'd grabbed his ankle with my hand as he flew past me.' He snorted. 'And you saddos thought he was trying to make a joke.'

It suddenly all made sense. Of course, Tanner would have had a plan to make sure that he didn't lose to Will. He knew that his enemy was faster, and cleverer – even Tanner didn't think that Will would lose – so, Tanner made sure that Will didn't win.

But in the other reality, the reality I'd just left, something completely mad had happened. An unexpected news report. Tanner, distracted for a moment, had been denied his fast start. Will had grabbed the lead and Tanner had not been in the right place to murder him.

Tanner knew me well; he could tell I was shocked, even though I tried to hide it. He was loving the power.

'Do you remember that game we used to play?' He asked. 'How to plan the perfect murder?' He smiled, but it wasn't a friendly smile. He was so ridiculously pleased with himself. 'Well, I did it in front of about seventy witnesses – and no one had a clue.'

He was on a roll now. He wasn't even using the story as a threat anymore. Once he'd reached the point when he realised that he'd lost my friendship, he had taken the second prize. The chance to tell me how clever he'd been. And he hadn't finished.

'So yes,' he smirked. 'I've committed the perfect murder.' He paused like a comedian waiting to deliver the punch line. He delivered it. 'Twice.'

This time I didn't even try to hide my shock.

'Do you know anyone who knows more than me when it comes to tinkering with engines?' He asked. I was a bit surprised by the change of direction. My hesitation delighted him, and he was happy to taunt me. 'Do you know anyone who could break into a boat yard and sabotage a motorboat?',

I felt a little sick.

'Oh, don't look like Little Lord Fauntleroy.' He snapped irritably. 'It was brilliant. The Vincents were in dispute with a mechanic. He'd be the one in the shit. No one would suspect anyone else. They certainly wouldn't suspect me.'

I didn't want to ask the question. I didn't want to give him the satisfaction. But I couldn't stop myself.

'Why?'

I'd given him the satisfaction. And it showed.

'Rubber's boyfriend had died. If his parents died too, I knew he'd be completely lost. He might not have liked them, but he needed them. Two houses to look after, and no boyfriend to run to. After that, all he needed was a little persuasion. And I gave him a lot of that.' Tanner smiled at me.

He was evil.

Tanner must have seen my disgust. He said easily, as if he was excusing himself for dodging a twenty pence fee at a public lavatory, instead of justifying his murderous past. 'Well, my parents were going to make me homeless. I needed somewhere to live.' The terrifying thing was that it all seemed to sound so reasonable to him. 'It was very easy to persuade your twat of a father to help me, he just thought we were taking advantage of the situation to make a swift buck. Dodgy bastard.'

I'd always thought that he put my father on a pedestal, that he wanted to become another Jack Shawcross. I was wrong. Tanner respected no one. That much was clear.

We had reached Back Street by this time. I looked across at the pub we'd spent so much time in when we were underage. Such innocent days. At the time I never realised I was sharing them with a sociopath.

I took a deep breath. I couldn't believe how little I knew about my best friend. The real Tanner Hootley. It was time for me to wrestle back control.

'I know I can't prove anything about the murders,' I said. 'But I can still prove the fraud. And believe me, mate, if you're not on that train, I will prove it.' I paused. I wanted to give my next words extra power. 'And, if anything happens to Amy or me in the future, there will be links to that proof somewhere. You might not go down for murder, but you will go down.'

He was surprised by that. He had expected me to be intimidated.

I looked at my watch. 'You've got five minutes. Unfortunately, the footbridge is closed for repairs and you've still got to buy a ticket.' I couldn't resist a smirk of my own. 'You'll have to go the long way round.' I finished with a sarcastic smile. 'You'd better run, you bastard.'

Tanner looked at me, still not convinced. I tapped my watch, and we heard the muffled tones of the loudspeaker announcing the imminent arrival of the train to Exeter.

He still didn't run. He sauntered down the road as if he had all the time in the world. Just as he reached the closed off stairway, he put his hands on top of the six-feet barricade and used them as purchase to leap over it.

I saw a man walking up the road towards me, he glanced back at Tanner and gave a look of disapproval.

'No Tanner!' I shouted. 'Don't be stupid!'

Tanner didn't reappear.

I waited for twenty seconds. The lights on the bridge were beginning to show up as the day became more and more gloomy. Suddenly, they illuminated a figure in the bay window.

He looked towards me and raised one finger in defiance.

It happened quickly. I'm not sure which part of the bridge gave way first. I was aware of the look of panic when Tanner realised that he was just about to die.

There was a scream from someone. The streets, which I thought had been empty, seemed to be alive with people screaming.

They watched as a young man tumbled from the broken bridge into the early evening sky, cracking his head on the abandoned rails that used to carry the fast train to London.

Suddenly there was silence. People were trying to work out what had happened. I was aware of someone behind me. It was the man who had given Tanner the hard stare when he had launched himself over the barricade, just a few minutes before.

He mistook the look on my face. 'You tried to warn him.' He said soothingly. 'You mustn't blame yourself.'

I allowed him to comfort me, and I smothered my face into his coat. Tomorrow, at work, I would tell them that I'd discovered Tanner's fraud and that was why I wanted the afternoon off. I'd hoped I could convince Tanner to hand himself in, but he'd run away. Onto a crumbling bridge.

It was a tragic accident brought about by stupidity. He ignored the warning signs and paid the price. No one was to blame.

I even had a witness who would say I tried to warn him.

It was when I'd been driving to the bookshop, to pick up Amy, that I'd had the idea. I'd waited at three sets of traffic lights because they were renovating the station bridge. Fifteen years ago, after a tragic accident, they'd been forced to repair the same bridge in Carmichaeltown. But in Westcastle, there'd been no accident, so it had never been a priority. It had been rotten to the point of collapsing when they'd finally closed it.

I thought about Cooper-Wilson. The man who got most things right but a few things wrong. If he was wrong about this, I would still have the fraud to fall back on. But Tanner had been right. I would never feel completely free from the threat of him, while the bastard was still alive.

But – I wasn't prepared to serve time for killing him.

Buried into my new friend's overcoat, I allowed myself a small, sad smile. Tanner had thought he had got away with two crimes he'd committed fifteen years ago, not to mention the crimes he'd committed against Amy.

It had taken a lifelong knowledge of Tanner. He hated being made to do anything. I was certain he would never run for a train if I told him to. He would have seen that as humiliating.

It had taken a trip to another reality to learn about pre-requisites and a bridge that had collapsed fifteen years before.

It had taken the story of a boy, who'd tripped from a water tower in one reality and jumped from it in another.

Whatever it had taken...

I had just committed the perfect murder.

ACKNOWLEDGEMENTS

I first had the idea for *In Another Man's Shoes* a few years ago, when I was driving to work. I was driving through a village just like Sandelwood, when I nearly crashed into another car. By the time I'd swerved, stopped, and restarted my heart, the other car had completely disappeared. I then wondered to myself what could have happened to it, if it hadn't boringly disappeared around the bend. The seed of an idea had been planted.

This has certainly been a different story to write. Hence, the rather long hiatus while I was trying to mould it into the book I wanted it to be. I would wake up in the middle of the night, convinced that I'd got the worlds of Westcastle and Carmichaeltown muddled up in a particular chapter. I would then go back to sleep and, when I woke again in the morning, I'd forgotten which chapter I was thinking about!

I would like to thank my friends: Anne Andrews, Alexis Batt, Angus Bramwell, Karen Croft, Anna Difazio, Kath Fletcher, Rik Fletcher, Sarah Houchin, Sue Keith, Nicky King, Debbie Plows, Fiona Sharp, Jim Stephen, Sarah Stephen and Jane Thomas. They read this book in its infancy, and gave me some wonderful feedback.

A special mention to Barbara Barnes. She helped me with the proofreading, editing and was an invaluable extra brain while I was attempting to transcribe all the ideas from my head, into the written word.

I'd like to thank all my author friends for their continued support, especially Laura and Foxy, for spa days, cocktails, karaoke and bingo nights. All washed down with a healthy dose of book discussions!

To everyone who read *Postcards From Another Life* and *Killing Them With Kindness*. You gave me encouragement, feedback, and excellent reviews. Thank-you so much.

And as always, last, but not least: love and thanks to my wonderful partner, Ian Lawson. You have provided me with never-ending support with all matters technical as well as designing the cover and formatting the whole project. You also listened while I read the book out loud to you. That funny little noise you made, when you heard something you didn't understand, was invaluable. I knew that if I didn't hear it, then that chapter was good to go!

Printed in Great Britain
by Amazon